Praise for *A God Strolling in the Cool of the Evening:*

"Even though there is plenty of high-energy action, enough to make it a literate, page-turning thriller, Mário de Carvalho's *A God Strolling in the Cool of the Evening* is much more than that. It is also the story of a good man in bad times, a man who might be called noble except for his own irony and honesty that won't allow it. This powerful, moving novel, set in ancient times, is as vital and pertinent as this morning's headlines."

—George Garrett

"*A God Strolling in the Cool of the Evening* has messages for us on many levels. . . . In an age where our excesses could lead to the destruction of the life we are all enjoying, Carvalho's story lends a timely parable to those who would chase only pleasure without thought of the consequences."—*The Midwest Book Review*

"Beautifully crafted and written, it is a jewel."

—*Library Journal* (starred review)

"Carvalho, an exile during the last days of the Salazar dictatorship in Portugal, examines themes of dictatorship, repression, and futile resistance to the great trends of history as well as the natural yearning for human decency and spirituality. . . . *A God Strolling in the Cool of the Evening* makes the point that as history marches forward, we must look into our hearts—not at society and certainly not at our political leaders—for moral guidance. It is a high-minded, artful novel meant to touch and inspire."—*Richmond Times-Dispatch*

"Carvalho ponders the often conflicting riddles of responsibility and virtue in this exquisitely crafted fictional memoir. . . . Lucius struggles to balance his ingrained sense of civic duty with his innate sense of justice. . . . Timeless ethical drama."—*Booklist*

"Engrossing . . . The tension between Lucius' self-aware, measured, first-person narrative and the chaos that erupts in Tarcisis and in its magistrate make this a compelling and powerful novel."

—*Virginia Quarterly Review*

"Well-written and beautifully translated . . . The strolling god of the Christians remains imbedded in Lucius's memory as he retells his story, one of duty and conscience, enhanced by psychic foreshadowing of a Christian Portugal rising from the Roman ruins."—*Choice*

"A satisfyingly intimate look at a man torn between tradition and open-minded curiosity . . . A sympathetic, penetrating allegory of the humanist at bay."—*Publishers Weekly*

"Provocative . . . tightly structured . . . a chord has been touched by this story of a decent man who finds he is no match for civic indifference, ethnic superstitions, moralistic fanaticism, and wanton destruction."
—*World Literature Today*

A GOD STROLLING
IN THE COOL
OF THE EVENING

THE PEGASUS PRIZE FOR LITERATURE

A GOD STROLLING
IN THE COOL
OF THE EVENING

A NOVEL

MÁRIO DE CARVALHO

Translated by Gregory Rabassa

GROVE PRESS
New York

Originally published as *Um deus passeando pela brisa da tarde*
in 1994 by Caminho in Lisbon

This Grove Press edition is published by arrangement with
Louisiana State University Press.

Printed in the United States of America

FIRST GROVE PRESS EDITION

Library of Congress Cataloging-in-Publication Data
Carvalho, Mário de.
   [Deus passeando pela brisa da tarde. English]
   A God strolling in the cool of the evening / Mário de Carvalho ; translated by
Gregory Rabassa.
       p.   cm.
   Originally published: Baton Rouge : Louisiana State Univ., 1997, in series: The
Pegasus prize for literature.
   ISBN 0-8021-3774-1
   1. Romans—Portugal—Fiction. 2. Portugal—Antiquities—Fiction. 3.
Rome—History—Empire, 30 B.C.–284 A.D.—Fiction. 4. Rome—Civilization—
Christian influences—Fiction. I. Title.

PQ9265.A7717 D4813 2001
869.3'42—dc21
                                                                            00-046268

Designed by Michele Myatt Quinn

Grove Press
841 Broadway
New York, NY 10003

00 01 02 03   10 9 8 7 6 5 4 3 2 1

PUBLISHER'S NOTE

The Pegasus Prize for Literature, created by Mobil Corporation in 1977 and published by Louisiana State University Press since 1980, recognizes distinguished works of fiction from countries whose literature merits wider exposure in the rest of the world. *A God Strolling in the Cool of the Evening*, winner of the 1996 Portuguese competition, is by Mário de Carvalho. Originally published in Lisbon in 1994, the novel also won the Portuguese Writers' Association's Grand Prize for Fiction in 1995.

The Portuguese competition attracted 114 entries, from which an independent jury of distinguished literary figures chose this novel. Chaired by novelist and Portuguese Writers' Association president José Manuel Mendes, the jury included Lídia Jorge, of the Writers' Association; Fernando J. B. Martinho, of the Portuguese Centre of the International Association of Literary Critics; Luiz Francisco Rebello, of the Society of Portuguese Authors; and Richard Zenith, an American-born translator of Portuguese literature residing in Lisbon.

A practicing attorney who in his youth was active in resisting the Salazar dictatorship and so was exiled to France and Sweden, Carvalho returned to Portugal during the revolution of 1974. *A God Strolling in the Cool of the Evening* is his twelfth published work and was preceded by other novels, short story collections, and plays. That this novel was a best-seller in Portugal seems at first thought unusual considering that its setting is third-century Roman Lusitania, the province that centuries later became Portugal. The protagonist and narrator is Lucius Valerius Quintius, prefect of the imaginary town of Tarcisis. Steeped in the mood and thought of Marcus Aurelius, Lucius must contend with marauding bands of "barbarian" Moors from North Africa, and also with the rising power of the Christians within the city walls. Caught up in a time evincing both past greatness and present-day decadence and corruption, Lucius finds that he must still act with honor. His political convictions are sorely tested when he falls in love with Iunia Cantaber, daughter of a respected aristocrat but a fervent new convert to Jesus. And there lies the explanation for the book's best-seller status. Carvalho manages to subtly draw parallels to our own time, with the noble heroes of our history outshining the all-too-flawed figures who now lead us.

A God Strolling in the Cool of the Evening was translated from the Portuguese by Gregory Rabassa, renowned translator of two Nobel Prize winners. Mr. Rabassa was a founder of Columbia University's Translation Center and is Distinguished Professor of Hispanic Language and Literature at Queens College in New York. Equally adept in Spanish and Portuguese, he translated Gabriel García Márquez's *One Hundred Years of Solitude*—perhaps the single most influential work of fiction since 1960—and other works by García Márquez, including *The Autumn of the Patriarch*. He also translated Miguel Angel Asturiás's *Mulata* and four works by Brazilian author Jorge Amado, including *The War of the Saints*.

Grove/Atlantic, Inc., joins Louisiana State University Press in expressing appreciation to Mobil Corporation, which established the Pegasus Prize for Literature, and provides for the translation into English of the works the award honors. We also salute the twentieth anniversary of the Pegasus Prize, and the roster of international authors Mobil has brought to English readers. As publisher of this paperback edition, Grove/Atlantic also wishes to express gratitude to Louisiana State University Press, which has published all but the first of the Pegasus Prize winners in hardcover, for making this work available in English for the first time and for allowing us to join them in this endeavor.

For my grandson, João, who will be born one of these days

And they heard the sound of the Lord God strolling
in the garden in the cool of the evening . . .
—Gen. 3:8

This is not a historical novel. Tarcisis, or, more properly, the municipality of Fortunata Ara Iulia Tarcisis, never existed.

A GOD STROLLING
IN THE COOL
OF THE EVENING

I

THE SKY IS BRIGHT, night is slow in coming, time lags, life is dull, movement is languid. Beneath shimmering shadows I read and reread my books; I stroll, reminisce, ponder, wonder, yawn, doze, let myself grow old. I'm unable to find any great pleasure in this golden mediocrity despite the invitation and consolation of the poet who has given it his ear. Like the Orator, I, too, am embittered by idleness when activity has been forbidden. The days drag on, Marcus Aurelius has lived out his life, Commodus is emperor. I have endured what I have endured, a long punishment. How could I be happy?

Mara, farther off, is embroidering, seated in a tall wicker chair next to the steps to the door. A while back she was reprimanding the slave girls. Now she's laughing with the slave girls. Soon she'll be reprimanding the slave girls. From where I am I can't hear her, but I can almost guess the reasons for the laughter and the reprimands. It's pleasant to know that Mara is close by and also to have such a clear recognition of her expressions and her ways after so many years.

Moments ago, for no special reason, she came over to me with her pet, which is a gray cat now—she having lost, in a time of disaster, the very white turtledove that used to eat out of her hand.

This strange new animal, which they say is Egyptian in origin, is a kind of miniature panther that preserves all the fury of that wild beast and that, like it, takes pleasure in cruelty and unexpected scratches. Sometimes it's at rest, peacefully sprawled, drowsy, in an invitation to universal repose; sometimes it will leap, claws at the ready, ears flat, fur standing stiff, fangs threatening. It won't respond to its name, and despite its small size it earns the respect of the guard dogs when it confronts them. A merchant left it here as a token of recognition for the considerable, perhaps excessive, purchases Mara had made. I must confess that I look upon this foreign animal with some distrust. It's still not a member of the household, and I don't know if it ever will be . . .

Mara is surprised that I'm involved in reading the *Tyrrhenika*, an interminable collection of Etruscan stories by the Emperor Claudius. What benefit can the effort bring me, she asks, since we have so few guests to dazzle? With a facetious gesture she unfolds one of the rolls, spells out some words at random, laughs, and lets it curl up on the table. The cat's claws are immediately extended, curved and ready to scratch the papyrus in the same way previously they marked Mara's arms. She protests. Mara cuddles the creature to her bosom and runs off. A daily, familiar, trivial, and loving ritual. Delightful Mara, confirming her concern for me . . .

Mara has maintained a youthful vivacity that still amazes me. She never had the patience to unroll a book; she yawns and dozes when I call a slave to read some passage, even a light and witty one. She's bored in this dull town, but she would never admit that she's bored. It never occurs to her to complain. "Where Gaius is, there will Gaia be": that's how she was brought up. Under that merry and flighty frivolity, solid, ancestral principles stand guard along with a lucidity that only shows itself when weighty matters bring it forth. I've always been able to rely on Mara's strenuous loyalty, even though she probably couldn't define the word *loyalty* or expatiate on it or even use the term *strenuous*.

To be perfectly honest, Claudius' Etruscans have scant interest for me, and his prose is as garbled as his speech is said to have been. But I go on reading, page by page, step by step, with the application of a student under the torture of an assignment with the teacher's ruler standing watchful guard. I have no reason for this except to divert my tedium in a way that is probably more pleasurable than other occupations: hunter or tiller of the soil or stonemason or diligent manager of an estate; and better, too, than any of the pastimes available for one of my station . . . If the reading begins one day, it is imperative for me to carry it on to the end. Suggest a book to me? I have to read it!

On the green marble of the round table by which I am seated a square scar, scratched and obscene, mars the smiling profile of a meticulously carved Bacchus laden with grapes. Despite all attempts at scrubbing and washing, the black ashes of the fires that burned there once have been impossible to remove. Marks of the fury of the barbarians. Could this table—slimy with entrails, base for the flames—have been the chosen altar for their primitive rites? Or not even that, an unprotected object of their wrath, wounded because it was something human, the mark of a perfection that ignorance abhors?

I had seen this table arrive one day, wrapped in furze and straw, in a convoy of carts; my father was still young, and I was an urchin playing with a hoop. He was proud of that green, streaked stone, one of a kind, which had come from far away. I remember the exertions of a group of slaves to make the heavy, round piece of marble roll, turn after turn, up to the bower, which flourished in those days, leafy with grapevines. And there was my father's satisfaction as he proudly followed the lines of the chisel with his hands, explaining the genealogy, deeds, and attributes of Bacchus for my edification.

With the passing of the years and the distressing difficulties I shall speak about, I saw that stone lifted up by arms once more; I saw it rolled along in a series of great efforts and stubbornly replaced on its base with the help of hawsers and crowbars. It was no longer the same marble: it had been profaned, cracked, scorched. Like that, just the way it is now, it would remain till time immemorial, free of major damage or defamation. But every time my hand runs over its injured surface and I feel the roughness caused by the blows, the grime caused by the ashes, I feel the touch of a threat, undefined but brutal.

3

The great rolling stone reminds me of that king of Corinth, the temporary jailer of death, the eternal prisoner of fate. Who can say whether this green marble, overturned one day, will not return to what it was and be left just to fade away naturally, slowly, peacefully, from the measured abrasion of the erosion of the ages? Who can assure me that these bucolic afternoons, so quiet and tranquil, won't be shattered once more by the thunder of malignant shouts? Is what happened all past? Let me cultivate this lack of concern, the illusion that the world will go on forever unperturbed and imperturbable after a temporary disturbance of its order. I am a landowner, I am a Roman, I read, I learn, I follow the rhythm of the times in my bearing, my gestures, my words, my manners, my phlegm, my toga. Dignity. Gravity. Romanity. Humanity. Trembling fears and anxieties are resolved for us by the legions, and firmly, as behooves them. For me, now, my books . . .

But what could have gotten into those raw, coarse, brutish people to go hooting off from their deserts, from the companionship of scorpions and snakes, to cross the sea in their crude boats without oarlocks or sacred altars and fall upon Lusitania in a bloody foray, ravaging farms, houses, and people? What drive was given them by some obscure and resentful god, which spared neither wood nor stone, neither innocent nor guilty, neither freeman nor slave, and carried with it the sole aim of destroying and turning into desert the cities and farms so skillfully created by generations who spoke Latin, worshipped the gods, and obeyed the law? A conquering army plunders by turns, spares the conquered, rebuilds cities, collects tribute, reestablishes order. It makes what has been subjugated its own and maintains it as such. When the tumult is over it organizes patrols to preserve normal order. But when a horde passes through it leaves the mark of pure irrationality on the land, the relapse into original chaos, which turns talent into a threat, work into perversion, beauty into a dungheap. In that way columns are broken, baths defiled, corpses disemboweled in the light of conflagrations. There's not a man among them capable of shouting: Spare them, because all this belongs to us now! The devilish assault erases everything until the cold steel of a legion halts them.

In this town they slaughtered animals and slaves, who lay bloating on the fields; they destroyed columns, tore off tiles, shattered the household gods; they scratched the old paintings; they used furniture and upholstery as fuel for fires; even the hard-rock millstones were broken up by them. They uprooted trees, destroyed vineyards, trampled flowers. All books were shredded or burned. They even made their bestial marks on this inoffensive marble table. Why? In the name of what? If I knew, I would be the wisest of men and would be able to advise them to their advantage. The reason behind that demented urge to destroy must be the most carefully guarded mystery of all. The divinity didn't wish to reveal it to me, wished only that I should suffer its consequences.

When I returned, auxiliary cavalry detachments of the VII Legion Gemina were already patrolling the hedgerows, returning runaway slaves to their masters, and crucifying, on the nearest holm oak tree, Moorish stragglers or anyone who had been in league with them. The rule of the Senate and People of Rome was reestablished among the ruins, the moans, the putrescence, and the persistent plumes of smoke. My overseer returned, having hidden for a long time in a distant hut. Little by little, other slaves came forth from hiding in the countryside, waiting for the legions to restore order, which, harsh as it might be, was always less to be feared than the maddened scimitars that cut for the sake of cutting. Some livestock were recovered in the woods, as if they had been protected by some shepherd god.

The steward piously put the household gods back together and had them placed, tenderly, on their altar in the vestibule. Then he laid down mats in the one room left almost intact, lighted the remains of a small lamp, and only then let Mara and me enter. It was the return of the master and mistress. The slaves stood in formation in the atrium, some of them bruised or bloody from the terrible experience they'd been through. Eight soldiers were billeted in the remains of the granary. At night we could hear the snorting and stamping of mules on the pavement. But we were safe. Through the windows that had lost their frames the distant croaking of gloomy birds vibrated. The white moon made the signs of destruction all the more desolate. Mara and I, clinging to each other under my cloak, decided that we would redo everything exactly as it had been before. And at that point Mara began talking and talking and talking, and she talked until the sun came up.

❦

Few traces of the raid are visible today. It's difficult to believe that these buildings have been rebuilt after being almost completely demolished. When this generation dies, no memory will remain of the destruction that stained these parts with blood in times of distress. Accounts might endure in books that no one will read until the books themselves are destroyed through men's cruelty or lack of care. Let Mara and me enjoy peace now, and let us hope that until the end of our days the depredations we had the misfortune to witness will not be repeated. Even today I look with suspicion at anyone coming from the direction of the ocean. But will it be only from the beaches that dangers will arrive?

The other day I was startled by something I saw. It was a cool and pleasant morning, and contrary to my custom, I took it upon myself to stroll along the riverbank. Up on a fence a slave boy was picking mulberries and putting them into a knapsack. They wouldn't all end up on my table, needless to say. I normally close my eyes to these little transgressions. Nature gives us the bushes; they require no outlay or care. I only tried to keep my distance so the child wouldn't see me and become needlessly embarrassed. The boy stopped, sat down, filled his mouth with berries, picked up a stick, and began drawing in the sand: a curved line, another curved line from the same origin but bending in the opposite direction, then bowing back to cross the first. A third line to connect the ends. A dot: the eye of the fish.

"Who taught you to draw that?" The boy leaped up and looked at me, petrified, his mouth half-open, purple from the juice of the mulberries. He'd never seen his master so close. I must have seemed terrifying to him, threatening, like Jupiter the Thunderer emerging from the clouds. He knelt and instinctively held out a handful of berries to me while with the other hand he protected his head: "I'm sorry, master!" He felt he'd done something wrong, but he didn't know quite what. "Answer me. Who taught you that de-

6

sign?" It had been a wool comber who'd passed through. "One of mine?" No, master, it was a foreigner who was on a long journey to someplace. And the urchin was trembling, struggling to hold back tears. His mouth, tinted by the mulberries, gave him the pitiful look of a tragic mime. "Be off with you!" He disappeared through the heather on the run, leaving a trail of fallen berries.

I carefully stepped on the design with my half-boots of carded wool. A useless act. Realities aren't extinguished by the destruction of their symbols. Perhaps many miles farther along the wool comber's route, other designs have appeared and other memories been revived. Was the congregation of the fish extinct? I tried to convince myself that it was. What did I know?

⌖

It was a short time later that Proserpinus rendered me the surprise of his visit. I was at my usual place at the green marble table, going over accounts. I'd sold two iugera of land at one end of my property to free myself of a boundary dispute with a neighbor, a man whose manner was too rustic for my taste. The payment was mixed, figured in gold, measures of oil, and bales of flax. I wanted to check everything minutely because my trust wasn't too great. I verified the price of the material and decided to spend the morning working with the abacus and mathematical tables. When the dogs began to bark and dash toward the gate in the wall and a strange slave entered and set about driving them back with an iron-tipped pole, I took it to be my neighbor coming once more to wail and beg me to lower the terms. But right behind the slave, hunched over in fear of the dogs, that tall, crooked, nervous figure I knew so well and scorned a bit appeared. I felt an almost painful discomfort. Proserpinus! I got up, alarmed: what could Proserpinus be doing here?

Mara was already on the alert. She went down the steps quite serenely, calmed the dogs, and let the intruder greet her. She showed no surprise whatever and smiled at Proserpinus as if she'd seen him the day before. Mara was always on top of things. He arrived enwrapped in a large, fringed Asian cloak, covered with dust, wearing a wide-brimmed traveler's hat that he immediately removed respectfully. From his broad gestures I could see that he was asking

7

permission for his party to come in. Mara said something in a loud voice; slaves came running and pushed back the wings of the gate. The litter and the people accompanying Proserpinus passed between Mara and me and were led to the stables. While the procession was passing, filthy and weary, Proserpinus was seeking me out with his restless eyes. I had a perfect view of his anxious look and the contraction of his face as he squinted into the distance to see me. He took two steps, got a better look, and smiled. He'd recognized me. He made a vague, hasty bow in Mara's direction and ran toward me.

"Lucius, Lucius, greetings! How good to see you after all these years . . ."

There was Proserpinus, tripping over his misshapen cloak, almost crawling at my feet. What was I to do? I couldn't ill use a guest who'd showed himself to be solicitous even if uninvited. I hid my annoyance, suggested that he fix himself up in the baths. I kept him company. I asked his advice on my transaction. I invited him to the green marble table and listened with patience and courtesy.

Then I ordered two mules to be saddled and took him for a ride through my estate. Proserpinus was not too taken with the country, was completely oblivious to the beauty of an isolated cork tree in a clearing of yellow stubble. He'd never read Hesiod. He was passing through a sanctuary with indifference. But he kept quoting Virgil: "Happy is he who knows the rustic gods . . ."

He tried to impress me by going on about Mago and his treatise on farming. Could a Carthaginian like Mago have been endowed with sufficient sensitivity to expound on the agriculture of this side of the Mediterranean?

When he spoke, Proserpinus would suddenly throw open his right hand in front of him, almost touching the ears of his mount, as if he were incessantly working at an energetic casting of dice. He expressed himself in a detailed and pompous way, like a teacher of rhetoric, even on subjects about which he knew nothing.

How could a Carthaginian aspire to universality, even if he was only disserting about vineyards? Besides, everybody knows that the fruitful growth of plants depends on prayers to the local gods at the right time and place. Could Punic rites, established for Punic gods, ever persuade the divinities of Italy, or those who held sway over the fields of Hispania?

I reminded him that Mago was the only Carthaginian translated into Latin by authorization of the Senate and that therefore he must have some merit. Proserpinus launched into an elaborate disquisition on the Carthaginians, who, as is well known, have the peculiar quality of completely lacking virtues.

I let him go on, trying to guess what had really brought my visitor here. I was convinced that Proserpinus had looked me up so unexpectedly for some reason. I couldn't conceive that disinterest was part of his makeup. But I seemed to be wrong in that respect: he showed no sign whatever of asking for anything or of trying to extract any benefit from me. Nor did he try to wound or belittle me. It's the usual characteristic of inferior souls to use another's adversity as an excuse to exercise their condescension. They have scant esteem for their own worth, and they think they can increase it with the suffering they can extract by references, ambiguities, or inopportune mentions that trouble the one they are speaking to. Reviving the misfortunes of their fellow man lifts their spirits and gives them pleasure for reasons that escape my understanding. But there was no assault from Proserpinus: instead, advice concerning my affairs that was confused but useful, absurd ideas on agriculture, diatribes against the Carthaginians, some quotations from the Greeks gleaned from a textbook of rhetoric, pretended rapture over nature, and on like that all day long . . . always in a style that was legalistic, stilted, full of images, and pompous. He never tried to remind me of my exile or demean me with the memory of my troubles. Knowing him as I did, I couldn't help feeling grateful to him. And that for the second time in my life.

"Remember," I was saying, "it wasn't the Carthaginians who invaded us this time. It was the Moors from Tingitania."

"They're all the same: Carthaginians, Moors . . . flour out of the same sack. The wrong side of the Mare Nostrum."

⚬━━✦━━⚬

At dinner Proserpinus outdid himself over the cost of the dark silks and the delicacy of the perfumes. It was his way of paying us

9

homage, though he knew it was our custom to be frugal and restrained in our repasts. Mara still has the old habit, passed on by her mother in days gone by, of eating while sitting up on the edge of the triclinium—as natural for her as the archaic custom of addressing me as "friend." All that was offered was rabbit, mushrooms, river birds, bread, and some regional fish sauce. Our own wine. Serving us was the old slave who had waited on my father. A triple oil lamp for illumination, nothing else. I only gave orders that the cups and place settings be silver and that cinnamon sticks be placed in a glass to match Proserpinus' silks in their exoticism, so that he wouldn't take our simple ways to be a show of avarice.

When he settled down he made me a present, and with it a small speech thanking us for the hospitality. In a leather case he had brought a copy of the *Cato* of Curiatius Maternus, which he handed me with great solemnity. I thanked him with the appropriate words. Mara added some polite remarks after casually examining the rolls.

"I haven't read it, but I thought it would give you some pleasure," Proserpinus said.

It was, in fact, a fine gift. And that copy, those rolls with strange carved wooden handles, that case, must have cost him a goodly sum.

He told us that he'd traveled from Tarcisis to Vipasca to take care of the legal formalities regarding the affairs of a widow, a client of his. My properties aren't on the road to Vipasca; Proserpinus took a wide detour on the way back, off the patrolled highways, just to pay a visit. He'd come with some hesitation. He expected, certainly, to be received with haughtiness or brusqueness, and our generosity, he said, had moved him.

He recounted the details of his trip and didn't spare us the description of the matters that were his reason for taking it. From time to time I would sneak a glance at Mara as if to ask, "What does this one want from us?" Mara, always sharp, perceived what was bothering me and hastened to keep the conversation going. As soon as Proserpinus paused, she would immediately come up with questions and comments, keeping the talk away from the subject she knew could hurt me: Tarcisis.

Such tact, Mara's ... but I could see in Proserpinus, too, the wish never to touch upon the events in which I had been a participant years before. And it wasn't just because of a lack of opportunity, given Mara's close attention; it was clear that he didn't want to. In good conscience, I can't think of much to praise in Proserpinus. I've always felt an uncomfortable disdain for him, and I don't doubt that he knows it. But I see myself forced to recognize under that voluble, self-seeking, and crafty nature a few remnants of nobility that prevented him from embarrassing me.

Wasn't I curious for news of Tarcisis? Inside, though I wouldn't let it show, I was burning with curiosity. But in a contradictory way I was terrified by the idea that the matter would be mentioned, and all the more if by Proserpinus. I wanted to preserve my peace. I'd earned my right to still waters. It would be a great cruelty if someone, with me completely defenseless, came to poke around in old wounds.

But Mara and Proserpinus, as if there'd been a secret compact between them, mentioned Tarcisis only as a geographical notation: a starting point, a point of return, a spatial reference, nothing more. I can imagine how much Mara wanted to find out about so many things and how Proserpinus must have been anxious to shine there on my triclinium, exercising his mordacity at the expense of other people's lives. But the miracle took place. My curiosity wasn't satisfied, of course, but my pride—which counts the most—wasn't touched.

At a certain point Proserpinus, stammering now, set about singing my praises: "Never—are you listening, Lucius?—never have I come before a judge as upright and as wise as you. And I'm no longer a child."

"You didn't win many cases in my court ..."

"I didn't win, but justice did! No, in that city there's never been a more righteous judge, Lucius."

And Proserpinus held out his goblet to me in a sad salute, his hand trembling. He didn't insist on bringing up bygone lawsuits, one of which, he knew better than anyone, was the cause of my bitterness and discomfort. . . . He got entangled, rather, in elevated considerations of the meaning of existence and the rules of life adequate to the challenge of the uncertainties of fate.

We finished with Proserpinus questioning me on points of mythology. Only then, with a certain relief, did I satisfy myself that he would make no reference whatever to Iunia Cantaber. . . .

"Do you think, Lucius, that Minos, when he spared the Minotaur and imprisoned him in the Labyrinth, had already foreseen the deeds of Theseus through inspiration from the gods, or, on the contrary, that he wanted to preserve the monster in order to keep the material evidence of Pasiphaë's sin alive?"

I went along, answering with whatever came into my head. I submitted to a more and more obtuse interrogation about Achilles and Proculus, Morpheus and Halcyone, and the Seven Against Thebes. Proserpinus was no longer listening to my opinions. The nods with which he'd been accepting my words grew less and less pronounced until his chin was simply resting on his chest. His breathing had become regular and heavy. Mara called his slaves, who carried him to the cubicle that had been set aside for him.

Mara and I talked about banalities. Neither of us mentioned Proserpinus or Tarcisis. Later, in bed, I went over the questions I would have liked to ask and that my pride and the kind deference of Mara and Proserpinus had thwarted. I slept little and restlessly, anxious for my guest to leave.

<hr/>

I wanted to be the first one up, as is the norm: the master must be on his feet before his slaves. That was how it had always been in my house and in my father's. But the women were already lighting the fire in the kitchens and Proserpinus' entourage was making ready to continue its journey when I made my appearance in the atrium. I gave orders for them to be supplied with food for the trip, and I reinforced their escort for half the distance with four husky armed guards. Proserpinus was so effusive that he almost kissed my ground before leaving.

That morning I didn't see anyone. I ordered the sportulae to be distributed outside to the few clients who'd had themselves announced, and I set myself up by the green marble table with my quill, inkwell, and some fresh papyrus. After Proserpinus' visit, perhaps in compensation for what had been left unsaid, I resolved to write down the events that had taken place in Tarcisis during my term as magistrate. What I couldn't manage to remember I invented, with no scruples whatever: imagination is also a refuge for the truth. It might be that by writing I'll be able to settle my nerves, which would be of manifest utility for me. But I do want this book to serve as a lesson for the one who reads it. Let me be clear, then, precise, careful, truthful, skillful, imaginative, and in that way Providence will inspire me. And I'll not even refuse the intercession of a certain god who in the beginning, so it seems, was strolling in a garden in the cool of the evening . . .

II

In THE YEAR 213 of the Age of
Augustus, 928 from the founding of the city, with Marcus Aurelius
Antoninus as emperor, I was a duumvir in Tarcisis for the second
time and jointly exercising the magistracy with Gaius Cecilius
Trifenus, a highly esteemed citizen, who died suddenly and under
peculiar circumstances.

Trifenus was a jovial magistrate, liberal, benevolent, and a lover
of the games. He spent more time at meals than in the baths, not to
mention the court, but he had no problem with his obesity or the
style of life that maintained and increased it. He slept a great deal.
He read little. He thought less. He discoursed abundantly. He always left difficult matters for the morrow. He knew how to get a
good share of benefits over the course of time. He kept well away
from any pitfalls. He never got involved in my duties, but was very
pleased to involve me in his. He was on good terms with the governor, Sextus Tigidius Perenne, which was evidence of tact, patience,
and an elasticity of spirit. All this contributed, logically, to the popu-
larity he had built up, and which, in part, spilled over onto me.

The games he had organized some years back during one of his
earlier duumvirates to commemorate the emperor's first victory
over the Marcomanni were most certainly catastrophic. For lack of

a circus and with an urgency brought on by the rapidly approaching festivities, he had a wooden arena built, similar in appearance if not in size to the one Vespasian had erected in Rome in the gardens of the gilded mansion. Wild beasts and gladiators came from Emerita, charioteers from Mirobriga, and ropewalkers from every corner of Hispania. The games were never able to get started because the benches collapsed at the very moment Trifenus tossed his handkerchief into the arena, as if that had been the signal for a revolt on the part of the structure. There were many dead, and late into the night the undermanned urban cohort went about clumsily hunting down bears and mastiffs through the streets of Tarcisis. The builders disappeared and were never seen again.

A letter from the governor was severe with the curia, and it entailed them to indemnify the families of the victims according to the status of each, even though the games had not been, strictly speaking, a public undertaking. There were protests and demands. Something worse had occurred in Rome when the benches of the Circus Maximus collapsed under the eyes of the Emperor Antoninus Pius, killing 1,112 innocent spectators. But the municipality complied and paid.

Excessively crude epigrams were bandied about, jocosely attributing the collapse of the benches to Trifenus' weight. From that time on he became all the more fixed in his pattern of not making decisions. I found a fine pretext in what had happened to avoid any organization of games, and I ordered the construction of a theater, which was never finished in the course of my judgeships because all the stones and even the statues and inscriptions would one day be diverted for the rebuilding of battlements.

Trifenus' unexpected death brought on divergent comments: some understood it as divine retribution for the excesses of the life he'd been leading; others said they envied him such a sudden, painless passing, clearly the result of intervention by Apollo. In a general way everyone lamented the disappearance of a magistrate of good family who was merry, free-spending, a friend of the governor, and whom no one hated.

His decease occurred during a public reading at the home of a decemvir named Apitus. As was customary, one of the duumvirs presided. Habitually that honor, or to be more frank that affliction, fell upon me. On that day, however, I preferred to receive a certain Airhan, recently arrived in Tarcisis, who with great secrecy and urgent appeals had asked for an audience to give me the news from the south. So Trifenus settled into my place on the great official chair on the platform reserved for the duumvir.

According to what I was told, the session went on with absolute and dull normality. The first speaker announced that he would proceed to the reading of a variation on the famous question Demosthenes had proposed in Athens dealing with the sale of the donkey or of the donkey's shadow, a question that had been glossed in great detail by all jurisconsults.

Everyone was reconciled to suffering the question of the donkey, which was followed by a dialogue on the munificence of the Caesars and a heroic poem on the fall of Numantia. There was much yawning and nodding in that audience, and therefore no one was surprised to see Trifenus' head drift down and hang to one side, barely supported by the back of the chair, or to see that his outstretched feet had pushed his stool away. Only hours later, when the session came to an end and they tried to awaken Trifenus, first gently then vigorously, did they reach the conclusion that death—as they said—had taken pity on him and spared him the flood of words and gestures that had taken place there.

Even so the last speaker—Proserpinus—was accused by joking backbiters of having furnished apostrophes that were fatal to curule ears, and a few young wags even put together a nickname out of a Greek neologism that meant "he of the fateful word."

I'm not given to smiling when I speak of these events and their burlesque form, nor am I trying to amuse anyone. I simply want to accentuate the somewhat irreverent insouciance, silly in a way and absolutely merciless, that reigned in Tarcisis in those days. The notables took nothing seriously; the plebes didn't take the notables seriously. And in that lighthearted irresponsibility, all felt themselves protected by some great diaphanous but solid bell jar, watched over by benevolent guardian gods. It occurred to no one that the divinity of the Emperor was valid only in temples, that the authority of the Senate and People was tremulously guaranteed by the encampment of the VII Legion Gemina nine hundred miles away, or that the corruption of discord was already at work within the city's battlements—a certain man, weak-looking but with winged words, having entered Tarcisis.

Airhan was the one who brought him to my attention, offhand and in a vague and as if distracted way: "It seems that a foreigner's been going around there. They say he's a dealer in walnuts. . . ."

"Name?"

"Milquion or Melquion, I'm not sure."

Then he went on to something else without providing more details. Nor did I give the wanderer any great importance. What worried me at the time, the reason for calling Airhan in, was the rumor of disturbances and activity across the strait. From what he hinted, the situation called for concern.

⌖

This Airhan was my informant, the informant of my predecessors, and I don't know of whom else. I never liked him, a situation that was all right with him as long as I paid and didn't fall into any great curiosity about what could be called—to put it simply—his way of life. Airhan was accustomed to being detested, and he expected no other feeling—even from those in power, as I was.

He had a strong smell of half-cured leather and stable animals about him. No sooner did he enter than my chambers became impregnated with that stench, which persisted in contaminating the tiniest and most out-of-the-way objects even after his withdrawal. For a long time the very wax on the blinds revealed contact with this man.

Quite confusing were his national origin, the activities in which he was involved, and even the words with which he expressed himself—which, though lacking the solemnity of oracles, rarely pointed to a single meaning. His heterogeneous clothing (almost tatters), scraggly beard, thick trunk, and short arms made one think of those dockworkers brutalized by heavy work and fermented drink. He didn't remain still, there in my chambers facing me. He would take a step toward the window, then one toward me; then, about to turn his back, he would almost give me a blast of his sour breath. His eyes were continuously goggling, shifting from side to side and fixing onto some object or another, as if he suspected that a hidden threat lurked in a dark corner. And he never held his arms close to his body, was always spinning his hands open and away, in broad theatrical gestures that contrasted with his low, monotone speech.

I gathered that multitudes had been pouring down out of the Atlas Mountains and from the confines of the desert—driven sometimes by hunger, sometimes by warlike peoples—and spreading over the plains on the other shore of the Galpe. Volubilis and Septem Fratres didn't feel secure and were calling up militias and asking for reinforcements. The beaches and seas were being overrun by small, poorly constructed boats weighted down with people who, as far as was known, had sacked and burned a cargo ship and even dared board a bireme off Lixus.

But Airhan had heard the rumors in Gades, where life was going along normally. He hadn't seen anything with his own eyes. The tales were circulating, people in the ports were commenting on them, but my informant, for all his colorful additions, lacked any precise facts. He'd heard the story of the bireme in Vipasca, quite inland already. The others might have been rumors of the kind that run through countryside and city from time to time (starting from some tiny point of stimulation) to satisfy the human pleasure of invention, and are immediately forgotten and replaced by the first new item to put in an appearance.

Secretly I remembered with a nervous twitch as if it had been a great revelation, what I knew better than he: the military forces available in all of the south were scarce, almost nonexistent. Vigilantes, watchmen, public slaves: little else. If the Berber uprising were confirmed, the peninsula would find itself undefended. In the meantime, according to my wishes, Airhan was to leave for African territory to gather more detailed information.

It was obvious to me that this contribution by Airhan had a hint of bargaining about it. In some way he was trying to effect along the way some obscure dealings I didn't wish to go into any deeper, and which probably had to do with the traffic of precious metals to the disadvantage of the public treasury. But he kept trying to convince me that he was on a selfless mission for the good of the city. I gave him the equivalent of 250 sesterces. He stood there waiting, shuffling with embarrassment and looking at me with a supplicatory air. I gave him 50 sesterces more. Airhan sighed and dribbled the coins, one by one, through an ingenious opening into the wide leather belt he wore. It was during this meticulous operation that he distractedly mentioned the name of the stranger, the dealer in walnuts, again.

"They say he's a protégé of Maximus Cantaber."

"So? What about him?"

"Nothing special, duumvir. He's very superstitious, and he speaks well. I just wanted to bring you up to date."

He went on about the weather, about the vows he had to make to his protective gods, then saluted, made a courteous bow to the bust of Marcus Aurelius, and left. The next day I learned he'd taken off quite early with his slaves and his animals.

⸺✦⸺

Trifenus had been bountiful to half the city in his will: he freed a handful of slaves, left money to the temples and shrines, and spread his liberality around. His funeral ceremonies were widely attended. He left me three Greek books from his library, two being medical texts of uncertain authorship and the third the *Tyrrhenika* of Claudius. He also had exuberant words of praise for me, which gave me even greater pleasure than the books. Though Trifenus' will had been read in public at his triclinium, in the baths, in the forum, I would never have imagined that with his death those laborious phrases—which, and I don't exaggerate, placed me second only to the Emperor in worthiness—could please me so much. That's how it is with little human vanities. I reject them and deny them, but I acknowledge them. I was priding myself on words dictated by Trifenus—I, who used to grow impatient with his rambling and who'd made a great effort not to laugh when he told me one day that he intended adding the title of "philosopher" and perhaps that of "saint" to his epitaph. . . . But after all, Trifenus had come to his end; his ashes would be thrown into the Anas, far away. Let him rest in peace and with the honors of a philosopher, even of a saint; why not?

The decemvir Pontius Velutius Modus delivered an ingenious and lengthy funeral oration inspired by well-known examples, with touches of Plutarch, two complete phrases from Tiberius Gracchus, and an abundance of bold thefts from Cicero. If Trifenus hadn't deserved so much in life, he was completely undeserving in death. But what difference does it make if a funeral oration doesn't precisely fit the one being eulogized? If death hadn't whisked him away so early, perhaps even Trifenus might have gone on to accomplish the good deeds attributed to him. It really isn't the man who lived and whose remains are laid out there on the pyre in their helpless materiality to whom the eulogy is directed; rather, it is to the projection of the man that circumstances might have revealed. Everyone, including the party in question, would have liked to have knowledge of the last item. It is therefore legitimate and even obligatory for it to be brought out. An elaborate homage like that adds luster to the speaker, his auditors, and the city, enhancing it with the revelation of one more distinguished citizen, unfortunately deceased now, to whom before—to its shame—it hadn't paid attention.

It was in this frame of mind—or an equivalent one—that those present listened solemnly to the funeral encomia. Though Pontius had a husky voice, he knew how to modulate his phrases according to their content, to gauge his gestures to fit the emotion, and to manipulate other people's quotes to the increase of his own glory. It was a pity he didn't lean to brevity.

When, finally, one of Trifenus' freedmen ignited the pyre with a long torch, an event took place that I laid to mere chance, but that brought on movements of retreat and even a startled nervous clamor. Two of the upper beams holding the casket collapsed without being touched. Half the body dropped down along the firewood, an arm fell loose and dangled, and Trifenus ended up being cremated in that indecorous position.

I didn't put much credence in the rumors that immediately circulated by the wall there and considered what had happened an evil omen. Simple souls are always ready to prognosticate, to draw inferences from any slight event, and are most often unaware of the true premonitory facts accessible only to augurs, when gifted, or to someone who knows how to struggle with the sibylline books.

❦

While the beams crackled and the chorus of professional women mourners wailed their hair-raising lamentations, I summoned to the praetorium, either in person or through the lictors, all the decemvirs of the curia, taking advantage of their attendance at the ceremonies. There were mutters of protest and attempts at excuses: that it was ill-omened on the day of a funeral; that mourning togas were inappropriate for the conduct of public business; that it would be a great affront to steal away from the banquet; that the meeting was not being called with the customary formalities. I wouldn't hear of any excuses, and I held firmly to the order. They were all to appear at the praetorium an hour from then.

I waited at one of the upper windows of the basilica. The people were convening in the forum in scattered groups. A formation of armed vigilantes passed, off to somewhere with their boots sounding rhythmically on the pavement. Aulus Manlius, a centurion in the city's service, a position he held along with that of prefect under the orders of the praetorium, came from the decumanus, walking stiffly, displaying all his phalerae on his armor. He crossed the forum, returned the salute of the patrol, and slowly headed toward the basilica steps.

This Aulus was an institution in the city. He had served with Trifenus' father in the Dacia campaigns. One day during a barbarian attack an enemy horseman managed to vault the camp stockade and was immediately riddled with javelins. The horse fell on Aulus, a centurion from Hispania belonging to the tenth cohort, the most junior in his rank, who was left with a crushed left arm. The arm didn't have to be amputated, but he was never able to move it again. Trifenus' father, who was not to return from that campaign, took pity and sent the young centurion to Tarcisis with a recommendation to the curia. They made him prefect and commander of the urban cohort, which he, in his own way, enlarged and organized. He was a very tall man, of few words, and was considered to have iron-clad loyalty to the magistrates. So much so

21

that backbiters called him "The Dog of Sabinus," an allusion to the animal that leaped into the Tiber after his master, who had been thrown from the Gemoniae steps at the instigation of Sejanus.

The forum was coming to life again. Merchants were setting up shop. The poet Cornelius Lucullus appeared in one corner with his languid walk, then examined a chicken, holding it up to the sun for a long time, only to give it back to the vendor and go off in a harangue—accompanied by broad gestures—that he directed at a group of fellow loafers. Criers arrived; ropewalkers leaped about. In one gathering there was an altercation, a bustle, a rumpus, a reconciliation. And my magistrates were late . . .

They finally came, litter after litter, drawing after them a train of slaves, freedmen, clients, and gawkers. The gray and brown tones of their mourning togas formed a dark diagonal line that contrasted with the jauntiness of the crowd already strolling through the forum. The somber garments finally gathered at the foot of the steps like olives in the bottom of a bowl. The litters were lowered, the forum took on its flash of colors once more, and the eminent men came up the steps, heads down, grave, circumspect, leaving my field of vision.

⚬━✦━⚬

When they came into the hall of the curia I was waiting for them, standing by my chair of office. Beside me, Trifenus' empty seat. All around, as usual, a circle of stools. They were coming in now, conversing in small groups. Annoyed by such an unexpected summons, they wouldn't concede me any great importance. Some didn't even make a move to be seated, and the ones who did so, after Pontius had given me a vague wave of the hand, hadn't waited for my invitation to take their places. The remnants of interrupted phrases were still wandering about the room when Pontius settled onto his seat, cleared his throat, and smiled condescendingly at me: "So, Lucius Valerius, what are your orders?"

I was going to reply, but Pontius turned around suddenly. The Gobiti twins broke off their whispering, became serious, put their togas and their expressions in order. I couldn't catch sight of Pontius' face, but I guessed that his smile had grown in that way—which was very much his—of someone who gives commands without speaking. I'd always admired the serene way Pontius took charge by the mere effect of his presence, and he would calmly make everyone do his bidding without the need of anything but a look or a smile. A gift the gods had bestowed, no doubt, to balance the defects with which they'd loaded him down. And it was with a new variation of that same smile that Pontius asked again: "You were saying, Lucius?"

"I haven't said anything yet. But it seems obvious to me that with the loss of one of the duumvirs, a replacement is in order."

Pontius stroked his chin as if reflecting. The others exchanged glances. Abruptly all of them began talking almost at the same time and saying the same thing: No, it wasn't necessary; they praised my honesty, but the matter had no relevancy. It was only six months to the end of the term; it wasn't worth it for the city to incur the expenses involved in ceremonies, in a waste of energy and activity. There were plenty of precedents. Someone remembered the case of Tiberius Nero, who, under similar circumstances, held the consulate all by himself.

Synthesizing, Pontius slowly pointed out the disadvantages of an intercalary replacement. The curia backed him . . .

I reminded them of events on the other side of the strait, the threat they represented, and the need for strong government in Tarcisis. They all minimized the seriousness of the Moorish raids in Africa. I brought up Airhan's report. No one paid it much attention.

Africa was far away, my informant was exaggerating, and the Moors wouldn't dare invade Lusitania after the lesson they'd been taught before, at an enormous cost to them. The new walls at Volubilis barred their way, and, as a last resort, a squadron could always sink their boats . . .

"Don't worry, Lucius, no disaster of that kind is going to take place anytime during your term," Apitus concluded with a broad circular gesture.

Pontius artfully took advantage of the tumult to turn my argument around: "But should we concede, Lucius . . . hypothetically,

23

of course . . . that there were threats to the city, it's obvious that the slightest political change would be inopportune."

"We must comply with the law!"

"Come, now, Lucius. The law that matters here is the law of good sense!"

"There are other positions to be filled."

"The aediles? But my dear Lucius, who cares about the aediles? The only ones who aspire to those aedileships are the sons of freedmen . . . and even so, it's doubtful they'd be any more competent than the two useless types who now hold the position formally."

"I'm not in the good graces of the governor."

They all laughed. They remembered with amusement the answer I'd sent to Emerita, citing Tiberius, when Sextus Perene demanded an exorbitant and illegal tribute from Tarcisis: "A good shepherd shears his sheep, he doesn't skin them." Simultaneously I'd demanded an imperial curator, a common practice at the time, but one that wasn't very pleasing to governors. Perene was silent, but he let it be known that he didn't want to hear much about me.

"There are roads to Rome that don't pass through Emerita," Pontius calmly philosophized, his hands crossed over the bulge of his belly.

They showed themselves unitedly disposed to go against me, ably led by Pontius Modius. A mood of almost derisive indifference reigned regarding what I understood would afflict us all. Perhaps I'd moved too quickly in calling the curia together in that way, on that occasion, interfering with their comfort and causing ill feeling. But I was the chief magistrate, and I meant to take the circumstance very much to heart. There were obligations to fulfill, a right to be in control of my activities, a bond of loyalty to the Emperor, and threats to be confronted.

I perceived that I would have to make some concession, but without going against the constitutional order of the city: "Perhaps I should write to the Emperor, then, so that he can ratify what's to be decided."

"That's it. You write to Rome. We mustn't forget that you have privileged access to the Princeps," Pontius pondered lazily. "Then, at another meeting, we'll get back to the matter."

"Just a moment!"

Pontius had wrapped his toga about his left arm and made a motion as if he were going to get up, when he was surprised by my shout. He dropped back onto his stool, annoyed, and stared, measuring me up and down. I must have looked enraged and ready for a test of wills. I confess that my hands were trembling. Pontius gave a deep, benevolent sigh, raised both hands in a calming gesture, and began excusing himself: "Come, Lucius, you're certainly not counting on me. I've already been a duumvir of this city, and it almost ruined me. This basilica. Who was it who had it rebuilt at his own expense? In part, at least, eh?"

He looked around. The faces were tightened now. They were all looking down at their seats or letting their eyes roam the walls. Little by little, one by one, they brought up their munificences to the city, generously exaggerated, and the attrition that the course of honors had brought on in their fortunes, their health, their family harmony. This one had had the forum paved and the statues to Mars and Minerva erected, that one repaired the temple of Jupiter Optimus Maximus, that other one offered games for three days with four gladiators and seven wild beasts ... They all declared that Rome owed them more than they owed Rome. When I spotted the Gobiti, the whining had exploded into bursts of laughter, followed by jokes about the twins' effeminate habits.

"Well," Apitus observed, "it's time we were going. My wife is waiting in the litter, the slaves haven't eaten yet . . ."

Pontius was watching me out of the corner of his eye. He saw that I was getting more and more impatient, and he could see that the comedy was wearing thin. He became serious, raised his arms and imposed silence. Everybody in the room obeyed Pontius' gestures. He clasped his hands to his chest and began to speak in a soft voice, sadly, emotionally, staring at a spot on the floor where the mosaic figure of Laocoön was struggling with the serpents.

"Ah, Lucius. You know quite well that I'm covered with scars: on the body from barbarian steel; on the soul from a lack of understanding and consideration on the part of the Romans; on my estate from large, generous, and sometimes misunderstood expenses.

I'm sad, my friends, I'm disillusioned, on the road to old age. Look at these white hairs. Can anyone censure me for wanting, at the end of my life (without ceasing to respond when necessary to the call of duty), to enjoy at last the domestic tranquility that well-born patriarchs deserve?"

I was hasty. I interrupted him. It was a mistake. I said what he wanted to hear: "I've made sacrifices too, Pontius . . ."

Pontius looked at me obliquely, maintaining the same disconsolate pose and reflective tone of voice: "You're right, Lucius, you're an upright man. Isn't that so, citizens?"

A murmur of respectful agreement went about the room. I perceived the trap into which I'd fallen. Too late. Pontius stood up, carried away; pushing his stool aside, he lifted his right hand, raising two fingers in the solemn gesture of the orator, and roared at those present with an imperious tone: "I ask for the floor! Will you permit me, Lucius?" And he repeated, thundering, "Will you permit me, Lucius?" And then, with rhetorical inflections: "I propose, citizens, that the duumvir Lucius Valerius Quintius, here present, a model of piety, moderation, and wisdom, assume, with the approval of the curia, the double mandate, taking on the duties of the duumvir Gaius Cecilius Trifenus, now deceased!"

There was an outburst of applause. Pontius was smiling with rapture, hands posed on his broad chest, nodding his head to one and another as if thanking them. No one was paying the slightest attention to me. I was frozen. Only moments later did they notice that I was covering my head with my toga, stressing my silence and my protest. The applause and the congratulations ceased. I felt the hand of Pontius, who was gently pulling on my toga and trying to uncover my head: "Lucius, Lucius, well?"

Other voices joined in to convince me. Someone went so far as to state that his confidence in me was such that he felt it wouldn't be amiss to confer a dictatorship on me. No one spoke against it. They made the decision by unanimous assent and in a definitive way. It occurred to no one to raise any doubts or reservations. With equivocal waves of the hand and mumbled excuses, they began going off, leaving me to myself.

I remained for a long time at that table, downcast. What worried me was not only the doubtful legality of the situation or the added work and responsibilities it would bring me. It was the fact that the matter had been decided by my peers out of pure accommodation in an access of frivolous selfishness, to which the problems of the city, the interests of Rome, were completely alien. How could something like that have become possible? There hadn't been a single voice that brought into the discussion the public interest or any consideration of the threats hanging over Tarcisis or the slightest gesture to renounce the general idleness and faintheartedness. Was that, then, what my fellow citizens were like? My subjects, as I could almost say with propriety now?

That night I wrote until very late—not to Rome, but for myself, in the intimacy of my bedroom. I wanted to make note of everything before my memory lost it. Mara saw the light and came to be with me. She didn't say anything. She put her lamp on the floor and sat on my bed. Then she dozed off while I was writing. Mara wanted to let me know that she was aware of my concern and that she was with me. Discreet as always, watching me concentrate, she asked no questions and made no comments. But she wanted to stay beside me in that grave moment of mine.

Mara!

III

"I APPROACH the altar of the god!"

The chorus of young boys wearing the toga praetexta stood in a circle around me, scanning the ritual words as they resounded off the stonework of the temple.

"Behold, he approaches the altar of the god!"

Thick wine poured from a silver pitcher and filled the carved goblet in my hand. The flute player broke into strident music that came to an abrupt stop when I finished pouring the wine over the altar.

"I have made the libation!"

The chorus: "Behold, he has proceeded to the libation!"

I took two steps back and, speaking the prescribed words, announced that I was delegating the sacrifice to Aulus, who was already leaning over the victim with the ceremonial instruments. The stridency of the flutes broke out again, muffling the brief death agony of the first animal.

I have never liked blood. Avoiding the slightest error or the smallest false movement, I have always scrupulously and meticulously carried out the ordained ritual, whether public or domestic, of the Empire or of the city. When the moment for the slaughter and the nauseating handling of bloody flesh and viscera arrived, I would habitually delegate it, as the rules allow. Afterward, with my head covered, I would approach the altar to consult the god with the proper formula. As usual the god would respond, always with the same words, because that was how it should be.

A thick coat of dampness covered the stone of the temple walls and seemed to darken the environment even more and increase the chill of the place, though the weather was pleasant outside and the sun wasn't hiding away. I couldn't remember having seen that black and spongy stain before, and it stayed with me as a sign, perhaps the forerunner of others to be revealed later, more impressive than the display of steaming entrails. Cosimus, a decrepit, crafty haruspex, lifted his wrinkled head and made a gloomy signal to me, indicating that the entrails predicted nothing good. It wasn't the first time. I cannot remember old Cosimus ever drawing predictions of happy times from the innards of an animal. What is it about men who pride themselves on being the bearers of bad news? Why is it that the announcement of misfortune is more natural to them and gives them greater joy? Perhaps because adversities are more easily confirmed by life and last longer in one's memory. . . . Giving it some thought, however, I could see that all this was of no great import. It was only a matter of a ritual, a simulacrum, consecrated gestures.

A month had passed since my confirmation as sole supreme magistrate of the city. I went about performing my duties and working more than I had to. The two aediles, chosen more by routine than by any deliberated consideration, had yet to set foot in the praetorium. I had also taken the aedileship under my charge. As the days passed I was becoming aware that I missed the very indolence of the late Trifenus; his simple, peaceful (and irregular) presence would have been a support and stimulation for me.

Rumors of movements by the barbarians in the south were, meanwhile, growing more and more insistent. Travelers, merchants, and muleteers brought scattered news of raids and piracy, sometimes inconsequential, in most cases extremely exaggerated. Good conversation helps business, and the more fanciful it is, the better disposed is the customer's favor. The events were taking place off in the distance. They were the object of general curiosity, the same as events in Germania or Dacia. My fellow citizens, as was their ill-considered habit, took the stories for gossip and fabulation. They would look around and see wheat fields waving peacefully, birds flying, shepherds guarding their flocks, farmers bent over their plows, carts coming and going, lumbering over paving stones in the road. But every day I reminded myself that the Tarcisis garrison was under a hundred men, between vigilantes and gatekeepers, aged, inexperienced, softened by peace, and ill-suited for resolute action. And I was quite aware that the city walls, built in the time of Augustus, had never been kept in good repair. The sections that weren't crumbling or destroyed displayed the neglect and the depredations permitted by aediles too accustomed to the Pax Romana.

From the citizens' point of view, the most vexing source of nervousness could be found over the mountains. Active at that time were a bandit named Arsenna and his band of rogues, drawn to marauding, it was said, by the ruination of Arsenna's father in a disastrous lawsuit. This closer danger, which translated into missing carts and emptied purses, aroused more indignation than the distant and uncertain rumor of clumsy, coarse barbarians, unlimited in their fury but with respect for the legions. No one seemed to perceive, taken as they all were with blind confidence, that between us and the barbarians not even a cohort was encamped. A tiny auxiliary detachment was guarding the Vipasca mines to the west. Contemptible urban garrisons, as inept as ours, were loafing about in some municipalities. That was all.

❦

After the sacrifice, when the ceremony was over, the lively group of boys scattered pell-mell, joyful at seeing themselves free of the ritual and anxious to get rid of their togas. I had to hide my smile when I spotted the gorgon looks with which the soothsayer was trying to petrify the young ones. It was more than certain that Cosimus would go knock on the door of each one and complain to his parents. The matter would then be discussed with Mulnius, the teacher, who would promise scoldings and whippings over two mugs of indignant hot wine.

Back at the praetorium, the merry episode of the children and memories of childhood and school gave way to the disquiet of recent times, aggravated by the uncomfortable feeling brought on by that sinister stain of mildew on the wall. I know nothing of prodigies or presages except for the obvious ones everybody knows: a statue that smiles, a snake that falls from the ceiling, an eagle that alights on a temple, a lightning bolt that strikes a tomb. . . . But I felt instinctively that I'd been warned things were not going to go well for me. I preferred not to consult the haruspices of the city. They were given to catastrophes, terrifying people with eschatological visions, and in a general way, I had doubts about their competence. It's difficult, furthermore, to believe in a soothsayer we come across arguing over the price of cucumbers in the marketplace or glimpse at not very sacred libations in the darkness of a tavern. No one is a prophet in his own land, the Jews are wont to say. I must admit that the same can be thought of priests—being one myself, which goes with my duties—who, after presiding over the sacrifice, wrapped in a toga, rise to decide matters of apportionments in court. Basically, we go along fulfilling the formalities without believing in anything, even when our civic feelings make us proceed as if we did believe. But fate always insists on compounding unforeseen situations that are immune to our rituals, gesticulations, and invocations.

<hr />

On my birthday Mara surprised me first thing in the morning with a rare present that I found at the foot of my bed: an onyx cameo with the embedded effigies of Marcus Aurelius, Lucius Verus, and Faustina. I made a decision—an uncharacteristically worldly-minded one, those who knew my makeup would say. I resolved to send out dinner invitations, breaking with the custom imposed on me, since my accession to duumvir, of not hosting anyone in my home. I made no visits, nor did I receive them: I limited myself, at daybreak, to seeing clients—fewer and fewer since my swearing had become known—and following the precepts of citizenship that the circumstances demanded. The magistracy relieved me—I felt—of paying my respects to anyone, no matter who it might be, within the city limits. And I paid scant attention to the railery they engaged in at my door during the Saturnalia: "Lucius, open up your brothel, what are you hiding?"

Senator Ennius Calpurnius didn't accept that behavior with good grace and never lost an opportunity to treat me as if I were his client, as my father had been before. I condescended to maintain the ambiguity of the situation in the same way I made other concessions dictated by the office I held. So as not to annoy others, I saw myself not rarely obliged to cease closeting myself; Marcus Aurelius himself had taught me that. But I was evidently a bad pupil . . .

The games and festivities hold little attraction for me. I avoid bloody rituals as much as possible, but I have always tried not to upset the people, not to go against custom openly, and not to offend elders. Our citizenship, which gives us so many reasons to be proud, is founded on this complex system of hypocrisies and balances. I was a magistrate, not a philosopher: if it was necessary to pretend in order to maintain peace and tranquility, I would pretend. The Emperor was a philosopher, and wasn't he compelled to involve himself in wars and intrigues that were brutal and perverse? What will, except the one that duty imposed, made Marcus Aurelius share the hard cheese of his soldiers, suffer wind and sun, witness the decapitation of hairy barbarians? Or vengefully break up the conspiracy of Avidius Cassius? Or preside over cruel spectacles that have never succeeded in taking the place of the Greek games? None, I presume. It simply had to be. It had to be borne! But with what limits?

Later I shall speak of the "illustrious" Calpurnius, the only one in the city to wear the purple stripe on his toga and a gold ring on his finger and to have himself attended by three lictors, while I made use of only two. Today I shall speak of the dinner to which I invited Aulus, his wife Galla, and even Cornelius Lucullus, that vagabond poetaster, a frequenter of taverns and the forum, who'd been going about lately reciting verses in my praise.

I received them as if they were my equals, with the same deference on the part of the slaves, the same quality of wine and food. I don't think Aulus felt himself particularly honored. He was a simple man; he limited himself to complying. He was invited? He obeyed. I'll wager that he would have preferred his daily routine to that dinner the magistrate, with whom he was involved all day, had burdened him with. The little poet, however, immediately showed his delight: he was killing his hunger, a hollow, devouring, ancestral hunger, and he would be able to go about the city boasting that he'd been admitted to the duumvir's triclinium. Perhaps that would garner him sufficient prestige for some benefactor to have his poems copied . . .

If on the one hand I needed some distraction after that strange upset in the temple, it was also up to me to please Mara, whom I'd never refused the pleasures of diversions and company that she deserved. That dinner party wasn't exactly what Mara was after. Though she never would have confessed it to me, she would have preferred conversation at Calpurnius' table in the company of the decemvirs and the city's most honored landowners. On that occasion oratorical pieces would be read, dancers and flutists would frolic about, and, in the midst of spirited comments, Mara would know how to make her lighthearted enchantments shine. But I didn't want to give Calpurnius such a great honor, enhanced as it would be by his sense that he, rather, was honoring me. I never spoke to Mara about the matter, but I'm quite aware that each of us knew how to guess the motivation of the other. An intermediate way was found. Haven't I said that our life is wisely made up of balances and implicit understanding? What is marriage if not one of the tiny stitches in that tangled weave?

But why not confess this, too? I think my invitation to the centurion and his wife was due to my egotistical gratitude. I've never forgotten Aulus' conduct immediately after the meeting at which I was invested—I dare to say it—as dictator. Even before the last decemvir had left, Aulus had come into the hall of the curia and was painstakingly going about a chore that was not part of his duties— picking up and putting in order the scattered tablets and papyri. We exchanged glances. We remained looking at each other for I don't know how long. Aulus seemed to understand the vacillation that was distressing my spirit, and I interpreted that look as a mute display of solidarity, worth all the words I would never expect from him. It was important to me to know at that moment that I had the understanding and esteem of a poor centurion, even if that was all.

Now my reasons for choosing the poet were a bit perverse, I must admit. I knew he'd tried to get close to Calpurnius, having sent him some verses by a borrowed slave at the time of the senator's triumphal entry into the city. The following day, early in the morning, when he presented himself in Calpurnius' atrium, aspiring to his patronage, he received instead of the coveted gratuity the returned verses with corrections in red ink in Calpurnius' own hand and the admonition not to do it again. I wanted to show the Pater Conscriptus, the senator, in some way that his rejections and also his affirmations were not conclusive in Tarcisis.

I was told later that Aulus had borrowed the ill-fitting attire he wore that night so as not to appear at dinner in his usual military garb. Reclining, he almost dozed off after the first goblet of wine and made a valiant attempt to stay awake. He was looking at the little poet out of the corner of his eye and not hiding the profound disdain he felt. Mara had received the guests festively, as if it were a great occasion in her life. She overdid it a bit, I think, especially when, still in the atrium, slave women tossed rose petals over the new arrivals.

Mara explained to Galla in detail the seasoning of the dishes that were served, showed an interest in the poet's epigrams, and never lost a chance to direct a friendly word his way. Galla accepted everything quite naturally, as if she'd been accustomed to those attentions, and she let herself recline on the couch alongside her husband, not noticing that Mara was sitting up. Cornelius felt lifted up to the empyrean and didn't stop filling his mouth and his napkin—more ample than was called for by custom—which reached across to his flanks.

Galla had her conversation all prepared, and sometimes she would make use of recherché expressions of problematic meaning. She was trying to shine. She even got to quoting something in Greek, a language she didn't dominate. She spoke discreetly about slaves, flaunted a knowledge of wigs and cosmetics, and joked somewhat wittily about the several religions she'd gone through, with no respect for the mysteries and secrets that each one obliged her to keep. One had to understand Galla. Aulus was getting bored, glum, taciturn. She had to babble for the both of them. It must be added that Galla was radiant over the distinction the invitation brought and couldn't always manage to measure her words. She caught Cornelius' attention; I noticed that as he became more sated and uninterested in food, the bard cast his eyes on her, pretending to listen with the rapture of raised eyebrows, exaggerating.

"I went from Isis to Mithras," Galla was prattling. "I never liked those female cults with their processions, whispering, and backbiting. Osiris spends his time dying and reviving, and it's all one big monotonous bore. I converted to the son of god, Mithras, sent to earth by his father, Aridman, to drive the shadows away and lead the just to heaven over the Milky Way. It's a shame that women aren't admitted to the mysteries . . ."

Galla's words received acquiescence but no enthusiasm. Mara is supremely removed from religious matters. She limits herself to doing what everybody does, but without according it much significance. Our door, our bolts, our house are entrusted to the competent gods, I can't remember too well which they are. A candle is always burning by the threshold, and an oil lamp smokes on the altar of the lares. The divinities entrusted to Mara's care, among whom Trebaruna stands out, never lack for anything. Mara does her duty, imitates, carries on the tradition. She conducts herself at home as I do in the city. The ancient rituals were enough for us to care about without concerning ourselves with the hordes of new gods, local and foreign. For my part, I've always avoided priestesses with shaved heads and pleated tunics. I've learned that the world is complicated and diverse enough and doesn't need the efforts of men to make it any more intricate. I would prefer for the gods, whichever and wherever they are, to keep on busying themselves in their proper places. And for their priests to be closer to them than to us . . .

I tried to rouse Aulus out of his reticence by mentioning the bandit Arsenna and some perfumes and unguents that the city's female population had been waiting for greedily for months and that, it was suspected, were now embellishing the bandits' lady friends in those notorious hostelries out there. I knew that the mere mention of Arsenna was all that was needed to infuriate Aulus, who'd been chasing him for years, and to whom the brigand's crimes were a personal affront. Coming to life, Aulus turned the conversation away from insipid matters of religion just at the moment when the poet was on the dangerous verge of perorating on astrology with regard to the resurrection of Osiris.

But Mara wouldn't let Aulus deliver his speech and immediately cut off the only burst of liveliness that night: "Oh, no, my friend, I won't allow any serious matters in my triclinium. You people have plenty of time to talk about that in the praetorium. Let's talk about frivolous things instead."

At that moment, all at once, a downpour began. The rain resounded on the tiles of the roof, roiled the water in the impluvium, swirled whitish dust up in the peristyle. There was a short silence in the triclinium as if in homage, with some apprehension, to that manifestation of the elements. The air cooled. A door slammed.

Cornelius Lucullus gathered inspiration from the event. After a few moments he raised his cup in Mara's direction while he fastened his eyes on Galla and recited: *"Hearing the sound of yon sweet nymphs, the waters rush with avid roar."*

It was the poet's moment. . . . He'd been invited to entertain us, and the moment had come to fulfill his charge. A young slave with a small harp inlaid with mother-of-pearl settled down next to Cornelius and accompanied the verses with soft, slow chords that could barely be heard over the noise of the rain. They may not have been the greatest verses in the world, and they certainly didn't merit having someone take on the job of copying them, but their sound was just right for the moment. All of us, in gentle drowsiness, withdrew into ourselves and became fixed in our own thoughts. Aulus immediately dozed off.

Confusedly, I caught the sound of creaking doors, the clank of metal, of raised voices out by the entranceway. My quartermaster was beside me now, whispering respectfully into my ear. I was urgently wanted in the vestibule!

I shook Aulus and ordered him to accompany me. The alacrity with which he got up and stood by my side was almost comical, with such energy that he startled and silenced the poet. If Galla's look was of vague curiosity, Mara's was anxious, trying to probe—staring now at me, now at Aulus—what was happening. I excused myself and left the triclinium. I heard the poet timidly pick up the thread of his declaiming.

The rain was beating down so fiercely on the tank in the atrium that a fine foam clung to our clothing as we passed and had a strange effect on the oil lamp I was carrying. A lugubrious gurgle was coming out of the drainpipes and from the bottom of the cistern like an interminable death rattle. Indifferent, exhausted, a young slave was already drowsing leaning against a column in his half-drenched tunic.

In the vestibule, beside the half-closed door, a shape was moving back and forth as far as the narrow space would allow. The drops of water that covered his cloak were glimmering in the light of a torch. As we approached, Airhan took a step in our direction. His clothing was sopping wet. Water ran across his beard in threads.

"They've crossed the strait. They've been driven back for now, duumvir! But tomorrow, who knows?"

IV

THEY HAD crossed the strait in
tall, slim boats with triangular sails and in the dampness of dawn
had established themselves on crags along the sea. Habitually
using metaphors like all Orientals, Airhan compared them to the
clouds of locusts that in years of infestation follow the same route
over the waves, flight after flight. And just as those creatures make
their depredations and leave fields of green stubble, so, too, these
invaders were coming to ravage the lives and estates round about
in ever widening circles. Their mandibles were crude weapons of
stone and bone, and the mark of their passage was the devastation
left by their fires. No settlement or sanctuary escaped their fury,
and there was concern that they would become emboldened enough
to attack cities. There was confirmation of the boarding and burning of Roman ships and a blockade of the Pillars of Hercules by
swarms of small boats bristling with weapons. An improvised
troop recruited hastily from slaves and freedmen in Gades and
Septem under the command of a retired primipilus had engaged the
barbarians in indecisive battle, scattering them but not wiping
them out, in the region of the Galpe. Landowners had fled their
fields for the uncertain protection of the cities. Messengers were
already on their way, bearing the fears and pleas of the populace, to

find the VII Legion Gemina. There were those who swore that an imperial procurator was about to be appointed to take command of the offensive.

And Airhan's deplorable looks—soaked to the skin, his dirty beard shimmering in the reflection of the lights, eyes bulging and roving about, open hands gesturing wildly—brought to that narrow vestibule the preview of a horror that had only been postponed. In that same light Aulus' hardened and glabrous features seemed to reproduce the faces of ancient Romans on statues, so worthy, firm, and serene, though inept at flights of the imagination. There I was, between the two, aroused now by the flamboyant gesticulations of the one, calmed then by the imperturbable immobility of the other. It was up to me to make a decision. Airhan's description redounded with details that were more than enough for me.

I ordered him to go back and keep me informed of everything he saw or found out. He opened his arms, showing his soaked clothing, raised his hands to his beard and then held them out, damp, rolled his eyes upward as a sign of the great sacrifice he was going to make once more for me—and only for me—and, finally, he bowed. Then I spoke to him prudently, with many well-planned hesitations: "If by chance—only by chance, obviously—you, who've been to so many places and slept in so many beds, were to obtain useful information from someone who, let us say, is outside the law, I would understand, Airhan . . ."

"Fortunately, duumvir, I only have contact with people who are loyal to the Emperor, whether Romans, slaves, or even rustics."

If, however, there happened someday to be a surprising exception . . . Airhan scratched his head. We understood each other: perhaps Arsenna and his band might still be useful to me.

I had no money on me, and I didn't want to involve my quartermaster in that transaction. I remembered a small silver statuette of Minerva that usually adorned a table in the atrium. I went to get it and tried to give it to Airhan.

But he reacted almost as if offended. He became quite agitated, refused with great affectation, and protested—looking repeatedly at Aulus—that his loyalty to Tarcisis and to the magistrates of Rome came ahead of any material interests. I noticed that it was a bit difficult for him to speak these high-flown words; his eyes would light on the gleaming silver from time to time and divulge the greed that was his nature. In those glances the statuette had been measured, weighed, and priced more than once. What was taking place in Airhan was a painful conflict between reason and impulse. His present refusal, we both knew, would result in a future recompense much better than the value of the object. Airhan was counting on my not forgetting his show of disinterest in refusing the gift; I would have to credit it to his bill for services rendered. He took his leave hurriedly, not wanting to add any words to the ones he'd spoken and thus to compromise their effect, and he went out into the rain. The stench that his wet clothes exuded, even stronger than usual, lingered and in a certain way maintained his presence inside the house.

When the door slammed shut, Aulus, who'd listened to everything without blinking, finally moved. The festive clothes we were wearing must have seemed to him inappropriate for the occasion. He took the garland off his head and dropped it to the floor, and his good hand slipped down over his chest, tugging at his clothes. He missed the leather lorica he customarily wore, and that was how he showed his discomfort, as if he were tormented by some blame for wearing banquet garb and being unarmed when the barbarians were announced.

"What orders, duumvir?" he asked. The stance and the martial question, thrown out almost as a shout, clashed with his embroidered, colored clothing. I must have slipped into a smile, because I remember Aulus' stupefied look when I took him by the arm and led him through the atrium: "Orders? Yes . . . to return to the triclinium!"

On the far side of the impluvium, behind the streams of water that were swirling more violently and splashing in the tank, was the outline of three shapes, rigid, as if part of a group sculpture. Mara, Galla, and Cornelius, not daring to approach the vestibule, were watching from the rear of the atrium. Mara was holding a light quite high, and they were all waiting, petrified with fear, for us to return. This time—something unusual—Mara's nervousness had overcome her feelings as hostess. She hadn't resisted, in view of our delay, taking a look to see who'd arrived and what was going on. The others had followed, drawn by curiosity, and there the three of them were between the columns, embarrassed now, looking at each other with indecisive expressions, not knowing what to do.

But that soirée was irremediably ruined. When we settled again in the triclinium there was no way to continue the conversation. It seemed that the room had become chilled in our absence. The fish steaks seemed drier and less inviting, the fish sauce was lumpy and pasty, the vegetables had lost their glow. Also our appetites had waned. A few circumstantial phrases were spoken that aren't worth remembering. And, not moving, we concentrated on the beating of the rain as if our edification and spiritual consolation depended on that sound. Our guests were impatient to leave. I was desirous to be freed of all constraints, and Mara was anxious to ask me the questions that social conventions wouldn't permit at the moment. When the storm abated—it was late now—Cornelius took his leave in a jumble of disorder, with the little slave and his lyre prancing after him, carrying the napkin so swollen with victuals that it looked like a soldier's knapsack. Aulus waited for the poetaster to go and then, in a fury, almost dragged Galla to the door.

"Friend," Mara asked me, leaning on my arm, "what's going on?"

"The barbarians have crossed the strait, Mara. They've been thrown back for now. But they can return."

Mara had an unexpected reaction. She called to the slaves in an ill-tempered way and scolded them for not having been quick enough in removing the silverware from the triclinium. And she redoubled her orders with all the severity possible, given her fragile bearing—none of which succeeded in terrifying anyone. With her back turned, she didn't seem to be paying me any heed as she gave orders for this one to dust, that one to sweep, the other one to put the tables away.

I gave orders to light the tablinum, and I spent some time there at the table by myself, thinking. Through a small gap in the half-open curtain I saw Mara shifting about among the slave girls as if busying herself with household details. Every time she passed by the door she would throw me a quick, fleeting, frightened look and continue on. And then she would come back.

41

The agitation and the rumors going about the house finally ceased. The water left by the rain was now dripping into the impluvium, slow, weary, mournful. I thought Mara had retired by now and that everyone was in bed. I woke the slave who was crouched by the entrance to the tablinum, dozing, and told him to bring my cloak, my boots, and to light a torch. But, coming from I don't know where, Mara emerged to meet me: "Lucius, where are you going?"

"Don't worry. I just want to see if everything's all right."

"Why shouldn't it be all right?"

"You understand, Mara . . ."

She gave a quick smile of agreement, which was negated, however, by her anxious look. It was, in fact, unprecedented for me to want to leave the house in the middle of the night. But my wife made no comment. She adjusted the cloak lightly around my shoulders and stroked my beard, ever so softly, with the back of her hand.

"Don't be long!"

◦━━✦━━◦

The slave pushed open the double doors, and bronze echoes resounded down the narrow alley. I hadn't been out at night on the streets of Tarcisis since I was a boy. At that hour the city lay stretched out, deserted, as if perpetually abandoned. The moon, skipping between dark clouds, drew lines from time to time on the walls, on the outlines of fountains, and on the weave of the tile roofs, which still dripped. The slave went ahead softly and solicitously, lighting up obstacles and puddles of water, which reflected the quivering flames of his torch. Over the crackling of the resin and the moaning of the wind on the signboards of shops, the thumps of the iron-tipped staff the man carried in his right hand could be heard on the paving stones. Then, in the distance, a dog barked.

With impulsive anxiety, I didn't want to leave my inspection of the city for the next day. I was impatient to reach the wall quickly and get an immediate impression—which drowsiness would have a hand in shaping—of the state of the defenses. Along a stone stairway, quite worn now, that rested against the chipped wall of a lookout, we went up to the aqueduct in order to avoid impediments on the ground or unwanted encounters and to reach our objective more easily.

Seen from above—as the gods must surely view it—Tarcisis was growing smaller now as it slept, moving away from me and the feelings of everyday life. It was taking on a neutral materiality, objective and a bit disquieting. The deserted decumanus, over which we were passing; the forum, with the rigid monotony of its colonnades and the imposing temple of Jupiter; the concave space of the unfinished theater gleaming white in the distance; the maze of alleyways along which round, thatch-roofed indigenous houses had survived among the lookouts with loose tile roofs that almost wavered above them. Everything here had been entrusted to my responsibility. I could take in Tarcisis with a look now and easily imagine that I could touch it with my hands, as if it were a model made of wood and plaster. The basilica where I worked each day, the interior of which I was capable of describing down to its darkest corner, looked to me at that moment, with its distant stone frigidity, like a structure from another world, alien, motionless, dead, with an inaccessible soul. . . . A strange city, in short, that one there. The truth was that I, who went through Tarcisis every day and decided its destiny, had just discovered that I didn't know my city.

The sharp sound of the tipped staff with which the slave was marking the time of his steps went echoing across the rooftops, awakening the unease of dogs here and there. I imagined that seen from below, the spectacle of two men wandering by torchlight across the archways over the city must have looked like something ghostly. What would a night owl say if he recognized his duumvir walking along the aqueduct as if on a tightrope? What wonders would be thought up? What rumors? What alarms?

"Be careful with that staff! Don't make any noise!" I ordered the slave.

We were approaching the hill called "Tumultuaria," one of the high points of the city, formerly the camp that had been its origin, so they say, and which held the manor of the Cantabers on one of its slopes. The aqueduct was at the level now of the rows of houses; farther on it joined with a reservoir that in turn would be subdivided among the various districts. The distance from the ground lessened until the rooftops were on a line with our steps, and rose above us farther ahead.

Near the reservoir the torch revealed broad sheets of whitish smoke that took the shape of a tenuous but gigantic spiderweb that went along casting off slow shreds of itself to dissolve in the cold breath of the wind. Along the way the area was impregnated with a thick smell of cooked meat and vegetables. The smoke was hovering over our heads now, slipping lazily over the roof of one of the two-story houses that faced the reservoir. On the ground floor of that building, wide open, with the boards removed, there was a light. Outside, a firebrand stuck in the wall dimly illumined a painting I couldn't make out. There was no sound except the distant barking of dogs and the crackling of my slave's torch. When we got to the platform of the reservoir I could make out some motionless shapes by the entrance to the shop, their backs to me; their slim shadows, projected from the interior and affected by the flickering of the firebrand, snaked along among the puddles on the ground. I went down behind the slave and, hidden by the stone corner as much as the glimmer of the torch would permit, spied on what was going on there. Filling the shop, on a level above us now, a gathered crowd was looking inside, their eyes on the stairway to the upper floor. Nobody was moving; nobody was talking or making the slightest sound.

"What's that there?" I whispered to the slave.

"Rufus' shop."

"A tavern?"

"Tavern and bakery . . . Rufus is the one who supplies the bread for your house, master."

The silence didn't last long. The stairway creaked: someone was slowly descending. There was a wavy motion through the crowd. People were changing position; bodies tightened against each other. I caught sight of some sandals on the upper steps—decorated around the ankles with strips of scarlet cloth—and the fringe of a toga that fell over them. One, two, three steps, slowly. The whiteness of the ceremonial garb dominated. Finally a face, broad, crowned with flowers. A heavyset man, smiling, stopped halfway down the stairs. He was wearing a toga so bright that it glimmered as it caught the light of the oil lamps. Suddenly the crowd grew excited; shoulders were lifted, arms raised, and an ovation broke out that resounded throughout the area.

"There's Rufus!" the slave announced crisply. And I noticed that he was eagerly attentive, enrapt, wishing perhaps that he, too, were in the tavern among the mob listening to the words of that Rufus, who, with a broad wave, arms outstretched, making his gleaming toga swirl, proclaimed at that instant: "I, my friends, cannot speak Greek!"

The crowd laughed, but the authoritative man, with an imperious gesture, imposed silence again. He had a clear voice, and the words followed each other effortlessly and without hesitation. A born orator, even if his speech was infested with mistakes and low expressions and the Hispanic accent prevailed here and there despite his efforts to hide it.

He didn't speak Greek, that Rufus . . . unlike the nobles with their fine manners, who didn't want to be understood by the masses, who closed themselves up in the luxury of their mansions and in the snares of their prejudices. He, Rufus Glycinius Cardilius, was one who knew the language of the people quite well. He'd amassed his fortune at the cost of hard work; he wasn't ashamed to say that his father was a freedman, his grandfather a slave, and that he himself toiled with his hands. But was it or was it not the truth that he baked the best bread in Lusitania?

At that point Rufus lifted his chin. His eyes seemed larger, and his face was trying to express wounded dignity. There was a clearing of throats, a nodding of heads, but no one dared answer or applaud.

Rufus changed his tone: without compromising himself, he skillfully mocked the aristocracy, who wouldn't admit him to their houses at mealtime and lived in idleness and in weakening pleasures, far removed from the real problems of the people, many times spending money they didn't have.

"This white toga," he shouted and threw his arms forward, sprinkling the area with sparkles and spreading luminous splotches over the ceiling, "is the sign of my candidacy for aedile, which, here and now, I solemnly announce to you!"

The house erupted with the crackle of applause, but Rufus' voice was powerful enough to rise over the clamor. He raised his pitch and speeded up his speech: "To you! To the people! Here in my shop and not in the praetorium! The people have the right to be the first to know!"

At the top of their lungs, the gang began to chant: "Rufus! Rufus!" He smiled and came down a few steps more. Then he lifted an arm, and the chorus fell silent. "There's bread and wine for everyone!"

The uproar started again, less warlike, more jovial. Rufus mingled with the crowd, slapping someone on the shoulder, whispering to another, listening circumspectly to a third. Small amphorae of steaming wine were already making the rounds, and greedy hands went after the mixture with cups that had been laid out on the tables. The crowd was obviously happy. Loud laughter echoed, and facetious remarks flew from one end of that den to the other.

It was then that they caught sight of me. Unconsciously, whether drawn by the slave's interest or by my own, I'd inched closer, and at that moment I was between the reservoir and the tavern. The hubbub died down, the faces turned toward me, the remnants of conversations ceased, cups and glasses were lowered. With slow movements the crowd drew back, took flight, and left Rufus abandoned, gleaming right in front of me. In the rush I thought I caught a quick glimpse of the fringed tunic of Proserpinus disappearing behind a pillar.

I felt just as uncomfortable as most of those around. Rufus, on the contrary, was very sure of himself; he inclined his head slightly in a quick bow and then looked me boldly in the face. I must confess that I wasn't sure what to do, but I thought it imprudent to intervene—without an escort, without lictors, and lacking any mark of authority—in what was going on there. Rufus and his people hadn't been blocking my path. I was the one who'd appeared without warning, coming out of the night like a phantom.

I preferred, however, not to continue on along the aqueduct. I turned my back on Rufus and walked along the pavement. The slave, hanging back, left me in the dark for a few moments before running up to light the way. No one followed us in a procession. On other occasions, without the unexpectedness of this one, I might have considered such an omission an affront. Farther on now, I could still hear noises from the direction of the tavern. After that I heard laughter, mingled with indistinct sound, starting up again in the distance. Then the echoes disappeared around the curves of the ever more sinuous streets, and a menacing silence weighed down all around.

We'd entered a chaotic district of narrow, crooked alleyways. On the unpaved ground the slime was mixed with putrid garbage. The stucco on the lookouts, which seemed almost to touch the moonlit skies, was crumbling, chipped away, exposing the ulcers in the blackened and eroded tile roofs. Innumerable graffiti of the most obscene kind, indiscernible in that light, made the walls even grimier and more miserable. I got the impression that my slave was slackening his pace. Was he hesitating? But then he chose an alley where the two of us could barely fit side by side. The ground and the walls gave off a damp, unhealthy smell.

A feeble light was coming from between two buildings ahead. On my side, next to a door, I could make out a whitewashed mark, a kind of design: a fish swimming amid circles that represented a series of hoops or maybe loaves of bread. When we passed, I took a look down the blind alley on the left to see where that light was coming from. In a filthy courtyard, under a porch, several men were sitting around a wooden table in silence. One of them, with a twisted beard, very stiff-backed, stared imperturbably in our direction. A clay oil lamp was swinging on an iron hook a bit above his head. I noticed that there were pieces of bread scattered over the table.

A few steps farther on I asked the slave what house that was.

"*Episkopos,*" he answered me.

"Supervisor of what?"

"He's a merchant in dried fruits. A foreigner. A priest or something like that . . ."

The slave shrugged his shoulders and went ahead, pushing aside a pile of trash with his stick: "Careful, master, don't step on that!"

47

The uncomfortable and disquieting feeling of strangeness that had been dogging me now grew stronger. Because what, after all, did I know of my city? I didn't even recognize the filthy and slippery streets I was walking now. The name of the person who supplied my bread had seemed unimportant; it had never occurred to me that the rabble stayed up at night and held political meetings in his tavern; it would never have entered my head that a freedman would throw himself into a candidacy for aedile, nor that the aedileship could be so coveted by the lower classes. And to top it off, the man appeared in a white toga, an article of clothing that in Tarcisis none of the duumvirs, as far as I could remember, had ever worn, even at the most magnificent ceremonies. What impulse was behind that idea? How could anyone take pride in not knowing Greek and be applauded? Could I have been mistaken in recognizing Proserpinus among that convulsive mob? What could Proserpinus, a lawyer, a decurion, a frequenter of my court although not of my house, be doing there among drunkards and revelers? And that mysterious silent banquet of rigid, stonelike men over chunks of bread? Under the sign of the fish when the zodiacal influence at the time was that of the lion? *Episkopos?* Supervisor? Merchant? Impostor? He surely must have been the fellow Airhan had told me about. But what did they want, what did those people want?

With a steady step, going ahead, torch held high, leaning forward, my slave would slow down sometimes, lighting up a stone or a puddle with an expert sweep of the lamp before going on. His name is Lucidomus, in homage to my name, and he'd been born in my house. I could still remember it. But who was he? What was he thinking? Why did he look at the meeting in the tavern with such interest? How did he know about the sign of the fish and that bizarre assembly? I was almost unable to hold back from speaking to him, asking him too much . . .

I was recognized by the guards at the main gate, who were warming themselves around a fire in robust merriment. They saluted, startled to see me there. There were women and idlers chatting, who quickly slipped away into the shadows. No one asked me for the password. A gatekeeper presented himself, sloppy in appearance, sword over his shoulder, winy breath, wanting to escort me along the wall. I refused. I had crossed the city without being intercepted a single time: I hadn't run into a patrol, nor a vigilante. I wanted to show my displeasure by refusing him the privilege of my company. Later I would ask for an accounting from Aulus.

But scarcely had I started on the path along the wall when Aulus came to meet me with his improvised staff. I was surprised to find myself suddenly surrounded by guards, oil lamps held high. Curiously, Aulus—who'd had the same idea as I, an impulse to inspect the walls—didn't seem nonplussed to see me there. Whatever I did represented normal behavior for him, who always accepted everything from his uncontested and incontestable superior. Did I appear in the middle of the night with a slave to look over the defenses? I had my reasons, and from Aulus' point of view they must have been the best ones, all the more so as they coincided exactly with his course of action. If I'd been sleeping at home, Aulus would have found that, too, to be quite natural and fitting for the duumvir to whom he owed respect and obedience. If I got mixed up, he would cover for me. If I proceeded in the proper way, he would approve. If I did nothing, he would take it upon himself to act in my place.

Aulus came over to me after a quick salute, as if I'd been close by all along. He was wearing his old Greek armor now, and, insensitive to the cold of the night, he wore no cloak. "Come, Lucius Valerius, come see."

We didn't have to walk very far to verify, right under our feet, the disrepair of the walls, one of the signs of the more than obvious negligence and incapacity of the successive generations of aediles. In those times it was felt that the walls served no purpose and even hindered the city's growth. Where we were standing, the way around went down abruptly to ground level in the midst of stones scattered haphazardly on the pomerium. How ironic it was that every day we followed the ritual of closing the gates and keeping watch over them, with passwords changed daily, while there was

V

DURING THE DAYS that followed I spent almost all my time in the praetorium in frantic activity that I had been unaware I was capable of. All the responsibilities of governing, not just the usual routine of office, court, and religious ceremonies, but the urgent and increased tasks that the threats to the city imposed, fell on me. The decemvirs rarely took the time, always with the subterfuge of taking care of their clients' affairs, to appear in the basilica. The aediles were as if nonexistent.

It fell to me to negotiate with crafty contractors for the rebuilding of the wall, reaching the point of threatening to jail one of them, exceeding my rights, because he was asking too much for the only heavy hoist in Tarcisis.

The praetorium slaves, whom I knew to be indolent and given to shooting dice in my absence, now found themselves busy copying edicts, letters, and accounts without any time for the usual follies that I would have felt obliged, under the circumstances, to punish severely.

Heralds made announcements on street corners; messengers galloped through the surrounding countryside and gave warnings at crossroads. All the inhabitants of the outskirts of Tarcisis were advised to take refuge in the city with their goods, their livestock, and their people. I requisitioned, I confiscated, I threatened. I'm not sure whether I managed to create a feeling of alarm among the citizenry or whether, on the contrary, the majority of them considered the demands of the duumvir to be exorbitant. But with conviction or without it I was getting results. If my words weren't effective, Aulus' activities in multiplying by ten the small urban cohort caused some impression and had some effect.

I would go off to the praetorium, sometimes without an escort, as soon as the sun came up. I ceased seeing clients at dawn. I fed myself on a little cheese, some goat's milk, and figs. I almost never saw Mara.

The exigency of a decision that had a controversial aspect led me to summon the curia day after day. The city's new defenses, planned with the weakness of the garrison in mind, called for the improvisation of sections of the wall in a narrower perimeter. Some property owners would have to be prejudiced by the construction, and the damages wouldn't be small. I understood that I shouldn't undertake that decision on my own. The lictors and the municipal slaves searched out the decemvirs from door to door: they shouldn't be absent, it was urgent, I needed the participation of them all.

❧

I was leaving the house quite early one morning when I heard someone coughing. A shape, half hunched over, came out from under the projection of a wall: Cornelius Lucullus, not having been let into the atrium, was waiting for me outside. I told him gruffly that it wasn't the time for me to see anybody because I was in a hurry.

But the poet insisted, pitifully. He looked emaciated, stooped, and his poverty could be seen in the darning on his old, faded cloak. He was dragging a sandal whose thongs had split, making him limp as he walked, and he carried a thick roll of papyrus in his hand that he never let go of and that was a kind of baton, representing his power over words. He told me he'd tried to speak to me several times but had been sent away, either at the praetorium or at my home. He hadn't dared approach me in the forum or in court because of the lictors and the escort. He was especially afraid of Aulus.

What did Cornelius want, then? Alms? A meal? With no time for reveries or trifles, it was no problem for me to tell them to give him the leftovers in the kitchen.

The man stood there facing me and didn't seem to grasp what I was saying. At the rear of the alley a potter was noisily dragging out his clay and beginning to set up his merchandise on the sidewalk. The city was coming to life.

"So?"

Cornelius suddenly began, in a very confused way, to explain himself, bowing and tugging at his tunic over his chest. Almost in tears, he begged me to forgive him.

"But what for?"

He'd been one of those at Rufus' tavern when the owner gave his candidacy speech. He'd seen me appear, my way lighted by a slave, but, embarrassed, he'd mixed in with the crowd instead of coming to greet me. Moments before, through my benevolence, he'd been in my house and honored in my triclinium. After leaving in a corner of his hovel the remains of the dinner, well-hidden so that no one would steal them, he'd run to the tavern to return the clothes he borrowed from Rufus. He stayed on. After all, he was a poet. He was supposed to capture feelings, phrases, emotions, atmospheres . . . But when he spotted me he felt ashamed at being caught in that place listening to those words, and caught by the distinguished person who just a while before had done him the honor of having him as a guest. He should have greeted me and gone along with me as courtesy demanded. But, tipsy from the flow of wine, he couldn't answer for his actions anymore, or, either, come staggering after me . . .

From time to time, as he let his laments flow on, he would lift his eyes from the ground and look at me with fright. He was uselessly searching in my expression for some sign I'd recognized him that night. He wasn't sure. I could perceive that doubt had been gnawing at him over those last few days.

I didn't feign ignorance, and I doubted that Cornelius' prostration was sincere. Had he come of his own free will after pondering his interests, afraid of having offended the duumvir, looking to put himself in good standing again and to forestall any retaliation? Or had he come because somebody had sent him?

53

A heavy covered cart rolled by on the street, making the paving stones rumble. Each of us drew back on his own side. The poet shook his fist and cursed the driver: "Hey, you miserable heathen! Do you know who this is? Show some respect!"

He was answered by a loud laugh amidst the noise of the wheels.

"Do you forgive me, then, duumvir?"

"What is there to forgive, Cornelius?"

Cornelius almost threw himself to the ground, insisting on his loyalty, toadying. He wasn't seditious; he was on the side of the duumvir, the aediles, and the curia. He didn't want to be confused with those others whose words had been blown up by ambition, or spite, or wine. He persisted in showing me his respect and dedication. Cornelius swore that never again would he ask for anything from Rufus or frequent his tavern. I felt uncomfortable, impatient, and undecided.

I looked straight at him and told him he should understand that some men stray from their natural bent while under the influence of wine. But I couldn't see any good reason why he should keep away from Rufus, who, after all, was only exercising his rights. The son of a freedman offering himself as aedile? There was nothing against it. And I repeated: "Do you understand, Cornelius? I would rather have you follow your customs. After all, a lot of interesting things happen in taverns . . ."

As he left me I was still subtle: "Tell my steward when you need something to eat or to wear, and come see me whenever you want to get something off your chest . . ."

He halted for a moment, stroking his chin, and then I think he followed me to the basilica at a distance, because for some time I could hear the drag of his broken sandal. He was a man of slow reactions, that Cornelius. For the moment I wasn't sure he'd understood my proposal. I would give him time to reflect . . . so whether he was sincere or whether there was duplicity in his intentions, my liberality would incline him toward the public good.

❦

On my tablinum in the praetorium, drawn in black on a goatskin stretched over a frame, the plan of Tarcisis appeared just as it was on the stone by the main gate. In blue were the new houses, built just a few years before, which now extended beyond the pomerium and the walls themselves. A rather long red line cut one of the corners of the city's square shape, this line being the sketch of the new wall that would leave half a dozen buildings outside.

I'd spent hours on end in secret conference with Aulus and one of the contractors before reaching this unavoidable conclusion. It was necessary to erect an epaulement with a wooden stockade along that red line as soon as possible, and afterward to raze the outlying houses and build a stretch of wall using the material from the demolitions. It wasn't an easy decision to make. We had to take into account our forces present and future; the terrain; the state of the old fortifications—all that along with the damages the citizens would have to bear. When everything had been thought out, I opted—instead of sacrificing heavily populated sectors, bringing down the wrath of the people and causing the demoralization of the city—for sacrificing the mansions and gardens of Pontius and the land of two or three notables, as well as a few semi-abandoned buildings of scant worth. The governor would indemnify the property owners later on if the city treasury was unable to come up with a just recompense.

I waited all morning in the hall there, sitting in my chair beside the frame. Runners came bearing messages: one decemvir was ill, another had urgent business, a third had planned to use the morning for hunting. The majority gave no justification. No one appeared. I was listening to the sound of stalls being set up in the forum, hawkers, the noise of carts, the bustle of commercial life. Facing me was nothing but a group of empty stools and a lictor leaning against a column, yawning. I took advantage of the delay to take care of petitions, claims, letters. The sun would light up a spot here, disappear, and spread out farther on—glimmering on the copper of a lamp, making suspended dust sparkle—and then off it went. It was midday. I'd waited long enough.

I drew up a somewhat laconic message, which I sent on tablets with a wax seal to Pontius Velutius Modius. I announced to him that given the unfortunate circumstances, his house stood in the way of the new wall and therefore would have to be torn down. I assured myself with pride of his anticipated agreement and praiseworthy trust, letting it rest that I had taken it under consideration all by myself and that there would be no further discussion.

I had probably gone too far with my irony, and I left little margin for negotiation concerning a matter I already considered decided and closed. It would have been easier simply to publish an edict or to write Pontius a comminatory letter. But my style was made ponderous by the hours I'd waited for the decemvirs in an empty hall, across from a bored lictor: it was weighed down by my annoyance and by the suspicion that Pontius, who wielded considerable sway over his peers, might have been the one responsible for the curia's indifference.

It wasn't long before Pontius, wearing a toga, burst into the tablinum like a whirlwind. He was accompanied by Proserpinus and Apitus, both wild-eyed and shaking their fists: "Have you gone mad, Lucius?"

Pontius was adjusting his fallen-down toga and panting. His booming voice echoed in the four corners of the room. He fell silent for a few seconds in a visible effort to moderate his anger. Then he sat on a stool. The others remained standing.

"This has got to be a joke, Lucius Valerius."

No, it most definitely wasn't. The decision had been made. I appeared brusque, did nothing to calm their tempers. I limited myself to showing that there was no other solution. I pointed to the map, tried to be meticulous, got ready to reprise the whole discussion I'd had with Aulus and the contractors; but Pontius' fury erupted once more, and he wouldn't let me go on.

"I don't want to hear any stories! Nobody's going to touch my house!"

"You won't be left without a place to stay, Pontius! You've got other houses."

"It's not a question of that! It's a question of principle."

Apitus and Pontius began to speak at the same time. I tried to convince them with the threat of the barbarians. They spoke to me of sacrosanct property rights: "What barbarians? You're using those phantom Moors that you invented yourself to strengthen your power and humiliate your peers!"

Proserpinus tried to find a way out. While Pontius was waving his arms in a whirl of irritated gestures, he was examining the map minutely. He was quite myopic, couldn't see a thing. He pretended. "Let's see, Lucius, why don't you rebuild the wall the way it was before? Here and here, eh?"

"I haven't got the time or the people or the materials!"

Apitus, triumphally: "Are you planning to make use of the ruins of our houses?"

"I'm only taking back the stones that were taken from the wall."

Proserpinus, conciliatory, opened his arms in a grand theatrical gesture. It was the moment, he thought, to intervene fully: "There's nothing that can't be negotiated among well-born people," he exclaimed.

From the direction the talk was taking, I surmised that they thought I was putting on an elaborate act in order to strike a deal, maybe do some extortion. Probably Proserpinus, Apitus, and Pontius had already exchanged ideas about the matter on the way over. So that was what my fellow citizens thought of me. . . . They were projecting onto me the traits of their own characters, as if, in the end, we'd been made from the same clay. I got up in a fury. Pontius took a step backward and began to roar: "Don't you insist! It won't be worth the trouble! This is a scheme! This is the result of the hate that Lucius Valerius Quintius has always nourished for me. And do you want to know why?"

He was purple with rage. His extended forefinger was drawing close to my beard.

"Envy!" And he repeated, to my astonishment: "Yes, envy, Lucius! You should cover yourself with shame!"

Proserpinus, perturbed, stepped in now. He hoped it would all end in an arrangement to which he could lend his learned contribution with memoranda, juridical formulas, and sacred oaths, rather than ending in wild and ear-splitting shouts. Pontius' fury had already gone beyond the limits. In spite of everything, Proserpinus had sufficient respect, if not for me then at least for institutions, to abhor such convulsions in the praetorium. All the more so because Aulus, alerted by the noise, had appeared in the door and was watching, mistrustful, ready to intervene. With a quick glance at Aulus, Proserpinus said: "You must understand, Lucius, I have to represent the interests of Pontius Velutius Modius. Citizens have rights: to enjoy, to use, to misuse. Pontius' new house is the pride of the city. Something rural within the walls."

He expressed himself pedantically, almost condescendingly, as if trying, in that predicament, to teach me the law that I applied, facing him, twice a week, often against his mandators. But this apparent serenity was becoming a bit ridiculous with his tall, unsteady figure interposed between me and Pontius, who was huffing and seemed ready to run over Proserpinus to get at me. Apitus, immobile, bewildered, didn't know where to put his hands.

"It's not a question of law," Pontius was roaring in a ringing voice, "or of originality or of the prerogatives of beauty! What's before us here is the insane persecution against me on the part of Lucius Valerius Quintius, instigated by envy, blinded by despotism, perverted by the abuses of power."

Pontius succeeded in brutally shoving Proserpinus aside and advancing toward me with clenched fists. Proserpinus grabbed him by the waist and got his head all entangled in Pontius' toga. Apitus joined Proserpinus in his efforts. For a few seconds the three of them were pushing and shoving. When Proserpinus succeeded in calming Pontius down and extricating his own head from the rolls of cloth, Aulus was standing at my side.

Pontius had momentarily desisted from attacking me. Fatigued, he was rearranging his clothing. The veins on his thick neck could be seen as they throbbed. With a quick swirl he covered his head with his toga.

"Careful, Pontius," Proserpinus advised. But Pontius wanted to continue railing at me. He'd given up hostile movements but not hostile words: "Don't count on my submission! I'm going to appeal to Rome, I'm going to appeal to the Emperor, I'm going to destroy you, Lucius!"

Proserpinus was trying to pull him outside now, whispering to him, looking now at me, now at Aulus. Maybe he was trying to establish in an unmistakable way that it was he, Proserpinus, a devoted hero of order, who was doing everything to calm that fury—an attitude that would do him credit in the annals of the city and in the mind of the duumvir. Retreating step by step, Pontius burst forth with: "I'll never leave my house, Lucius! I'll stay there buried in the ruins to your shame. But the whole city will know, all Lusitania, Rome!"

"Let's go, Pontius, let's go!"

Now energetically, now gently, Proserpinus and Apitus were leading him to the door. They passed the thick curtains showing the she-wolf of the Capitol embroidered in strong colors over the standard *SPQR*, and these draperies swayed for a few moments.

But I could still hear the raucous drag of sandals and Pontius' insults from the other side: "Wretch! Tyrant!" which didn't cease until they mingled with outside noises and became indistinguishable.

Aulus discreetly disappeared, and I was left wondering whether I'd shown myself too harsh, even excessive, in the language I'd used with Pontius. Perhaps my desire to redress the curia's disrespect had moved me to intemperance in my choice of words. For a long time, examining my conscience, I tried to recall the words exchanged. Maybe I should have been less curt, more persuasive: it behooved me to seek justice, not retaliation. There would be no lack of occasions on which to repair the lapse.

⌀━◆━⌀

From the window of the basilica, I could make out in the distance over the roofs of the houses the plumb lines of the large hoist being set up beside the walls. I decided to go out. Aulus went with me when he spotted the movement of the lictors and bearers, who leaped down the stairs after me.

The crowd drew back when we reached the foot of the huge vertical drum that was joined to a winch by a shaft and where hawsers were wound up, supporting the large, still-empty baskets that swayed above, hanging from the lines. Men in rolled-up tunics were pounding on heavers with mallets; others were letting out ropes. The baskets came down, and two slaves got into them, sitting one on each side with their legs dangling out. Inside the drum, a team that climbed up the transverse slats made the great wheel turn with an infernal squeaking. Swaying in the baskets, the others gave out hoots of merriment, which seemed rather strange to me, given their status as slaves, not to mention the relative danger in which they found themselves. The wheel was suddenly blocked by a lever. Some of the men lost their balance and fell inside the drum. Those two up above, suspended, shaken, were making faces and antics to the rhythm of the rocking.

The contractor came over to me. He wanted to talk. He seemed to have forgotten our arguments and my threats and was smiling, visibly satisfied, pointing to the hoist as if it were a spectacle presented in the circus. He had small white teeth in regular rows, like those of a child. I remained seated in my chair, listening. He confided to me that he'd sacrificed fourteen ouzels to Endovellicus so the god would help him in his undertaking.

"Why Endovellicus?" I asked.

"Ah, I know that Endovellicus isn't directly involved in works like these, but I'm certain that by paying him homage I'll at least get his intercession with the gods who are, using his prestige."

To my right, leaning over a groma, was a mapmaker, one of those recently arrived from Vipasca, making broad signals to another who was outside my field of vision. Two oxcarts loaded with stone brought from the new theater arrived, creaking, and stopped beside the wall. Carpenters went by with thick crossbeams on their shoulders. There was a racket of hammering and shouting in the dusty air. Everything seemed to be going along well.

I spoke a few words of encouragement to the contractor, heartening him regarding the favors of Endovellicus, inquiring about deadlines, urging him on; and then I took my leave. I called Aulus and asked him to stay there while they carried me to the baths.

It was a spur-of-the-moment decision brought on by the bustle I was witnessing beside the wall. I knew that at the baths I would find a happy unconcern that would contrast with the arduous chores beginning now. I would have wagered that the majority of my curia, so busy, annoyed, and unavailable when it was a matter of public affairs, would be found prattling beside the pools. And perhaps I'd have an opportunity to speak with Pontius again and make him understand the interests of the city in a less austere, more neutral atmosphere than that of the praetorium. I would then have a chance to mitigate the harshness of my words. I was subjecting myself, it was certain, to a public uproar. But I had faith in myself.

Only a half-dozen houses in Tarcisis had private baths: my own, that of Calpurnius, that of Maximus Cantaber, and not many others. There were those who, although they owned a bath, never heated up the fireboxes of the hypocaust and preferred the promiscuity of the public ones, either as a matter of avarice or out of fondness for company.

The large baths had been remodeled under Claudius, much enlarged in the time of the Flavii, and restored and enriched thanks to a generous donation from Marcus Aurelius in times when the palace was still able to squander. In all the rooms the walls were covered with pink marble, which reflected the light and the glimmer of the water, creating with the steam from the caldarium and the perfumed aromas from the massage room an atmosphere of almost ethereal luxury, completely freed from the travails of daily life and completely out of proportion to the importance of a small city like Tarcisis. At the entrance to the dressing room a small boy in marble was mounted on a dolphin, which, from a smiling, upturned mouth, gave off a spout that took on various colors according to the substance added to the water in a concealed tank. In every room a life-size sculpture in white marble gave men the company of gods and nymphs. Some niches lined with mother-of-pearl were still empty, their figures missing. It was the most pleasant place in the city, a refuge, repose, the propitious comfort that brought on enchantment and a lack of care. The coarse apostrophes of the forum aren't heard there. Though they speak loudly and jovially, the citizens are careful with their words, as if they are in a hallowed place, the holy of holies of the great temple that is the city. A limitation of space had reduced the exterior palestra to a colonnade that ran over a narrow expanse of turf. The library on the upper floor had been empty ever since it was built, as no benefactor had considered it a high priority to furnish it with books.

Among the numerous litters left on the steps by the entrance, I recognized that of Calpurnius, which was inlaid with gold vine leaves and covered with a purple canopy. His three lictors were waiting for him beside the great bronze doors, their fasces laid down—away from the slave bearers, who were fraternizing in noisy gangs. Well, Calpurnius at the public baths?

I didn't let them dress me. I went through the steam room among lazily moving shadows, and in my toga I entered the tepidarium, crowded with people at that hour. Some recognized and greeted me. Curiously, the ball games halted, and there were those who tried to hide their nudity with linen towels.

There was the head of Calpurnius, visible in the second tank between the shoulders of two slaves who were supporting him under the water with crossed wrists. On nearby benches, alongside the senator's mat, some decemvirs were gossiping. A sculptor, removed from it all, was working on a plaster bust, shaping it with a spatula. I waited, standing, for Calpurnius to finish his bath. He seemed to be in deep concentration, looking straight ahead and not paying any attention to me. The decemvirs gradually began to disperse. They greeted me casually and stole away, some to the frigidarium, others to join the groups forming farther back by the door.

Finally the slaves, stirring up the water, brought Calpurnius over to the stone steps on one side of the pool. The old senator's legs, extremely thin, paralyzed, waggled like loose reeds as the slaves effortlessly carried him. They put him down, supporting him, on a high stone bench and wrapped him in an enormous embroidered towel. Only then did Calpurnius seem to notice me, and he called to me with a wave of his hand: "Look, Lucius. I brought my sculptor. I'm so old and sick that I can't give myself the luxury of wasting any time. Come, sit down here beside me."

Calpurnius seemed to be smiling in a wry way, his wide quadrangular mouth allowing a glimpse of some tiny teeth, surprisingly well-preserved for his age. The reflections of the water, lighted by the circular window of the dome, made iridescent glimmers leap out of his damp and wrinkled face. He put his hand on mine. I felt the roughness of his heavy senatorial ring.

"I haven't seen you in a long time, Lucius."

"You know how busy I've been."

"Not even a short visit . . ."

What was I supposed to say after that? Calpurnius was treating me with indulgence, was broadly displaying the magnanimous understanding of a great lord. With a wave he dismissed a slave reader who was approaching with a case of books, and he looked disdainfully at the sculptor, who, hunched over, would scan his patron's features in a glance and immediately return to his plaster model. Before I could ask him, he said to me: "You must be surprised to see me in the public baths. My physician is given to understand that these waters are the best thing for one's blood. As long as I avoid the frigidarium, of course . . ."

The waters for the baths come from the same aqueduct that supplies the baths in private residences, the fountains in the streets, and the cisterns in homes. Calpurnius only wanted to avoid my plunging into questions about the reasons for his presence there. His beady eyes, dull, half-closed, indicated a sagacity intimately given to twists and maneuvers. In Rome, although a senator, he'd never been completely accepted in the senate. In Tarcisis he'd almost been promoted to divinity.

"Pontius Modius is quite angry with you, Lucius."

"It's impossible to please everyone."

"I sense that the citizens are quite restless."

"That's natural when barbarians are on the move."

"Ah, you're changing the subject, Lucius."

He laughed with a muffled chuckle that was like a dry cough. Then he suddenly became serious and snapped his fingers at his slaves. They picked him up, laid him down on the bench, and began to massage his back. He called me over and said into my ear: "It's important to maintain harmony among important people. Isn't there some way you and Pontius can get together?"

"It's a matter of the city's defenses!"

"Come, now, Rome's not about to be conquered at this moment. Rome is eternal, as Virgil prophesied. Who are these Moors, after all?" He paused and ran his tongue over his teeth. I heard a loud smack from the hands of the slave rubbing his shriveled skin. I didn't know whether the twitch of displeasure Calpurnius gave then was for me or for his masseur. The intense smell was filling my nostrils. Calpurnius cleared his throat, changing the subject: "Listen, Lucius: if it were a matter of my house, would you also order it torn down?"

"Yes."

He spun his head toward me and fixed me with a stare for an instant, face to face. His countenance hardened, and the inelegant trapezoid that his mouth usually formed was converted into a thin and mobile line. Then he pretended to react to another vigorous action on the part of the slave, stretched his shoulders, and went back to smiling. "Does Rome have need of any more Catos?" And, changing from a reflective tone to a natural, unworried one: "I'm sending someone to have a talk with you tomorrow. Receive him well, I beg you."

"Who?"

"You'll see. Oh, massages make me so sleepy . . ."

He rested his head on his folded arms and pretended, still smiling, to doze off. The slaves were now scraping the oil off his back with their strigils. The sculptor crept over, took another close look at his features, and went back to his slow task.

When I lifted my head slightly I found myself in the midst of a strange silence. All that could be heard was the dripping of water from a stone face into a tub. Standing off to one side, the people there were looking at us, suspended in curiosity. When I arose they all acted busy with little chores. I caught sight of a very pale man in the neighboring tank who quickly began to splash water over his back with a seashell. None of the decemvirs could be found among the bystanders now.

At the end of the street I lifted the canopy of the chair and looked behind. Calpurnius' group was just leaving. He hadn't waited long. His nap had been brief.

⚹

That night Mara came looking for me. I told her how my day had gone.

"Friend," she said, "why don't you spend one of these nights in a temple? Maybe a god will appear and inspire you."

"Have you gone over to believing in the gods, Mara?"

"I believe in what's advantageous, Lucius."

We could hear carts passing on the street, rattling the paving stones and the walls. It seemed as if the flame of the lamp quivered to the sound of their heavy wheels. It was cart after cart seeking refuge in Tarcisis. The gatekeeper had orders to facilitate their entry, even in the still of the night.

Perhaps it was then, while I was holding Mara in my arms and chatting with her, that Maximus Cantaber's carts were trooping along the street as he fled his estate with his family and servants.

Iunia Cantaber had arrived in the city, then.

VI

"Rufus Glycinius Cardilius!"

Standing before me, he inflected his name with a slight nod of his head and placed a basket full of loaves of bread, covered by a thin, transparent cloth, on the table. The gleam of his white toga contrasted with the somber tones of my tablinum, even reflecting off the marble bust of the Emperor that was keeping watch opposite. This, then, was the man Calpurnius had promised to send. He hadn't appeared the next day but the day after.

Through the window I could see alongside the new wall in the distance the top of the scaffolding, the lifted arms of the hoists, and the fumes from the large kettles of molten lead. The work, I assured myself, was proceeding at a good pace, and at that moment it would have been more fitting for me to check on it rather than to receive this fellow Rufus. But I decided that my consideration for Calpurnius called for conceding the baker a few brief minutes.

"Is that an offering," I asked, pointing to the loaves, "of the best bread in all Lusitania?"

"You mustn't have any doubt about it, duumvir. And I'll repeat it as many times as necessary."

"So why do you come before me in that bright toga, baker? Or should I say instead 'tavern-keeper'?"

"My name is Rufus Cardilius! It is my great honor to inform you of my candidacy for aedile and of my readiness to contribute to the public treasury."

He was insolent; he'd brought no prepared speech. He trusted in a natural capacity for extemporaneous reply and in his experience in commercial dealings. As he spoke he maintained a rigid stance with his toga neatly folded and tucked, indifferent to the obvious fact that his attire was magnifying his haughtiness in my eyes.

"There are two aediles functioning already."

"One never gets out of bed, and the other suffers from the sacred illness and is delirious. In addition to that, they're both bankrupt."

"Their terms aren't up yet."

"I'll wait. But there's nothing to stop me from putting myself up now. Unless, duumvir, you have some objection. In that case I will bend to your will."

"What about the other candidate—where's he?"

"Domitius Primitivus has delegated me, and he sends you greetings through me."

"What does this Domitius do? Is he a baker or a tavern-keeper, too?"

"He's worked with his hands, yes. Today, they say, he could pave the street between the two farthest gates of the city with money. If his trade had been base, that's been washed away by now with the touch of gold."

I kept feeling uneasy as I faced that man. I was seated at the table, and he was standing, as was called for by our different stations. I didn't like the secure and slightly disdainful look that he was giving me from above. I could get rid of him if I wanted to, allege disrespect, have him arrested, close his place, find some pretext to confiscate his goods. But there was Rufus Cardilius, confidently presenting himself, answering me without any hesitation, resplendent in his costume-party toga, raising before the magistrate his right to civic existence and public renown. How could he have guessed that I'd be incapable of making use of my prerogatives to throw him out, jail him, have him whipped? Among those whose opinion mattered, no one would be upset if I went beyond my formal jurisdiction. Calpurnius, when he ran into me, probably wouldn't even mention the matter. But I wouldn't be able to forgive myself if I stooped that low.

But how could he be sensing all that? Among figures of the lowest birth there sometimes arises a strange appetite for risk capable of exploring any path whatever and venturing to the edge of the abyss. Rufus certainly wasn't counting on my being intimidated by the protests of a gang of drunkards that Aulus could sweep away with a half-dozen guards. And it certainly wasn't his grotesque figure dressed in those bright trappings that belonged to a career of honor (and that so ill suited him) that made him think I would be susceptible. He was wily, he had no illusions about Calpurnius' protection. Why did he dare speak to me in a tone that, without being disrespectful, still didn't show sufficient respect? I stood up so as to avoid the uncomfortable feeling of finding myself on a lower level than he. I frowned, wrinkling my brow, and asked: "Why have you come to announce your intentions to me, Rufus? Weren't you satisfied with the ovation you received at your tavern the other night?"

"That was an informal talk among friends. Now I want to make it official, in front of the magistrate . . . and I've humbly come to ask for your support, Lucius Valerius."

"Isn't the protection of Ennius Calpurnius enough?"

"The senator's not involved in the affairs of the city. The city's too small a thing for him; he doesn't consider it proper to make his position public. However, he recommended your kindness to me."

"And what qualifications do you have, Rufus, to present yourself as a candidate for aedile? The fact that you don't know Greek?"

"It's true that I don't know Greek. I can barely write Latin, too. When you heard me from where you were hiding the other night I was speaking to the masses. I wanted them to identify with me. I told them what they wanted to hear. That's why I put such great store in my ignorance. The people are children. You've studied rhetoric, you must know that better than I."

"They say that the Emperor writes his thoughts down in Greek . . ."

"I bow before Marcus Aurelius Antoninus. But he's in Rome, the center of the Orbis. I'm in Tarcisis, at the far end of the earth."

"So why do you want my support? Because you bake the best bread in Lusitania? Because you can't speak Greek? Because you own a tavern filled with supporters? Or do you have some other qualifications, perhaps? Money? That shining toga?"

"I have a decisive qualification that's never been lacking in the best of Romans. Will and persistence, duumvir!"

"Ah, so you identify yourself with the best of Romans. Like your grandfather, perhaps?"

"I'm not ashamed of being the son of a freedman. The law doesn't stop me from being a candidate. Trajan himself recommended merchants for the curia in Ephesus, which is a great city. Maybe someday, who knows, the sons of freedmen will be able to become emperors. But if you look down on me, Lucius Valerius, I will suffer your scorn with resignation."

I'd moved away from the table and made a wide turn behind the pedestal that held the bust of the Emperor. Rufus was turning, following me with his eyes. Not a wrinkle sullied his toga, and he did not make the slightest movement or get rid of the impassive disdain that was showing on his features. Nor did I note any concern in his voice. I stopped, quite close to him, and stared into his eyes. He didn't blink. "Because, frankly, I don't like you, Rufus Cardilius."

"That's an attitude for which I'm all to blame: it must be because of my faults. But I can repair them if you would just tell me what they are, since my poor freedman's intelligence deprives me of that instant recognition."

Sarcasm. The descendant of a slave, unlettered, fearless, dared to be sarcastic before me in my praetorium, on the lookout for some disorder in my gestures or my words. That most certainly was what he was after. To make points so that, facing him, the magistrate would lose his composure. His brazenness extended so far that he went on freely even though he had no witnesses in his favor and was at my mercy, two floors above the ergastulum.

It wasn't wise for me to prolong my talk with that man, no matter what tone it took: he would always be the one to profit from it.

He had no lack of verbal resources with which to maintain the initiative and was probably capable of drawing arguments, phrases, examples from a store that was inaccessible to me and that would provide him with uninterrupted verbiage destined to conquer by weariness, the way legions steadfastly besiege towns. Win? Conquer? That was all Rufus was after, in the flourish of a gesture, in a certain hesitation as he finished a sentence, in a tiny touch of a frown. What response could I give, not wishing to commit any excess unworthy of my office or improper in those of my order, and yet vulnerable to his skillful advantage?

Aulus burst furiously into the tablinum with huge strides, carrying my folded cloak, and he saved me from that hesitation only to plunge me into an even greater entanglement. He shot a withering glance at Rufus, drew me into a corner, put my cloak over my shoulders, and whispered breathlessly into my ear: "It's Pontius. There's no time for explanations. Come!"

When he brushed by the table, Aulus' cloak knocked over the basket Rufus had put there. As we left the room a small white loaf of bread came rolling along behind us across the mosaic floor.

⁕━━✦━━⁕

There was no chair; there were no lictors waiting for me. Aulus was in a hurry. Counter to all convention we mounted two mules that a slave had just tied up at the entrance to the basilica. Amid the noise their hooves made on the pavement, Aulus gave me terse news of what was going on. They were halfway through the demolition of Pontius' new house, and he refused to leave the atrium, first in the company of his wife, children, and slaves, then by himself, despite appeals by Aulus and the contractors.

"Did he send for me?" I asked.

"No, duumvir. I took that liberty. Pontius call you? Did you hear what you said?"

Looking over my shoulder as we turned a corner, I had the impression that Rufus, tripping over his gleaming toga, was running after us, pushing his way through the onlookers, who were emerging from doors either because they smelled that something was up or to watch the duumvir pass by on an unaccustomed ride through the city.

We arrived at a place of great agitation among demolished walls and piles of stones. A stew of men was laboring all over the area, digging in the ground, carrying cut stone, hoisting materials. There was the deafening noise of mallets pounding on walls. Farther on, next to the main gate of Tarcisis, the great hoist was trembling and creaking with the effort of the slaves who were suffering inside the drum as huge rocks were lifted to the top of the walls. In a tremendous confusion, amidst shouting and cursing, the line of carts entering the city mixed in with the carts of those working on the project. Country people, with their outlandish appearance, could be seen everywhere; barefoot, dressed in filthy clothes, and with shaved heads, waiting for someone to organize them for the work in progress. A large stockade fence that formed a backing of driven stakes was there, along which the new stretch of wall would be built. Earth and rubble had been scattered across a vast extension that came to an abrupt stop by the half-demolished walls of Pontius Modius. There an abandoned battering ram, hanging by ropes from a pyramidal scaffolding, was swaying in the breeze across from a large gap that it must have opened some time before.

We pushed through the onlookers who were crowding by the gate watched over by two guards and went into the atrium. The light coming in through the compluvium and through the large breach just opened, where a swirl of dust was hanging, blinded me. My eyes needed time to make out the shapes. On the side some half-naked men covered with dirt were leaning on large iron mallets and wearily awaiting orders.

Before the now dry tank of the impluvium, motionless, sitting on a tiny stool with his back to the vestibule, his head sunk between his shoulders, loomed the rotund figure of Pontius. He was wrapped in a brown funereal toga. He didn't react to our entrance, which brought on some agitation and murmuring among the workers and the people massed outside. We approached slowly. Finally I said something: "Pontius Velutius, what's going on, what are you doing?"

Slowly, at my voice, Pontius turned his head. His graying beard was untrimmed, ragged. His loose, sagging cheeks were the very image of fatigue and wear. He looked at me vaguely with his dim

71

eyes, then stared at the pavement of the floor, which was covered with dust and debris. Despite the din and bustle from outside, his words were quite clear to me: "I'm not leaving!"

Pontius didn't raise his voice; his tone was neither challenging nor arrogant. He pronounced that sentence in a neutral, indifferent, hoarse way, addressing not so much me as the walls, the ground, the dust, or, who knows, his own disposition. I tried to temporize: "Pontius, be reasonable."

"It was my house," Pontius muttered gloomily, his back to me. A roll of papyrus fell from his lap. Pontius reached out with his left hand and bent to pick it up, but then he stopped. His hand came back again and spun in a gesture of demonstration, hanging in the air for a time in an elegant way, but also with great detachment. "My will," he sighed and withdrew his hand. He kept the other hand concealed in the folds of his toga.

Aulus thought it a good time to intercede: "Come, now, Pontius Velutius, let us take care of you."

"It's no use, centurion!"

He stood up laboriously and turned toward us, smiling. He gave a shrug of his shoulders, and his toga slipped off and fell to the floor. Pontius was clutching a Spanish sword against his tunic. He grasped the hilt up high with both hands and turned the weapon against himself. He paused briefly, measuring us triumphantly with his look. Then he suddenly doubled over. And he uttered a kind of sob, brief and cavernous.

Aulus and I rushed to him, but Pontius had already fallen onto the sword, whose triangular tip was now protruding from his back along with dark bubbles. Behind us, the crowd closing in around the door was abuzz. That enormous body looked grotesque to me, indecorous, crumpled there on the floor like a pile of discarded rags. Aulus turned him over hurriedly. The head rolled over, and his eyes, wide open, seemed to be staring at the people crowding into the vestibule. Dead. A trail of blood went along the floor, staining the dust and soaking his will.

I felt the chill of a shudder. It was hard for me to control my movements as I walked, as slowly as possible, toward the exit. The throng opened up to let me pass. I got the feeling that they were all staring at me with a superstitious terror. I sighed deeply and leaned against a wall before everything around me began to spin.

When I raised my eyes, a resplendent figure was rising over a divided altar and haranguing the crowd. There were moments when I heard the orator's lush droning, higher, lower, closer, farther away. But I couldn't disentangle the words or the meaning. Very slowly the outline of objects and the import of the talk began to become clear. It was Rufus. His arm in the air, hand open, he was shouting with quick, fluent words a speech that had now reached this point: "Horror! Horror and shame! Hear me, men and women of Tarcisis! Citizens! Pontius Velutius Modius, the most distinguished citizen of all Lusitania, crowning light of equity and protector of the poor, great in wisdom and munificence, no longer exists. He lifted a sword against himself and called down death. Why? Because an unjust offense had been made against him! Shame on the one who humiliated him! Know ye that Lucius Valerius Quintius, the supreme magistrate of this city, a duumvir who talks about the law, was his killer. Oh, no, it wasn't the duumvir's arm that sank the sword. Instead he armed and urged on the hand of the suicide." And on like that . . .

I didn't turn to look at Rufus. I kept trying to restore my composure, distancing myself from the scene on foot without waiting for Aulus to get me transport or an escort. Rufus' words were fading away amid the clamor of the onlookers and the noise of the work. I don't know how many people may have been listening to him. Out of courtesy, as was the custom, a group followed me, going along almost to the door of my house. I don't even remember going in.

⟡

I didn't return to the praetorium that day. I let myself stay in my tablinum until nightfall. I didn't take anything to eat. Mara, when she sensed I was home, came to be with me and, respecting my silence, withdrew to a corner in the shadows, quite still, her hands in her lap.

When they came to light the lamps, I finally became aware again of Mara and the sacrifice she had been making with that motionless expectation all that time. She must have heard everything already. She didn't want to leave me; she guessed my state of mind and stayed there, seated, breathing softly so as not to disturb me. I

73

think she perceived that my silence hadn't been motivated by indifference or cruelty. It was quite hard for me to speak without my voice faltering or my gestures getting out of hand. I tried to think about everything that had happened, pondering questions, making plans, but all that came into my head was a chaotic swirl of images and painful sensations. My body told me not to move. There I stayed, outwardly serene, perhaps, but with an inferno in my soul.

"Is it night already?" I finally asked Mara with some effort as the slave went about lighting lamp after lamp, looking at one and then the other of us, waiting to be told to stop. Mara's face was illumined by a wick that sputtered at the same moment I asked her the question. I saw her sigh with relief and smile softly. And that peaceful and friendly gesture was pleasing to me.

"You know what happened, don't you, Mara?"

"What can you do against fate?"

The slave, curious, was taking his time with his chores, feigning difficulty in closing his wineskin of oil. He finally went off after a commanding look from Mara, who hastened to draw the curtain.

"I never hated Pontius," I said. "I hadn't been his friend over time, but the gods are my witness that I never wished him any harm. And he attacks me in this way, laying his death on my shoulders."

"It was his decision, Lucius. He was a selfish man. He didn't know how to play the role that belonged to him. He was sick, didn't you know?"

It was a known fact, Mara went on to tell me with a certain emphasis—as if that would change the essence of the matter—that Pontius' body was covered with black blotches and that his end was probably not far off. How did she know? Gossip from the slave girls.

"I could really do without these duties," I sighed.

"Nobody's stopping you."

"No, I can't quit! Once the wine is poured you've got to drink it. Right now Pontius' house has to be torn down. I can only tell you how all this upsets me."

"I'm right here, Lucius."

The conversation on that theme had reached its end. Mara had come to the end of it. She never questioned me. If Aulus accepted all my decisions in the name of discipline, dedication, and the sense of a chain of command, Mara accepted them in conformity with the values she'd picked up in her father's house. I was fulfilling my obligations; I was proceeding according to her idea of what it was to be a Roman. Mara found it proper.

If I were to give up my principles in an attack of madness and abandon my duties and renounce my honors, Mara would accompany me wherever I might go, even to the most disastrous fate. She would do her duty without hesitation, but she wouldn't cease pointing out any breach in mine, even if it was in a subtly symbolic way: a phrase cut off in the middle, a vague gesture, a brief onset of sadness. Her obligatory dedication as a wife would thus be shadowed by the discreet censure of the daughter of a citizen. Her father—Mara always thought deep inside—would approve or disapprove of this or that behavior, and along the way she would measure his approvals and disapprovals. Her affection for me was something apart, dictated by her heart, not her head.

"The Cantabers have just arrived." Mara roused herself, changing the subject. "Maximus brought his daughters, Clelia and Iunia. It's too bad it's not a time to invite anyone."

That last phrase was couched in an interrogative tone. Mara knew of my long-standing friendship with Maximus Cantaber, and she was hinting that she was ready to receive his family, for my pleasure, but she was leaving the final decision to me, since it had to be considered with regard to the events of the last few days. I didn't reply. I didn't intend to issue any invitation; I would wait for Maximus Cantaber to look me up, wanting him to visit even though circumstances would appear to forbid it. And heavy sleepiness suddenly came over me.

◦━◆━◦

Late in the night now, in my bedroom, we were startled by strong knocking on the door. They'd come to tell us that Rufus Cardilius was waiting, that he was asking to be forgiven for the lateness of the hour and the inconvenience he was causing, but that he had to speak with me urgently.

I went out to deal with Rufus in the vestibule, where he was huddled against the wall. His tunic was torn and dirty. He was bleeding from a cut on his forehead; his lips were swollen. His appearance was pitiful, his expression miserable, his speech babbling. He didn't look like the same man who in his radiant toga had spoken so haughtily to me in the praetorium and had insulted me with harsh, oratorical outbursts by Pontius' house.

"I didn't want to wake you up, duumvir, but Calpurnius suggested I come see you. His slaves have given me protection this far."

Voices could be heard outside speaking softly. I wanted to know what it was all about.

"Lucius Valerius Quintius, I have taken it upon myself to bother you and tell you the following: I'm quite aware of my place and status. You don't have to use any violence with me."

It was mocking, that tone of voice, in spite of the sobs. Rufus bent over in a broad bow and looked at me again with a grimace on his bloody face: "Your lesson has had its effect. Never again will I use any word that might sound bad to your ears. I got your message, Lucius Valerius."

He bowed to me, bowed even more deeply to my manes, moved backward and, before the door closed behind him, repeated once more: "Never again, Lucius Valerius!"

It seemed to me that he was dragging one leg. For a few moments I could still hear voices in the street. Then quiet returned. A fish leaped in the impluvium. Only the slave who was lighting my way showed a great silent surprise on his face.

Mara, who'd witnessed everything from the shadows, took my hand and whispered: "Watch out for that man, Lucius."

⊂━━✦━━⊃

When I left that morning, the poet Cornelius, who'd become accustomed to hang about my door, replacing the clients I never received, came over to me, all anxious, and signaled that he wanted to speak to me in secret. I listened to him, and I flew to the basilica. The litter-bearers had to run behind me.

From what he had told me, I would have to demand an accounting from Aulus a short time later in the praetorium. I was angry, and I'd forgotten the kindness with which I usually treated my centurion. I asked him if it was true that he, on the preceding night, accompanied by two men armed with spears, had gone to Rufus' tavern.

Aulus confirmed everything Cornelius had told me: yes, he'd proceeded toward my redress because he'd understood that this Rufus fellow wasn't going to get off without a lesson. Aulus was a soldier; he wasn't a man to let stand an affront against his superior.

He'd appeared in the early morning, when the freedman's son was preparing to close up shop and fasten the shutters. He threatened Rufus with the spears, swung the iron tips within two fingers of his face, made holes in the wall and on the electoral graffiti. Aulus beat him with the handle of the weapon. Then he'd gone into the tavern with his men, torn up and burned the notorious white toga with a torch. He'd managed to scratch Rufus' mouth with the tip of the spear and to extract a promise that never again would he open it against the duumvir as he'd done so boldly that day. Everything was exactly as Cornelius, who had witnessed it all from the shadows, had told me.

"And you, Aulus, what do you expect me to do to you?"

"Whether you approve or not, duumvir, I acted as I saw best for you and for the city. I will not allow them to accuse and insult in public the magistrate I am under the obligation to respect and defend."

"How could you have dared?"

Infuriated, I threatened Aulus. Motionless, his arms slackly at his sides, he was ready to accept my fury impassively. Fire and lighting could rain down, the thunder of Jove could rumble away; Aulus would bear it all. I would never succeed in getting it out of his head that he'd acted properly, even though against my wishes. At that moment my rage was such that I would have horsewhipped Aulus if I'd had a lash. He would have borne the beating or whatever fate I had in mind. Deep inside, stubborn, his conscience told him that he'd done his duty even if the extent of his retribution was beyond me.

"But Aulus, you poor fool, do you have any idea of the consequences of your act?"

"Rufus is a swindler!"

"So he's a swindler!" The blow I gave the table resounded throughout the room and upset the inkwell. The sound of the metal rolling on the floor was a warning for me that I was going too far. I tried to hold back my impulses: "My duty is to respect the right of free speech for swindlers, especially when they're aspiring to public office," I finished in a softer tone.

"A stinking freedman, Lucius Valerius. How can you let him slander you?"

"It is my centurion who's making the decisions for me now? Be quiet, Aulus, and listen."

I put my arm around the bust of Marcus Aurelius while I spoke, as if I were expecting inspiration from that cold marble: "This is the divine Marcus Aurelius Antoninus, your lord and mine. Can you imagine the Emperor persecuting those who make up epigrams about him, those who plot intrigues in the palace, or those who disagree with him? Marcus Aurelius is a philosopher, and he lives surrounded by philosophers when circumstances don't force him to put on his helmet and armor. His actions and his figure ought to enlighten the acts of all magistrates of the Empire, because they are the image of moderation and justice."

Aulus was frowning, with respect for me and for the invocation of the Princeps, but it was easy to see that inside he was sticking to what he thought, and he didn't think thrashing Rufus had been a waste of time. It was for me to be leery of that excessive dedication.

"Is it up to me, a minor local magistrate, to place my vanity above the law? Think about it, centurion. This emperor was sent to us by Providence. Be attentive to what ingratitude our being unworthy of him would represent."

My running on like that, useless perhaps, was deeply sincere. The intonation and vehemence that I put into my words may have made an impression on Aulus. As for the content, I have my doubts . . .

Aulus' withdrawn equanimity worked me up again. I reminded him that his duties consisted in something more than giving a scare to a tavern-keeper and that we were all still hoping a certain Arsenna, a highwayman, would be subdued through armed force, a better use for it than any disrespect within the walls. Or would I have to pay the bandit hunters Senex or Irenaius out of my pocket to free me of that fellow?

I'd pricked his pride, touched upon the matter that was most painful to him. He finally blinked his eyes, wrinkled his forehead. He waited in vexed silence for me to have done with my reproof. When he perceived that—with arms folded, facing him—I had nothing more to say, he gave a military salute and went off.

✦

At nightfall an under-officer of the urban cohort presented himself and asked for the password. He told me that the centurion, under arms, had left the city secretly with a few men, not all soldiers, not all free men, and he didn't know when Aulus would be back.

After the annoyance that followed my perplexity, I thought I could guess where Aulus had gone in the still of the night and without my authorization. And I was almost sorry for having wounded his vanity and stimulated his obstinacy.

VII

Had I done wrong in watching Pontius' funeral discreetly from a window in the basilica, half-hidden by a curtain? Was I dissembling? Was I a hypocrite? I've pondered that many times, keeping the problem open just to myself, since I haven't even confided the matter to Mara.

I'd decided not to attend the funeral. The last thing the city needed at that time was seditious talk or outcries. My leading the cortege, which would fall to me because of my position, would do more harm than my absence. Would they accuse me of timidity, fear of public censure? So, let them accuse me . . . The mob would, inevitably, insult the only authority in Tarcisis were he present.

I think it obvious that my recourse to informants like Airhan or Cornelius was proper when in the public interest. But . . . should I have been spying myself? No action should be undertaken without good reason, and even if I did have valid motives for not taking part in the funeral, I unfortunately can't justify my giving in to childish curiosity like that. I'll add it to the none-too-short list of my worst moments.

Pontius' will, stained with blood most certainly, was unrolled and read on the steps of the basilica to a respectful and togaed audience. Calpurnius himself appeared, supported by his slaves and surrounded by a substantial delegation of mourners. Nor was the poet Cornelius missing, if not because he was anxious for a legacy then perhaps with the expectation that he would be called upon to furnish some sundry verses for the epitaph. From where I was I couldn't hear a word, but I discovered later, to my perplexity, that in the dispositions of the will that Proserpinus was bellowing out at the top of his lungs there wasn't a single attack directed at me.

The cortege finally arrived and made a turn around the forum. In the light of day the flames of the ceremonial torches swirled in the air about the coffin, clouding it, and through the haze the shapes of objects and men quivered. Pontius' slaves, freedmen, and clients took part, carrying the plaster masks of his ancestors and, in an unusual display of posthumous petulance, even the bust of the deceased himself. The shawms burst forth with their shrill, metallic tones, which immediately clashed in the air with the convulsed shouting of the professional mourner women. Seeing things through, Proserpinus stayed in the litter beside Pontius' widow, gravely consulting the tablets on which he had his speech written.

I caught sight of Maximus Cantaber, standing quite unsteadily. I hadn't seen him for many years, and in spite of his age and frail look, Maximus still had an enviable head of hair, though it was completely gray, in singular contrast to the dark tones of his ceremonial toga. I felt a certain joy as I recognized him, even from a distance, because the presence of an old friend in the city gave me some comfort in those difficult times. Among the people of Maximus' group a young woman with blond hair stood out as she tripped along, a note of discrepancy with the solemnity of the moment, and went over to give him her arm, speaking into his ear. It must be one of his daughters, probably Clelia. Where could the other, Iunia, be?

And off went half the city in mourning to the cremation ceremony outside the gates, in the shadow of the wall. The forum was left deserted, the tents taken down, the stalls closed up. Only two municipal sweepers were sleepily dragging their osier brooms over the pavement. A mangy, pitiful bitch crossed the stones, followed by a gang of restless watchdogs.

A while later a column of black smoke swirled into the sky. The retinue would be returning, commenting on the splendor of the funeral and the eloquence of the officiant. The banquet would follow at the dead man's old house. Pontius wasn't popular enough to merit the stoning of temples, nor was I hated enough to justify the stoning of my house. I would learn later that Proserpinus' speech by the pyre was long, learned, modest in its terms, and absolutely silent regarding the circumstances that had brought on Pontius' death. Nothing against me came from him.

◦═╳═◦

Absorbed in thought, I paced for a long time between my tablinum and the meeting room of the curia. A praetorium slave appeared in the door with some tablets for a ruling. He could see I was in no mood to receive him and discreetly disappeared.

Pontius had sat on that stool at the last meeting of the curia, wielding his thunderous voice and his dominating gestures. He had leaned on the pedestal of the imperial statue, trembling with rage, when I confirmed the destruction of his new house. Behind that drapery he'd roared and shouted with words unworthy of him and of me. I couldn't get Pontius out of my mind. A stupid remorse was tormenting me, sharp, obstinate, implacable, all the more unbearable because it was unjust.

Mara's recommendation occurred to me. Why not spend a night in the temple? Not that the sacred surroundings could free me of my bitterness. What was the temple? Four ice-cold walls, columns, darkness, a few statues. And who, deep down, believed in those gods except slaves and simpleminded plebs? But if a night in the temple wouldn't appease the gods—because they hadn't been offended—or set me right with myself—because my state of mind wasn't dependent on where I spent the night—perhaps it would reconcile me with the city. Politically useful. That definitely was Mara's intention when she suggested it. Objectively it was good advice if I was able to get all the consequences and benefits of a public display of piety out of it.

When, at the age of thirteen, I gave up the bulla and the toga praetexta and my father put away the clippings of my first beard,

82

he determined that I should spend a night in Apollo's sanctuary, outside the city at that time, so that the god would inspire me with dreams. On a cot in the corner, far from the votive statue, a Greek slave from our house slept, not so much to protect me as to follow the principle that a person of my birth couldn't take a step without having someone nearby to serve him. The slave fell asleep before I did; I had trouble getting used to the cold and discomfort of the place. As I looked at it, the statue of the god stayed stone. I started to close my eyes, overcome by fatigue, and I ended up sleeping soundly. I didn't dream about anything.

I woke up frightened by the great row the slave was raising, tearing at his tunic, leaping about, calling out to everyone passing by. He swore that in the middle of the night he'd seen a bluish light land in a corner of the temple and slowly descend until it lighted up Apollo's crown. The god immediately moved, seemed to stretch, and took a few steps toward my bed. Then Apollo removed the crown from his forehead and held it over the head of my bed for a few moments while I slept. A chant accompanied by a deep rumble like that of a water organ arose then, resounding off the stones of the walls. Enchanted, I hadn't awakened. The slave had trembled and remained motionless while Apollo levitated through the temple, leading the music with his crown, which swung elegantly in his hand. Then the slave fainted out of sheer terror. He woke up to give everyone the good news that his young master had been gazed at by the god.

My father called in the haruspices to interpret the dream, and they predicted a glorious future for me, one filled with victories, with blessings for me and my long line of descendants. All the people around me were happy. My father organized games, made sacrifices, distributed alms to all the inhabitants of Tarcisis, and manumitted the Greek slave.

I, frankly, didn't believe a single word of all those offered on the occasion, and I doubted that deep down anyone had believed it. The future went on to show that my skepticism, and not the prognostications, was correct. My province was at peace, I wasn't a military man; the glories that fell to me were the ordinary ones befitting my career; I had no children with Mara; the two orphans I'd adopted after my father's death went on to die of fever, and I didn't want to go ahead with any new adoptions so as not to suffer any more disappointments. My line of descent ended right there.

I was accused of avarice at the time, but the decision had been thought out in consultation with Mara, who had also seen in those deaths a barrier put up by fate, one it would be foolhardy to pass. In order to quiet evil tongues I made a will leaving all my possessions to Marcus Aurelius, making Mara trustee. Even so, every so often I would hear disguised insinuations at public sessions or I would be the target of unfair epigrams during festivals.

Sleeping in the temple for a night might be an astute political act now, capable of recovering the good will of the city. Afterward I would tell what happened—or I would say nothing, accentuating the mystery even more and giving to understand that revelations of the future had been made to me that vouchsafed my actions.

That was how I would have proceeded had I been a skillful, prudent, and perfidious man. But the price of that action—a compromise with lying—would be most unpleasant for me, intolerable. What web of deceit would I have to submit to or engender, and for how long, in order to bring it off?

Everything must be done, of course, for the city's best interests. Though I didn't ask for any responsibilities, I was brought up to accept and bear them for the public good. But I also felt obliged, by unwritten norms accessible to all well-born men, to respect the limits of my inner honor.

No one would be able to force me to go deliberately against the truth and wound my conscience to deceive my fellow citizens and lead them along like a woman chivvying geese with her staff. And even if my peers were to accept that procedure or pretend to accept it in the name of convenience, it would be hard for me to live with the ridicule of having been a humbug for a few hours and with the risk of remaining a humbug for the rest of my days. No, Mara friend, I wouldn't sleep in the temple.

I called the slave to bring me the documents he was preparing, made a quick reading of the day, and gave orders to be taken to the works.

84

The new wall was taking shape in the confusion of the work area. The appearance of the duumvir in those precincts had become commonplace, and the spectacle of the lictors and the escort had ceased to impress the workers, who earlier would stop their chores to come and greet me. The contractors approached, to ask for more money, I thought. But this time, on a handbarrow, they were bringing me an offering covered with a purple cloth. Among the stones of the new theater begun during my previous mandate and still unfinished, which with unconfessed displeasure I'd ordered demolished in order to make use of its materials for the wall, they'd discovered a bas-relief with my profile and name. They were in a hurry to return it to me, with great respect. They unveiled the carved stone before me amidst broad smiles. I thanked them for the gesture but, against their protests, I ordered that the stone join the others in the wall at the place where it best fit, with the effigy on the inside.

On my way there I'd noticed graffiti showing a fish on several walls, and I concluded that the sect that worshipped fish was growing in the city. In times of danger—I thought at the time—oriental religions, given to zoolatry, proliferated, asking the gods of animals what the gods of men might not be able to grant. That Syrian fellow, a supposed dealer in dried fruit, was carrying out his duties quite well. And as there were followers of the fish among the workers on the wall, it would be fine if those repeated drawings animated them to work harder and better. Little did I know at the time the bitterness and troubles the symbol of the fish was to bring me . . .

The next night a small, very agitated crowd arrived at my door and demanded my presence with shouts. I went out to receive them. They were almost all drunk. They were carters, shopkeepers, and artisans, the dregs of Tarcisis—dregs, however, who had a very high opinion of themselves. They stopped their howling when I appeared, but they couldn't get rid of the vapors of drink, and uncertain movements, garbled voices, and stumbling steps abounded.

A certain Dafinus greeted me from a distance with a few words and explained at length that they had come in protest to ask for my intervention. Someone had drawn a fish on the electoral signs of Rufus Cardilius, which, in addition to being an affront to him, showed even more impious disrespect for the laws and customs of Rome and the city.

"Where is Rufus Cardilius? I don't see him in this delegation," I inquired.

He was shut up in his shop, overcome by the offense and waiting for justice to be done. I didn't reply right off. I couldn't deny that Rufus Cardillus might have reason on his side. But only he or his supernumerary, Domitius Primitivus, could present the complaint. Furthermore, I considered the use of that wild mob an obvious political expedient, all the more suspect because Cornelius had come to inform me that Proserpinus and some of the decemvirs were in the habit of going surreptitiously to Rufus' tavern and having long conversations with him in the corner.

"Tell Rufus Glycinius Cardilius to appear, if he so wishes, at the praetorium tomorrow, bringing along the guilty parties to be judged."

Protests broke out; other drunkards tried to say something, but my slaves, armed now, had taken up positions alongside me. I went back inside and could still hear the noise and shouting of the gang of idlers as they dispersed. The bronze doors resounded with the blow of a stone that someone had thrown in the darkness. There was running outside. Then the street returned to its silence.

<hr />

Rufus Cardilius didn't appear at the praetorium, but the matter wasn't forgotten. Two days hadn't passed when, with an air of great mystery, one of the public slaves brought me a letter that had just been delivered at the door of the basilica. Who had brought it? A vigilante, asked to do so by a beggar. Who was sending it? He didn't know.

I grasped the roll of crumpled papyrus and untied the faded ribbon around it. A small fish cut out of leather fell onto the table. I ran my eyes over the letter: a brief message, capital letters, words separated by dashes, a crude hand.

Next to me the slave was lingering, attentive, curious to see my reaction and hopeful of getting a hint at least of the meaning of the message. I tossed the roll alongside some others and ordered him out. I wasn't going to give slaves to understand that I would deign to read anonymous letters.

After he'd left I still hesitated a little. Appearances had been safeguarded, but should I give in to my curiosity and the demands of a cowardly anonymity? I decided that in my position as magistrate it would be imprudent to tear up the writing. Reading the letter would not mean yielding to a base and superficial curiosity; rather, it would reflect the concern of a governing official who couldn't afford the luxury of depriving himself of information no matter who the Mercuries involved might be:

"*Lucius Valerius Quintius, greetings. You, who closet yourself in your redoubt like Procrustes in his lair and, taken by fantasies of war and vain dreams of glory, disdain the company and advice of your fellow citizens, whom you let die, to the scandal of the city and to your shame, refuse to recognize the fact that in the house of your friend Maximus Salvius Cantaber obscene rituals are practiced, based on fornication and the adoration of impure animals. When they dare to sacrifice the first child—for they are known to go on to the sacrifice of adolescents—all that blood will fall on your head if in the meantime you don't take the steps that your duties call for.*"

Nothing more! I wasn't surprised by the stupid bad joke of the fish, the symbol of the new religious faction that was growing in the city and that some people seemed to fear; nor the insinuations and insults that were aimed at me, typical of the enemies I would always have because of my office; but I was startled by the allusion to Maximus Cantaber, a circumspect citizen, liked by all, withdrawn by choice from a public career and incapable, because of his solid civic formation, of having anything to do with oriental superstitions. Who, really, could be interested in making me have a falling-out with my esteemed Maximus?

Calpurnius would have no need to stoop so low; my clients and freedmen, so demeaned now, wouldn't dare resort to a show of disloyalty like that. Rufus Cardilius immediately came to mind, or someone under his orders, and at that point I almost regretted the dressing-down I'd given Aulus.

◦━◆━◦

It wasn't long before new signs of the discord already at work in the city arose. Toward the end of an afternoon I was in the baths at home when Mara came ahead of the nomenclator slave to tell me that a delegation of Jews was waiting for me in the atrium. She put on a look of puzzlement and left me alone in the warm water. Thinking I would be honoring them, I ordered the nomenclator to have the delegation come into the bath. The slave returned with the answer that their religion forbade them to enter those parts of houses where naked bodies were to be seen and that it was even contrary to Roman customs concerning baths. Their very presence in my atrium was strictly exceptional and would oblige them to undergo purifications: all of this mingled with a thousand formulas of respect and protestations of apology.

This Hebraic community had established itself in Tarcisis during the time of Claudius, when the emperor had deliberately expelled all Jews from Rome because of the desecrations they'd been accused of, desecrations brought about by an obscure agitator named Crestus. They lived in poverty, married among themselves, and were fanatically attached to their customs and traditions. They practiced their rites in a house set aside for them for which they adopted the Greek name of *synagogue,* and they never appeared before my tribunal. They didn't participate in public events, didn't keep the holidays, didn't attend the games, abstained from the slightest activity once every seven days, and managed their affairs among themselves, with their priests, I presume.

Relations between the local population and the Jews hadn't always been peaceful. When echoes of the wars of Vespasian and Titus reached here in times past, there had been troubles. The houses of the Jews were stoned, and some of them were found dead, which obliged strong intervention on the part of the governor, Pompeius Catelius Celer. Other tumults had spread more recently, in the time of Hadrian, on the occasion of the bloody revolt of Simon Bar-Kokhba in Judaea.

I never had any reason for complaint against that intractable community. I'd never been sought out by any of their number, and rarely did it even cross my mind that they existed among us. I was bewildered, therefore, by this embassy. I had myself oiled and cleaned and went to receive them in the atrium.

They were two old men dressed in heavy black tunics, with white beards hanging down over their chests and strange turbans on their heads. Strands of curled hair covered their ears and reached down to their shoulders. When I came out they bowed respectfully in oriental fashion and blessed me effusively.

I began by asking why they sought me in my house and not at the praetorium, since I presumed it not to be a personal matter. They gave me to understand that they were coming in secret and preferred that their words not be heard by anyone who might perversely distort their intentions. They were, in fact, looking with mistrust at the slaves going familiarly back and forth at their tasks. Accustomed to their small closed and bolted houses and the narrow intimacy of limited spaces and measured gestures, they didn't feel very courageous there in the open expanse of my atrium.

They showered me with praises in a ceremonious and highly exaggerated tone. They were visibly fearful of my authority, and they reacted attentively to my slightest look. They were afraid of offending the duumvir with some omission or poorly calculated phrase. It was obvious that only some quite powerful reason could have pulled them out of their milieu and brought them into my presence. I had to ask them outright to get down to their business.

While they were speaking I was puzzled by their gestures, which made me think of Airhan's: open hands, palms up, turning on the wrists. What they told me left me gloomy.

They protested that they were prepared to swear by their most sacred and inviolable oaths that they had nothing in common with the sect called Christians. They maintained that they'd never been invited—and even if such had happened would never have agreed to appear—to the rites practiced in Maximus Cantaber's house. Their people had been frequently and unjustly accused because of the Romans' ignorance of fundamental religious differences, and it was that eventuality—false recriminations—that they wished to avoid.

Calling themselves the worshippers of a single god, the so-called Christians, who venerated idols, were the prisoners of superstition and in full rebellion against Rome, always seeking to impute to the Hebrews the abominations that they themselves practiced.

"Maximus Cantaber's house?" I asked, concentrating on the items that seemed of the most interest to me in that whole rigmarole. "What proof do you have?"

"It's what people say, honorable duumvir. It's what's going from mouth to mouth all through the city."

"And what are those rites?"

The two Jews looked at each other quickly. They were fearful that I'd drawn from their revelation the hostile conclusion that they knew too much about these matters. Perhaps I was even suspicious of their presence at those rites. The older one hastened to explain: "We're poor, peaceful, and God-fearing men. We don't create conflicts among citizens; we don't visit their homes; we don't know what goes on inside them. We're only touched by the rumors that buzz and pass by us like the wind, which we can't escape. But you, illustrious duumvir, with the authority vested in you, with your recognized clearheadedness and the instruments of command that were conferred on you at a fortunate hour, you will know how to find out what we cannot. If, however, you come to the conclusion that in some place they are conspiring against the authority of the Senate and People of Rome and are practicing acts repugnant to its laws and customs, remember who gave you early warning, and spare us your wrath."

I sent the Hebrews on their way and felt all the more puzzled. It wasn't to be believed that those men had come at someone's command, and their worry of being confused with those of the other sect seemed sincere and reasonable. It was no longer just a base urban intrigue backed by an anonymous letter. There was another accusation against Maximus from a different source and, in its way, believable.

I decided to do nothing until I got more information, perhaps through Cornelius, who, it happened, had been appearing less and less at our morning meetings and was becoming increasingly laconic.

What Cornelius had to tell me about the Christians was vague, remote, and indifferent: they worshipped a single god whose name they never spoke, and this god from time to time would send one of his sons down to men as an emissary. That was what had probably been the case with heroes like Adam, Moses, Joshua, Isaiah, and Christ. As for their practices, Cornelius only knew what was said in taverns and brothels: they hated humanity, insulted the statues, and gave themselves over to orgiastic rites in which the flesh and blood were always a part.

⌀━✕━⌀

No sooner had the Jews gone off than the entrance door opened with a clatter, startling the doorkeeper, who had to leap back. Aulus crossed the atrium in a great hurry and approached me almost at a run. He was clutching his helmet against his chest with his good hand. From head to toe he was smeared with mud and dried blood. His useless arm hung down, fastened to his body by a thong at wrist level. His old Greek cuirass showed thin scratches that gleamed brightly, contrasting with the leaden, dull, and muddy appearance of the armor's engraved decorations—the curls and scowl of Hercules—which could scarcely be made out. His cape dragged along, trampled and torn. The mosaics of the floor were soiled with grime as he passed.

He stood at attention, facing me, panting, and he didn't even salute. He was smiling. He could hardly manage a word, such was the fatigue that weighed on his chest with a heavy throbbing that was cutting off his respiration. Finally, after an unsuccessful attempt that came out of him like an indiscernible gasp, I managed to hear: "Don't say anything, Lucius Valerius. Come with me!"

Aulus' blackened face, normally morose and hard, gave off such a radiant joy that it looked almost like the stylized grin on a comedy mask.

He took me by the arm and almost dragged me to the door. We flew to the praetorium through a tumult of soldiers and street people. When we went up the steps of the basilica, as the guards parted the crowd with their lances, an enthusiastic cheer broke out. Only then did Aulus whisper a single word into my ear: *Arsenna!*

Moments later we came upon the bandit, who was waiting, standing, bound, in a corner of the dungeon. When I entered the cell, its floor covered with rotting straw, the mob pressing against the semicircular gratings at street level broke into a howl of insults and curses against Arsenna. I went up to him. Silence closed in. Curiosity on the outside had borne the fury away.

"What's your name?" I asked in an almost officious way, showing no doubt as to whom I had before me, but following the routine required by any solemn act of the magistrate.

"You know quite well who I am."

He didn't have the terrible and eloquent look fame had attributed to him. Where one would have expected a strong, astute man of penetrating gaze stood a crestfallen rustic who was looking at me with fear. There was no subservience in the man, true, but neither was there the noble and haughty pose that the imagination of popular writings customarily assigns to highwaymen.

"What are you going to do with me, duumvir?" he asked fearfully.

The mob outside was making a wild clamor. The ones in back who couldn't see us were asking those pressed against the grating what was going on.

"Don't give in, duumvir! Don't have any pity on that monster!"

One voice, isolated and quite clear, shouted: "Let it be in memory of Pontius Modius!" And it began to chant: "Throw him to the dogs! To the dogs!"

The chorus immediately grew, angrier and angrier: "To the dogs! To the dogs!" The faces against the grating were agitated, flushed, red, open-mouthed, revealing such savagery that I began to fear for the strength of the bars. I thought I heard in that first call for torture the sonorous voice of Rufus Cardilius.

"I'll soon see. We have time!"

Arsenna bowed wearily and sighed: "Remember that I'm a man."

I ordered Aulus to take him to a corner of the dungeon that was less exposed to the derision of the mob. Arsenna, an outlaw, had no right to a trial; in that, he was more helpless than a slave. Later on I would think about what fate to give him. But I wasn't disposed to be cajoled unthinkingly by the bloodthirsty impulses of the common people. Shouts, snorts, and grimaces would have little sway with me.

Aulus, smiling with pride, told me as we went from one door to another how he'd managed to capture Arsenna. He'd left Tarcisis stealthily, on the night I'd noticed his absence, through one of the secondary gates. He was accompanied by a few vigilantes and slaves supplied, without knowing why, by their masters. The group took a wide swing through brambles and underbrush until it picked up the road to Ebora again some five or six miles to the north.

On the road to Ebora was a hostelry called the "Three Sisters" for the three harpies who practiced pimping there along with fortune-telling and harboring outlaws. They hadn't obeyed my orders to take refuge in Tarcisis and went about their business as if nothing were happening. They were probably more afraid of the duumvir than of the Moors.

Aulus had suspected for a long time that Arsenna was operating around there, all the more so since a cart returning to Tarcisis belonging to a freedman named Tobius had been attacked in the area after a delay for repairs on a cracked wheel.

Aulus remained hidden in the underbrush for two nights and a day with no sign of the bandits. Several times he sent some of those with him to the hostelry, disguised as travelers in broad-brimmed hats and capes, to see if there was any indication of Arsenna's presence. Nothing.

On the morning of the second day, since nothing out of the ordinary had occurred, Aulus decided to withdraw. In order not to reveal his failure or arouse false fears or rumors that would discredit him, he decided to make a detour, avoiding the highway. The disheartened detachment was going along at nightfall when they came upon two men who seemed to be resting and chatting under a cork oak. One of the men pulled out a sword and took sudden flight. He was immediately knocked down by the ball from a sling. It was Arsenna. The other man ebulliently greeted the patrol that had freed him from captivity. He sang, he gave thanks to the gods, he danced. He identified himself as a merchant whose life Arsenna had spared on the condition that he teach the bandit how to read. He was just beginning the lessons when Aulus surprised them. A board was lying in the shade of the tree with the alphabet drawn on it. Next to it were the abandoned tablets that showed Arsenna's first attempts in wax.

And so, in that easy and somewhat ridiculous way, Aulus' matter of honor, which for a long time had also been his frustration and despair, was satisfied without any great violence and without bloodshed. The dirt and the disarray of Aulus' clothing were due to the poor rations, the wild terrain, and the chase after a wild boar that had crossed their path, not from any armed exchange.

Even before Aulus passed through the gates, a small assemblage was waiting for him and demanding that Arsenna be handed over. The crowd had subsequently grown, led by Rufus Cardilius, and had become threatening by the doors of the basilica. Aulus found it more prudent to hold Arsenna prisoner under guard than to come and present him to me in person at home.

I couldn't help but congratulate my centurion and return the rare satisfaction that lighted up his face. I made no reference to his unexplained disappearance during those days—an act of disobedience that could have been harmful to the city—nor did I indicate that, in all truth and despite the harsh words of the other day, I didn't consider Arsenna's arrest to be a great priority at that time. Given the imminence of a barbarian attack, I wouldn't put aside the plan of negotiating for the services of the bandit, using Airhan as go-between.

I promised to draw up a proclamation in praise of Aulus, omitting the more burlesque aspects of his adventure, and to see that another phalera be added to the four he already displayed.

⊶✦⊷

When I left the basilica, scattered groups were still agitating in the forum. They ran over, congratulating me on the arrest, and shouted suggestions for a suitable end for the highwayman, each one bloodier and more spectacular than the last. Aulus patiently escorted me home. I found myself free of the excited, gesticulating troop only when the doorkeeper closed the thick bronze doors behind me.

Waiting for me was a surprise that immediately made me forget the somewhat equivocal taste of that victory. Mara, smiling, came to meet me, accompanied by a slave woman who was having trouble holding up an enormous pike by the gills. Its tail fin was brushing the floor.

"Look at this amazing fish we've been given, friend. I've never seen one this big."

"Who brought it, Mara?"

"I don't know. The doorkeeper heard two knocks, and when he went to open, the fish was there on the doorstep, wrapped in a mat. Next to it was a bag of beans. Someone wanted to surprise us." Startled by my look of rejection, she immediately added, "But what's the matter?"

"Don't ask me any questions, Mara. Have that fish thrown into the garbage!"

Mara hesitated: "It's a superb pike. You could make an offering of it in a temple, place it by the Lararium, give it to the slaves."

I refused, impatiently. Mara suddenly grew very pale; her hands began to tremble; her whole body shook. Then she ran to embrace me, paying no heed to the slave woman who was still there, open-mouthed, the heavy fish hanging from her hands.

"Poisoned?" she asked in my ear.

"Don't be afraid. It's a poison that doesn't kill."

Grasping me by the shoulders, Mara didn't take her eyes off me; she was trying to rend the reason for my anger from my expression. With a signal of the eye I reminded her of the presence of the slave, who was watching us curiously, bent over and holding the fish with an effort that was a bit self-conscious and embarrassed now. Mara told her to follow out my orders. As she left the atrium, the slave dragged the fish along the pavement, leaving a glitter of scales as they got caught in the mosaic.

No matter how much I wanted to forget or leave the Christians for later, someone would always come along to remind me of them. This time by means of specious symbolism: a fish whose other name, *lucius*, was the same as mine, a ravager and a cannibal that swallows anything alive around it once it's free, the ruination of ponds and hatcheries. And that funereal sign of the beans . . .

I decided to speak to Maximus Cantaber first thing the following morning.

VIII

COUNTRYSIDE IN the city was an enduring fashion inspired by the demented megalomania of Nero Claudius Ahenobarbus. Reduced-scale imitations of superb golden mansions were erected in olden times at the ends of the Empire, even after all vestiges of the matricide's structures had disappeared. Huge gardens, fancy pavilions, artificial lakes, stone nymphs peeping from behind exotic shrubs: that was what Maximus Cantaber's city home was like, built by an ancestor and remodeled several times since. When it was built it may have given those who dwelled there the illusion that they were living in the country, which, incidentally, was only two steps away, rougher and less stylized. With the growth of the city and the sprouting of islands of habitation, the enormous enclosure had been circumscribed all around by ordinary buildings reached by narrow streets, dark and uneven and dominated by the shadow of the aqueduct.

When I dismounted I told the lictors and attendants to wait beside the half-open iron gate, where large medallions fastened to the grillwork, medallions featuring the figures of Echo and Narcissus, were displayed in colors ill-treated now by sun and wind. At first glance the property looked abandoned. Rust and verdigris were collecting on the metal of the gates; the yellowing lime of the wall was splotched with ulcers where the tiles showed through, and there were tufts of grass at the joints. . . . But as soon as I went in I was intercepted by the gatekeeper, who spoke to me with fawning humility. The skinny old man, dressed in rags, was dragging fetters and a noisy chain that were linked to an iron stake driven into the ground.

"Sir," he whimpered, "have pity on me!"

"Why have they tied you up?"

"Because of a mistake I made not meaning any wrong. I beg of you, intercede with Maximus Cantaber for me. Remind him of the years I've served him and his father. Assure him that I won't go back to begging on the street."

Two quite thin watchdogs came out of the shadows and wagged their tails hesitantly, not daring to approach. The gravel path ahead led to a knoll, behind which could be seen the tile roofs of Maximus' house. Two slaves were cutting grass on the berms and tossing it into a bonfire. Morning was getting on, and it was already quite warm. The panting dogs' tongues lolled from their mouths. Bees, with their changeless spontaneity, were buzzing about the bushes of blue-flowering rosemary. By the edge of the path a small fountain in the form of an open scallop shell was dry and covered with moss and sand.

"Do you know who I am?"

"From your dress and escort I know that you can have influence with my master. People came this morning, and I didn't ask any of them for this favor because they didn't seem worthy of my request."

"People? Who? Clients?"

"People, sir."

I decided not to go forward, opted to walk around to the path inside the low wall that traced the compound's perimeter. It gave me time to think once more about what I would say to Maximus, to remind him of childhood play on that property, which I had visited almost daily in times gone by. To be more frank, the delay would let me postpone the inconvenience of the meeting a tiny bit. One of the dogs followed me timidly, his tail between his legs. The slave settled down in the shade, clanking his chains.

The mansion of the Cantaber family had been so sumptuous in times past that its gardens had been praised all over the south for the coolness of its lawns, the amazing engineering of the waterworks, and the exotic imported vegetation that thrived there. In those bygone days, brightly colored rare birds flitted about, paid for by their weight in gold; these would, not rarely, be sacrificed on feast days with pageantry. It was told, apocryphally perhaps, that Maximus' grandfather, of Turdetani origins, had ordered gold dust sprinkled in the hypocausts with the conviction that the outpouring of that noble metal would be beneficial to the body's humors. And such was their proud position that even the slaves wore embroidered tunics—of purple on the Lupercalia.

If the house wasn't in ruins today, and if the gardens still gave a hint of the old luxury by the shape of the flowerbeds, the skillfully placed rock gardens, the shaded paths that crossed, nevertheless weeds, the yellow withering of whole beds, the grime on the walls, and the awful disharmony showed the neglect to which the terrain had been subjected.

When, after the death of his father, Maximus Salvius took possession of his inheritance, he decided to retire to the family villa some twenty miles away, rarely putting in an appearance in Tarcisis. He left the property in the care of a decrepit slave couple who did what they could, which wasn't very much. The birds began to disappear, the couch grass took over, and a lot of trees died.

Along these walks I'd rolled my hoop; behind those rocks I'd pretended to be the fierce highwayman Coreolus; in the ponds, dry now, I'd caught carp with my hands in the merry company of Pontius, under the watchful eye of Maximus, the oldest of us. Still familiar to me was the age-old holm oak that shaded a curve in the path with its enormous spread and that was said to be already in existence in the time of Decimus Iunius Brutus. But on its knotty trunk, so familiar, I now saw sacrilegiously carved the design of a fish, its outline standing out in whitewash.

That mark among the signs of my boyhood was like a brutal, offensive profanation and brought into my spirit, so distracted by distant reminiscences, a sudden alarm. There was another power here, one stronger than that of my memories.

I could see the pavilion, modeled after the Etruscan style, hidden in the groves beyond where the wall curved. From where I was I caught a quick glimpse in the distance, among the shadows, of a naked woman standing in a tub. Someone was pouring water over her with a shell. The woman squatted, sat in the water, and two male hands were placed on her dripping hair. I stopped, startled. I hadn't expected to come across any nymphs of flesh and blood in those byways . . .

Cautiously I drew close to the pavilion, which stood at the end of a paved area, below the level of the path. Some twenty men and women were massed in front of a sacrificial altar of rough stone that I didn't remember having been in that place. On the altar was a small statue of painted clay showing a peasant with a lamb over his shoulders. The girl I'd seen undressed was shivering now, wrapped in a toga. The dog that had been accompanying me so tamely joined the gathering and stopped to scratch himself, unconcerned. I concealed myself in the shadows behind a poplar.

The group was mumbling some kind of litany. I noticed that those who didn't have their backs to me had their eyes half-closed as they said the prayer directed to a father-god who kept watch in the heavens. They held their arms out, palms up at shoulder level. It all looked rather ridiculous to me.

It was a mixed group: citizens, freedmen, and slaves, men and women, old and young. Tunics of pure linen, in soft tones, mingled with bright-colored estamin. The fish motif appeared frequently on the few adornments they wore: bracelets, pendants, earrings, a buckle. . . . I couldn't understand, then, what the relationship was between that obsessive symbol and the clay statuette peasant dressed in skins and carrying a lamb.

The prayer was over, but not the rite. A man approached the altar solemnly. I recognized him: it was the fruit merchant my slave had pointed out as the one who supervised that cult and who had been distributing the bread with helpers in an out-of-the-way courtyard. Airhan had been right when he informed me that this man frequented Maximus Cantaber's house.

He displayed the palms of his hands and began to recite a text in Greek: it was an oriental tale, full of antitheses, events that happened and didn't happen, animals that moved and stood still, objects that were but also weren't. Through the haze of its ornamentation, one could vaguely perceive in the recitation the journey of a person who in a certain city of Judaea was looking for a place where his wife could give birth. Of the free men there present, few understood Greek; of the slaves, none. But the fruit merchant went on monotonously, as if the fact that the majority didn't understand was absolutely irrelevant or, who knows, was convenient. His ecstatic figure, his repetitious intonation marked by pauses, and the soft swaying of the foliage around seemed to bring on a dull, halting, hypnotic conviction in that environment.

At that moment a woman in a light blue tunic pleated in the Greek manner turned toward me and fixed her hair. I don't know what impulse it was, whether provoked by spontaneous impatience or some sound I'd unwittingly made. With that movement the sun, passing over her very bright green eyes, almost lighted them up in a very quick flash. She stared at me for an instant, then turned away. I had no reason to feel any shame, but I found myself compelled to lower my face. When I lifted it again, the woman was looking at the officiant with the same attentiveness as all the others.

An immediate certainty came into my mind: that could only be Iunia, Maximus Cantaber's elder daughter. None of the free women there could have been dressed in such an expensive peplum.

When the recitation was over, silence fell. Another, older, man came to the altar with an unfurled roll in his hand and announced a letter from the community in Terash, on the other side of the Mare Nostrum. "Brothers and sisters in Christ, of wise and simple hearts," he began to read. It was Greek again, not of the best kind. Iunia turned her face toward me again, slowly now, looking for me in a forthright way. Her eyes, almost transparent in that light, suddenly widened and followed mine. One corner of her mouth tightened into a grimace somewhere between questioning and scolding. I made a silly gesture, pretending distraction, adjusting the strap of my sandal. Iunia's clear look went on until I went on my way again, disturbed, like a child caught at some sort of mischief.

I didn't continue on the route I knew so well. I preferred to get as far away as possible from the group celebrating those mysteries, so no one would think that a magistrate of the city had taken up the perversity of personally spying on the practices of citizens. I went almost completely around the perimeter of the property until I found myself on a path leading straight to the residence.

Several reasons for worry were working on me. That worship of the fish, peaceful and innocent although widespread and strange, was indeed being practiced in the home of a friend of mine and among his people, with the participation of his daughter. A foreigner was officiating in that act, someone from the lower classes who hadn't escaped the perspicacity of my informant Airhan. The denunciations, then, had been justified even though nothing had been seen regarding the basis of it all. On the other hand there was the slave tied to the gate, which, though it was legal, showed an unwanted poor judgment on the part of Maximus Cantaber, not to mention imprudence in those times, which were not suited for any dissatisfaction on the part of those in servitude. Who knows how many rebellious slaves were already mingling with the Moorish bands? That spectacle could only result in discredit to Maximus, and to my esteem as well, as his friend. Finally, there was Iunia Cantaber's haughty look, so innocent and yet so determined that it weakened and disquieted me without my knowing why.

I came upon Maximus sleeping on some pillows on a stone bench under an arbor. A pruning knife lay on the ground. His arm, resting on the edge of the bench, was moving softly back and forth to the rhythm of his heavy breathing. His head hung down over his chest, and his handsome white hair, which he wore too long, fell over his forehead. He was at peace, far removed from the world, in the land of dreams. I committed the cruelty of awakening him.

I whispered in his ear, going back to old bits of play: "Not rarely did good Homer nod!" Maximus didn't start. He opened his eyes, taking his time, straightened his head, and then lifted it up. My image must have been confusing to him in the counter-light of the sun beating down on the foliage. He had some difficulty in recognizing my features. Then he smiled and got up: "Lucius Valerius Quintius! In person! And my thinking you were part of my dream . . ."

"When friends don't visit me, Morpheus brings me to visit my friends. Here I am, your humble servant."

"Ah, Lucius, so many things have happened."

I declined the wine Maximus offered and sat down on the stone bench too. I commented on the pruning knife, which was gleaming brightly, with no sign of earth or thread of grass, and we both laughed at Maximus' arduous horticultural labors. At that moment I felt a real pleasure in being with him, and I almost forgot the reasons that had brought me there and the conclave I had witnessed along the way. I noticed, however, that Maximus, though he was trying to be cheerful and loquacious, would make sudden pauses in the middle of sentences. He would look at me then almost shocked, as if he'd lost what he'd wanted to say, picking up the thread of the conversation again with difficulty. Also, when the phrases seemed to flow and were well coordinated with his gestures, strange repetitions of entire sentences would occur, in successive waves, quite rapidly and in a dislocated tone of voice, as if the talk belonged to somebody else who was intervening quickly there and copying his speech.

But the conversation, which had begun in a carefree and merry tone, gradually began to get weighty, and Maximus' smiling visage gave way to a more and more somber dejectedness. He recalled the death of his wife years before after painful suffering, continued on about the stupid riding accident of which his son-in-law was victim. He picked up the pruning knife and began using it on the grass with minute and excessive care. There were long moments of silence now. Suddenly he observed: "Then poor Pontius, he went too . . ."

There was no censure in that phrase. It was in a small way the reaffirmation that we all depend on fate and that there's nothing we can do but submit to it.

"And now these Moors. Who could have guessed that they would try again? It's absurd, isn't it?"

"Ridiculous," I added. But Maximus suddenly grabbed my arm.

"Lucius, you're not going to tear my house down, are you?"

I explained that the new wall wouldn't pass that way, which was more than obvious. I worked hard at calming him. I leaned over, sketched a rough map in the sand. Maximus nodded gravely. He thought a bit before daring to ask: "What if it did?"

He took note of my embarrassment and quickly changed the subject. The words came out of him bungled and chaotic. They were about repairs to the house, their extortionate expense, the state of the hypocaust—which, in addition, he hadn't been able to heat up because his daughter Iunia was against it . . .

He fell silent, twisted his lips, and looked at me. Then he got up, took a few long, pensive steps, opened his arms, and came out with: "It's no use pretending. Let's get right to the point. It's because of my daughter that you're here, isn't that so, Lucius?"

"There's a lot of talk in the city."

"Isn't the cult free in the Empire now?"

He didn't let me answer. He came over hurriedly, uneasy, and sat beside me again. He was talking quite loudly now. That nervous tic of repeating phrases was getting more insistent and disturbing: "Lucius, the fault lies with that Milquion, who says he's a fruit merchant, but he looks more like a merchant of souls. Iunia's not well. She suffered with the death of her mother and was desperate over her husband's. This man convinced her that after the end the people we love can still be alive in spirit in some place in the spheres. Iunia, in good faith, turned the innocence of a spirit weakened by disappointment to him. Try to understand, Lucius."

"I've been getting denunciations. The citizenry mistrusts anything that seems different . . ."

"But what can I do? Shall I prohibit the celebration of these mysteries in my house and subject myself to knowing that my daughter is going to practice them who knows where? Did you see the people there? There are slaves among them! Slaves! I'd rather have them under my roof and my vigilance than in some shack in the city."

"But how is it that as paterfamilias you don't preside over the ceremony?"

"Because it's a crude religion, opportunistic, unworthy of people of good birth, and one that repudiates the family customs held by Romans. I know. I know! I received the merchant once. Take note, Lucius, only once. He speaks vulgar Greek, like door slaves. But could I throw him out? Lose my Iunia? See myself involved in shameful proceedings?"

"What do you intend to do?"

"You tell me, Lucius, you tell me. You're certainly more sensible than I am. What should I do?"

There was a sudden rustle, and a smiling, florid face emerged from the bushes. All ruddy, young Clelia came into view with an enormous bouquet of flowers in her arms, a garland of marigolds in her hair. With a leap she came easily between us and stood looking at me, all excited. Finally she took a deep breath and widened her smile even more.

Maximus seemed embarrassed and didn't know whether to scold or welcome Clelia, who was standing between us now, still staring at me. I made a slight bow, which I tried to make stern and proper. I felt annoyed by the girl's arrival. Her attitude seemed impertinent, but I waited in vain for her father to call her down. I'd recognized her immediately, having caught a glimpse of her at Pontius' funeral. I was far from expecting she would present herself in this way, so bold and so direct: "Sometimes I see you pass in the forum, Lucius Valerius. I almost never miss a session of your court. You, of course, don't notice me. Ingrate."

She pouted, feigning anger, and leaned against her father, who, taking part listlessly in the game, held her. With his free hand Maximus made a disconsolate gesture, imploring patience. Surprised, I searched for some compliment, some phrase that would simultaneously express my pleasure at seeing Maximus' younger daughter and my vexation at having her interrupt a meeting that dealt with important matters. Finally Maximus, with extraordinary softness, begged my pardon and invited Clelia to leave us.

The young woman laughed, her head thrown back. She was obviously accustomed to a rather free and easy relationship with her father and felt no qualms at embarrassing him in front of me. With an exaggerated effort she swung up the bundle of flowers and grasses that she held against her breast and pulled out a rose with her teeth. Then she took it between two fingers, supporting the bouquet with her knee, and ended up hanging the rose from a high branch: "Be careful, my father, always to speak *sub rosa*!"

Then, all cheerful, she gave me a sidelong glance, clutched the flowers to her breast, and ran off laughing, leaving a trail of crumpled petals. When she'd disappeared, Maximus' smile weakened. "What do you think I should do, then? Lock Iunia up in her room? In a cell?"

"I don't want any disturbances in the city. I don't want them stoning your house. Please, talk to her."

"Talk to her, talk to her! As if we haven't had so many frustrating and vexing talks. Iunia believes in that man! Or she's possessed by that god! How should I know!"

And, growing calmer, reflective: "When you come to think of it, Lucius Valerius, the divinities of our fathers limit themselves to enjoying their eternity. They don't compensate us for our losses. What interest do the gods, who live here and there, so close and yet so distracted, have in us? You make a contract, you make a sacrifice . . . 'I give so that you shall give!' Who guarantees you that the gods will fulfill their part?"

"Yes," I agreed. "Who guarantees it?"

But who was the guarantor of that oriental god? I didn't get to give an answer. I only noted that the celebrations in his house were public knowledge throughout half the city, beyond the wall. If they could find some more discreet way, at least, if they wouldn't let themselves be seen, would let themselves be forgotten for a time . . .

I was going to go on, but Maximus grew pale, moved his lips, and babbled: "It's getting very cold, Lucius."

It was around six o'clock; the sun was beating down strongly, and we were both perspiring. Maximus leaned against the back of the bench. It was with great strain that he said to me, articulating word by word: "I thank you very much, Lucius Valerius, for your friendly intervention. Will you forgive me if I don't accompany you to the gate?"

Stooped over, arms crossed on his chest, dragging his feet, he went toward the house. I called the slaves and tried to accompany him. Maximus refused. He straightened up, shook his head, embraced me, rejected the help of the servant, and went in.

I stood there for a bit, uncertain whether my visit had been a wise step. I felt inept, frustrated, and vaguely irritated by Clelia's

105

impudence. The rose she'd placed on the tree had fallen onto the marble bench like a bright red smudge, defacing the perfect smoothness of the stone. Only then did I remember the request of the gatekeeper slave. I'd forgotten the man completely, and that increased my discomfiture even more. On the way out I would have the poor devil whining after me with that horrible clanking chain leaving its mark in the sand.

Maximus was not one to punish a slave easily. Undoubtedly he'd summoned him, heard him out, let him defend himself formally in front of his people. If he applied that punishment, more of a stain on his own house than on the one punished, he'd certainly proceeded because of strong reasons. Had justice been done, then?

But I was feeling compassion for the slave, remorse for not having kept my promise, and resentment for having been upset by it all. Compassion is a noble sentiment that should only apply to those who are victims of an unjust fate. Separated from a sense of justice, it becomes simple faintheartedness, unworthy of a citizen.

Could the image of the shackled slave that obsessed me then and the intense desire to relieve his bad luck be a sign of softness? Could I be losing the qualities of citizenship? At that instant I recognized, in my recent behavior, deviations—some greater, some lesser—from what might properly be expected from me. In spite of everything I gave thanks that I'd noticed them before someone else had to point them out, which wouldn't have been long in coming.

◦—✦—◦

I was going toward the exit along the gravel walk, and I'd already caught sight of the old slave huddled on the ground by the gate, in the company of the two dogs, when I noticed someone waiting for me on one side of the path.

Leaning against a tree trunk, looking down, Iunia was rolling and unrolling the thin veil she'd been wearing moments before during the ceremony. There was no way to pass her by. She was clearly waiting for me, to stop me. I approached her, firming up my steps.

"Duumvir, why were you spying on our prayers? You don't have to be so furtive. I'll invite you anytime you want."

106

I hadn't counted on that question. Iunia's appearance, for which I was unprepared, troublesome after my disastrous conversation with Maximus, was completely inopportune. I would have preferred to forget her image—or at least to remember her only later, from a distance, or to meet her again, while defended by my retinue, in the course of the city's daily routine.

Under the serenity of her tone and the impassivity of her features, Iunia was hiding a provocative intent I couldn't manage to grasp. She dared to ask for an accounting from me when I was the one who should demand it from her. What business was it of hers if I happened to be passing by the place where those rites were being practiced? I replied, almost in a hostile tone: "It's not part of my duties to examine citizens' religion."

"Are you interested in my religion, Lucius?"

She was treating me familiarly, using my praenomen. Just as I had recognized her despite not having seen her since she'd become a grown woman, so perhaps she still remembered me from the few visits Maximus and I had exchanged years back.

"'Nothing human is foreign to me,' as the man said."

"My religion isn't human. It was founded by the son of God."

"Ah, of which one?"

It was the right moment to return the provocation and to show, in some way, my annoyance at having been accosted without plan or warning. But simultaneously, deep inside, I felt an indefinable alarm, which I tried—affecting disdain for Iunia's words—to evade. If I was disdainful she didn't seem to notice it. She was determined to confront the magistrate. That might have been—who knows?—an initial test. My manner didn't seem to mean much to her.

"The son of the almighty God!"

"And that one, does he have a lot of sons?"

"Only one. Whom he sent to Earth to save us and whom you people crucified."

"You people? I never ordered anyone crucified, nor do I have the authority for it. There's no ax-head in my fasces. Besides, it would be difficult to crucify a fish. Anatomically it's quite complicated."

At that moment the irritating placidity of Iunia's features, which didn't exclude a strange hardness, changed slightly. I sensed a slight puckering of her lips, a turning away of her eyes, and deeper breathing that was telling me—I thought—how big a mistake I was making: "The son of God took human form and came into the world to save us. You too."

"I don't care about being saved. Nobody would care, I think. And that fish you people go around painting, what is it?"

"*Ichthys!*"

"I know, I speak Greek too."

Dialectically, with affected patience, she explained to me, starting with the letters of the Greek word, that it was a matter of an acronym for Jesus Christ Son of God Savior. While she was speaking she kept passing the veil from one hand to the other. The story of that unruly Jew called Crestus, who in times gone by had provoked riots in Rome, came to me. I didn't want to ask if it was the same person; the religious conversation was of much greater interest to Iunia than to me. But the truth is that, paradoxically, I had no wish for her to stop, because Iunia's presence was making a more powerful impression on me than her words.

"Wonderful! May he be welcome to the Pantheon! There's room for all. So much the better if he doesn't have the shape of a fish. And what is it that he has to offer?"

"Goodness and mercy." These words she flung out like an accusation, in vivid contrast to their gentle meaning. I was finally exhausting Iunia's patience. In an almost childish way I considered it a small victory that could be seen now in her tight face, her rigid lips, the harshness of her voice. Goodness? Mercy? The shackled slave was there, pitiful, sitting in the shade. I pointed to him and said something in a tone that tried to be ironic.

"I wasn't talking about the slave!" Iunia said in a nettled tone.

I put on a face that simulated great surprise. Iunia's voice rose in pitch, dry and exasperated: "I was talking to you about salvation, and you come back to me with household matters. Can it be you're like peasants who are only interested in the petty appearances of life? Who think their crude gods live in the woods?"

"What I believe in tells me to respect myself, and nothing more. Don't you feel any pity for your slave?"

"Don't you want to hear me? Good-bye, duumvir."

With a jerk Iunia drew the veil she'd been clutching around her neck, turned her back, and started off. I took a step in her direction and began talking again quite rapidly. I gesticulated, I think. I wanted to tell her to be careful, to warn her about the ill will in Tarcisis against those of her sect. I swallowed my words, was flustered. I wanted to tell her all that, yes, but most of all I didn't want her to go . . .

"Don't worry, duumvir. I'm quite well guarded!"

And Iunia, before she broke into a run, turned and showed me the gold pendant in the form of a fish that she wore around her neck.

❦

As I'd expected, the slave, as soon as he saw me approach, crawled over to meet me. I had to step aside to stop him from throwing himself at my feet. He was shouting in a howling, tremulous voice, thrashing his arms about in such a way that one of the dogs, all excited, started barking aimlessly and baring his teeth, squinting with his snout in the air.

"I spoke to him, I spoke to him," I mumbled, giving the slave a wide berth as I passed.

I didn't want to look back, and I continued on my way, for some time hearing the clanking chains and the moaning of that man, who seemed to be placing a layer of fictitious suffering over one of real suffering.

My escort hurriedly reassembled. The lictors stood at attention in front of the litter; the bearers hid the dice they had been furtively amusing themselves with and picked up the handles as the others shaped up behind. As soon as I got in, the litter swayed and left the ground.

But before I could give the order to march, the curtains on my right were suddenly drawn back. Sitting on the wall, young Clelia was holding out her hand, grasping the curtain and looking at me in all her ruddiness.

"I saw you talking to my sister," she said.

"So? That's no reason for this insolence!"

Clelia was embarrassed; she didn't know quite what to say. She kept holding the curtain back with her right hand, which was trembling. I crossed my arms impatiently.

"Did Iunia try to convert you to her religion?" she ended up asking, with a timidity that belied the free and easy gestures with which she'd interrupted my conversation with her father.

"And what if it were so? Why do I have to tell you?"

Clelia leaned a little closer. I was afraid she would fall. She whispered: "Poor Iunia. Forgive her, duumvir. My sister is completely taken up with all that. They put slaves in tubs and pour water over them. 'Bapetismos,' they say. They almost only speak Greek. Even the slaves go around here saying things in Greek. I think I should protect her. Try to understand, duumvir."

Clelia, unexpectedly, was almost weeping. I tried to keep my face very stern. I ran the back of my hand over her face paternally, closed the curtain, and snapped my fingers for the slaves to start up.

Through the translucent curtains I could for some time still make out the shadow of young Clelia on top of the wall waving to me. We turned into the alley. And it was Iunia I was thinking about along the rest of the way to the forum.

That afternoon I presided over the tribunal in the tumultuous nave of the basilica. With a ferocious look Proserpinus was calling, in the name of a client, for the eviction of a shop tenant, whom he had made to stand there, held by the arms by his slaves. The matter took up the whole afternoon, and I would be lucky if it didn't go on into the night. The litigants were whining and trying to get my attention. Those present applauded or hooted according to their sympathies.

It was so hot and the place, closed in by drapes, was so filled with incense that we were all perspiring. The flies were going about aimlessly, stickily. The very wax of the tablets seemed softer and less resistant to the incisions of the stylus.

Proserpinus, with loud shouts, was demanding two water clocks; the representative of the other side laid claim to the same. In the back, not interested in the decision, Rufus was strolling through the basilica between two citizens. He would listen circumspectly and then stop, making a speech to those around him. He left my field of vision. I awarded a clock to each litigant, indifferent to the customary protests, and leaned over the table to listen to Proserpinus' allegation.

It wasn't long before I caught myself sketching a fish on the wax tablet.

IX

"Is THIS A MOOR?"

The bloody, mud-encased corpse was rolled along, rocking, on a wooden handbarrow with crude wheels affixed to one end. The apparatus was handled by three men who were laughing and euphoric and expressing themselves in rustic speech. The owners of the curiosity, they were asking for coins from those who had gathered in the forum, brought there by news of the event. The peasants were attempting to keep the remains concealed under a burlap cloth, uncovering them only for those who paid, but soon the crowd was so large and so curious, tugging at the cover from all sides, that in spite of the yokels' efforts, the body was exposed for all to see. When I got there, accompanied by Aulus, there was a citizen asking questions with an air that was between inquisitive and anxious: Is this a Moor? My, how he stinks!

Everybody drew back so the duumvir could have a look. Silence fell. One of the bearers rolled up the burlap and folded it, leaving the corpse in full view.

The Moor was short in stature, so slim and weak-looking that one might think he was incapable of life, of wielding a weapon. His tight, black, curly hair, sprinkled with earth and pieces of underbrush mixed in with coagulated blood, was like a paste on the left temple, where he had caught the blow that brought him down. Hollow eyes, dark now, dimmed by the shadow of death; a low, furrowed brow; a flat nose; a long neck; strangely protruding cheekbones; he wasn't so different from the peasants hereabouts. His complexion was, perhaps, a bit darker; his skin had a yellowish cast, accentuated by splotches of decomposition.

He wore a simple necklace of painted shells, and wrapping him down to his bare feet was a kind of striped tunic of coarse wool, all wrinkled and torn, grimy now. Next to him on the stretcher lay a cap of soft leather, lined with grasses, which had served him as a helmet. Tied to his left wrist was a thin strap of unknown use. The corpse's greasy, sweetish smell made the faces of the onlookers tighten, and it dissuaded them, after the first movements of curiosity, from drawing any closer. Only the peasants seemed indifferent to the stench.

"Did he have any weapons on him?" Aulus asked.

One of the rustics removed a heavy bundle from his back and unrolled it on the paving stones: short spears with hammered copper tips, several cudgels made of round stones embedded in wood, an Hispanic sword, a bag of sling stones, two bows, arrows with fire-hardened tips, and some mysterious objects of clay and metal that might have been amulets or idols . . .

These were the weapons captured from a band that had attacked refugees from a villa not far from Vipasca. This dead Moor had acted like the chief—according to the peasants—even though he wore no insignia that showed him to be such. Fate had favored us: at dawn, when the wailing marauders fell upon the carts, they were immediately surprised by a crew of laborers who'd been keeping an eye on them for several hours.

The other barbarians had been left hanging from trees, impaled, both as an example and to strike terror into those who might try again there. The villa's unharmed owners who took refuge in Vipasca, with base ingratitude thanked their saviors with only a half-dozen sesterces and an amphora of oil. The peasants dragged along the Moor's remains so everyone could see what had happened and so they would be congratulated and properly rewarded for their deed. They intended to exhibit him through all the villages round about, collecting as recompense the money that generous citizens might see fit to dispense, as they are accustomed to do with the carcasses of wolves and bears.

I gave orders that each field hand be given a hundred sesterces and clothes and footwear, at my expense. As for the corpse, they should toss it into one of the municipal garbage dumps because it was already reeking and stinking up the forum.

I would learn later that the peasants were treated to a banquet at Rufus' tavern and that he gave each one four hundred sesterces and made a speech of thanks to the "brave defenders of the highway" who had been treated with such ingratitude by the notables.

As had happened before, nervousness and excitation ran through the city, and rumors were at a boil. The dead Moor was transformed in people's imaginations into a levy of prisoners captured in a military skirmish. The encounter on the Vipasca road was multiplied a hundredfold. Many citizens were convinced that the south was teeming with barbarians devouring territory, cities, and fields, like lava from a volcano. That night statues spoke and laughed, cocks crowed at off hours, glowing ghosts appeared on the roof of the temple of Jove, and all the portents usually held by popular fantasy had occasion to show themselves.

It didn't take long, given the inconstancy that is part of the makeup of simple souls, for the agitation to slacken, for the signs to become rarer, for women to cease seeing the blazing eyes of Moors in the darkness of backyards and peristyles, and for people's attention to return to the petty affairs of the city: Rufus' campaign became more and more widespread, the provocations of the Christians more and more brazen, and the cases before the tribunal brought up nasty matters as always. A load of fish sauce and fresh sardines that arrived without the carters' reporting any surprises or foreign presences along the coast seemed to belie any barbarian danger. The people's spirits calmed down, stretched, and dozed off.

But if the public is by nature fickle and pusillanimous and inclined to credit the outer appearance of things, inattentive to thought and foresight, it is up to the magistrate to compensate for those weaknesses of spirit, because in the event of a disaster, the responsibility lies with the magistrate and not with the hoi polloi.

They were still dragging the Moor out of the forum when I set about convoking a special meeting of the curia for the next day. Municipal slaves were to appear immediately at the homes of every decemvir with a letter from me, and the summons was to be enforced by lictors so that there would be no later allegations of any slight on my part. And I arranged with Aulus for the means of assuring the presence of all at the praetorium so as not to undergo another humiliation from a summons that was ignored.

The wall, in the meantime, had been almost entirely rebuilt. There was no longer any trace of Pontius' house or of the storehouses and ruins that had been torn down, except where the remains of columns and decorative stones, hastily incorporated into the wall, stood out here and there. These would soon be buried by cement and plaster. The crowd of workers seemed sparser and slower now; the refuse was being burned; scaffolding and hoists had been dismantled. Singing could be heard.

Aulus made a point of showing me an old device rescued from the debris that now crammed a rundown barracks building beside one of the gates. It was a small catapult, the kind they call a "scorpion," which propels darts through a tube with a force capable of piercing bronze plate at two hundred paces. It was damaged, with one of its supports split, but the essential part of the mechanism—the sturdy iron springs, the steel bow, the tube—could, although rusty, easily be repaired even in Tarcisis. That machine had probably never been used in combat; they'd put it off in a corner during the same distant era of peace that had rendered the walls dispensable. Little by little, the catapult had been covered by junk and trash. Aulus saved it from destruction when slaves were preparing to burn it on a pile of old wood. He ordered them to carry the weapon to the battlements, and he tested it by aiming at positions with it and calculating the distance of the horizon.

Satisfied and proud, my centurion explained to me in detail how the "scorpion" worked, and he demonstrated by placing a tube inside the guiding mechanism. Unfortunately there wasn't the slightest possibility of making a series of copies to arm the walls with a battery of "scorpion"-type ballistas. The springs had been manufactured in Rome, and no blacksmith in Tarcisis had either the skills or the shop for such complex work. But perhaps they could try making imitations that would hurl stones or clay balls instead of darts.

I was amazed to see Aulus so animated, chattering on glibly, almost joyfully, about matters that (though germane to his duties) seemed to me of insufficient import to demand the time and attention of one who was neither a military man nor a blacksmith. I let him talk on, more for the pleasure of seeing him unburden himself with an unsuspected loquacity and show the capacity for an unusual initiative than from any interest in technical trifles. Could it be of use for the city's defense? That was all I wanted to know. But when would that centurion of mine cease to surprise me?

<hr>

No sooner had we come down from one of the towers by the main gate than a strange cortege, somber and slow, turned a nearby corner and came on with measured step. Men and women were walking in a group, close together, dressed in dark colors. Upon the shoulders of four slaves a stretcher was swaying, carrying a body wrapped in a shroud. A flutist was playing funeral music to all sides with a continuous repetition of tones. As a repugnant stench filled the air, contorting the gatekeepers' faces and making everyone beside the gate draw back, I caught sight of Iunia Cantaber at the head of the procession, on foot in the manner of the common people. The Moor's corpse was what they were bearing.

Once again, as I saw Iunia, I felt a sudden, intense, and almost painful frisson pass through my whole body. I didn't want another confrontation with Maximus Cantaber's daughter. For a few seconds I considered the chance to get away from there and leave the matter in Aulus' hands, avoiding her. It was what I should have done, but I didn't. I felt strangely immobilized, fastened to the ground, unable to take my eyes off her.

The group stopped mournfully beside the gate. The flutist stowed his instrument in the leather box of his profession. The fruit merchant took a place ahead of the stretcher and stood there conspicuously with his arms folded. No one was blocking their way. But all those around, including the guards and Aulus, had their eyes on me, as if awaiting my word. I covered my nose with my cloak. The stench of decomposition was becoming more and more unbearable.

"Are you blocking my way, duumvir?"

I wasn't about to block anyone's way; I just happened to be there in the performance of my duties, and I couldn't turn my back just like that and go on my way now. Onlookers had begun to gather at some distance. I had to address my reply not to the fig merchant but to Iunia, who because of her social position was not to be ignored. Besides, it was her presence that had brought out the man's daring bravado.

"What are you going to do with that body, Iunia Cantaber?"

"I'm going to bury it, Lucius Valerius."

"The times of Antigone have long since passed."

"This man was my brother."

Iunia was challenging me. To accept the challenge would mean demeaning myself, and it was foolish to continue the conversation. Whatever I said would only serve the designs of Iunia and her clan of proselytes. In the background the gawkers, with a muttering that was growing louder and harsher, were waiting for the duumvir to take a position. The flute player, his assigned work finished, was going off phlegmatically with his case under his arm.

"Aulus! Have that man buried outside the wall!"

Silence fell. The flutist, without stopping, looked back. Then the gabble started up again, a bit more intense perhaps. Standing beside me, Aulus took charge of the operation and began to shout orders. He immediately assembled a half-dozen vigilantes with picks and shovels, and these men joined the cortege. The slaves who had been carrying the body were replaced, somewhat rudely, by city guards who, showing disgust, marched through the gate to Aulus' cadence.

I stood there watching. In the distance the retinue hesitated and made a few useless turns. Outside, Aulus was shouting mercilessly, as if commanding a military formation—pointing out a place. The procession struggled over to the spot, and the guards began to dig.

On the way back Iunia passed by, looking straight ahead, trying to ignore me. I took her by the arm, forcing myself to smile, and brought her over to my litter, which was waiting by the gate. Iunia made a motion to resist, then looked at the bishop and the others, but all of them, seeing themselves surrounded by guards and my people, preferred to consider the incident concluded. During those moments, without losing my smile, I continued talking to Iunia in a soft voice about absolutely insignificant matters, only so the people would take note that the duumvir had not suffered an insult and that the incident had been resolved in a good way. Iunia was silent; she didn't return my affability, but she docilely let my attendants put her in the litter and escort her home.

⚬━✦━⚬

Mara had already heard about the episode when I got home. She helped me into the bath and dined with me, quite simply, at the table in the tablinum, as was customary when there were no guests.

"What do you think of that Iunia Cantaber?" she asked casually after a few desultory domestic comments.

"Obstinate."

"Do you know what Galla told me?"

Days before, Iunia had caused a scandal at the door to the baths during the women's time. When Galla and others approached, Iunia Cantaber had her litter cross in front of them. She got out and spoke to Galla and her companions in a very agitated way. Nudity in the baths was indecorous, she said; everything was adornment and vanity; they should all return home immediately and reflect on the punishments of Gehenna.

Galla had confessed she felt puzzled and upset at seeing a person of rank expose herself that way—in the middle of the street—to the jeers of the women. The other women, in fact, hadn't spared Iunia. They'd laughed, almost shoved her. It was her younger sister Clelia who took her by the arm and led her back to the litter, delivering her from any more abuse. The two of them went off with their guards amidst general laughter. But every afternoon from that day on, as soon as the bell was rung for the women's bath, there was Iunia at the door. She gave no more speeches, but she posted herself on the steps, dressed drably, without makeup, her arms crossed so that everyone could see her. And she impassively endured the raillery and sarcasm of the women going in. When someone or other would speak to her, usually in a cynical or mocking tone, she would go on at length about her god. She would lift up her eyes and prophesy. Nearby, not intervening, her sister, concerned and impatient, strolled about in a veil—a futile attempt at disguise.

"She's a strange woman, isn't she, Lucius? What do you think of her?"

"Stubborn, as I said."

"Cults," Mara reflected, "usually celebrate according to some ritual: the faithful fulfill their mysteries, have their processions. Even the Jews keep their ceremonies to themselves without bothering anyone. But this proselytizing on the public square is so . . . vulgar."

As she spoke, Mara was looking at the table and flattening a bit of bread with a knife blade. She seemed completely absorbed in the task, as if transforming a ball of bread into a flattened mass was the most important and exacting objective in the world. Two small wrinkles had formed on her brow. A drop of oil ran down from a lamp, hesitated, lengthened, and fell to the floor. Mara grabbed the bread and rolled it between her palms vigorously until she had a spindle-shaped mass. Then she suddenly turned to me. "She's very pretty, isn't she?"

I didn't know if I should answer that question. I would probably have to agree. It bothered me to detect behind Mara's words the signs, slight as they were, of anxiety. Mara, attentive to all things. Her reactions were invariably more visible in her expression or gestures than in her words. A matter of good taste: for Mara, states of mind are not to be verbalized. She leaves them for others to guess.

She raised her eyes, surprised, and I sensed a presence beside me. That disagreeable odor I knew quite well, that low, hoarse voice: "The rear door was open. There was no one there. I ask your forgiveness."

Almost leaning over me, Airhan was stroking his beard and looking uneasily toward the door through which he'd entered. I asked Mara to leave me alone with the man—not because I didn't trust her, but because I didn't want to afflict her with the bad news Airhan was no doubt bringing.

The news was indeed bad. Hordes of barbarians, joined by many slaves, were crossing the strait continuously and heading north. The garrison at Septem had withdrawn into the city and had not, because of insufficient forces, even attempted to clear the countryside of Moors. The waters in the vicinity of the Galpe were once more clogged with boats. It wasn't a matter of isolated bands now but of a huge and disorderly multitude that included women and children. Once on the Peninsula, they'd driven back by sheer strength of numbers the volunteers who confronted them, and it was feared they would lay siege to Gades and Ossonoba. The road to Emerita would soon be cut off, so many were the bands that were crossing the countryside freely farther north. These were acting, if there was any order or organization discernible among the invaders, as the advance guard.

<hr>

It was precisely in those terms that Airhan expressed himself to the curia the following morning under my orders. All were present except for two aediles who, for their usual casual reasons, preferred not to attend. The decemvirs had been obliged to come under force of arms, one by one, as I had arranged with Aulus the evening before.

I had a lictor announce each one solemnly as he entered, between guards. They glumly went about seating themselves on their stools, avoiding any glance at me. When I ordered the guards to withdraw, Apitus, by dint of being the eldest and the richest now, asked for the floor: "Never has there been seen, Lucius Valerius Quintius, such an affront to the notables of the city as you have just perpetrated, obliging us to appear before you and harassing us with the force of arms. The governor will hear of this."

"Does anyone propose replacing me?"

"No, Lucius Valerius. You must be deposed by a higher authority, and with all the shame you deserve, when it is the proper time. And no one will take the floor because we, despite being free men, are here under restraint. The guard brought our bodies, but not our minds. Be content with our casings! Therefore I am silent, and all will be silent."

Apitus raised his toga over his head, and all the decemvirs did likewise and averted their eyes from me. There was a flurry of waving cloth. Motes of dust rose and swirled in the air. Apitus had composed that speech on the way there: such had been his fright when he saw himself escorted by the guard without knowing my intentions. It wasn't bad, that antithesis of bodies and minds. And that bit about "casings," where could he have picked that one up?

I conducted the meeting—if my monologue could be called such—as though I hadn't heard Apitus, as though the heads hadn't been lugubriously covered, as though amity and the spirit of cooperation reigned over an ordinary meeting of the curia.

I began with a long report on the work at the walls, including expenses and salaries; I spared no detail about materials and construction options. I called for sacrifices. I set a rather high contribution from each of those present, expecting that at that point someone would at least bristle or give a hint of irritation or protest. They remained as they were.

I sent a lictor to call Airhan, who was waiting in my triclinium, and, contrary to custom, I ordered him to relate before the curia what he'd told me the night before. It evoked no reaction. Not a single brow was wrinkled.

After dismissing Airhan, I read a note of praise for Aulus for the capture of Arsenna, I put libations in honor of the emperor's numen on the agenda, and I decreed a general mobilization, including slaves and peasants, with accelerated military training for all those mobilized. Everything to be carried out posthaste.

As I finished each point I didn't neglect to inquire if the worthy and most holy decemvirs were in agreement and if anyone wished to say something with his enlightened and enlightening speech.

I kept them until the tenth hour. Finally I pronounced a few solemn words of exhortation and adjourned the meeting. They rearranged their togas and left without a word. I could hear the smack of sandals in the corridor and then, farther on, when nothing inhibited them any longer, the sound of voices.

That afternoon, having hastily taken the necessary steps to translate the deliberations of the curia into action, I decided it was time to call in Milquion, the leader of the Christians.

Perhaps I should have taken that step long before. I'd postponed contact with the man as long as possible, on the one side because I didn't consider him worthy and on the other because, as he was under the protection of the Cantabers, I thought it unwise to question him without first talking to his sponsors. I suspected that Iunia's intransigence derived to some degree from that Milquion. I intended to stir up the cause, at least, in order to divert the effect.

The lictors were late. In the meantime, sitting beside me, Aulus was industriously checking the census lists of Tarcisis with one of his men who was more adept than he at reading and writing. He was filling in the gaps from memory, mentioning recently acquired slaves, sons who'd abandoned the toga praetexta, people away from home and dependent in one way or another on their paterfamilias. The census totaled some fifteen hundred men. If we managed to enlist half of those it wouldn't be bad.

From the praetorium I could clearly hear the criers who were announcing the mobilization at different spots in the city, sometimes to the sound of trumpets, and were ordering all able-bodied men under the age of fifty to present themselves on the terrace by the temple of Mars the following dawn. Groups were becoming excited and chattering noisily in the forum, casting furtive glances at my window from time to time.

Night was falling when the lictors brought in Milquion and a slave, in a miserable state. Their disheveled rags were so soaked that there were puddles forming around the pair.

"We had to pull them out of the old cistern," a lictor explained. "They were close to drowning."

I ordered a brazier to be lighted so the men could warm up. They were tired and shivering. The slave unhesitatingly squatted down, extending his hands over the coals. I thought their discomfort would help in the conversation we were going to have, so I held off

having them brought dry clothing. I was waiting . . . "I'm all ears,"
I finally said.

"You're the one who ordered us called, duumvir," the bishop
said, expressing himself in bad Latin. "I've already given thanks to
God, and I thank you, too, because your lictors were His instrument in saving our lives."

I didn't move, waiting for an explanation that was slow in coming. Milquion finally said with a sigh, "We'd fallen into the cistern."

He pulled his shredded tunic from his body and held it over the
weak heat of the brazier. He was answering me while completely
preoccupied with drying his clothes, amid puffs of steam—as if it
were the most natural thing in the world for someone to drown in
the cistern.

"Who are you?"

"You order me to appear and you don't know who I am? I am
Milquion, sir, a merchant and the bishop of the Christians."

"Show me your title of citizenship."

"I'm not a Roman citizen, duumvir. I'm a Syrian."

"Interesting. We must continue this chat. Explain to me now,
foreigner, how it happened that you were, if I may say so, so ab-
sentminded as to fall into the public cistern. Were you philosophizing?"

The slave, identifying himself as a servant of Maximus Cantaber,
asked permission to say something. The bishop, owing to his innate gentleness and sense of charity, had left out certain facts.
They both, in fact, had been brutally thrown into the cistern. By
whom? By a gang led by Rufus Cardilius.

"Is that true?"

Milquion faced me finally and ran his warmed hands over his
beard. He was a man of my age, taller, with regular features, a short
jaw, a tangled, graying, unkempt beard, and curly hair, also graying.
He didn't speak a word that he didn't ponder first. He spoke in an
elementary Latin quite contaminated by Greek. His gestures were
long, slow, the result of a restraint learned not from the cradle but
along the steps of life. His features weren't oriental. Blue eyes, but
with a sad gleam. He could easily have passed for a Macedonian or
a Lydian.

"It's true, duumvir."

The slave loosened his tongue. He understood that the bishop's attestation was the signal for him to unburden himself of his complaints to the magistrate. Milquion lowered his head and let his companion talk.

His community, under the direction of Iunia Cantaber, a virtuous woman and the slave's mistress, was collecting money for widows, orphans, and unprotected laborers who could no longer work. Milquion and he had already gone all through the city appealing to the charity of some, bringing consolation to others. In addition to the statuette of the good shepherd, they were carrying a pot of paint and a bar with which to mark the doors they had just visited with the symbol of the fish.

They were on their way back to Maximus Cantaber's house, where they held the alms collected in safekeeping, when on Rufus Cardilius' street they were intercepted by a gang of lowlifes. They blocked the way. They shoved them. They insulted them. They banged their heads against the electoral notice on Rufus Cardilius' door. Then, with a great to-do, they hauled Milquion and the slave inside the tavern—which, in addition to the obvious violence, was even a sacrilege since their religion forbids them to go into gambling houses.

Rufus Cardilius himself presided over a kind of trial. They were accused of the most infamous practices, and neither their protestations nor their pleas were of any use. Their persecutors smashed the statue of the good shepherd against a wall, and Rufus took the purse with the money, which he went about counting, coin by coin. In the middle of that farce Rufus asked his chums what they should do with their prisoners. The slave had reminded them that he belonged to the house of Maximus Cantaber and that his master would surely take personal umbrage at any harm done to them. They doused him with wine and burst out laughing. They amused themselves for a time by suggesting the most obscene and brutal punishments. Rufus finally announced the sentence: a bath! Ahead of the group, in a hail of jeers, they were led to the old cistern without anyone's raising an objection. Rufus threw the moneybag to

Milquion. That money, close to seventy sesterces, was now lying in the mud of the cistern.

I couldn't formally accept the testimony of a slave and a foreigner against Roman citizens. They should try to get Maximus Cantaber, on whom it was incumbent—if he wished so—to initiate the process and bring the miscreants to trial. Milquion replied that Rufus and the others would be judged by a justice higher than that of Rome, though he himself, from the depths of his heart, had already forgiven them. And he solemnly added a quotation in Greek: "I give my back to those who wound me and my face to those who pull out my hair. I do not hide my face from those who insult and spit on me."

I shrugged, then interrupted Milquion to say that if I had sent for him at what was a fortunate time, it hadn't been to listen to him complain against citizens or recite prophetic versicles, but to advise him to abstain from attitudes and behavior that might cause disturbances in the city. I'd just found out that I'd acted too late and that another fracas had broken out. The next time, and in spite of the consideration that Maximus Cantaber might deserve from me, I would throw Milquion into jail.

I am sure the speech was a trifle unjust in view of Milquion's small portion of the blame in those actions. I must confess that I was moved by a certain irritation with the foreigner, by the influence he already held over Roman citizens, but also by that tranquil arrogance, based on false knowledge, that made him utter grand phrases and carry on about the fate of the world. And, most especially, because he'd managed to get closer to Iunia Cantaber than I had.

I'd called him to warn him, to recommend moderation in the activities of his cult, to caution him about the city's curiosity, which was more often than not malevolent. Now that I saw myself confronted with an open disrespect and because I felt a strong antipathy toward Milquion, I had no good reason to soften my words!

"I've been hearing talk about you for a long time now, foreigner. I don't think your arrival in Tarcisis has been all for the good."

"But what harm have I done, duumvir?"

"Discord . . ."

"But what I've brought is the truth."

"Then why do you pass yourself off as a merchant, bishop?"

"Because it's the way I earn my living."

"And the disguise with which you enter houses and insinuate your superstition. That gives you some control over the weak. You're looking for power, even if only over the defeated and the downtrodden. Isn't that so, Milquion?"

"No, that's not how I am. I'm not a Roman!"

"That's your bad luck!"

I ordered the two men escorted to Maximus Cantaber's house, by a route avoiding Rufus' place. I resolved to pay more attention to the foreigner from then on. His hands were broad and knotty. That Milquion had already lived seven lives, and they hadn't all been well-lived.

"What do you think, Aulus?"

Aulus shrugged his right shoulder to express disdain and distrust. "A hunter after opportunities. The city got along fine without him," he finally said.

And he called my attention to the crowd that had gathered in the forum. Rufus again, in a gleaming toga, had climbed onto an empty pedestal and, his back to the basilica, was making a harangue: he, and all the people of Tarcisis, were there to denounce the perfidious sect bent on undermining trust, corrupting customs, and leading citizens into wayward practices improper for humanity. A wooden placard that someone was waving showed a twisted fish run through by a trident. The poet Cornelius was circling around nearby. The man with the placard pushed him scornfully.

"He talks well, that he does," Aulus observed, spying between the drapes. And then, after a pause: "Would you like me to clear the square?"

"Never mind, night's coming on."

"That Rufus is getting bigger and bigger . . ."

Aulus prepared to make his rounds. He buckled his belt with great tugs, settled his cape. "The password for tonight, Lucius Valerius?"

"'Eagles don't hunt flies,' " I answered, laughing.

126

I started hearing discordant steps, running, across the atrium of my house. Then a mewing of voices, higher, lower; immediately thereafter, a sudden beam of light slipped under the door.

I came upon Maximus Cantaber sitting in the atrium, visibly fatigued. In the weak light illuminating the painting on the wall, he himself seemed part of the scene showing aged Priam surrounded by mourning women and saddened old men lamenting the death of his son Hector.

Mara came over at the same time and, seeing Maximus' state of prostration, took his hand.

"Tell me, Lucius Valerius, tell me, Mara, have I ever provoked my fellow citizens? Can anyone lay any indignity at my door?"

The flames of a candelabrum were lighting up his tear-filled eyes. Mara squeezed Maximus' hand harder.

His speech came out irregular and imperfect: "They killed my dogs, Lucius. They killed all the dogs in my house. What have I done to deserve this?"

Head down, he huddled against the wall as if overcome by cold.

Mara, commiserating, dried his face with a handkerchief.

X

"I DON'T KNOW why you came."

"I don't know why I came."

I'd gone to meet Iunia in the garden behind the house that was surrounded by colonnades in the manner of a peristyle, opening onto the lawns. Chaotic rosebushes, on which withered petals mingled with living ones, climbed the columns, supported by twine. Iunia was sitting on a bench formed by the brick projection that ran along the wall underneath the columns; and she was reading, I didn't care to know what. The slave women keeping her company went off slowly and reluctantly, chatting and giggling, to the other end of the colonnade. At that moment, next to the city's main gate, across from the small temple dedicated to Mars, operations for the recruitment and training of the Tarcisis militia were taking place. I'd decided, without much hesitation, to leave the square for a time in order to speak to Iunia. I departed in such a hurry, right after the sacrifice, that everyone must have thought I'd been called away on some urgent matter. As I went up the paths of the Cantaber house, all by myself, I already felt regrets. When I caught sight of Iunia I got the strange feeling of a shock, a kind of start, as if my whole chest were tightening; and I forgot everything else, even the guilt that was gnawing at me for having abandoned my duties in order to appear before her.

She received me coldly, carefully rolled up the papyrus, tied a bow on the two red ribbons, and was quick to dispatch the slaves to wake up her father, who was resting inside. I wouldn't let her. I wished to talk only to Iunia—though what I had to say would cause perturbation on my part and annoyance, perhaps, on hers.

It was hard to broach the subject that had brought me there and to get beyond the greetings, because Iunia would keep silent for long intervals, then drily lead the conversation toward irritating banalities completely devoid of interest for me or her: how much the roses had grown in such a short time; how cold the nights in Tarcisis were; how the streets around hummed with sound . . . I ended up plunging ahead without any forethought, and with a phrase that, later on, didn't seem to have been the most appropriate one: "I know what happened in your home yesterday. They killed your dogs."

"We'll have to punish the gatekeeper. He didn't keep watch over anything."

Iunia was answering mechanically, with the neutrality proper in any matron dealing with trivial domestic matters, deliberately misconstruing my meaning.

"You can't expect much dedication from a slave you order chained."

"Do you think he was involved?" she insisted, with the same officious tone.

"That's not what I said."

"Oh, I misunderstood."

I pretended patience, was didactic: "You have to be careful with slaves. This isn't any time for punishments. The presence of the Moors so close can bring on temptations to revolt."

"I'll pass on to my father what you're telling me."

Iunia shrugged. I choked back my annoyance and turned my eyes away. Through the columns I saw in the distance young Clelia, in a cart meant to be drawn by geese, playing in the company of two boys, one of whom was still wearing the toga praetexta. The boys pretended not to have the strength to pull the cart, which would tip over from her weight. A tiny brindle pony was grazing peacefully nearby. This time Clelia showed no interest in me; she didn't even come over to greet me. But at certain moments I noticed that she would be distracted from the game and look toward us in a very serious way.

In the meantime my talk with Iunia was threatening to become completely sterile and pointless. I felt uncomfortable at being so inept. There was a silence. The laughter of Clelia and the boys could be heard distinctly. Another tumble. The scroll Iunia was clutching crackled.

"Are the baths an evil place?" I asked, to provoke her.

"In what way?"

"You're the one who said so!"

"Did they tell you that?"

"It's my duty to be informed. I want to know: are the baths evil?"

Iunia hesitated and ran her tongue fleetingly over her lips. She didn't seem quite sure that the direction the conversation was taking was in her best interest. Then she made a decision, raised her eyes to me in a brusque confrontation, and said: "Baths . . . spectacles . . . banquets . . . adornments . . . tricks of the devil to lead souls away from God, since you ask me . . ."

"There were baths in the time of my forefathers, there have been baths as long as Rome has been Rome . . . and there always will be. The baths are one of the advances of Romanness. One of the things that separate us from the barbarians."

"And who are the barbarians in the eyes of the one God? How will the ones shamelessly exhibiting their nakedness be judged?"

"But what does this have to do with you?"

"Nothing human is alien to me, also—to quote the obscene Terence as you like to. What happens in this city calls for attention on my part. Somebody has to denounce the scandal so that people won't come along saying that no voice was raised. Maybe God will take pity on the others, knowing that there are a few just people in Tarcisis. You yourself, duumvir—who knows?—might draw some benefit from it."

The speech had taken such an extravagantly vulgar form, so childishly subversive, that I held back my words and gestures and just stared at her in stupefaction. Iunia clutched the papyrus to her breast, almost to the point of crumpling it, and she went after my perplexity: "Does the answer satisfy your inquiry? Or do you have more questions, duumvir?"

"Some citizens feel offended by the behavior of a foreigner you're sheltering. A certain Milquion. They threw him into the cistern. But you know that better than I. Aren't you going to enter a complaint?"

Iunia folded her arms and passed the papyrus lightly across her face. She leaned her head forward, lifted it again, and bit her lower lip. She held back a smile. "In the court of men? Oh, forget about it, Lucius Valerius. Milquion is resigned; he forgives and blesses the ones who mistreated him."

"That's not the question!"

"'I give my back to those who wound me and my face to those who pull out my hair. I do not hide my face from those who insult and spit on me.'"

"I've already heard that quotation."

"Isaiah."

"Who cares . . ."

Iunia moved her shoulders exasperatedly. She'd had enough. She was obviously looking for a pretext to send me on my way. I decided to thwart her. I tried to get Iunia to think about me: "Listen to me: I'm a just man, don't you think?"

She took her time, smoothed the papyrus, fixed its bow, searched for words. "I don't want to offend you, duumvir. I respect the friendship my father has for you. But I can't lie to you. You're not a just man. You could only be that if you renounced the life you lead. You're only a pagan. Worse, you're the symbol of the pagan power of Rome."

"Pagan?" The ugly word sounded absurd and offensive to me. I, who was wearing a toga . . . I almost laughed in Iunia's face. She remained indifferent, as if she hadn't just proffered an insult. But I'd already noticed that Iunia's language, not to mention her feelings, didn't coincide entirely with mine.

My face tightened. I tried to be more blunt. I exaggerated a little. She squeezed her hands together, crumpling the scroll once more, ready for whatever might come.

"You and your sect can think whatever you want, but I will not allow you to provoke the people's anger, even though you feel the right to provoke mine. As far as I'm concerned, I can bear up under it quite well. But I will not allow any acts of disrespect in the city."

"It's always been the just who fall into misfortune when those in power don't recognize God."

What could I have replied to that? I wasn't there to get embroiled in any ridiculous religious discussion. I appealed to Iunia's sense of citizenship, reminding her of the mortal danger surrounding the city. The barbarians were already on the scene! But Iunia was a temple without doors; I couldn't find any way in.

"The Moors," she went on. "Those poor Moors, who are even denied burial, are also God's creatures and are moving under His orders. Do you think they just happened to appear now by chance?"

"Is this some kind of prophecy?"

"The Moors are an instrument of God. They've come to show the world how fragile, transitory, and condemned the power of Rome is."

"How do you know that? Has Providence confided its designs in you personally?"

I think I shouted. Clelia was watching from afar, anxious, shading her eyes. Her companions laughed. I lowered my voice and tried to hide my face behind a column so that the young people wouldn't see my expression. Unconcerned, Iunia continued: "The plague in Rome, do you think it happened by chance? And the revolts along the Danube? And the floods on the Tiber? And the earthquakes? Do you think evil happens just by chance? Do you think moral decay can go unpunished in the eyes of God?"

"You must be really terrible, you, to deserve the misfortunes that have come your way."

I was swinish, I recognize that, and overly cruel in that personal allusion. But Iunia didn't perceive the irony, or didn't want to. As she well knew, her behavior till then had been—and the testimony of everyone who knew the Cantabers supported this—most worthy and irreprehensible. There was no reason for her to have deserved the vengeful wrath of any god and the misfortunes that had befallen her. Yet she didn't think that way: "It was terrible, no doubt about it! I followed the iniquitous path of a pagan and sacrificed to false idols! God punished me. Justly."

I was indignant at her resigned acceptance of a fate that had been woven to be worn under the skies of Judaea—a fate so unfitting for Romans.

"Remember, you're a free woman and the daughter of a Roman!"

"A servant of God is what I try to be."

Iunia tightened her lips, twirled the papyrus between her outstretched hands, looked at me sidelong, and then lowered her gaze as if the tips of her sandals had awakened a sudden interest. She seemed unsure whether it was worth going on. But she started up again in a clear voice, affecting patience, stressing her words with small taps of the papyrus on the marble: "Listen, Lucius: in the time of Tiberius the son of God left good news on earth before he was crucified . . ."

I was resolved to frustrate the sermon. I'd noticed that Iunia would soften her voice when she turned to religious propaganda, as if at those moments she wanted to assure my attention and guarantee my silence. She condescended to be gentle with me as long as I listened to her preach. I was vexed by the expedient. I interrupted: "I'm in no mood for oriental legends. What I want is for you not to oblige me, keeping in mind the respect I have for your father, to proceed against you."

The artful maternal mildness of one telling the story of miracles was ripped away, and Iunia turned aggressive again. "So, proceed against me if you find me guilty, or even if you don't. Go ahead! We're prepared for all and any iniquities."

"Consider the consequences of what you're saying, Iunia."

"What difference does it make what happens to us in this earthly life, which isn't even the true life, since later on we'll be the only ones to look upon the face of God? I'm not from here, duumvir!"

"Isn't there some way we can talk? Doesn't this preoccupation with challenging me seem childish to you?"

"Childish? You're the one who's like a child, duumvir, someone who still hasn't opened his understanding."

"Try to see it, Iunia."

"You don't want to listen to me."

"You listen to me!"

"The son of God came back to life in Judaea! You can't go along as if nothing happened! The world has changed, duumvir! It's changed!"

I tugged forcefully on a tendril of grapevine. Two or three grapes fell and were squashed on the ground. I took a deep breath and tried to contain my anger. The leaves of the arbor continued trembling and rustling for some time after I'd calmed down.

It was then that she shrugged and said, "I don't know why you came." And I agreed: "I don't know why I came." There was nothing more to say. I don't think Iunia had any special interest in antagonizing me. My words were fumbling, certainly, inadequate against the exaltation she was making her way of life and that was defeating me once again. Why had I insisted on seeking her out, abandoning my duties, taking a moment off when I shouldn't have?

When I left I had the hidden feeling that this wouldn't be the last time an unexpected, irresistible impulse would draw me to that woman, as had just happened. And this didn't sit well with me. Iunia had started off by being only the wayward daughter of my friend. A name, a vague memory. A problem for him. Now she was company that I liked, in a dim sort of way, without quite knowing why. A problem for me. A kind of obsessive challenge was imposing itself on me; to try to reach Iunia, the real Iunia, Iunia's humanity behind that thick tangle of phrases and attitudes. From her point of view—I sensed it—I was nothing but an object for the application and exercise of proselytism, as if she wanted to test herself, her power of resistance, her capacity for persuasion. Iunia was at best *deigning* to confront me, and she didn't seem to rule out the possibility of my conversion. We were both deceived regarding the other's vulnerability. She, because it wasn't because of her extreme piety that I was taken by her. I, because if I dug deeper behind Iunia's defenses there might be nothing else there.

Clelia waved good-bye to me from the grove as I was approaching the gate. The old shackled slave was no longer suffering there;

instead, there was a muscular black man wearing a military belt and sitting beside two spears stuck in the ground.

It was at that moment that off toward the reservoirs, behind a high wall, I caught sight of a slave up on a ladder carrying water for a lead tub being washed. The slave was boldly staring at me, his work suspended, with the vessel in his arms and a half-smile on his lips. Then he made a quick motion with his chin. The head of Rufus Cardilius appeared for a few seconds alongside the slave. Our looks met in a flash. Rufus disappeared.

"What wall is that over there?" I asked the black man guarding the gate.

"The back of Rufus Cardilius' place."

I returned with apprehension to the square, where Aulus and his soldiers were still working on the recruitment. Dozens of men were grouped around several improvised tables at which the praetorium slaves were registering names. Aulus, going back and forth, was weary from shouting. The agitation halted when my litter reentered the square, and I went over to a kind of platform where, by myself because none of the decemvirs had wished to accompany me, I presided over the operation.

<hr />

Very early in the morning I'd overseen the sacrifices in the temple, with the attendance of all the notables and many of the common people out on the square. Calpurnius' absence hadn't caused me any worry, given his illness and the special status he enjoyed. I was more puzzled by the absence of Maximus Cantaber, who was missing an occasion to show his piety. Later on I supervised the noisy beginning of the mobilization for a few moments. Every recruit who didn't have weapons was issued a pair of spears—or a bag of clay balls if he preferred. As they were being taken care of, the men sat on the ground in groups. Rufus Cardilius, in a gleaming toga, appeared at the head of a throng of slaves, all dressed alike and armed with javelins and short lances. He greeted me from a distance, ostentatiously laid some coins on a table, and gave the names of the slaves one by one. Then he withdrew, with only a few companions.

Immediately after that I ran to the house of Maximus Cantaber to speak to Iunia, far from suspecting that Rufus was aware of everything that happened in that garden as viewed from the rear of his place. And once again, and with additional reasons, I considered my conversation with Iunia ill-advised.

When I returned to the platform, the training in arms was beginning amid a certain unconcerned confusion into which Aulus was energetically trying to instill some discipline. In the center of the square they'd set up stakes holding strips of cork bark. The men lined up and ran by with great merriment, throwing their spears against the bark. Nearby, in the pomerium, the enormous new war machine was being assembled and tested: it vibrated, clattered, buzzed, and banged.

The slingers were practicing in the fields outside the walls under the command of Aulus' subalterns. Mingling in the air were laughter, joy, and a lack of care, as if it were a matter of games or festivities.

There was nothing more for me to do there. No sooner did my bearers lift me than a clamor arose on one side of the square. Calpurnius' lictors were approaching grimly, violently pushing aside the knots of gawkers. Immediately behind, swaying slowly, came the senator's sumptuous litter, decorated with silver and purple, on the shoulders of eight slaves, who carried it to the center of the square. Behind was a retinue of expensively dressed slaves and freedmen. Applause broke out. Attention was divided between Calpurnius and the duumvir, with the people curious to see how I would react to the presence of Tarcisis' most important citizen. I approached the litter, but Calpurnius, in a toga, was already getting out with some difficulty, held up by two slaves. A third picked up a spear and put it in his master's hand. The slaves ran with Calpurnius as if he were in the saddle, and it looked as if they were carrying death itself, pale, skeletal, and bent, dragging his flapping white shroud. Calpurnius, rising up a little with evident strain, went on to sink the spear into one of the pieces of cork bark. The point slipped out, the spear fell, but cheers broke out. Only after acknowledging them did the senator come, still on the backs of the slaves, to greet me.

He declined to sit on the platform. He treated me with deference, outdid himself with excuses, and addressed me very serenely,
smiling, with a few brief pleasantries. He was aware that everyone
in the crowd had admired his gesture and that all eyes were fixed
on him. He invited me, in a low voice, to stop by his house when I
could because he urgently needed to speak to me.

When Calpurnius' litter left the square, amid cheers, I noticed that
the men flinging spears were showing more determination and better
aim. Their throws were more vigorous and the impacts louder. The
civic intervention of the old senator, overcoming his age and infir-
mity, had lifted spirits and lent majesty to what under my super-
vision hadn't gone beyond a mere exercise, unusual and recreational.
The genius of the Senate and the People of Rome had passed over the
rabble gathered there. I had to be grateful to Calpurnius, and it
wouldn't have been good for me to ignore his invitation, which he'd
known how to make honorable in front of the assembled plebs.

⚭

I still had to stop by the praetorium and take care of routine matters. The forum was almost deserted, populated only by a few
women lingering here and there to chat. Without the color of the
tents, the crowds in the porticoes, the noise and agitation of the
everyday, the statues' timeless gestures prevailed, their silent faces,
their hollow eyes.

Any statue—it is a well-known fact—contains a vital principle
that some say derives from the artist who made it, others from the
entity it represents, still others from the vigor of the stone itself,
which, despite having been cut and extracted, continues being
born and growing in quarries. That apparent rigidity of form might
be illusory. The statue is probably observing what goes on around
it. It sees, hears, and stores everything away. But it only acts at propitious moments, which are rare and significant.

That being the case, there must be a secret way to penetrate the
souls of statues. A gesture, a word, a pious thought brought out at the
right time and the right astral conjunction. Or perhaps only a stipulated person, one chosen by the favor of the gods, is capable of reaching the soul cloaked in stone. Does every statue have its Pygmalion?

137

And what about Iunia's soul—would it be possible to reach it? Obtain some sign? Even the tiniest one, meaning *I look at you, I see you, I recognize you, I understand you!* All I ask for is a moment in which our words, instead of clashing and reeling off in conflicting directions, bristling with harshness, will succeed in converging.

How can Iunia have interpreted my visit, my insistence, my vehemence? Could she, too, have been resentful over the persistent absurdity of our encounters? What did Iunia really think? What did she think of me?

And me, what was going on with me? What was happening to me? What was it I wanted? Iunia was what she was; she behaved as she understood she should. What right did I have to expect anything from her? Anything might happen, even her interrogating me. I'm not going to stand next to the pedestals and niches in the forum, interrogating the statues, nor am I going to waste any time with their secrets. I did my duty with her as a friend and as magistrate. I was prudent; I disclosed what had to be disclosed. I tried to be persuasive. I insisted. I took great pains. I went so far as to interrupt the exercise of my duties. I spent hours of my precious days on it—more time than was advisable to spend. All right. Matter settled!

But Iunia's look in that glance at the sun a few days before, her so-white hands that were nervously holding the papyrus scroll today, her stern, almost grating, voice, the coldness of her words, the obsessive return to themes of her oriental superstition, were taking over in a swirl of contradictions that fused delight with displeasure.

I tried to escape it through work. I had a session with the treasurer, left written instructions for Aulus, made a fair copy of a sentence, inquired about the prisoner, scolded a praetorium slave who came to tell me that a kind of bluish ignis fatuus was appearing every night near the new wall at the spot where Pontius Modius had committed suicide.

❦

I arrived home weary. When I emerged from the bath, Mara told me, in a whisper, that one of our stablemen, Luciporus by name, was a Christian. The others had seen him pray, off in his corner, three times a day. He would fast. Sometimes he would steal off to the house of a certain Milquion. Mara was worried. "What if he poisons our water? They say so many things about them. They spit when they pass in front of a temple, did you know that?"

And she told me that several indignant citizens had thrown Milquion and another one into the old cistern after having caught them committing a sacrilege on the square by Jupiter's temple. They were strange people, with aggressive impulses. Who knew if they didn't practice human sacrifices? And if they killed or mutilated our slave, what would we do? But what surprised Mara most was that the Cantaber family was connected to that sect.

"I think there's something I should tell you." Mara hesitated. "Don't you find it strange that Maximus Cantaber was absent from the ceremony in the temple?"

"It might be that he wasn't feeling well. Maximus is old; he's ill."

"He didn't seem all that incapacitated yesterday when he came on foot to complain about the dogs."

Mara slowly put her forefinger between a bracelet and her wrist. Then, quickly: "They say his daughter wouldn't let him leave the house."

Iunia, her slave women, and other members of the sect had—so the rumor went—blocked her father's way, wailing, moaning, tearing their clothes. Maximus, upset, had turned back.

And right there, in the apparent quiet of my house and by means of Mara's mouth, Iunia was coming to upset me. I don't know if Mara noticed my confusion. In a kind of superstitious defense, I couldn't pronounce Iunia's name: "I can't see her wailing and tearing her clothes . . ."

"Who?"

Could it have been malice on Mara's part to make me pronounce the name I wanted to leave out? What was certain was that she'd asked the question in a calm, natural way, without any intention showing on her face. But I knew my wife as she knew me.

"Iunia Cantaber."

"Oh." A very long pause. Mara fixed her hair a bit and adjusted the clasp of her tunic. Then she smiled at me and shrugged. "It's what they say . . . What shall I do about the slave?"

"Have the overseer keep an eye on him and not let him out of the house. Unless he's needed at the walls."

But Mara, as if she'd completely forgotten the discussion about the Cantabers now, took me by the arm and led me solemnly to one of the rooms that was normally unoccupied. A bluish light was coming from inside. Between two oil lamps suspended on ropes, a suit of armor that had belonged to my grandfather—and had never been worn—gleamed on a wooden hanger. Mara had hunted for it all morning and had finally found it riddled with rust spots and verdigris in a chest. She'd spent the afternoon polishing and cleaning it with the help of the slave women. The plates of the cuirass showed the residue of liquid polish. The helmet's red crest was still damp.

"Don't touch it; let it dry."

The sword, with a gilded silver hilt in the shape of a horse's head, had been sanded and sharpened. I hefted it casually in my hand. And there was Mara, her timing impeccable as always, reminding me of the coming emergencies: "You can't imagine what a hard time I had finding this armor, Lucius."

She sighed, folded and unfolded her arms, gave a fleeting half-smile, and then scurried out of the room so that I wouldn't see her tears.

❦

The next morning when I finally headed for Calpurnius' house I brought along some tablets for trials to study in the litter. I passed a detachment of recruits with spears on their shoulders whom Aulus was instructing in close-order drill. Among the men, sagging under the weight of the weaponry, dragging along and arching in a painful effort to show some military dash, was the poet Cornelius Lucullus. It was the last time I would see him alive.

Calpurnius lived a long way from the forum, in a mansion in the middle of one of the city's poorest and oldest districts, where it coexisted with the ancient round huts of the peasants and the rundown streets of the destitute. The house didn't follow the usual form of a domus, but was a labyrinth of peristyles, parlors, and corridors built at different times, often making use of the coarse stone of ancestral structures. There was no vestibule, and entry was through a kind of covered atrium dominated by a huge rectangular pool that left little room for passage. The pool had no use whatever. The water was rarely changed and gave off a musty smell. The darkness of the square wouldn't even permit fish to be bred there, as they say is the custom in houses in Africa.

After going through this strange atrium—decorated with paintings of birds aligned in double rows: birds of prey (diurnal and nocturnal) up by the ceiling, and sparrows and jays along the edge of a greenish skirting board adorned with vague or imaginary plants, this board now crumbling with age—one came to a peristyle with a dry tank and a few parched tufts of grass. Then an accompanying slave who wasn't a nomenclator went ahead of us, turning to the right and passing through a string of rooms in which—lying exposed and covered with dust—were statues of all sizes, some from very distant regions. Coming after this was a new peristyle, wider and better cared for, with small goldfish swimming in the tank and fluted columns glimmering in red through which the hushed sound of voices could be heard. Beyond this peristyle, framed in the wall, was a disproportionate kind of low triumphal arch of pink marble, which I knew led to another atrium that connected directly with a side street. There Calpurnius received his clients in the morning, a good reason for my entry from the other street, thus showing my higher status.

Sitting in a rush chair, Calpurnius was listening to his reader slave, who was reciting selections from Menander in Greek. When I entered the peristyle, which was bathed in strong sunlight, the slave fell silent. Off in the shadows I heard the clicks of a chisel; the sculptor was continuing his work on the senator's bust, but directly on stone now. The plaster model was resting, as inspiration, on a tall stool. When he saw me, Calpurnius signaled me to come closer, but he didn't send the reader away immediately. He was smiling, delighted, still savoring in his thoughts the dialogues he had just heard. He obviously wanted me to wait a bit.

Then Calpurnius dismissed the man, who meticulously put the papyrus into its case. And he showed enthusiastic enjoyment, opening his arms.

"Ah, at last! I've grown impatient waiting for you, Lucius!"

XI

I RECOGNIZED that affability and that solicitude. It was the same broad and open smile with which in his house in Rome ten years before Calpurnius had welcomed our delegation from Tarcisis, which had traveled all that way to thank the Emperor for a donation of a million sesterces for the restoration of the forum, the baths, and the temples. At that time paralysis hadn't touched Calpurnius' limbs yet, and he was able to descend elegantly the few steps that divided his atrium in two and to greet us festively, opening his toga wide in order to display the purple of the laticlave.

We were put up in Calpurnius' house while we waited for the Emperor to receive us on the occasion of the games being celebrated in the Circus Maximus for the third birthday of the young prince Lucius Aelius Aurelius Commodus. Taking very much to heart his renown as the protector of Tarcisis, Calpurnius outdid himself in attentions and refinements. He made each of us feel individually the influence he'd used to gain the munificence of Marcus Aurelius. It was all false, as I came to discover later. Despite the luxury in which he lived, his laticlave and his gold ring, Calpurnius had no prestige whatsoever either in the Palace or in the Senate. He'd assumed staggering debts and had involved himself in some ill-advised business deals in association with wealthy freedmen, foreigners, and other people of low estate.

But if Ennius Digidius Calpurnius represented the dross of the Senatorial Order in Rome, he gleamed in the clouds alongside Jove in the eyes of the humble delegates from a city hidden away in Hispania. We all felt overwhelmed by Rome's sumptuous brilliance. The splendor of the notables of Tarcisis, their haughtiness and fatuousness, seemed small and contemptible beside that world of purple, incense, and silver. What was the Cantabers' golden mansion when compared to the ruins of the real one? Our baths, squeezed between narrow, crooked alleys, when compared to the baths of Trajan? Our tiny forum, deficient not in size but in splendor when compared to the various forums in the capital? Even Rome's plebeian suburbs, despite their filth and misery, seemed to possess infinite grandeur when compared with the base poverty of our districts of native huts and squat buildings. With the innocence and awe of provincials, we were almost ready to exchange our whole city for the stinking hovels of Subura.

On the appointed day we were ushered to places along the flanks of the imperial platform, where on such occasions senators, hostages of quality, princes, and ambassadors were seated. We were placed in the last row, a little below the passageway where richly garbed Parthian archers walked back and forth with quivers and arrows at the ready to riddle any man or beast who didn't respect the prescribed limits. Calpurnius led us to our places very graciously, but he didn't relinquish his seat among those of his Order, those with purple-hemmed togas. He was sitting by the aisle; his peers paid him little attention.

It was the rule—repeated often, forgotten even more—that Roman citizens should wear togas at spectacles. From what could be seen in the huge expanse of seats in front of us, however, dark or colored clothing dominated. Only in the sections set aside for the common people, at irregular intervals like patches in the lining of a piece of rich cloth, the not-always-immaculate white of rented togas would sometimes stand out.

Hours passed before the Emperor arrived on the platform. From sunrise on, after the procession of images, men and animals were killed in that arena at the whim of the lanistae and organizers of the games. I've only been able to retain the image of a gladiator on metal stilts that seemed to be coming up out of his sandals, who, armed only with a short spear, disemboweled three fierce wild boars as he whirled like a dancer. I don't know if it was only my impression, but it seemed that after a while the damp, salty smell of blood was overcoming the aroma of precious perfumes that impregnated the rows where we were sitting.

I repeat, I've never been a lover of the games, even when reduced to the more modest proportions of my corner of Hispania. I'm not proud of this strange antipathy of mine, not always openly declared, which still persists in spite of all attempts to quell it. I get to thinking that there's something odd in me because I can't share the feelings of my fellow citizens. I had a good view of the avidity of the senators and rich foreigners in front, applauding, growing excited, waving their arms, standing up, shouting, howling, to the point that I wondered if they might not be straying from the gravity and composure demanded of them in public. The senator who would speak to me later with condescension, using clipped and slightly disdainful phrases, was the same man who was now standing up, dancing, wailing frantically, his toga in disarray and his face fiery red because the retiarius had got the myrmillo entangled. And my countrymen from Tarcisis were singing in a chorus: "I'm after a fish, not you, why are you running away?" Were they not feeling that they were living the culminating moment of their existence as their hearts beat in rhythm with the heart of the city?

All the colorful activity in the arena, the shouts, the blows, the intermissions, the pompous display of armor and expensive clothing, were monotonously repeated over and over; likewise, the sand was turned and smoothed every time it became soaked and stained with blood.

Except for some quick flashes, a few indistinct flights of color and noise, and apart from the memory of that gladiator on stilts, the only thing still sharp in my memory is the yellow fringe on the heavy drape that gave our seats a bit of shade and showed our privileged status on a day when the velarium hadn't been extended.

I can remember with absurd exactitude the thickness and pattern of the very heavy weave, the hem of ingeniously interwoven gold threads, the misty red, the gray folds with tight curls that decorated the open spaces, the slight waving in the breeze of a fringe of reddish-purple cords that fell down over a column as a burst of breeze moved them. I can even remember the sharp snapping sound as the drape flapped.

I must admit that it seems strange for someone in a favored seat in the Circus Maximus to remember a drapery. At one time one of my young country slaves was brought from the villa. He was to be apprenticed in the triclinium as a replacement for a servant who had died. When the overseer, for the fun of it, asked what had impressed him most in the city, the slave answered a small ceramic oil lamp in the kitchen, with the design of a lily on it. The streets, the forum, the tall buildings, the bustle of the market, the baths, the luxury of the house itself, the paintings, the peristyle, the meals—none of that had aroused his interest. Only a little lily designed on the disk of a cheap lamp. That's what simple people are like. That's how simple I felt—and how ashamed—as I faced the renowned and celebrated splendor of those games.

The muscular gladiator who had entered with uplifted arms to an eager ovation would leave minutes later, dragged off by his feet after his skull had been crushed with a mallet by officials of the arena dressed as Charon. Soon after, at one time or another, the same thing would happen to the one who had felled him. "Give it to him! Cut his throat!" the whip-lashers bellowed as they leaped around the combatants, scourges in hand. Hungering, the rabble joined in with a chorus of "Knock him down! Stick him!"

What did the spirit of the prince being consecrated that day need with all those victims? What would it do with them? Of what use are corpses to divinities? Since the fighters are men accustomed to death and skilled with weapons, would it not be better to utilize those special proficiencies in the republic's service? Did the Emperor have enough praetorians and foreign guards? Were the twenty-eight legions of Rome so sufficient that these reserves could be discarded lightly? Were there enough young, healthy, robust lives? I never heard anyone ponder those questions, nor would I ever dare to voice them—coming as I did from the hinterland of Tarcisis, I didn't attribute to myself any extraordinary gifts of clairvoyance. I did have my inner self, however, and could resign myself to carry on with my erroneous thoughts.

❦

First four Germanic guards, very tall and blond, wearing armor of golden scales and pointed helmets with scarlet plumes, came to take their places in the imperial box. A praetorian tribune appeared next. Then the trumpets sounded, the people rose, and Marcus Aurelius stood for a moment, waving to the crowd, which was producing a great roar of acclaim. Behind him the consuls, the praetors, the flamens, the vestals—the whole court—was spreading out over the platform according to careful protocol until they formed compact groups around the Emperor, who wore no adornments at all. He was wrapped in a heavy blue cloak and stood out among his entourage precisely by the modesty of his dress. And it was so distinct and individualized that no one dared copy the Princeps or transform his simple garb into a style, though in the court such imitation tends to occur naturally.

Faustina, dressed in a long, saffron-colored chiton, took the little Commodus by the hand and settled him on her lap for an instant. Then she handed the child to Marcus Aurelius, who lifted him high, arms extended. The people, standing, applauded ceremoniously. The Emperor returned Commodus to his nurse, who was waiting in the rear; then he sat beside Faustina and signaled the consul for the games to start up again.

The charioteers came into the arena in a procession with their equipment and crews. In our section two slaves were distributing tesserae and noting the bets on tablets. A nervous thrill ran through the seats. Some couldn't hold back and sought out the slaves before they drew near. I saw Calpurnius in the middle of a cluster, gesticulating and tugging the tunic of one of the slaves.

I must have been the only one in that section who didn't place a bet. I hesitated, let the slaves pass. Trifenus' father, who was sitting beside me, stood up and leaped into the whirlwind, but I abstained. No one took down my name, nor did any tessera reach my hand.

146

After the trumpets blared, indicating that the chariots had taken their places at the starting line and were ready, the consul finally showed his handkerchief to the public and with a gracious nod asked for the Emperor's authorization. Then he leaned over and dropped the handkerchief into the arena. The crowd roared. The twelve gates opened simultaneously, but only four chariots left. The greens and the blues went down the track in a churn of dust.

I noticed that the Emperor, while the race was at a boil down below and captivating everyone's attention, was taking his chance to dispatch some business. He had a wooden slab on his knees and was looking over some documents. Then someone came over with a bundle of tablets, and Marcus Aurelius, holding a stylus casually in one hand, spoke into his ear. The little silver dolphins on the spina marked the fourth lap. Everybody suddenly stood up; the stones reverberated with the clamor of the crowd. There were screams and moans. The strident sound of afflicted whinnying was sharp in the distance. I had to stand up too, a bit annoyed because what was going on up on the platform was of greater interest to me than all the rest. On the track an overturned chariot was still sliding along and making deep, semicircular furrows in the sand. At the same time there was the flurry of a horse's hooves waving in the air like the legs of some gigantic insect that had been squashed and was dying. The blue charioteer had been unable to control his chariot at the turn by the spina or to cut the reins wrapped around his body in time. His trunk and his loose arms, lifeless now perhaps, stuck out from under the chariot, one wheel of which continued turning for a long time with a sighing drone that grew less and less piercing.

With loud musical chords the bigas, the quadrigas, wagers, and arguments all followed along. From my vantage the races seemed all the same: more falls, fewer falls; more skill or less skill on the turns; more ability or less ability of the trace-horses; more speed or less speed in the straightaway. But everyone was avidly observing the slightest movements of the charioteers and the horses. They knew them all by name. They shouted suggestions. They were quite knowledgeable about technical details. My countrymen, who knew as little about races as I, were already shouting "Go it! Hold on! Hang on!" as if the games at Mirobriga, where they'd gone once or twice, had made them the equals of the enthusiasts in Rome.

It seemed in the end a very unlucky day for the blues and the reds and one of triumph for the greens and the whites. Of the Tarcisis delegation, some were lamenting, and others were smiling as they displayed the coins they'd won. Either way, they considered their day well spent. They were taking away something to talk about, and the sesterces they'd lost would be credited to their reputations.

On the platform Marcus Aurelius continued writing. I saw him speak to a slave, with a frown, and I noticed that at one point, perhaps to restrain Faustina's enthusiasm, he put his hand on hers. For me it was more exciting to be able to make out the gestures and behavior of the Emperor among all the bodies moving about on his platform than to share in the ersatz thrills of the chariot races. I was probably the first to notice when Marcus Aurelius stood up and left. At that moment, in the arena, a troupe of buffoons dressed in bright colors was cavorting in acrobatic leaps while the sand, glittering with malachite, was being raked and watered again.

Not much time passed before a centurion came to summon our delegation, whom the Princeps was prepared to receive at once. We looked at each other in surprise. Pontius turned to the praetorian with a befuddled look, as if he'd been awakened from a dream. Calpurnius, I don't know how, had sensed that we were being called and came running along the benches above, shoving his way through.

We were led to a subterranean passageway lighted by torches stuck in the walls, this passage connected the imperial platform with the outside. Here—I was told later—the conspirators Cassius Chaerea and Cornelius Sabinus had executed the tyrant Gaius. Apitus' adoptive father, Geminius, who was to speak in behalf of the delegation, seemed unnerved and was whispering protests that he hadn't counted on being taken into the presence of the Emperor so suddenly and was afraid he hadn't memorized his speech too well. We turned to the right, still escorted by praetorians, and before going up some steps we were all, including Calpurnius, carefully searched. There wasn't a fold in our togas that wasn't inspected by the agile fingers of a slave under the vigilance of the soldiers, who wore no armor but carried heavy spears.

Finally, from the landing on the stairs where barbarian soldiers of imposing look were standing guard, we entered a quadrangular room that had a large window to the outside. All the notables I had seen on the platform, from consuls to flamens, were waiting for us, with the exception of Faustina and the other women. The Emperor, standing beside a table, turned when he heard the sound of footsteps, made louder by the iron-plated boots of the praetorian; and he greeted us graciously, raising a cup. We were all frightened and openmouthed and almost clinging to each other when a nomenclator, in a thunderous voice, announced the delegation from Tarcisis in Lusitania. Calpurnius himself, though more accustomed to these surroundings, showed embarrassment and limited himself to designating old Geminius with a clumsy nod.

Geminius made his speech—long, as was called for. Marcus Aurelius listened without any sign of impatience. It was a conventional oration of thanks; it added nothing to the annals of rhetoric. The Emperor replied with a few words, simply. He mentioned the love he felt for the people of Hispania, where his own family had its roots; he mentioned the bonds of Romanness that joined the remotest city of Lusitania to the farthest military post in the mountains of Bithynia in a uniformity and cohesion that our presence there proved. And thus, just as the soul of every man was a piece of the universal and general spirit—he added—so every city of the Empire, no matter how small or how distant, partook of the genius of Rome.

The light from outside was striking the opacity of the windowpanes that were mounted on iron lozenges, giving the glass soft and iridescent colors and making the grains of silicon shine in a mobile and irregular constellation of flashes. The luxuriously dressed figures who were drawn up all around, with touches of the Greek and the oriental in their garb, were peering at us with an airy serenity that wasn't far from being ironic. After the Emperor's brief speech, they broke the stiffness of their posture and groups, and conversations resumed. Calpurnius understood that it was time for us to go. Marcus Aurelius took leave of us with a smile, and we were awkwardly withdrawing to the door. Calpurnius had warned us that in no case were we to kiss the hand of the Princeps, and so we weren't quite sure what form of courtesy to use. As two soldiers pushed back the doors so we could pass—and as I was breathing a sigh of relief, anxious to be somewhere else, even if it was the turmoil of the circus—I heard, quite clearly, the Emperor's voice calling, "Lucius Valerius Quintius!"

I couldn't believe it, but when I turned I saw that indeed it was for me, because the Emperor was now giving me a signal to approach him.

"Would you please come over here?"

I was left without a drop of blood, alarmed. For a second the world around me disappeared. The surroundings, the shadows, the chiaroscuros, the dazzling window, all gradually took shape again. My praenomen, nomen, and cognomen clearly enunciated by the voice of Marcus Aurelius himself. How was it possible? What could I have done? Who had denounced me? Because of what?

With stupefied and unsteady steps I approached the Emperor in answer to his wave. Marcus Aurelius took me by the arm and led me to a corner. Everybody moved away. Calpurnius and the delegation from Tarcisis were standing stock-still at the door, looking at me in amazement. I was either going to be mysteriously honored or was, also for mysterious reasons, lost.

"There's no reason for you to be afraid of me, Lucius Quintius. Why are you trembling?"

"I'm not trembling," I pretended. "I feel surprised and honored."

"Honored? I don't see why. I'm only the official who's most burdened with duties in Rome and a mere tenant of the Palace. Don't Caesar me . . . ," and, changing his tone, "Do you like the blues or the greens, Lucius?"

"The blues or the greens? I don't know what to say, sir."

"One citizen doesn't call another 'sir.' I'm not your master."

Marcus Aurelius' face, in the opaline light of the window, which was giving his profile a touch of color, was imperturbable; his clear, articulate voice was reaching me without inflection, either hostile or friendly. His eyes, saddened, almost inexpressive, bespoke an age-old weariness. His beard, coming to a point in a torrent of precisely curled ringlets, reflected more the care of a barber than the insouciance of a philosopher.

"Don't you care about the teams?"

I hesitated, searched for the proper words, but my provincial embarrassment wouldn't let me find a phrase sufficiently ambiguous to get around the question graciously. The genius of courtiers, through some special divine gift, is to succeed in guessing and parrying the thought of princes. I had no such gift—I, who had never dreamed of coming into the presence of the Emperor someday. In all truth, this little interview was more uncomfortable than festive for me.

"Of the gentlemen in your section you were the only one who didn't place a bet, Lucius Quintius."

"I missed it."

I didn't dare say that I hadn't noticed the Emperor himself placing a wager. My rapt attention to the platform might have been interpreted in a bad way. But he was smiling now, right in front of me. With his back to the light, his face was shaded—in contrast to the multicolored reflections of the glass, reflections that would vary with the slightest movement of one's eyes. He seemed to have guessed my doubts: "I didn't bet either, Lucius Valerius. But my . . . let's call it 'position,' which some people would like to be divine, allows me to be immune to human passions and authorizes me to be indifferent to the difficulties of the greens, the blues, the reds, or the whites. If I appreciate the races or not, that's my private prerogative. But you saw me there, presiding . . . So, what do you want to answer me?"

"In these games I saw only blood, slaughter. We Romans forbid human sacrifices, and yet . . ." I immediately felt I shouldn't have said that. One should never confess a thought to someone who's not an intimate. Why is it that my stupid sincerity always ends up having its way? And before the master of the Empire's destiny. I wasn't chatting with the philosopher privately in the haven of my home. It wasn't a man waiting in front of me; it was a candidate for divinity. I cut myself off and blushed.

151

"You didn't fool me. You don't like the races, Lucius Quintius, and you think you have the luxury of not having it noticed. Look, it's not true that we Romans have done away with human sacrifice. We've only changed the way it's done. What we've prohibited for subjugated peoples are their peculiar formalities for killing. And we consider them Romanized and fortunate when they adopt our rituals, which are these."

I remained silent, embarrassed. I knew that I shouldn't contradict the Emperor or prolong the conversation. I lowered my eyes and waited for Marcus Aurelius to go on. Outside, the din of the crowd was thunderous. The lots had been cast. It was time for the beasts.

"Do you hear, Lucius Quintius? There you have the people calling for blood. Does it disgust you? Do you think it would be good if the Senate and I put an end to the races, the fighting, the beasts?"

I murmured something about the power of the Emperor, the excellence of the Patres Conscripti and their sagacity; but he was speaking to me instead about good sense: "Do you know something? The thirst for blood is so great that if they didn't sate it in the amphitheaters they'd do it in the streets. If I proscribed the spectacles, we might go back to civil wars and banishments. Other Caesars would rise up. Should I run that risk?" The Emperor lowered his voice. "Things are the way they are, Lucius Quintius. Bear up under them, and forget about indignation. A philosopher can't impose himself on every citizen and make him follow his path. And since you, from what I know, are a young man of promise in your city, never show either through act or omission that you're far removed from the feelings of the people. You might break an established balance in the natural order of things, into which your convictions would intervene as nothing but a personal whim, alien and disturbing."

He took a step back, advanced to the table and lifted the cup to his lips again. It was rose water he was drinking, not wine. The groups that were conversing here and there opened up, spread out, almost dispersed. Some heads turned toward us. But Marcus Aurelius had something to confide in me still, in private. "You must be wondering how it is that I knew you hadn't placed a bet." He brought his face close to mine. I could feel his breath, smelling sweetly of roses, almost nauseating. "Another duty of a public man is to know everything that's going on around him. Don't forget that."

The smile of the Emperor as he drew away a little and pointed out the exit with a gracious flourish was a sign for me to leave. But he held me back for one moment more to tell me, "Write to me whenever you want to, Lucius Quintius."

Those last words were spoken in a voice sufficiently loud for all to hear.

◦═╪═◦

That night at dinner in Calpurnius' house my companions behaved in a strange and unusual way toward me. They pressed me to tell them about my conversation with the Emperor, knowing that I would, out of discretion, be unable to do so. They all showed themselves uneasy in their words and their miens, and I was the target of cryptic observations, of specious irony. These remarks made no sense in isolation, but, coupled with my companions' expressions and gestures, displayed distrust and—it's hard for me to say it—spite. I was the youngest of the group. I didn't know how to defend myself from that elaborately perverse antagonization.

They got enmeshed in malevolent gossip about Faustina; they had doubts that young Commodus could be the Emperor's son. They laughed at "government by philosophers." They ridiculed and imitated Fronto and Rusticus; they repeated witticisms of Avidius Cassius, quoted the epigrams of the buffoons.

In the midst of all this they made subtle insinuations with recondite allusions about commissions the Emperor must have charged me with and which implied some treacherous vigilance of their affairs. Within the mood of laughter and high spirits, mingling friendly and soothing words with their dubious comments, they did everything they could to make the dinner disagreeable for me. "You, who are an intimate of the Emperor," Trifenus' father got to say as the others guffawed. Calpurnius remained almost entirely silent. I remember his moody, sidelong glance over the cup he was raising to his mouth.

XII

He was motioning me now to sit beside him. He ordered the slaves and the sculptor to leave. I went to sit down on a stool, but he stopped me with a quick gesture, a weary face. Then he turned around and shouted that the duumvir needed a chair; he wasn't to sit on the stool so recently occupied by the reader. Fearfully, they brought in another rush chair, and Calpurnius promised the lash to the slave who was carrying it.

"Forgive me, Lucius, the wretches take advantage of my old age."

"I've come to thank you."

"Thank me? I don't know why. You haven't let me do you many favors."

"For your participation by the temple. It helped lift morale."

Calpurnius took a clay cup full of small, twisted, and dark-colored roots from a small table. He pulled out a handful and chewed them, making a wry face. The corners of his mouth glistened with a greenish drool.

"Why is it," he asked, "that medicine always has to be bitter and hard to swallow? Doctors think that suffering with the illness always has to be exacerbated by suffering with the cure."

A flight of doves passed with a flutter of wings. The formation broke up, and they went to alight on the roof, one by one. The boldest dropped and pecked among the grasses in the flowerbeds.

"But I summoned you because I wanted to absolve myself. My pains were such in the morning that I was unable to appear at the temple. I want you to know that I sacrificed at home, by my home altar, for your purposes."

I was going to make some circumstantial comment, but Calpurnius cut me off in a commanding way, raising his hand. He leaned slightly toward me. "We've got to see which way the feelings of the people are going—the way sailors see which way the wind is blowing. It's necessary for the plebs to see that we're sharing in all the city's troubles. That's why I feel guilty about not having appeared. Will you forgive me, Lucius?" He lowered his eyes, almost closed them. His features showed remorseful humility.

"Forgive you? I should thank you. I've already told you that."

Calpurnius lifted his head and smiled. He seemed satisfied with the path the conversation was taking. He ran his still-greenish tongue over his upper lip and grasped my tunic with two fingers.

"I'm going to be sincere with you, Lucius. If nothing else, my . . . ancientness allows me to speak a few frank words. They tell me that you're isolating yourself from your fellow citizens. You don't receive your clients, you don't get along with the curia, you don't frequent the baths or other people's triclinia . . ."

"I haven't the time or the inclination. The barbarians are running all through the countryside round about. It doesn't seem to me the time for any social life."

"Ah, yes. I think I underestimated those Moors once. And there we have them, as people say . . . Absurd, eh?" Calpurnius shook his head with displeasure. On one of the columns a gecko climbed rapidly, weaving among the fluting. "But do you know, Lucius? It's precisely at difficult moments that the affirmation of Romanness is most urgent. The people have to be united around leaders that they recognize."

"I didn't ask to take on the duumvirate. I've already put my position at the disposition of the curia."

"Which, I might add, treated you in a way that was . . . a little, let us say . . . discourteous. But you've performed very well as duumvir. No one has censured what you've done—even in spite of the tragedy of Pontius. What people have questioned are things you haven't done, which, in the end, are the simplest part of your duties."

"Would the affairs of the city run any better if I wasted my time receiving clients, distributing alms, presiding over games, spending my evenings at dinners?"

"You'd only be doing what's expected of you! Lucius, my dear Lucius, you've been seen going about on foot! And sometimes all by yourself!" And he asked me a question I hadn't foreseen: "Who won the last race on the last calends? The blues or the greens, the whites or the reds? Maybe what was left of the golds or the purples?" He refused to heed my impatience and kept on: "What's the name of the glorious charioteer of the blues? What's the name of the immortal horse of the greens who's already survived seventy races? Ah, you don't know any of that, Lucius."

"And I don't care to know. I don't think it's important. As for the rest of it . . . it's the way I am."

"And the people are the way they are. They're restless, divided. There's whispering, there are plots. Have you heard the talk about Pontius' ghost appearing by the house you demolished? Have you done something to exorcise the spirit?"

"I don't believe in ghosts, Calpurnius. And you don't either."

"It's not a question of what we believe. We read books. We can give ourselves the luxury of private doubts. I'm referring to the people of Tarcisis."

Calpurnius picked up another handful of roots, but this time he didn't raise them to his mouth. He crumbled them on the marble table. He wouldn't let me interrupt; he had his speech all thought out. "You've got a bandit in jail. You're the one who's feeding him, I presume. Why don't you sacrifice him in the arena as the people demand? These are risky times. We have a war on the horizon. You could dedicate games to Mars at this point. You, who've never sponsored games as your duty calls for."

Calpurnius' lordly and paternalistic tone was evolving, sentence by sentence, into the harshness of a demand and a reproof. He was reminding me of my obligations with senatorial authority. "Come on, answer me, Lucius Valerius!"

"Do you know what the bandit said to me when he was brought in? 'I'm a man.' I don't want to shed the blood of a man at such a decisive moment for the city."

"It's debatable that a bandit is a man. I can't conceive of a man who stands outside the city and outside the law; but, after all . . . why shouldn't you throw a guilty man to the dogs?"

"Because I remember the aversion the Emperor has to blood. Do you remember many years ago, that time in the Circus, when he refused to manumit a supplicant slave who was exhibiting a man-eating lion? It's even been said that he secretly ordered the weapons of the gladiators to be dulled."

"Lucius Valerius, my friend, how ingenuous you are. Every ruler has his peculiarities. This one has given himself the fantasy of government by philosophers. Yet never have I seen so much misfortune. The gods must be upset by the excess of philosophy. There was an earthquake. A plague even fell on Rome. The Moors are running wild across its territories. Poor Marcus Aurelius . . . he'll pass on like the others. He'll rise up to heaven in apotheosis and take his philosophy with him. But the Senate and the People of Rome remain."

"The age of the Caesars is over. Avidius Cassius' conspiracy was broken up."

"And was that to the good?" Calpurnius stared at me with a very serious look. Thoughtful, he rubbed his face with his senatorial ring, gave a glimmer of a smile. Then he broke into laughter, almost convulsively, to the point of choking. "Do you know who Commodus is? Lucius Aelius Aurelius Commodus?"

"I know he's been educated by Fronto and the best philosophers in the Empire."

"Lucius, my dear fellow, try an experiment. Buy two Greek philosophers in Gades. Set them up in your stable and put them to discoursing to your pack mules for several years. Maybe in that way you'll succeed in the miracle of a philosophizing mule."

"What do you mean by that?"

"That Commodus is stupider even than your mules. He spends all his time in the amphitheater with the gladiators. Like Nero, his greatest aspiration is to be a charioteer. He strangled one of his friends with his bare hands just because the man recited a verse he thought equivocal. Nothing has stuck to him, either from Fronto, Rusticus, or the others."

"That's not possible!"

"It's true, Lucius. And Marcus Aurelius refuses to see anything. He never knew how to evaluate those closest to him. He exalts Fronto, and Fronto is a numbskull; he glorifies Faustina, and Faustina is nothing but an irritating and unfaithful hussy; he plans to bring Commodus into the government, and in all probability Commodus isn't even his son. If you live long enough you'll have Commodus as emperor. And then you'll see the return of the age of the Caesars. You'd better prepare for it."

"The great virtue of this emperor is that you're allowed to speak this way, without being *sub rosa*."

"I speak freely because I'm very old. In the time it would take for a denunciation to reach Rome and for the executioner to come for me, I'll probably have gone on my way. Besides, Lucius Valerius, your loyalty and sense of decorum are so strong that they seem almost pathological. You'd never be capable of denouncing me, even if you repudiate my words."

He was right. It didn't take much perspicacity to see that I would never betray . . . I won't say a friend, but someone who'd entrusted me with a secret. Calpurnius was smiling, and he gave me a soft pat on the hand.

"My dear Lucius, respect the popular will. The people want the bandit? Give them the bandit. The people want the Christians? Give them the Christians. But keep the people on your side."

"I do what I think just, not what will flatter the plebs."

"Just is what the rabble accepts as just, not what Lucius Quintius thinks."

Calpurnius had his arms folded now and was casting his small, faded eyes on me. He'd begun, now, to parry all my opinions in an almost sportive way; and this game of give-and-take seemed to afford him immense pleasure. "They say you're much too tolerant with that abominable sect of Christians."

"One god more—what's so terrible about that?"

"They spit on the temples, they sacrifice children, they worship monstrous animals, they plot to poison our drinking water, they organize incestuous orgies . . ."

"I have no proof of that."

"It's what they say. It's what's going around. The inhabitants of Tarcisis despise those people. The hatred of the citizenry is the proof. Isn't that enough for you?"

"I'm a magistrate. I depend on the law, on the Senate and the People of Rome. I'm not a satrap!"

"Do you know why Maximus Cantaber didn't appear at the sacrifice?"

"Maximus Cantaber is free."

"No, he's not! He would be free if they'd let him proceed according to the duties of a knight. But those Christians forcibly prevented him from going to the temple."

"He hasn't complained!"

The dialogue was moving very swiftly. Calpurnius had let go of my tunic and was pounding the marble table with both fists, alternately. The moment for attack had arrived, and he was letting himself go, revealing the whole string of accusations he'd been gathering in secret. Suddenly he pointed his wizened finger in my direction. "I know! You, Lucius Valerius Quintius, you've been bewitched by Iunia Cantaber, and that's the source of your evasions. Not from your mind, but from your heart. These evil sects have arts and enchantments that are capable of destroying a man's judgment. I'm giving you a warning, Lucius."

It was too much. I got up suddenly. The chair fell, and the cushion rolled off.

"What are you doing, Lucius? Listen to me!"

Calpurnius was shouting now. And I just stood there, alarmed, leaning against a column, looking at him. *Iunia*, in the mouth of Calpurnius, had scandalized me. I wasn't ready to share Iunia with that corrupt mummy. Slaves appeared in the doorway at the sound.

"It's your sense of Romanness that I'm appealing to. Wake up, man! Despite everything—take heed—despite everything, I prefer to see a well-born citizen like you heading this city rather than the son of a freedman like Rufus Cardilius. But if Rufus defends the interests of the people better, then let it be Rufus."

I took my leave with a curt nod and hurried toward the exit. I had never expected anything like this from Calpurnius. I knew that sooner or later we would enter into conflict, but the mention of Iunia had seemed a low blow, one in extremely bad taste. I'd never spoken about her to anyone. How did that decrepit and debauched rogue dare mention the name of Iunia?

"Airhan! Airhan!" Calpurnius was bellowing behind me.

Airhan appeared. He bowed slightly and accompanied me to the exit. I thought nothing of it, I was so confused. We passed through room after room in silence; the sound of our sandals resounded icily through the empty space. At the door, finally, without my asking him anything, Airhan bowed again and tried to explain the situation: "I'm working for Ennius Digidius Calpurnius now. Steward and proctor. Your servant, Lucius Valerius."

"I don't think I paid you for your last service, Airhan."

"You don't have to pay me anything, Lucius Valerius. What Ennius Calpurnius gives me out of the goodness of his heart is more than enough."

"That silver statuette I promised you . . ."

"Please, keep your statuette."

I think I saw a quick gray flash run across his hair. A louse. The embroidered clothing Calpurnius had given him hadn't taken away his stench; the proximity of the senator hadn't driven off the vermin. Airhan waited by the door, quite sure of himself, until I got into my chair and left.

What bothered me on my return was perceiving that, underneath it all, the advice of the Hispanic senator Ennius Calpurnius had coincided almost point by point with the observations of the philosopher Marcus Aurelius ten years earlier.

❦

At the praetorium, at last, orders from the governor awaited me. The messenger, weary and dripping with sweat, was dozing against the door of my tablinum. From Emerita, where he'd made a hurried trip, Sextus Tigidius Perenne had sent me a letter. In Greek prose that was like a cipher—its overrefined oriental style made it difficult to tell where the cautionary note began and the bombast of the phraseology ended—he gave an account of the invasion of the Moors, whom he described as "hordes of unreconciled barbarians," advising me to have the citizens from suburbs and villas brought into the city, to reinforce the walls, and to follow up with sacrifices. Only now! I awoke the messenger and asked if he'd run into any Moors on the road. He said he had, that he'd spotted a group behind a hedgerow but that they hadn't chased him, probably because they didn't have mounts.

"Are you going to risk returning to Emerita?" I asked.

"It's my duty. I have to bring an answer back."

I called in a cartulary, dictated a note, in Greek, to the governor. This communiqué was a touch ironic and enigmatic, acknowledging receipt of his message and briefly sketching the measures taken in Tarcisis. Then I dispatched the bearer, who had a long ride ahead of him.

Aulus waited for me to send the man on his way before giving me the bad news: Cornelius Lucullus had been found dead in a yard under the aqueduct, on the slope where the highest section crossed. The night before, after a drinking bout at Rufus' tavern, he'd apparently taken the risk—with the confidence that wine gives—of staggering along the aqueduct. The people at the tavern had seen him leave, but from what they said, none of them had imagined that Cornelius would take a chance on following that narrow way, which, besides, didn't lead to his house. Maybe he wanted to take a shortcut to the prostitutes' street, one of his habitual destinations.

"That's what they say, duumvir. But there's something even stranger. They found a dead fish in Cornelius' clothes."

"Do you think he was murdered?"

"Maybe. But nobody knows anything. Nobody saw anything."

"Can the fish be a sign?"

"Who knows?"

"And why not Cornelius' meal the next day?"

Aulus shrugged his shoulders ambiguously. "There are people capable of anything out there, Lucius Valerius."

Poor, unfortunate, pitiful Cornelius. Dead without having attained fame or fortune, reduced to the abject state of being a beggar in Tarcisus, stupidly done in by machinations beyond his control and understanding. It wasn't the time to probe the circumstances of that death, which I, with rage, was sure had not been accidental. I wasn't going to interrogate all the habitués of Rufus' tavern or Rufus himself and raise more suspicions and anxieties in the city. It was a matter of a retaliation against me. The sign of the fish was directed at me. Any investigation at that moment might be awkward and bring on the mob's derision. It would wait for later on, when there was an occasion . . . I wasn't disposed to let Rufus Cardilius get the better of me.

Aulus stood before the bust of the Emperor. He was still imperturbably waiting for me to make some decision about Cornelius. I remained with my elbows on the table for a long time, but it wasn't about Cornelius I was thinking. It was about Aulus.

I was pleased by that discreet taciturnity, the precise gestures, the scarcity of words. I'd never been intimate with Aulus. The invitation to my house once had been an absolute exception—though I knew that Galla had done everything to be received by Mara and to share confidences. My reserve toward Aulus, which never ceased to point out the difference in status, seemed to suit him perfectly.

Aulus never led me to suspect any corruption, and at a time when venality was almost synonymous with the centurionate. But his fidelity—so constant and humble, like that of Sabinus' dog—seemed at times based on a conformity and a coldness that were beginning to worry me. Who was Aulus after all? Were there no cracks in his rigidity? Why had he been so equivocal moments before?

"What do you think of all this, Aulus?"

"There wasn't as much divisiveness before, duumvir."

"Before what?"

"Before these Christians . . ."

I hesitated before asking him the question, almost without thinking: "Aulus, has anyone approached you recently?"

He thought for a few moments. It could be seen from his wrinkled brow that he was trying to unravel the meaning of the question. But contrary to what I expected, he only answered, impassively: "No one, duumvir."

Then he asked permission to see about burial arrangements for Cornelius, who hadn't belonged to any funeral confraternity or left anyone to accompany his coffin. Aulus had always detested Cornelius, and his generous solicitude seemed odd to me.

✦

The surprise of Iunia in the praetorium. She pushed back the drapes and approached my table in silence. I stopped breathing and stood stiffly until my hands stopped shaking. I must have turned pale. Then I felt the blood flowing into my cheeks. I may have blushed. Iunia, ignoring my upset, looked at the bust of the Emperor for a moment.

"Where's the marble from?"

With gestures, puzzled, I confessed my ignorance.

"Hmm, it's not from here. It must be from Italy. . . . The marble from here has broader veins and a grayish tint that tends toward the greenish."

She glanced out the window and spun around, came over to me, smiling. I felt strangely embarrassed. I hadn't expected to see Iunia in the praetorium, invading my domain, and I wondered about the mundane and indifferent way she had gone through the meeting room and the slightly mocking tone with which she was speaking now, fiddling with the corners of her veil, uncovering her face completely, then hiding it partially. I resolved to remain silent lest I say something wrong. Iunia's broad smile was so unwonted that it changed the image, always serious and composed, that I had of her. Fearful of breaking the spell, I didn't dare ask how she got by the guard or what she wanted.

"I need your authorization to visit the prisoner."

Decisive, crisp, unexpected. I really don't know what I was expecting. Perhaps only that Iunia would let herself stay a while. Perhaps that she'd sit down and remain across from me there so I could look at her, only look at her. Perhaps even that she'd come to resume our interrupted arguments, in which I—always the loser— saw myself obliged to recognize a secret, unconfessable pleasure.

But this request took me completely by surprise. A heavy dark cloud fell over all objects. The face of Marcus Aurelius suddenly seemed saddened. My hands grew icy.

"Arsenna the bandit?"

"Arsenna the prisoner."

"But do you know Arsenna?"

"I don't. I don't even know what he looks like. I know only that he's a prisoner, that he hasn't got anyone else, that a horrible end awaits him, and that he needs consolation and charity."

"Do you want to convert him to your superstition? What for? Aren't there any slaves left in Tarcisis? You're going to talk to a man who's destined to die. What can you gain from that?"

"Do you refuse to let me see Arsenna?"

I could have said, "I refuse!" It would have been the proper rejoinder to such an improper demand. On the personal level it would have represented a pardonable revenge to counter the disappointment Iunia had provoked in me.

But I heard myself calling a lictor and giving him the order to take Iunia Cantaber to the prisoner. She didn't even thank me. She left rapidly, ahead of the lictor. I could see through the half-drawn curtain that she'd joined her slave women and that the group was descending the stairs that led inside.

<hr />

I arrived at the tribunal late; I'd allotted time for Iunia to leave. The presence in the city of idle people was filling the main nave of the basilica with agitation and rumors, and even though the trials constituted the only possible entertainment in those days, I didn't cease to wonder why my court should be so crammed with people. On that day the secretary had put on the calendar the case of a woman accused of slandering another and that of a woodcarver who'd neglected to keep the street in front of his shop swept: simple and quick matters on which I didn't plan to waste much time. No sooner had I settled into my seat and seen that the parties were present than Rufus, accompanied by Proserpinus and a large group, formally dressed, presented himself. And Proserpinus, with broad gestures and the tremulous voice he reserved for important occasions, asked to be heard urgently, requesting priority over the cases on the docket. He had obviously bribed the other litigants; when questioned, none of them was opposed. I gave permission, and he, adjusting his toga, theatrically unrolled a sheet that fell down with a clatter. We had papyrus, disbursement, solemnity, complications. I made ready to listen to the accusation that I guessed (correctly) was against Maximus Cantaber, his daughter Iunia, and a list of people whose names, with the exception of Milquion, were unknown to me.

Rufus Glycinius Cardilius, represented by Gneius Solutus Proserpinus, was formally accusing Maximus and Iunia Cantaber and others of acts of impiety; with incitement to rebellion against the Senate and the People of Rome; with sacrilege to the gods of the republic through acts and omissions; with the practice of obscene and repugnant rites and clandestine festivities; with illicit and unauthorized association; with violation of imperial edicts; with treason against the city by giving funeral rites to its enemies; with social promiscuity in the celebration of mysteries in which slaves take part; with witchcraft in the expulsion of demons and predictions of the future, matters reserved for augurs; with disrespect and violations of the peace; with injury to the political liberty of citizens. All of which would be further developed, explained, and proven in a judgment.

Proserpinus added to that, in a loud voice, something that had just been whispered to him by Rufus: collusion with bandits, abusing the benevolence of the duumvir by visiting them, encouraging them, and conferring on them the dignity that law and custom deny such scoundrels. It was a perfidious insinuation of complicity that I, in my position as judge, couldn't refute.

A lictor took the allegation, which I placed on the table without unrolling it. Let it be registered—I said—I would make a decision at a later date.

A rancorous, hostile murmur arose that was immediately transformed into thunderous acclamation for Rufus and Proserpinus, who thanked the crowd triumphantly. They left my court with their retinues to enthusiastic cheers. Remaining before me were only the forsaken protagonists of the current cases.

I'd deluded myself about the duration of the cases, which the lawyers artfully prolonged until dusk. It was already night, and I rushed on foot to Maximus Cantaber's house, accompanied only by a slave. We had to pound on the iron gate to wake the keeper, who was slow to respond. After that noise, I could hear the doors of indignant or curious neighbors opening across the way. Maximus received me in the deserted atrium, bewildered and with trembling hands. I looked around. I didn't see Iunia. A few faint lights were sadly illuminating the area. Above the compluvium, a dark sky with sleeping stars. In the back the triclinium, without lights, was closed off, dark and silent.

"There's been an accusation of impiety against you and Iunia."

I felt sorry for Maximus. He sat down slowly on a chest, looking at me mutely.

"By a certain Rufus Cardilius."

"The baker? The son of the freedman?" he finally asked, almost in a whisper. His dejected manner seemed excessive to me. Maximus had slaves, freedmen, clients, and the means to face up to any trial brought on by Rufus Cardilius, even if the latter had the support of Calpurnius and his people. Under normal circumstances Rufus wouldn't even have been able to make him appear in court. But Maximus was showing himself to be profoundly weary, in a state of prostration where any annoyance took on the aspect of a catastrophe.

"But why? Because I didn't go to the temple yesterday?"

"Yes, among other accusations. I wanted to warn you so you wouldn't hear the news from somebody else. As for the rest, I've postponed the preliminary decision. Under the present circumstances I think it prudent to suspend all judgments."

"No, I will go to your court, duumvir!" Iunia's voice, like a sharp jab stabbing my chest. I felt my heart jump. I probably shivered. In that light no one could have seen it. I hope I didn't make any superfluous gesture or change my expression. Iunia came out of the shadows and walked toward us in her slow way. She ran a loving hand over her father's hair and stood stiff before me, ready to take charge of the situation.

"You don't give the orders in my court, Iunia."

"But I want to appear. I'm going of my own free will."

A while before, when I was talking to Maximus Cantaber alone in the discomfort of the gloomy atrium, I realized that there'd been something false about my haste in coming to warn my friend at this late hour. In fact, once again, it wasn't Maximus I wanted to see. I'd deceived myself.

When I heard Iunia's voice and became aware—after the initial upset had subsided—of her presence, the tenor of everything seemed strangely altered. An intense sensation of fulfillment came over me. I felt myself a companion of the gods, a conqueror of horizons, a lord of the seas; and I no longer cared about the seemliness of my being there. I stopped seeing Maximus, who was still seated on the chest; and Iunia's cheeks, in the bluish glow of the lamp, filled the whole place. From far away, from deep down, diffusely, some kind of fear was gnawing at me—with a touch of remorse, I didn't know quite for what. And Iunia was there to dispute me, as always: "You have no right to spare me. If they want to judge me, let them judge me. I'm not asking for your protection."

"Nor would I give it to you. I just don't want any complications in the city while it is under threat. Tomorrow I'm going to announce the suspension of all judicial activities."

"Your concern for the city . . . Tarcisis shall not be left with one stone on top of another, Lucius."

"I hope you won't be responsible for that. I'm doing what I can to fulfill my duties and keep it intact."

"Is that why you order grotesque sacrifices to be made in the temple and wet a spear in the blood of the victims?"

"Yes, it is!"

"Poor, condemned Tarcisis. Another city will come to take the place of this one. The new Jerusalem has already been foretold. Priscilla of Pepusa saw it for forty days up in the clouds." And Iunia, folding her arms, recited: "'The wolf also shall dwell with the lamb,' Isaiah prophesies, 'and the lion shall eat straw like the ox, and dust shall be food for the serpent. They shall not hurt nor destroy in all my holy mountain . . .'"

I interrupted and retorted with Virgil: "'By themselves goats will bring home their udders heavy with milk and the flocks shall not fear the huge lions. By itself your cradle shall spread tender flowers. The serpent will die, and false, poisonous grasses shall die. Assyrian amomum will come forth roundabout.'"

"It doesn't have the same meaning!"

"No?"

"Maybe you'll come to understand someday, duumvir."

"Are you still making a scene by the doors to the baths?"

"Haven't your spies informed you?"

"You cause such a scandal that I don't even have need of spies."

Maximus' voice, weak and faint, as if struggling up from remote depths, broke in: "I'm so tired!"

He raised himself with a great sigh and leaned on the arm of Iunia, who didn't turn. She and I, staring at each other, fired up with anger, almost brushed faces. Iunia's was hardened, and I presume mine was too. We only paid attention to Maximus when he laughed courteously, snapped his fingers, and said, "Well . . ."

<hr>

Back home I caught myself still marshaling arguments against Iunia. Against the words she spoke, against the ones I imagined she could have spoken. New quotes occurred to me, poetry, lines from tragedies, myths. I was pestered by the idea that I'd missed saying something to her and that the unfortunate hostility between us stemmed, in the end, from an incomprehension that might be got rid of by reasoning, demonstrations, words. I thought of phrases, attitudes. I gesticulated to myself. And underneath it all, I knew that all of this was nothing but the product of my imagination . . .

My room was too small to walk about in remembering and ruminating arguments. I spent a long time in the atrium. I sat by the tank and tried to concentrate on a practice that, though useful before, hadn't been doing me much good of late: the examination of my conscience. Had I won the joust? Had I lost? And the image of Iunia, looking at me obliquely, with an air between ironic and mistrustful, kept interfering and disturbing me.

I ended up going to Mara's room. She woke up as soon as she sensed the light of the lamp. Nonplussed, she smiled at me and fixed her hair.

"Mara," I asked, "who won the last races in the Circus Maximus, the blues or the greens?"

It was a while before Mara—still not convinced she was awake—answered: "The blues five times, the greens twice."

"What's the name of the most popular charioteer?"

"Censonius."

"And the trace-horse of his team?"

"The one on the spina side? Polydoxos."

"How do you know that, Mara?"

"Everybody knows it, Lucius."

XIII

Before daybreak a placard
was hung by the door of the basilica. It reminded people of the im-
minent danger and the necessity for joining efforts and exercising
vigilance in defense of the city. It stressed the exigency for citizens
to enlist along with their people and announced that until further
notice, all judicial activity was suspended. Plaintiffs would have to
wait; interest on debts was held in abeyance; private jails were declared prohibited.

I can't say for sure that this announcement was the cause of the
climate of excitement that returned to Tarcisis, but sometimes when
all the conditions have accumulated and are just right for a determined event to take place, the only thing needed is some small oc-
currence, most often negligible and inappreciable, to undo the effec-
tiveness of opposing arguments. In the last few days popular feeling
about the Moors' advance varied between arrogant and ill-humored
blather; flighty and irresponsible alienation, almost putting it out of
one's mind; and a hysterical, half-terrified fury. From what I'd seen,
the pendulum of public mood was prone on any given day to swing
back and forth, with wild variance, between sunup and sundown.

On the day in question the people in the forum behaved unusu-
ally. The movements of the buyers were quicker and more nervous,

the clowns with their bears were almost unable to catch anyone's attention; everyone seemed to be in a hurry. When my litter passed, the bystanders saluted me with a strange, expectant curiosity, and not many fell behind to form a retinue. Contributing perhaps to the tension in the air were the regular thuds from the big catapult next to the wall—fully installed now—which I was on my way to inspect.

From street to street a sharp, protracted squeaking was becoming clearer, followed by a brief pause and then the hollow blow that, after a powerful rumble, finished with a metallic shaking that whizzed over the rooftops, making the air thunder and reminding citizens of the eventuality of war.

They called that machine the "onager," the wild ass; no one knows why. If the small slinger Aulus had discovered could put one in mind of a scorpion, taking into account the horizontal narrowness of the tube, the bow for the head, the raised lever for the tail, this one bore only an abstract resemblance to its namesake: one had to imagine the animal's size, brutishness, and corpulence.

They'd made use of the plumb-lines from the hoists and the beams from the scaffolding. Pulled by counterweights, the tall wooden arms, supported by metal plates that hung from ropes, would strike against a crossbar in a leather shock absorber and shoot off projectiles over a very irregular and uncertain distance. Close by the device, black and shapeless, pyramids of thick stones were waiting to be placed on the plates. Slow-moving lines of slaves and peasants, sunburned and exhausted, were piling the masonry from the demolitions within reach.

It was a matter of an ingenious and fearsome improvisation that filled the contractors of Tarcisis with pride. On top of the amounts owed for the renovation of the walls, they expected recompense for their dedication to the defense of the city with the sacrifice of their hoists and the diligence of their foremen.

The bustle of stonemasons and craftsmen, that could have been seen about the walls a month earlier, was now replaced by a swirl of people carting stones, chopping underbrush, or marching in formation to the sound of military cadences from Aulus' officers. I made a small speech to the contractors, distributed presents, and promised emoluments after the contingencies that were ahead of us.

171

On my way back, because of the shortsightedness of the lictors, I crossed paths with the funeral of Cornelius Lucullus. My litter stopped, and I was reprimanding the lictors for not having chosen a better route when from out of the small group around the stretcher a woman leaped and threw herself onto the ground with horrific shrieks, twisting about, wallowing on the pavement. That was more than was called for from a professional mourner. Aulus, who came over, tried to move the cortege along, but more and more people were gathering, drawn by the woman's cries, which were growing more and more strident. I got out of my chair and went over. The ones who recognized me made room so that the woman, in her agitation, was almost rubbing against my feet, her breast bared now from the tugs she was giving her clothes with her twisted hands. Her reddened features were twitching in grotesque, frightening grimaces. Two men tried to take her by the arms, but they were pushed away and repelled. Alarmed, the crowd drew back. The woman was resting on her elbows now, arching her body and breaking into a hoarse wail that seemed interminable. Suddenly she fell silent, sat up, her arms crossed over her breast, and she fixed her eyes on a man who came forward from somewhere and stationed himself in front of her. It was Milquion.

Awkwardly, the woman rushed at him, shrieking, but Milquion lifted his open hand and she stopped, whirled about, and fell kneeling to the ground, gasping. Complete silence reigned all around. No one dared stir. All that could be heard, in the distance, was the rumble of the shots from the catapult. Then Milquion spoke, and his calm voice, which his accent made all the more otherworldly and solemn, echoed up and down the narrow street: "In the name of the Lord I command you to declare your name!"

The woman, eyes on the ground, began to convulse with laughter. Her mouth had the mocking rictus of theatrical masks. Viscous threads of drool were running down her chin. And her voice, high-pitched and shrill before, changed suddenly to a grave, almost masculine tone. It was in the midst of harsh laughs that she pronounced a name and repeated it over and over: "Belmorot!"

Milquion extended both arms over the head of the possessed woman and commanded: "Belmorot, filthy serpent, in the name of the Father, the Word, and the Son, I order you to leave this body!"

As he spoke the last word, the woman went into horrible convulsions again, intermingling Celtic and Latin words, laughs and grunts, shouting insults and melifluous obscenities until, suddenly, she rolled onto the ground, inert, in a deep drowsiness. Other women surrounded her and lifted her head. Her face was transfigured; it showed the serenity, the peaceful and innocent breathing, of sleep.

The procession grew active again. Cornelius' body was hefted onto shoulders once more. To the shrill of a flute the pitiful cortege continued on its way. Before leaving, unemotional and triumphant, Milquion looked at me over his shoulder. The woman was adjusting her clothing. She seemed ashamed and was speaking softly to the others, who hugged her and took her along.

Going back to my litter I asked Aulus, "What do you make of that?"

My centurion shrugged: "If there weren't any exorcists, there wouldn't be anyone who needed to be exorcised."

⊶———✦———⊷

On my table in the praetorium was a small package; two sets of wax tablets, a stylus, a wooden slab with the letters of the alphabet carved on it, a tiny blue glass flask with an unguent—all in a small cotton sack.

"They brought this from Iunia Cantaber for the prisoner Arsenna," the cartulary explained. "We thought it best not to give him anything without your authorization."

"Bring him here."

"He's filthy and smelly, duumvir. All those days in the straw."

Then they should wash him first! When Arsenna arrived, fettered, his hair was still wet from the bucket of water they'd thrown over him.

"Somebody sent you this," I said, and I spread the contents of the sack on the table. "Give me a good reason why I should give you these objects."

Arsenna showed his wrists with a clanking of the chains. The rags that covered his arms were stained with blood from the rubbing of the fetters.

"A reason for the unguent? Fine. What about the tablets? And the stylus?"

"I want to learn how to read, duumvir."

"But you're going to die, Arsenna. Learn to read for what?"

"You're going to die too, duumvir. To live for what?"

"I'll always leave my small works behind."

"I'll leave my fame."

He was cockier than the first time I'd seen him. But in any case, looking at him the way he was—thin, small, with unexpressive features—no one would have believed that as the leader of a dozen scoundrels he'd made the highways of Tarcisis and Ebora unsafe. I quickly handed him the flask and the writing material. He picked them up, held them against his chest, and didn't thank me. I motioned to the jailer to take him away. But Arsenna still wanted to say something: "Duumvir, I beg you to thank Iunia Cantaber in my name for these kindnesses. I've asked her god to protect her."

Always Iunia! Even that miserable reprobate pronounced her name and held over me the power of making me think of her.

"Of course! On your way!"

But Arsenna, near the drapes, still tried to turn back. His face was anxious, his voice tremulous and pleading now. "What are you going to do with me, duumvir?"

"You'll probably be crucified in the place where you were taken. That's the custom!"

Arsenna shuddered, tried to free his arm from the jailer who was holding it. The fetters clanked again. He tried to approach me: "What if I told you where our spoils are hidden?"

I refused to listen to the enumeration of Arsenna's tempting riches. I wasn't prepared to let the bandit disenchant me any more. I shouted for them to take him away. The jailer, helped by the lictor, pushed the prisoner, whose grimy tunic was torn even more. They finally went out with a sound of clinking metal. The sack containing the presents from Iunia spilled to the floor. Arsenna still had time to shout, "Don't throw me to the dogs, I beg you! Have pity on me, duumvir!"

Arsenna, a highwayman, under the protection of Iunia Cantaber. There was no place I could turn where Iunia didn't assert her besieging presence. If only I could sweep the city clean of that cursed sect with its perverse tenacity in creating dilemmas, dividing minds, attracting attention. If only I could get Iunia to listen to reason, remember the elementary actions and words of Romanness. If she would only listen to me at least . . .

It would be even better if I never heard Iunia mentioned again. If she would stop surprising me, troubling me, robbing me of my peace. If I could only forget her once and for all!

I didn't deserve that. I needed a free and disciplined mind. On that table all the city's problems were laid out. On my right was a pile of tablets and scrolls that I had to take care of. Why did Iunia have to interfere in my life like this?

I felt myself hating her with a feverish rage. It was up to me to put her in her place. Make her see her insignificance. She was a woman, subject to the power of her father! I had an obligation to convince her once and for all of the inanity of her beliefs, the ridiculousness of her ideas, the futility of her proposals. There were arguments that hadn't occurred to me during my last meeting with her. New points were coming up now. I could question her about her conversation with Arsenna, about the disturbing magical powers of her *Episkopos*, about . . . About . . . About . . .

Everything that was happening converged, in the end, on Iunia and was taking me to Iunia. I stopped, ready to leave; I already had my chlamys on, and the lictors were lining up beside the door. It couldn't be. What was I doing? I had no right to be so blinded by that creature. What was she, after all? A widow, the daughter of a rich father, who, to console herself for the disappointments of life, had decided, taking advantage of her status, to promote a silly, esoteric religion, similar to so many others that plebeians and slaves join. It would be preposterous for the duumvir to appear in the house of the Cantabers and engage in disputations, discuss points of doctrine, with one of the daughters of the paterfamilias.

On the other hand, maybe I could get her to see the light, persuade her to abstain, at least during these uncertain times, from the public manifestation of her convictions. I would say, "Iunia, enough!" And maybe she would put on that look of patient condescension, fix her hair, sigh, and . . . If I were to explain that our city was in crisis—and couldn't, with a Moorish attack impending, withstand any more disturbance and commotion—she would come to understand. She was a Roman, the daughter of a knight. Even if I had to speak slowly, enunciating the syllables with great care . . . Would she understand? Obviously not! She didn't want to understand. Hateful Iunia. Iunia was a plague the gods had sent me. What I had to do was defend myself. Iunia deserved to be scorned, looked down on, with great severity.

Of course, I could seek her out under some pretext or other and treat her coldly or even rudely in front of her slave women, the better to humiliate her. No, no discussions. An order, a prohibition, a shout. After all, I was the city's supreme magistrate. I had treated her till then with indulgence, and she had abused my patience and confidence. All right, was it shouts that she needed? I'd give her a couple of shouts. I was capable of that too!

There I was again, getting entangled with Iunia. Imagining her gestures, her features, her ways, her words. And everything was always so contradictory, so inconclusive, so unbearable. I absolutely had to do something, find some distraction, banish her from my thoughts. Passing through the forum, men in formation were making their boots resound on the pavement. Voices of command could be heard. A marching song rang out. Where were the results of the last military census? I shuffled the wax tablets, irritated. Some fell to the floor. I leaned over to pick them up.

But there was the sound of an indistinct altercation coming from the door. There was yelling, the sound of running. Before I could get hold of myself, Iunia Cantaber was facing me and saying, in a quite natural way, as if she'd been summoned and was answering a question, "My sister has disappeared!"

Maximus—behind Iunia—stooped, greeted me, and made a vague gesture of introduction for a man in a toga, someone I didn't know, who had not, apparently out of shyness, come forward from beside the drapes. Then, in a distraught tone, he began to tell how Clelia had left early that morning, in the company of her custodial slave and a young man whose company she was in the habit of keeping, Vispanius by name, son of the citizen of that same name. Hours had passed, and nothing more was heard of Clelia, who had—contrary to her custom—missed the afternoon meal. The Cantabers had already gone all through the city, bothering neighbors and acquaintances and mobilizing all their slaves for the search. The other slaves, when questioned, didn't know where the young people were going or where they were.

There was no evidence of misadventure, but the Cantabers' mistrust was increasing. Maximus remembered the day his dogs were killed, remembered that a slave and a frequenter of his house had been persecuted, remembered the offensive accusations that had been lodged against him in public speeches.

"We suspect Rufus Cardilius and his people," Iunia summed up, definitively and drily.

"But with what intention?"

"To cause injury and upset. The motivations of the devil don't have to be reasonable."

"Iunia, just let me govern this small world of men. Devils belong to a different jurisdiction. Your favorite, Milquion, seems to know about those things."

Before she could interrupt, I guaranteed Maximus that I would have searches made and try to unravel the matter. I accompanied them to the door. I tried to appear optimistic and did everything to dispel Maximus' despair. But as they were leaving, Iunia fell behind. She obviously didn't want me to have the last word. Holding the drape half-open, she whispered, "You suspended trials, didn't you? I warned you. I preferred a thousand times appearing in your court to creating a situation where they would molest my sister. And all this because of me! Are you trying to humiliate me?"

"Don't judge yourself so important."

"Everything gets paid for, duumvir!"

And she pointed an accusing finger at me. Standing in the rear of the gallery, Maximus and the others were waiting. I watched her go down the corridor to join them, walking with a slow and sovereign step. Before they left, Iunia gave me one more long look, which I took to be a mute admonition.

I decided to speak to Rufus at once, no matter how much it might upset me. A short time later I went into his lair, leaving the two lictors by the door, one on each side. Rufus appeared in an apron still stained with the wine he was decanting. When he saw me his eyes popped out. He raised his arms, looked down at his clothing, and lamented, "Please excuse me, duumvir. I wasn't expecting your visit. I'm a working man."

And he looked sincerely concerned at finding himself taken by surprise in that gear. The Rufus before me now, embarrassed, bore little resemblance to the cocksure dandy whose activities at the forum met with such acclaim. The tradesman with an ignoble profession surprised at his menial chores was demeaning the candidate for aedile favored by the gods and dressed in a white toga. I almost felt pity for Rufus Glycinius Cardilius. In the tavern at that hour were only a half-dozen drinkers, absorbed in their lethargy. Rufus saw no chance to assert himself. He needed crowds in the same way that the giant Antaeus needed contact with the earth.

"Where have you hidden Clelia Cantaber?" I went right to the point and shot the question out, gaining an advantage over Rufus, who was desperately wiping his hands on his apron. He looked alternately at me and at his customers. He stared with a furrowed brow at the lictors waiting with their fasces. He finally asked me, challengingly, what was going on.

"You're an enemy of the Cantabers!"

"I'm not an enemy of the Cantabers! I'm against evil superstitions, *that* I am!"

Rufus, frowning, seemed to be formulating rapidly all the hypotheses that might explain my coming there with lictors, so unusual and unforeseen. His last phrase had been uttered in the dull, reflective tone of someone stalling for time. He tried to add something, but he hesitated and his voice stuck in his throat. Then he took a deep breath, swallowed drily, and seemed to regain his calm: "Duumvir, please explain to me what brings you here."

I understood immediately that Rufus was innocent. Briefly, I explained that there were suspicions that he might be involved in the disappearance of Clelia Cantaber. Rufus reacted with indignation. He took off the apron agitatedly, called his slaves with loud shouts, and ordered them to open all the doors in the house so I could look wherever I wanted to, down to the most private nook, to the bottom of the last amphora. He himself ran to the door to call the lictors so they could proceed with the search! Rufus' startled workers were appearing here and there with great fright. The drunkards awoke from their torpor and regarded us with piqued interest. It was obvious to me that I'd made a misstep. All that was left to do was leave, which was a little embarrassing. "Watch your step, Rufus Cardilius!"

"You're the one who should watch your step, duumvir, because there are those among us who want to create discord among the citizens."

"We still have to clear up the death of Cornelius Lucullus."

"Ah, so any reason is good to use against me!"

The real Rufus was coming to the surface. His voice had lost its quaver, and now he was thundering to the whole tavern: "Has Clelia Cantaber disappeared? Have you made sure yet that the Christians haven't sacrificed her during their monstrous mysteries? Among them, you must know, son doesn't respect father, brother doesn't respect brother . . ."

I left Rufus to his peroration, delivered with oratorical verve to the scant customers in his den and to his slaves. Passersby stopped as I went by, turned their heads, and greeted me with surprise. I hadn't gone far when a harsh voice croaked behind me: "Duumvir!"

The man was grotesquely trying to run as he staggered along. Twice he bumped his shoulder against a wall. The distance from Rufus' tavern wasn't great, but he was panting as if he'd been running for miles. One of the lictors grabbed him when he stopped. He was a bald, filthy tramp with a rough voice, who was addressing me, it was clear, against his wishes.

"I dare to speak to you because Rufus ordered me to. I just told him that I saw Clelia leave the city this morning in one of Tobius' carts. And Rufus made me come tell you."

"Do you know Clelia Cantaber?"

He didn't know her. But it had been strange for that girl and that boy, well-dressed, laughing, in a rented cart, completely indifferent to the swarm of refugees around them, to be there. She was wearing a saffron-dyed, embroidered chiton. It could only have been Clelia Cantaber. Tobius should be asked if one of his carts was missing . . .

⊙══◆══⊙

The vagabond was right. And it wasn't necessary to look up the freedman Tobius. He appeared at the praetorium a short while later to report that one of his rental carts hadn't been returned. And he suspected, though he couldn't guarantee it, that Clelia Cantaber had rented it for a short trip. Hours had passed; there were rumors in the city; and he, before sending someone out to look for the cart, had thought it best to report what had happened.

Aulus found out from one of the keepers on duty that morning beside the gate facing the Emerita road that he'd let Clelia out despite the express prohibition because she'd guaranteed that her friend and she were only going to take a turn around the walls, fulfilling a promise to Apollo. All upset, the man threw himself at Aulus' feet with his hands together in the posture of a supplicant.

At that moment the people who were concentrated outside the wall started running and came together at one spot. The lines of slaves carrying stones and the formations drilling on the terrace broke up. Something had happened up ahead that was arousing curiosity and causing excitement.

I wasn't long in finding out. They brought young Vispanius into my presence, naked, exhausted, his face flecked with dry blood. They sat him on the base of the catapult and covered him. He seemed about to faint at any moment. With great difficulty, writhing in pain, he told what had happened.

Clelia had got the notion for them to continue to the shrine dedicated to Endovellicus, a shrine hidden in the middle of a holm-oak grove quite far away, where there was a spring, almost always dry in summer, that came forth in a bucolic little temple. It was a place that wasn't visited often except for pilgrimages; it was so much feared because of the presence of worrisome vibrations that

180

few men dared pass close by when alone. What she had wanted to ask the god for, the boy couldn't explain, but from the looks of it there was something that involved a magical sign so she could choose one of several boyfriends—a lighthearted and whimsical bit of mischief that she imposed, with promises and threats, over the objections of the custodial slave and the one driving the cart.

When they entered the temple, which was in the shadow of a high cliff covered with very ancient inscriptions, they noticed that the offerings had been removed and broken and that the remains of a recent bonfire were on the altar. They grew anxious. What unnerved them more was a sound in the underbrush outside. The slaves ran toward it, thinking it might be some animal, but they immediately drew back and fled, panting. A small gang of barbarians, five or six of them, came out of the bushes. They chased and attacked the slaves, who were brought down, one run through by a spear and the other knocked down by a rock. Unarmed, the boy had placed himself in front of Clelia, who was screaming, desperate. The last image he remembered of the predicament was of a laughing barbarian raising a club over his head. He had lain unconscious for hours in a ravine. Then he'd crawled along aimlessly until a peasant picked him up and brought him to the city on his donkey.

For almost an hour after that, against the wishes and the advice of Aulus, I rode over the heath at the head of a posse of armed volunteers. For the first time in my life, I'd put on cuirass and helmet. Mara helped me tighten the lorica and buckle the sword-belt. She made no attempt to dissuade me from the expedition, but her opposition was quite clear in her tense face and trembling movements. Everybody considered that patrol under those conditions a useless bit of madness. It was the middle of the afternoon; the sun was already going down, and night wouldn't be long in coming. No one had any hopes that we would free Clelia. But it was up to me to forestall Iunia's taking the initiative and dragging her old, infirm, and tormented father with her. And it was quite a job preventing them from accompanying us. In the group beside the gate that watched us leave, I caught sight of Iunia's anguished look.

Beside the shrine—after we traversed ten or eleven miles of deserted and dusty heath—lay the decomposing corpses of the two slaves, which we buried sufficiently far from the altars so as not to offend the god. I thought it best to forgo cremation so as not to give ourselves away with the smoke. Then we went ahead, following the cart's tracks, which swerved over the barren fields.

One of the men riding up front at full speed was seen suddenly to rein in his mount, so abruptly that he caused it to rear, on top of a hill that overlooked the plain. He came back down the slope even faster than he'd been riding before. "Duumvir!" he shouted when he got within earshot. "It's best we went back!"

Aulus and I took off at a gallop for the summit where the man had stopped. And I was given to witness one of the strangest spectacles I have seen in all my life.

About five or six stadia away, the plain was covered with men and animals in motion. As far as the eye could see, thousands of figures were advancing in a slow and disorderly manner over flats and gullies. Nothing that looked like an order of battle of a legion on the march. It resembled, rather, a swarm of insects, weakened by the heat, their wings lost, scattering about with difficulty after their nest had been demolished. Individuals and groups were dragging along, some carrying bundles, others bristling with rudimentary weapons, others leading donkeys, some on horseback, the great majority on foot, a very small number in carts. There was neither a forward nor a rear guard, neither velites nor impedimenta. It was a haphazard mass moving at random all across the heath. And their clothes were so dark and shabby that the barbarians looked as if they'd been born of the earth and were of the same matter as the scrub and dry grasses they were walking through. I had never imagined that the aggregation of invaders could have been so extensive or that the remote deserts of Africa could have produced a multitude capable of darkening our fields up to the horizon in such a vast way. I thought I saw a group on horseback assembling in the distance. They'd probably seen us. It was time to go back.

⚬══╬══⚬

No one chased us. When we arrived, at night already, I ordered trumpets sounded at the observation posts on the walls and that pickets and guard details be organized. Excitement ran through the

182

city; lamps were lighted in all the houses. Waiting for us, Iunia and Maximus hadn't left the area of the gate. It was painful for me to go up to them as soon as I could give them my attention. Milquion, looking very priestly, stood behind Iunia—he was conspicuous, at a time when all the men were hearkening to the voice of command or reporting with their weapons. I gave the Cantabers the hope that Clelia might be alive. I told them about the cart tracks, the corpses of the slaves, and the absence of any trace of her. Two tears ran down Iunia's silent face as she hugged her father strongly.

Maximus didn't reply and went off slowly, leaning on Iunia. Aulus intercepted Milquion, who was following behind, grabbing him rudely by the arms. "And you, what are you doing here? Aren't you supposed to be on the walls? Which is your group?"

Iunia immediately turned back, addressing me: "Milquion is under my protection, duumvir. He's a foreigner; he doesn't fight!"

But they were already calling me from one side. Maximus, Iunia, and Milquion disappeared into the darkness of the streets. Someone tugged at my cloak and swore that lights had been seen in the distance. I climbed up to the battlements. In fact, the skies looked pinkish all along the horizon; the barbarians were lighting their fires.

In Tarcisis nobody slept. At a late hour, at a point on the walls away from the gates, a bell began to sound the tocsin. Outside, there was a trooping of horses at full speed, their way lighted by torches. Thrown with force, a small bundle flew over the wall and fell onto a roof. A band of barbarians went off howling, chased by a volley of stones.

It was Clelia Cantaber's veil, wrapping a lock of her hair. A stone had served as a ballast.

XIV

"ARE THERE a lot of them?"

Mara was holding a platter of chestnuts and figs out to me as she reclined alongside, contrary to her custom. After making certain that everything was in order and putting Aulus in charge of the walls, I'd gone home to get a few hours of sleep. Mara had made me eat: I wouldn't be back home all that soon. My slaves had distributed food along the walls, and I'd have some of that.

"They cover the whole countryside, Mara."

"But isn't anyone coming to our rescue? Are we being abandoned?"

"The legions move slowly. And they have to come from far off."

"Lucius, take care of yourself, friend."

And Mara wouldn't let anyone else help me put on my armor. She herself tightened the straps and buckled the sword-belt once again. It was like an investiture, slow and solemn, in which Mara might have been trying to show some power over me while I, to my sorrow, couldn't stop wondering what Iunia Cantaber was doing at that moment.

Disobeying the order not to go out, a few citizens shinned down the walls on ropes, as soon as the sun came up, to catch a glimpse of the enemy. We found out that the Moors were advancing along the road when, outside, a crowd of unarmed peasants made a tumultuous rush toward the city's main gate, which was slammed shut behind them. With the creaking of the winch, the hum as it slid down, and the impact of the portcullis as it hit the ground, the city was shut off, closed to the countryside. All that was left for us to do was wait.

Finally they began to show themselves. Long, slow rows of men with a somber, hairy look were gathering opposite the gates, beyond the necropolis, in the area between the cleared land and the edge of the marshes and the trees. They had the inoffensive look of weary people trudging along in some kind of miserable procession to a shrine. If one stood out here or there because of the color of his clothing, in the midst of the brown of burlap and sackcloth, it was evidence of the fruits of pillaging in Roman territory. The horsemen, on mounts most certainly stolen when they ravaged the countryside, mingled indistinguishably with the crowd, where no difference between superiors and inferiors, cavalry or infantry, civilian or soldier, could be noted. The barbarians displayed neither insignias nor standards. Little by little they were mustering in confusion at a distance of three or four arrow shots. The ringing of bells at other points on the wall signaled other approaches, other mobs.

For hours that human mass was spreading out opposite the walls, always beyond the range of arrows and stones. At some points they were more compact and strong, at others sparse and scattered. And the silence of that crude concentration was as impressive as ours as we watched from behind the battlements. On the plates of the big catapult, swaying ominously from the ropes, heavy quarried stones awaited an order from me.

Suddenly, in the thickest part of the barbarian mass, there was a bustle, shouting. The crowd changed the direction of its march; there was a milling about; gestures became more animated. A cart was making its way through, the horses led by hand. It was parked in the first row so that it could be seen from the city. It was Tobius' rental cart, from which the canopy had been removed. Tied to a beam placed vertically between the sideboards, Clelia Cantaber was twisting about. Maximus had stationed himself on the walk-way around the wall, near Aulus, and he couldn't take his eyes off his daughter or his hands off the merlons.

There was agitation and altercation in a tight group around the cart now. Then a man, alone, was brutally pushed along. He stum-bled, almost fell, got up, and came on toward the walls. He was dressed Roman-style, in the dark tunic of a slave; but over his shoulders he wore a wolf skin, and in his hand he carried an olive branch, the traditional Celtic custom for a parley. He moved in an odd way, as if limping, dragging one leg. It was soon seen that he had one ankle tied to a long, knotted cord that someone in the crowd was unrolling. The weight of the cord made walking more and more arduous. He stopped thirty or forty paces from the walls and raised both arms, holding up the olive branch. He was coming to negotiate. Bows and slings were at the ready. I leaned over the battlements.

"Who speaks in the name of Tarcisis?" the slave asked, one hand cupped to his mouth.

Those of us on the walls looked at each other. Didn't those people have a chieftain, a delegation, anything that would spare the hu-miliation, greater for them than for us, of speaking through the mouth of a prisoner slave? As they sensed my mute question, the decemvirs who were close by lowered their eyes. My arm was gripped by Maximus' trembling hand: "Lucius, ask how much they want for my Clelia!"

I gently removed Maximus' hand and decided to parley with the slave. I couldn't risk rushing things. Later on I might be criticized for it, but right now it was what had to be done. "Who are you?"

The man was close to bowing at the sound of my voice, relieved that he was being spoken to instead of having spears hurled at him from above: "I am a servant of Aponius Sosumus of Volubilis, and I was captured by these barbarians because I didn't take refuge in time behind the defenses of the city. I'm acting as interpreter out of force and coercion, as everyone can see, and I request that this be noted for when better times return." And the slave lifted the ankle held by the large leather cord. There were impatient shouts from the Moors. I myself had to silence the clamor already arising along the walls.

186

"What do they want?"

"They say they come in peace and that they're hungry. They guarantee that if you open the gates and let them enter the city to get supplies, they will spare all lives, properties, and buildings. And immediately after, when they've eaten, they'll leave without having caused the least bit of damage. This is what they declare."

"They don't deserve an answer! Go back and tell them to go away."

Once more the pressure of Maximus' fingers on my arms and his heavy breathing: "Ask about Clelia, Lucius, please!"

The slave clenched the olive branch between his teeth, took the leather cord in his hand, and turned back, coiling it onto his arm as he went. He knew the answer couldn't have been otherwise; he shrugged his shoulders, considered his role fulfilled.

"Slave!" I shouted then. "Tell them to free at once the girl they have prisoner."

There was an exchange of shouted words in an unknown language between the slave and a group of Moors standing apart and surrounding the cart to which Clelia was lashed. The dialogue, with harsh and guttural words, indiscernible from that distance, lasted for some time. Then the slave came back toward the city. He dragged along for a few steps and shouted, "They say they'll free the girl in exchange for all the offerings of gold and silver there are in the temples of Tarcisis." He repeated the words over and over, like someone hawking his wares, as he hobbled toward the walls again.

I ignored Maximus, who wouldn't release my arm and was calling me in a low voice: "Lucius, Lucius." I moved away a little from the battlements and sought the consensus of all the decemvirs present, looking fixedly at them one by one. They all lowered their eyes. Only Aulus was looking at me straight on, ready to do whatever I ordered.

"Lucius," Maximus was whispering frantically. "Give them what there is in the temples. I'll give the city everything I have, I'll put myself in pawn, I have friends . . ."

I called Aulus aside. In a foray we wouldn't have the slightest chance of rescuing the girl alive, and we'd put the city itself at risk. Turning over the gold of the temples was a sacrilege and a cowardly act; negotiating with the barbarians, giving them gold or silver, would represent payment of a tribute. We would all be brought up on charges of treason. The slave remained waiting there below, resting now on one foot, now on the other. I returned to the battlements. "If they want to be fed, let them hand over the girl, lay down their arms, and line up seated on the ground."

The slave made a disconsolate gesture, resigned, already calculating the parley undone. This time he didn't communicate our answer immediately. He retreated to the limit of where our arrows could reach, still dragging the cord that held him; and, near the rows of Moors now, he spoke in a low voice. There were movements and gesticulations. Twice the slave came to the middle of the terrace with other proposals and prices. Maximus, maddened, tried to take me aside to speak to him. He proposed negotiating Clelia's price privately. Paternal despair wouldn't let him see the utter futility of his words. Aulus and the decemvirs almost dragged him into the nearest tower.

"So nothing can be done?" the slave asked, with an air between insolence and indifference.

I ordered them to throw him a sword. "Free yourself and run to the gate!"

The Moors roared and grew agitated. The slave didn't pick up the blade that was gleaming in the dust at his feet. He shrugged: "It doesn't matter to me whether I die on one side or the other."

He'd made the wrong choice. The Moors killed him with spears as soon as he was within reach. They hadn't forgiven him his lack of success. Or they'd done it out of spite because of their desperate impatience.

"Catapult!" Aulus shouted after a signal from me.

From inside the wall a rough sound of creaking metal and braces arose. The thick arms of the "onager," pulled by the gathered ends of the winches, leaned back and swayed with the weight of the projectiles the attendants had slipped onto the plates.

That flurry of sinister sounds roused the Moors, who moved about with the chaotic rush of a disturbed anthill. Immediately, in the first rows, a wave ran that agitated the whole mass of barbarians, and at the crest of the wave, the cart to which Clelia was bound teetered. Several Moors positioned the cart, with its shafts in front held by a wooden framework, directly before the gates, so that their captive would be clearly visible. They began to load firewood into the cart. Each man placed a branch or two, as if he were taking part in a sacrifice, in a slow and measured way. And then a barbarian, to great cheers, ran all along the perimeter of the crowd carrying a burning torch high, as if it were a casting rod.

Aulus and those manning the "scorpion" understood my look. I saw them move and painstakingly adjust the machine, inch by inch, with furrowed brows and minute attention.

Now, clinging silently to the wall of the tower, Maximus, in suspense, was watching all the preparations: theirs and ours. It was impossible to quell the yelling on the walls now. Weapons were raised, fists shaken; roars of indignation thundered in our ears. Amid the screaming I could make out the voice of Maximus, who was calling to me: "Lucius, Lucius!"

The Moor with the torch touched off the wood. A flame burst forth at Clelia's feet, rolled along, grew smaller, disappeared, then broke out again, grew, climbed. The girl's cries made the air shudder. The arrow in the "scorpion" was aimed. The men were huddled over the machine. Before Aulus gave the order to fire, Maximus grabbed him by the arm. And it was he himself who released the lever of the machine that whistled its projectiles through the air as smoke enveloped the cart. The arrows followed one after another, still unleashed by Maximus, frantically, until the chute began to smoke. That was how poor Clelia died.

❦

Without warning, Maximus, completely undone, ran, climbed onto the parapet, and dropped over the side. At the last moment he was grabbed by someone. He struggled, suspended by his clothing, which gave way to his weight and tore but eased his fall. We thought he was unconscious, but he got up with difficulty, limping, and dragged himself shouting to the place where the sword rejected by the messenger lay. He took it in his hands and continued on, stumbling pitifully, with the weapon pointed at the Moors. At that moment everything fell silent, and the silence

189

was so heavy that far and wide we could hear the crackle of the cart in flames.

It was like a signal for a charge by the hordes. That surge of people, howling, brandishing their primitive weapons, stormed toward the walls and darkened the terrain around. From other battlements the sound of bells and the blast of trumpets broke out. The attack raged wildly in every direction, without order or logic. The catapults were vibrating and thundering with their hollow roar. Arrows and balls cut through the clamor and the clash of weapons with their whistling. In a rush against the gates, tree trunks served as battering rams; other trunks, crudely carved, were laid against the walls, and immediately swarms of barbarians were on them, trying to reach the parapets.

It was as if on a ship with high sides we were suddenly besieged by masses and masses of dark and curly waters, as when Neptune becomes enraged and calls on all the gods of the sea against poor humans.

Stones and assegais were falling on all sides. Near me a gang of barbarians appeared between the merlons. I remember very clearly that hairy head dripping with blood, a hallucinatory look in its eyes, a sword in its mouth, that emerged two steps away from me, bringing death. It was Rufus Cardilius who, before I could react, cut it off with one sure stroke.

Many of us were wounded. A stone took the crest of my helmet off. Some of our people fell from the walls. Others were brought down by projectiles and were moaning now on the path around the wall and on the pomerium.

After an hour had passed, the multitude—in the same way it had rolled up and attacked the walls with a drive that seemed overwhelming and unstoppable—flowed back. They abandoned weapons and equipment, leaving behind their tree trunks and crude devices; their war whoops devolved into sporadic cries of pain, and they retreated to a distance where our weapons could no longer do any harm.

At the bottom of the wall the bodies were heaped, some motionless and broken, others twisted in final gestures. As far as the eye could see—more scattered here, more dense there—dark patches of corpses stood out among the pools of spilled blood. At that moment, when the catapults ceased their flurry and the loud signals coming from other parts of the wall indicated the Moors' retreat, I was amazed, and I'm certain we all had the same thought, at the relative ease with which a garrison so tiny and unprepared had repelled that compact body of attackers. Among the corpses I couldn't make out that of Maximus Cantaber. No one could, despite my requests and promises.

The Moors seemed contained for now, in the distance, letting loose a series of howls and hoots, when people came to tell me that some interlopers had made it into the city by a rope near the aqueduct and were running defenseless through our streets. I saw that Rufus was already ahead of Aulus and leading a squad that leaped down the steps, weapons at the ready, and were lost in the darkness. Among those following Rufus I recognized some decemvirs, who seemed more and more to be transferring their authority and responsibilities to him.

They told me later that they'd intercepted a group of Moors who, already on their way to the forum, had been headed off and chased by defenders. Rufus' squad overcame the intruders almost without a fight, running them through with spears. The corpses were still displayed over the city gates that afternoon, hanging by their feet on the portcullis—and evoking a frenzy in the barbarian ranks.

There were still fitful attacks by the Moors, who advanced on the wall in clusters and launched sling stones or arrows. But after the collapse of the initial wave, that effort, though it obliged us to remain vigilant and sometimes to redeploy our men from one spot on the wall to another, no longer represented the earlier danger of overwhelming us.

When night fell, several bonfires were started on the enemy side, and the whole space between the city walls and the surrounding marshes was almost instantaneously ablaze with lights. Some of those lights, isolated and scattered, were coming at a zigzag toward the city. Others were joining them. But from the irregular and dispersed way they moved, we surmised that they weren't the forerunners of new attacks. The barbarians were only picking up their

191

dead. I stopped our people from putting the "scorpion" into action as the men were getting ready, almost merrily, to shoot the barbarians wandering about; and I gave instructions that no one was to shoot until there was a new order. The gathering of the corpses was beneficial for the city as it removed pestilences to the other side. All night we watched that antlike activity whose distant echoes reached us, along with strange chants to the rhythm of drums. At dawn the fields were almost clear of bodies, and the mob of Moors seemed thinned out, not so much because of the losses they'd suffered, but because for every one who remained another had left, to plunder the countryside or seek better targets farther on. The assaults against the wall were few and lacking in spirit. The Moors seemed to have opted for a prolonged siege, though no one could see what advantage they would have from it. Miserably encamped under canopies of skin, they kept on beating their drums, which echoed in the air. A waft of breeze brought us their choral songs from time to time. Otherwise, it was an extended and miserable encampment of nomads.

We cremated our dead with a minimum of ceremony. The wailing music that wavered in the distance was answered from the city by the moans of the mourners, the playing of the ceremonial flutes, and the laments of the relatives of the fallen.

On the second day, at the seventh hour, Calpurnius—with a touch of pomp—paid a visit to the walls. He was accompanied by Apitus and other decemvirs. On foot alongside him, immediately behind the lictors, was Airhan, wearing iron armor and with his helmet hanging from his belt. He carried saddlebags filled with money on his shoulders and went about distributing it to the combatants. Slaves of Calpurnius had already gone through the streets handing out alms to relatives of the dead and wounded according to the social status of each, more to the more rich and less to the less rich.

On the shoulders of his bearers, Calpurnius rose up the steps of the wall and, before peering out, waited for me and Aulus to come and greet him. Someone had placed a helmet on his head, which, in contrast to his purple-hemmed toga, gave him a singularly ridiculous look. He slowly contemplated the encampment of the Moors, made some disdainful comments about their poverty, and directed a few bland words of congratulation to me. Then, without transition and without changing his tone of voice, he asked, "What about the hero, where is he? Show me the hero."

Aulus and I looked at each other. Only when I noticed the triumphant attitude of the decemvirs did I understand that he was referring to Rufus Cardilius. Apitus was already leading Rufus by an arm, but the freedman pretended embarrassment and resisted. He gave the senator a deep bow. The square iron plate that he wore over his chest dropped down and covered his tunic.

"Rufus Glycinius Cardilius," Calpurnius proclaimed in a booming voice. "In due time and with the proper ceremonies, Rome will know how to pay you the homage you have a right to. Permit me, however, right now and with the authorization of the duumvir here present, to make you the offering of a modest gift, not at all proportionate to your deeds, but that signifies the appreciation you deserve."

Airhan brought out a basin of gilded silver decorated with a relief of Silenuses. Rufus hugged it to his chest with feigned bewilderment.

"As for you, Aulus Manlius, you too will not be forgotten for the self-abnegation you have shown."

Aulus blushed and averted his eyes. Calpurnius gave the helmet back to its owner and went down the steps on the shoulders of his men. There were cheers. The fable was over. We returned to our posts.

<hr/>

During all that time when the populace was active and visible, whether backing up the combatants or loading the machine or tending the wounded and weeping for the dead or urging our people on or cursing the enemy or offering their chests to barrages and attacks or helping in a small way in the rear guard or sacrificing in the temples or simply affirming their Romanness through the daily routine of movements, words, and gestures against the threat that wished to violate it—during all that time, Iunia hadn't appeared. Not even to shed a tear over the sight of her sister's charred body or to grieve over the slaughtered remains of her father.

I hesitated a long time before going to a man who hadn't abandoned the walls since the first Moorish attack, but who, deliberately or by chance, had always kept a slight distance away from me. A young man, probably his son, was fighting beside him, helping him. A wide board the man had tied on with a length of cord served him as a shield. In his hand he held a dagger. The son had nothing. That man, in situations of the gravest peril, with the tumult all around, had wielded his dagger. In moments of rest he stood guard like the others. He celebrated victories, slashed about with his short weapon during attacks, roared when it was time to roar, moaned in bad moments. He had a streak of blood on his scalp from an arrow, but I never saw him leave the walls to have it treated.

I wasn't sure at first that I recognized him, nor was there an appropriate moment to go over to him. But with the passage of time and after several glances I realized that he was one of those taking part in the ceremony I'd come upon in Maximus' garden. I took my first chance to speak to him: "What's this, Christian? Have your comrades abandoned you, or have you abandoned them?"

The man, who'd pretended not to have seen my approach and who at the sound of my steps had leaned against the wall, looking out, turned in mock surprise. He seemed suddenly afraid that the dagger in his hand might be considered a sign of disrespect, and he tried clumsily to hang the weapon on his belt. His chubby face, stained with blood and grime, blushed. Then he began to speak, hurriedly: "They stayed behind to pray, duumvir. I . . . I couldn't. God forgive me. For better or for worse, my place is here, alongside the others."

"What's your name?"

"Squila, duumvir!"

"Where are the other Christians?"

"Please, duumvir, don't make me tell you. You know." At once, very anxious, he grasped my cloak and then immediately withdrew his hand, regretting his boldness. "I don't believe, duumvir, I can't believe that God's intention is to wipe out this city, or that those miserable people out there are His instrument. The will of God, I think, to my humble understanding, would be to preserve what

194

men have built by using the intelligence He gave them, not the opposite. The divine citadel isn't to be built on ruins. That's the way I see it, duumvir. Besides that . . ." He got closer and whispered; "They adore images, statuettes. I'm against the worship of images."

"Where's Iunia Cantaber?" I asked.

The man went mute with fright. I came to my senses and went away.

XV

A STRANGE CALM had taken over the Moorish encampments outside Tarcisis. From the walls we watched the people going from tent to tent, carts and horses moving about, confused clusters here and there, the domestic activities of hauling water and cooking something or other—we even saw arguments and altercations. They didn't seem to evince any interest at all, now, in the city; they simply stayed put. The horde was still too large, however, for us even to consider trying to wipe them out with a sortie.

With the Moors hunkered down like that, Tarcisis grew accustomed to the situation; the city settled in for a siege visible only at a distance, quite beyond its defenses. The aqueduct was intact; the barbarians hadn't been interested in cutting off our water supply. There were wells and cisterns in sufficient number, and there was no lack of food for a lengthy siege, even by an enemy more skilled and disciplined than the one that faced us. With the passage of time, routine took over. The barbarians came to represent less a threat of destruction than an inconvenience, as though a flood or an unseasonable snowfall had cut off access to the city. The rounds of guard on the walls followed each other according to schedule and without anything new. Life inside Tarcisis resumed up its ordinary course. Even the market reopened. Temples filled up. Business at the praetorium went on as usual. There was even a litigant who came to protest formally when he found the court closed.

And just as the circulation in the bedouin camp looked like the activity that would be ordinary in a camp of nomads that extended to the horizon, so, too, daily life within Tarcisis conformed to the routine of any provincial municipality. There were two abnormal normalities gaping at each other.

Little by little, we began to realize that our resistance to the great invading swarm of barbarians, which at the time seemed for the participants nothing but fleeting moments of whirlwind, confusion, noise, blood, bewilderment, could now, as we pondered it with a coolness and circumspection the maelstrom of events had not allowed before, be viewed as a heroic feat of war. And, separating the essential from the secondary—which were the personal, diffuse, and quite subjective impressions of each man present—it turned out that Tarcisis' chief savior, whether for his readiness to rush to the points of greatest danger or the resolute will with which he faced enemy strikes, manipulated his weapons, put his intelligence to the foresight, tactics, and cunning that make a military leader, was Rufus Glycinius Cardilius. The others would give way respectfully when he strode onto the walls; they bowed when they addressed him in a low voice; they hung laurel branches over the door of his tavern; they spoke of him with rapture, adding imagined deeds to his proven acts, raising the brave man to hero, the hero to demigod.

When Aulus watched him pass, my centurion's features almost softened now, and it wasn't difficult to perceive the admiration that was increasing hour by hour. At the start of the siege Aulus had gone so far as to suggest, to my horror, in a crude and not too discreet way, that it would be easy to take Rufus' life, making it look like an accident or seizing any chance that might come along. At that time I had to appear extremely severe with Aulus. But now it looked as if he'd forgotten his former hatred of Rufus. He even got to the point of acceding to his wishes and looks.

At the end of the day—which had passed calmly and without any incident except for the shouting of the prisoner Arsenna, who, driven by his wish to take part in the city's defense, almost assaulted his jailer—two men came in running, panting, asking me to hurry to Maximus Cantaber's house, where there was trouble.

I ran with Aulus and some armed men. A crowd, composed largely of women, was milling about in the gardens in a threatening way. There was shouting on all sides. It seemed that the people of the house were inside with Iunia while outside the rabble was taunting and molesting them. I heard stones bounce off the walls of the house, and in the light of the torches I caught, here and there, the reflection of weapons. Some of the men in the crowd were still carrying their shields. They moved aside when I arrived, but they kept on shouting. It seemed as if my presence was making the riot louder and more compact.

I don't think those inside saw me. I have to judge it a coincidence that the doors of the house opened when I drew near. The crowd fell back with a hostile murmur. Iunia, dressed in white, appeared, surrounded by a group of slave women who were holding up lamps. Behind, like a theatrical chorus, in two or three rows, came Milquion and some others.

"Witch! Father-killer!"

Almost at my side, the voice of Rufus rose up over the shrieking and brought on a silence of curiosity. Iunia looked toward him and remained motionless, her arms folded. In the reddish light that made his white tunic stand out and the metal plate over his chest sparkle when he touched it, I noticed that Rufus had glanced at me out of the corner of his eye. He knew I was there, but he ignored me and didn't restrain himself from speaking in a sonorous voice with the tone of an orator: "You, Iunia Cantaber, are responsible for the deaths of your father and your sister! You wanted the spirit of the city to be offended! You brought down curses and misfortune! You brought on the enemy! You poison the air and hearts! You must answer before the people!"

Iunia limited herself to saying, in a low voice but in a way that could be heard all around, "Get out of my garden, tavernkeeper!"

A whispering was gradually growing louder, rumbling and spreading like a wave. The mob became excited once more and began to chant rhythmically, "Witch! Witch!"

I grabbed one of the men accompanying me by the arm, and it was Squila, the Christian who'd chosen to fight. He was watching everything, armed, his mouth open and his eyes wandering about, as if he was unsure which side to take. I whispered very sternly in his ear, "Go to the wall and sound the alarm!" And, since he hesitated, "Now!"

Only then, after my show of impatience, did Rufus give signs of noticing me. He gave me a slight nod, raised an arm, and, when the crowd didn't fall silent, he took a shield from someone close by and pounded the leather repeatedly with his fist.

"Listen! Everybody listen! The duumvir has deigned to be present! And before the magistrate those accused of treason to the city, and of other felonies that have already been brought up at the praetorium, are lined up. None of the men you see in front of you, free, freed, or slave, appeared at the walls or helped in the defense of the city. Iunia Cantaber instigated this treason. See, the magistrate has certainly come to make sure that justice is done, as his duty demands! Let us allow the magistrate to proceed."

Rufus approached me, step by step. Someone brought over a torch. In the coppery light his features took on a respectful expression when he arrived beside me and whispered, in an almost friendly way, "I've done everything possible to hold them back, Lucius Valerius. It's good that you got here. You can see how discontented the people are. I don't know if you'll be able, all by yourself, to stop them from taking the law into their own hands."

In the meantime Aulus placed the men in his escort in a cordon separating the crowd from the people with Iunia. The deployment of the armed men brought on jeers and howls. Spears were raised; clumps of earth were thrown. Aulus placed his good hand on the hilt of his sword and looked my way. But then the voice of Iunia, who pressed to the front of her group, could be heard:

"There are no weapons among us! What counts is the word, not weapons."

Her words evoked a crude hooting. The mob grew tighter; fists were lifted, torches waved; Aulus' men raised their shields.

"Do you hear, Lucius? Do you see, Lucius?"

Beside me, speaking into my ear in a familiar way, Rufus seemed to be hinting some sense of complicity. He dared address me by my praenomen. And when the tumult grew and the catcalls became angrier, he jumped forward and stood beside Aulus, his open hand in the air: "Have some respect for the magistrate, who is among us!"

Iunia, imperturbable, answered him as if she were speaking to one of her slaves: "How dare you, tavernkeeper! This is my father's house. It seems that there are those who consent to your disturbing the peace of my home. Not I! Off with you, all of you, out of here!"

"What we don't understand is why you are still free! Does Rome ,assent to its own decay? Who will answer before the Senate?" It wasn't Rufus who was speaking this time. It was that Domitius Primitivus, his supernumerary in the candidacy for aedile. And he aroused a growing chorus of curses. I was the one being accused now. The reaction was such that I felt obliged to speak. I let Aulus' men push back the most agitated, and I improvised a speech.

I praised the valor with which the inhabitants of Tarcisis had defended their city, valor that was to be put to the test many times, because the barbarians were still in view in dense packs and so unpredictable that there was no guarantee they wouldn't attack again, catching us unawares. It was against the Moors that our vigilance and vigor should be turned first. Once that danger was removed, we could turn to internal dissensions in conformity with custom, the law, and the Senate and the People.

I was trying to gain time, anxious for them to ring the tocsin, which I was counting on to disperse the gathering as it grew more and more menacing. But the mob dared to interrupt me. Under the cover of darkness, several voices rose up: "How can we be safe on the walls if the city's ruin is being plotted behind us?"

"The enemy inside is worse than the one outside."

"You speak well, but aren't you going to do anything, duumvir?"

The hue and cry among the multitude broke out again, rising. The words were mixed, some coarser, some more brutal. They wanted to make prisoners of us, they wanted us dead, they wanted us handed over to the barbarians, they wanted us hanging from the walls.

Rufus, next to me, his arms outstretched, pretended to pacify the crowd. But it wasn't difficult to discern, even in the uncertain light of the torches, his look of triumph. In a show of solidarity, he muttered, "It's getting ugly, duumvir."

Then he began bellowing for them to listen. They all knew him, they'd seen how he put everything aside to defend the city, they all knew his readiness as a responsible citizen to contribute his wealth and his intelligence for the public good. He wouldn't permit any lack of respect for the duumvir or the magistrates of Tarcisis. The men and women you see there, the celebrants of abominable mysteries even while the city was being besieged, had already been properly accused by him and would soon answer in a trial. Did they want justice? Then justice would be done! In the meantime, he humbly asked the duumvir to place the accused under protection from the understandable agitation of the people.

Rufus was going to go on, but the alarm bell rang. The crowd stirred, confusion grew, and men began to run with the same volatile energy of a moment before. Rufus disappeared from beside me. I quickly explained to Aulus the expedient that had saved me, and I don't think he agreed with the idea. But if the majority of the men were running off with their weapons and shields, the women remained, and, drawn by all the screeching and haranguing, more had joined them. So that my ploy of the alarm signal, which hadn't foreseen that female torrent, ended up being a very dubious success.

What it meant was that the turn of the maenads, the Harpies, and the Furies had arrived. It seemed that all of the women of Tarcisis, from the highest to the lowest estate, were gathering in that garden and insistently insulting and attacking the Christians. Iunia, quite serene, was the target of the most vulgar epithets. Obscene verses could be heard. More than once the men of my small escort had to use shields and lances to hold back the bustle of women that contained in its front ranks the scum from the city's foulest streets.

"What shall I do with them?" Aulus asked me, referring to the Christians.

I couldn't leave those people at the mercy of the rabble, nor could I let them disperse through the city. In that atmosphere of aroused spirits I was running the risk of persecutions, deaths, riots in every neighborhood. I had to give the inevitable order: "Put them in the jail in the praetorium."

I went over to Iunia, who was holding herself very stiff and wouldn't budge from the spot her slave women were lighting up. The hooting and execrations redoubled. The situation in which we found ourselves had become laughable and degrading. "Come to my house, Iunia. Aulus will stand guard over the people under your protection!"

"Do you mean you're really going to arrest them?"

"Do I have any other solution?"

"No? Then I'm going to jail too."

"I'm not going to put the daughter of Maximus Cantaber in a cell."

Iunia turned her back, called Milquion and his followers over, and told them the pagans planned to separate them, but that she wouldn't consent to it. At a gesture from Iunia they all clasped hands and began to intone a chant, which roused the ire of the women around them even more and accentuated my feeling of discomfort and, above all, ridicule.

We went down the street to the forum with the women of Tarcisis trooping behind us, insulting us in the most uncouth and exuberant way. And the more they shouted and jeered, the louder the Christians chanted their psalms. I saw Iunia, walking beside me, head up, singing at the top of her lungs with apparent joy, not paying the slightest attention to me. As had happened before, I was being overcome by a feeling of rancor that I tried to master at all costs. Especially because in her ecstasy Iunia was dropping back, encouraging her coreligionists, without even passing her eyes over mine. There I was, the city's supreme magistrate, reduced to shielding a cult from storms of indignant women at night in Tarcisis, which was surrounded by an enemy. And the blame, without any doubt, belonged to Iunia, who seemed always to enjoy acting in a way calculated to cause me the most trouble.

When we reached the praetorium, as the door of the corridor to the dungeons was opened, Iunia tried—amid an explosion of joy on the part of the women around us—to slip in among the first group. I had to get ahead of her, blocking her way with my arm. Aulus understood my intention and stationed himself between her and the Christians, who were entering, still intoning their repetitive verses. It was necessary to use a little force to restrain Iunia when the iron door closed behind the last man. The sounds of the psalm were lost down the corridor. Only then did Iunia stop singing and struggling. I allowed her to push free. Aulus' guards were patiently holding back the women, who were still lingering, silent now.

"I'm not going to let you stay in a cell. Remember who you are."

"I'm no more than they."

"Come to my house, Iunia."

"Duumvir, if you take me to your house by force, you should know that I won't eat, I won't drink, I'll scream all the time, and you'll be sorry for your despotism."

"Come, Iunia."

"If you make me, I'll resist until they kill me."

"Nobody's going to kill anybody, Iunia!"

"I dare you!"

Her challenge rang through the forum. The torches that were moving away, providing glimpses of the stone gestures of the statues here and there, halted. I pushed the man who was lighting the entrance away so that eyes wouldn't fall on Iunia and make our dispute all the more painful because of public leering.

Iunia was leaning against the doorjamb with her hands crossed over her breast, bending slightly forward. Relying on her defensive position, she seemed ready to resist any force that might be brought to bear—which she seemed to imagine might be terrible, but which was made up only of me. I sensed how vulnerable she was, and I felt sorry for her. I got the sudden impulse to hold her to my chest. But without any transition I went back to detesting her when, immediately thereupon, in a voice trembling with rage, she threw a grand phrase out at me: "No matter what you do, you won't destroy us, duumvir!"

"Come, Iunia, please!"

"You have no right to separate me from my brothers and sisters! I want to be put in jail!"

And she pressed more tightly against the door, as if under attack, as if ready to resist a threat that was only evident in her own determination and demeanor. I waited until the receding lights passed through the forum and were lost around the corner. When it seemed that the crowd had dispersed and there was nothing more to be seen or heard, I tried again to persuade Iunia to come out of the doorway. I spoke to her softly and affably, the way one cajoles a child; and Iunia replied in monosyllables, with the stubborn obstinacy of a child. I should let her go in, or she'd stay right there. Let her stay, then! I ordered one of the men to remain close by with a light, and, accompanied by Aulus, I headed for the walls without a glance behind.

I can't remember what Aulus said to me on the way, because the fury and the feeling of absurdity that had overcome me were so strong that I wasn't aware of anything. And it was with my mind still fuddled that I vaguely heard someone saying how the Moors, after the sounding of the alarm, had appeared beside the walls in groups and that there was a commotion and an exchange of arrows and stones.

There were no wounded on our side, and the bedouins didn't seem to have sustained any major losses in their disorderly foray. Off in the distance, the Moorish encampments once more took on their calm of dying bonfires and dozing tents. I took a turn about the city, first by the roundabout path, then by the pomerium. There was nothing new. Men were sleeping beside the turrets. The shifts at watch changed according to schedule. From time to time I felt my pace was too hurried, so I forced myself to slow down, to go into a tower here and there, wake up the men, ask the sentries for news, peer out at the enemy terrain in order to offset the urge my body had to lead me back to Iunia. I looked and didn't see anything. I spoke with this one and that one and didn't hear anything. I roused a sleeping sentry, and I don't even know what he said.

Hours later I was able to be alone. I went to the forum in the dark. Under the propylaea of the temple of Jupiter, hidden in the shadows, I couldn't resist spying on the basilica. On one side was the soldier, almost asleep, leaning on his lance under the now half-consumed torch that was casting its glow on Iunia. I could make out her hazy figure, bent over, hands in her lap, sitting on the doorstep. I crept up slowly. Could she be sleeping?

Iunia put out one hand, pulled up her veil and arranged it about her body. Then she crossed her arms. She lifted her eyes and lowered her head again. I withstood the temptation to make an appearance before her once more. I had the feeling that once she noticed me, Iunia would clench her fists and, on guard, would resume her struggle against this disinterested opponent whom she, in her proselyte's imagination, seemed to have elevated to the status of a terrifying monster. But I couldn't let the day dawn with the daughter of Maximus Cantaber shivering in a doorway of the praetorium.

⚬═══✦═══⚬

Mara, when she was awakened, gave me her usual smile. She must have found it peculiar that I, impulsively and in a somewhat addled way, was telling her more about Iunia Cantaber than about the siege. Mara's smile was fading, and without my having asked her, she understood what she had to do.

In a short while, wrapped in a cloak and accompanied by a pair of slaves, she went down the street toward the forum. She was going to talk to Iunia and try to prevail upon her to take shelter in our house. I was unable to wait in the loneliness of the atrium; it wasn't long before, all alone and disguised by the darkness, I followed the slave's light and witnessed, from a distance, Mara's meeting with Iunia.

Mara exchanged a few words with the soldier on guard, and he withdrew a few paces. Iunia got up and let Mara kiss her on the cheek. Mara was talking now, and Iunia was crossing her arms. Then Mara delicately took Iunia by the arm, and Iunia gently freed herself. It was Iunia's turn to speak. Symbolically, one of her hands rested against the iron door. The other was opening and closing slowly in Mara's direction. The conversation was long. From what I could make out from the pantomime, Mara's efforts were of no avail. She shrugged her shoulders, ran her hand over Iunia's hair in a light caress, and went off on her way home, where I would find her a few moments later. "I did what I could."

"I know, Mara."

"You know?"

Mara folded her cloak over her arm, sighed, and went to her room. I lighted her way myself. She sat down on her bed and finally looked at me. "What are you going to do?"

I told her I'd witnessed the conversation from a distance and that I'd surmised her failure through the gestures. I was ready to order Iunia escorted—against her will, and using force if necessary—to the Cantaber house, to be held there under guard even if it cost me the use of a few men. Mara dissuaded me very tactfully. It seemed more sensible, she said, to let Iunia have her way: have it explained to her that she wasn't a prisoner, that she could wander through the praetorium at will. The duumvir would be showing empathy for Iunia's affection for her slaves and for her compassionate spirit, and he would allow her to prolong her visit for as long as she wished. That, in Mara's opinion, would get rid of any basis for Iunia's aggressive behavior, and it would let me appraise the city's state of mind and give some thought to the Christians' fate.

"How did you find her, Mara?"

"What difference does that make?"

I decided to proceed as Mara had advised. I didn't even look at Iunia Cantaber when I ordered the attendants to open the door to the cells, and let her go in. She must have looked exultant, radiant, in spite of her weariness. I didn't see. I made it clear to the workers in the praetorium that Iunia's status was that of a visitor to the prison, and I did so without speaking to her, but in such a way that she would hear quite distinctly.

When I returned home, without having exchanged a single word or look with Iunia, the sky was already brightening, and the wife of the potter on my street was putting her vessels out on the sidewalk. Mara pretended to be asleep.

XVI

I WAS JUST ABOUT to leave
when I was told that fire was already climbing over the roof of the
Cantabers' house. One of Rufus' slave women had given the alarm.
The flames were rising high. A human chain was futilely passing
buckets of water, which, as it struck the hot walls, seemed to give
more life to the flames and smoke. They'd managed to free some of
the animals. Clelia's pony was grazing nearby, indifferent to the
blaze that was lighting it up from a distance. An empty chest made
of precious wood, seared on the corners, lay wide open and abandoned, pillaged perhaps. It was useless to go on wasting water; to
me, it seemed more important to keep the flames from spreading
to the garden and the trees and to keep the wind from carrying
sparks into the neighborhood. Hoes, picks, and axes were more effective than the pails of water.

It wasn't long before the roof caved in with a roar of sparks and
flames, taking along one of the walls. The beautiful golden mansion
of the Cantabers and all its treasures were scorched and melted
now. And overseeing the work, his tunic raised, his legs covered
with mud, was Rufus Cardilius, making a show of his efforts.

I was afraid the sight of the fire might rouse the enemy to bold
action, but from what I was told, the barbarians were gathering in

large curious groups to observe the blaze, which, burning on one of Tarcisis' highest points, was easily visible from outside the walls. No hostile movements against the city were noted. The hordes remained there in wonder, far out of catapult range—evidence that immediately defused any suspicion that the fire had been the work of raiders.

Rufus was running past me barefoot, an ax in hand, barking orders—showing off with rhythmic shouts and energetic dash. He pretended not to notice me, turned his back as if the agitation of the moment had clouded his vision. He monopolized all attention, took on the air of command even though I was in charge. I grew suspicious that Rufus Cardilius was not entirely unconnected to the fire. Now he was sweating from his exertions, dirtying his feet in the mud and ash, outdoing himself with verve and shouted orders. He'd probably been on the lookout for the right moment, had provided concealment to one of his slaves, had supplied the oakum and the spark, had covered the arsonist's flight. And yet, as in the case of Cornelius Lucullus' death, I hadn't the slightest bit of evidence against him.

As Rufus passed, I put out my foot and made him trip and fall miserably face-first in the mud. I must confess that I now consider the act a foolish piece of revenge, unworthy of my office, and motivated by a primitive impulse that I was unable to resist. In good conscience, a reproachful gesture. But at that moment I didn't care whether anyone had seen the duumvir in that juvenile prank. The matter was never mentioned in front of me, though many opportunities would arise for blackening my character—from which I presumed that only Rufus had noticed it.

He rolled over, turned his soiled face toward me, and smiled. Then he got up limping, picked up his ax, and resumed his chores of chopping here, hammering there, and issuing orders. Not another glance, even out of the corner of his eye, did he give me.

And then Iunia was at my side. She'd come from the jail all by herself and, with her hands crossed over her breast, was observing the flames. She was breathing heavily and pursing her lips tightly in an attempt not to weep, but she couldn't hold back the tears that soon slipped down her cheek: "Everything that God has taken away from me, God had given me. Blessed be the name of the Lord."

The harsh breath of the flames, touched by the breeze and swirling now into the air, could be felt where we were standing. The fire had brushed slightly against a tree, but they immediately chopped off the branches. There seemed to be no danger of its spreading beyond the area that was cleared and dug up around the house. No one had noticed Iunia, who left now as silently as she'd appeared. I went with her, following a few steps behind. She didn't even turn around when she said to me, "I'm going back to the jail. Unless you'd rather have me stay by the door, like yesterday."

I knew there was no use insisting. I almost asked her, one more time, to try to explain why she was acting that way. But what came from my mouth was the asperity of resentment: "Well, go ahead, and be quick about it before you cause any more trouble."

I waved at the man guarding the door. The bars clanged behind Iunia.

◦═╪═◦

Different rumors, some quite fantastic, were going around concerning that fire. There were those who'd seen a flash of lightning forking across the cloudless daytime sky and striking the Cantabers' roof with a tremendous roar; there were those who'd seen three Moors sneaking into the city and lurking behind hedges with torches in their hands; there were those who had heard from a reliable source that the Christians, either in collusion with the barbarians or simply giving vent to their destructive fury, had set the blaze.

The three versions together had led the people to search out all the Christians left in the city—and those merely suspected of belonging to the sect—and dragging them, badly beaten, to the praetorium. They'd hauled slaves out of their houses without respecting the will of their masters. Disregarding the hostile bedouins who encircled the city, many abandoned the walls and went to join the mob. It seemed that every priest from every cult was shouting incitement. Battered and bloody, more than a dozen men and women were put in the jail. From the window, I recognized among them my own stableboy. I'd forgotten that I, too, was the owner of a Christian.

209

The man almost fell to his knees when they brought him to me. I couldn't even remember his name. Standing by the window, half-hidden by the curtains, I saw that the crowd was dispersing for lack of any more Christians. Several groups were chattering in the forum and seemed to have an intention of advancing toward the praetorium again. I thought then that those men and women who'd just gone into the jail owed their lives to me without knowing it. If I hadn't imprisoned Iunia's sect the day before, perhaps today Christians and others would have been slaughtered on these streets because of their incendiary acts. With the leaders in jail, the mob opted to follow the duumvir's peaceful example.

"How did you come to end up here?"

"I was on the walls by your orders, master. A group of citizens appeared and accused me of attending the meetings where Milquion divided and distributed the bread."

"Was it true?"

"Yes, master."

"What's your name?"

"Luciporus."

"Who gave you that name?"

"Your overseer."

"Were you born in my house?"

"Yes. At your villa. Your father had bought my father."

"And that business of the bread, was it so important?"

"It was the body of the god."

"You people eat the body of the god?"

"Have pity on me, master. I'm a poor slave, I don't know anything."

"What am I to do with you, Luciporus? It seems that you wanted to poison the water in our house."

I remained impassive, watching him wallow on the floor, weeping, entreating, tearing at his tunic with both hands. I felt myself in the skin of those somewhat daft learned men who observe and take notes on the behavior of animals. And his despair and lack of control, quite normal in a slave, bothered me.

"Get up immediately, and let go of me!" He'd grabbed my leg with one hand, and with the other he was holding my wrist and lavishing my hand with kisses. I saw myself obliged to push him away with disgust. "By what right does one of my slaves"—I used the current expression "boys," also part of his name—attend meetings and practice oriental religions without his master's authorization?"

"I was wrong, master, I can see that, and I ask your pardon. But . . . they tell me there are signs that the world is coming to an end, and the proof of this was the resurrection of the Master in Jerusalem. There'll be a new world . . . everything will be different."

"And just by eating the body of the god you'll be made divine too, like the Caesars?"

"After I die I don't want to go on being a slave, master. That's why I made a promise to the god. I took baptism."

That was the longest conversation I have ever had with a slave. I wanted to slip in some query about Iunia Cantaber, but it seemed a profanation to me, almost obscene, to hear the repulsive mouth of my stable slave pronounce Iunia's name. I asked him one last question and told him that it was, indeed, the final one: "Would you rather stay down below with the others or go back home? Take heed; if you go back I never want to hear any talk about you again. At the tiniest complaint I'll sell you in Vipasca for the mines."

The man stood there bewildered, looking at me for a long time with a vacant gaze. His nervous hands were opening and closing along his thighs. He was searching for the right answer. He finally decided: "I don't know what I want. Do whatever you want with me, master."

I sent him home in the company of a guard.

⟵✦⟶

I wondered how Iunia was faring down there in a cell, between grimy walls and on damp straw. What could I do so that her situation wouldn't cause me so much anguish? Was she willful? Impertinent? Obstinate? Provocative? Absolutely! But being in that tablinum—so close to Iunia and yet so far away—was becoming almost unbearable for me.

I searched through the praetorium for furniture that might be of use to her. I ordered the only two slaves who hadn't been mobilized (because of old age) to carry a cabinet, a stool, and a screen down to the dungeons. I had them buy a cot from the cabinetmaker, whom they had to track down at the walls, where he was serving at the catapults. I would ask Mara for a change of clothes.

The jailer had let Iunia leave. Our encounter at the burned-out house was proof of that. But had the man been advised that she wasn't a prisoner and could come and go as she chose? Without restrictions? Everything indicated so; but why, then, did Iunia confine herself to the jail and not put in an appearance? It was best that I assure myself personally that my orders were being carried out.

Before I was halfway down the steps, I was already questioning myself, annoyed. It was quite clear, yes, the jailer had carried out my instructions, and the furniture certainly hadn't gone astray. What anxiety, what haste, was this? What was I doing there? And it was with that musing, more a self-censure than a question, that I reached the barred door that led to the jail. The jailer, a huge, stooped rogue in a frayed tunic, came over to me reverentially. I signaled him to be silent. I didn't want the prisoners to see me. I didn't want Iunia to know I was there.

I spotted Iunia over the jailer's shoulder, perched on the stool I'd sent, leaning down and speaking softly to Arsenna. She had the board with the alphabet in her hand; and the bandit, sitting in the straw, his head near Iunia's knees, was working intently over a wax tablet. All the others were squatting in a circle around them. Suddenly Iunia dropped the board and looked toward the door. I don't know whether I managed to slip away in time. When I passed by the bars again, the screen was hiding her from my sight.

I was most displeased by that harmonious and friendly closeness of Iunia and the bandit. What probably seemed to the jailer an ideal state of order in the lock-up was for me disorder and subversion. I had a burst of fury and an urge to summon Iunia to the tablinum, to give her some advice, to recommend that she keep well away from Arsenna, who was unworthy even of her words. I could transfer the highwayman to another cell, but I didn't want the public exposure of the bandit to foment any disturbances by the window, as had already happened once.

I ended up deferring any decision until later, when I would feel less confused. I went upstairs. But what attraction could Iunia feel for Arsenna? Her interest in sending him the tablets and the stylus; her words in his favor; now that close, almost intimate proximity . . .

⊷━╪━⊶

The ruins of the Cantaber house were still smoldering. Slaves with pitchforks and hoes were raking the earth around it. I would soon have to order the place put under guard because the mob, always attracted by misfortunes and greedy to scavenge, wouldn't be long in coming to search among the ruins for any precious metals they could salvage. I tossed a handful of soil into the air in homage to the spirit of the Cantabers and also for my memories, equally laid waste by the fire.

I was walking along the path by the wall now. It was a time of war, a time to put formalities aside. I'd always been ill at ease riding about in a litter in conformity with custom in a city where destinations were almost always close by. The use of the litter required at least four slaves, not to mention the lictor and the drove of clients who felt obligated to form a retinue. It was slow. It made me impatient. What did I care about the remarks of Calpurnius and the others?

Aulus hurried toward me. "There's nothing new, Lucius Valerius!"

"How do you know there's nothing new if you're coming from inside the city?"

Surprised by my untypically captious question, Aulus just stood there. With his free hand he tightened a strap that didn't need tightening. I was sorry at once for my brusque tone, so rare in our relationship. He wasn't to blame for my state of mind or for the stupid suffering Iunia Cantaber's conduct was causing in me. I was on the point of asking his forgiveness or making some kind of friendly gesture when Aulus' worried face and embarrassment held me back. And before I could ask just what it was, Aulus hastened to explain with a rapid flow of words that he was coming back from the house of Ennius Calpurnius, who'd requested, confidentially, that my centurion keep him informed of the situation in the city.

"I hope you haven't any reason to be against it, Lucius Valerius. If I did wrong, tell me."

"No, Aulus, there's no reason for me to be against it."

Aulus saluted me, lowering his head, and started up the steps of the wall. I kept standing in the same spot, and when Aulus, halfway up, sneaked a peek back, I didn't recognize his expression.

Mara was puzzled that evening. Galla used to come every day to chat and tell her the news, but she'd missed the day before. Could she be ill?

⊙══╪══⊙

That morning the trumpets rang out happily from turret to turret. The barbarians had left, slinking off in the still of the night. As far as the eye could reach there wasn't a living soul to be seen around the walls of the city. It looked as if they'd even carried off their campfires—so clean was the terrain of any vestiges, as if it hadn't been occupied and trodden upon for days and days by that unruly mob. Through a side door beside the portcullis a few men ventured out, fearfully, slowly. They were wary of a surprise attack. Some joked that they were looking for a wooden horse. But shortly thereafter, emboldened to go farther, they climbed up rises and trees and came back with confirmation of the happy news. There were no Moors in the surrounding territory, nor was there any trace of them.

The celebrations were still mingled with signs of perplexity when two horsemen, one behind the other, appeared on the terrace opposite the gates. They'd come at a gallop from the hills, happily prodding their mounts on in a whirlwind of dust. Amid the thunderous cheers on the walls and among the throng forming outside, they seemed to take delight in a kind of circuslike display, raising their weapons in both hands and obliging their animals to make some risky turns with dizzying speed. One horseman wore a regular cavalry outfit with plumed helmet, cloak, buckler, and sword; the other was a Celtic auxiliary, bareheaded and with a red beard waving in the wind. He wore trousers that were tied at the ankles under a crude leather tunic. They were the advance scouts of the approaching VII Legion.

The gates were thrown wide open; everybody ran out to the riders in ebullient joy, and the two men quickly found themselves

214

submerged in the crowd, which was forcibly trying to honor them, touch them, offer them things. With difficulty they finally extricated themselves from those cheering them and went back at top speed. The free and easy horsemanship of those two scouts was the most beautiful spectacle anyone could have offered us at that moment.

In midafternoon the velites began trickling in. They carried small, round shields strapped casually to their backs and, in their hands, bundles of light spears. They were all waving to the citizens quite merrily and festively. They immediately began to clear terrain for their encampment at a fair distance from the gates, precisely at the spot where Clelia had died.

Someone went over to advise them that the place was ill-omened. The men hesitated, consulted, and picked up work again farther on, near the highway, clearing brush and starting fires. Hours passed before the three cohorts of Marcus Scaurus, adjutant to the imperial procurator Gaius Valius Maximianus, marched within sight of Tarcisis, standards in front, armor gleaming, in close formation—and accompanied by the sound of cymbals and fanfare. The legion's impressiveness owed more to its gleam than to its numbers, and the jubilant crowd gave way to let the soldiers pass. Many people helped the men dig trenches and drive stakes for the encampment. At the very end, after a long delay, the supply train, the pack animals, and the rear guard of auxiliaries arrived.

The cohorts, after marching in so demonstratively, to our people's delight, were settling into their quarters. The first tents were going up. It wasn't proper for me to greet the military commander before the troops were settled. I would visit him afterward, at the time stipulated by protocol, to invite him into the city.

During that interval I went to the praetorium and ordered the jailer to free Iunia and all the others except Arsenna. The atmosphere in the city was lighthearted, and the legion offered security. It wasn't likely in that climate that anyone would bother to persecute the Christians. But the attendants came to tell me that some of them didn't want to leave: Iunia because she had no place to go and because, aware of the accusation against her, she wanted to be at the disposition of the authorities; others in solidarity with

Iunia's position, or fearful, perhaps, that the prohibition of private jails would be lifted and Proserpinus would rearrest them for trial.

Most impressive in the words that the praetorium slaves transmitted to me was the complete lack of interest of those religious fanatics to the liberation of the city. While the populace was singing and celebrating, praising the rescuing legion, they kept themselves shut up in the musty obscurity of the jail, immersed in their prayers and ritual practices in a way that seemed to be the expression of a challenge, with its touch of dementia.

Should I speak to Iunia now? Go down into the prison? Summon her? Take advantage of her audience with me to expel the Christians from the basilica with lashes? And I vacillated between the pleasure I would feel at seeing Iunia again under these new circumstances and the displeasure she always created in me under any circumstances.

<hr/>

"I'm not leaving, duumvir!"

"You've got to think about rebuilding your father's house."

"My poor father's house was a monument to the pride of the pagans. God willed for it to be destroyed, a warning of what will happen to this city and to Rome."

"You have a very confiding god, who always seems to let you know just what his intentions are."

"Don't blaspheme, Lucius Valerius."

"Iunia, be reasonable."

"Duumvir, be brave."

"What will happen if I give the order to have all of you put out?"

"We'll stay by the door waiting for the people to finish us."

"Why do you defy me, Iunia? Why do you hate me so much?" This time I had managed to surprise Iunia. She frowned in a meditative silence. She remained that way for a short time, pressing her hands together—thinking of an answer.

"But you're mistaken. I don't hate you, duumvir. Try to understand that my choices have nothing to do with you personally. It's a matter of values. And what's at stake is what could be the most important thing for a human being: eternal salvation."

And that was how Iunia dealt with me, crushed me: she scorned my insignificantly subalternate position as a human; she contemned my despicable existence, squashed as I was in the colossal clash between good and evil, with eternity behind it all. While I was trying to disentangle the reasons for her stubbornness (which she called "steadfastness"), they came to tell me that the decemvirs were all waiting for me in the praetorium and that they urgently wished to speak with me. Iunia went away, I couldn't hold her back; she herself closed the door.

XVII

APITUS: WHO rejoiced at the
return of normality, proving that Rome never abandons her children;
that there should be a holiday celebrated with municipal festivities
dedicated to the Emperor and that games and sacrifices should be organized as part of them; that all doors should be decorated with
roses and laurel and a painted wooden arch be erected on the main
street; that early in the morning a delegation should go to the tent of
the tribune with greetings and expressions of Tarcisis' gratitude; that
the tribune should be formally invited to enter the city with the appropriate ceremonies, with the distinguished Ennius Calpurnius, in
his position as senator, awaiting him by the gate.

I: of course, and it was indeed a pleasure to see the decemvirs
busy with public affairs again, because an onset of awareness, even
when sparked by the sheen of weapons and inspired by the tips of
spears, is always good in the knightly order.

Apitus: differences and misunderstandings between citizens of
quality should be eliminated. He, Apitus, would forget all offenses
during this moment of rejoicing, and he hoped everyone would do
the same. And if on some day, in the heat of exaltation, he'd spoken harsh words to Lucius Valerius, he was there declaring solemnly
that he retracted them.

Others: that it was essential to reopen the baths, the court, and to resume the usual course of public life; that among the delegation of notables of Tarcisis, Rufus Glycinius Cardilius should be present because, despite his inferior origins—the privations of which only increased his merit all the more—he had shown boldness and valor that deserved some reward.

I: that I would not join any delegation in which Rufus Cardilius was included.

Apitus: with the surrounding area pacified, it was time for luminaries to be reconciled, heroes to be glorified, and traitors to be judged.

I: that I would definitely not accept Rufus Cardilius in the company!

The chorus of decemvirs became conciliatory, valuable, and understanding. Rufus Cardilius would, after all, always be the son of a freedman. He did of course have qualities of leadership, obvious military abilities, and a fortune appropriate for a decurion. But if Lucius Valerius objected . . . it wouldn't cost anything to do without his presence for now. Afterwards we could see. With regard to misunderstandings in the curia, this wasn't the moment—since it was one of general euphoria—to touch on unpleasant memories.

One of the Gobiti twins muttered bitterly that the new wall, which had cost so many sacrifices, hadn't shown itself to be of any great use during the siege. Someone else added that the ghost of Pontius Modius still hadn't been exorcised.

Before I could answer, Apitus interrupted authoritatively: those painful matters should be left for a later occasion; satisfaction over the liberation of the city shouldn't make us lose our sense of statesmanship. There were citizens and slaves in the jail in an undefined juridical status, treated, furthermore, with benevolence because of circumstances known to all. Prudence advised that those who hadn't contributed to the city's defense, and who therefore wouldn't have any part in the popular rejoicing be held under arrest until a time better suited to deliberation. He raised his hand to his mouth and cleared his throat before adding that this applied as well to the daughter of Maximus Cantaber, who, though descended from knights, hasn't shown herself worthy of privileged treatment.

"Are you suggesting that I put Maximus' daughter in a jail cell?"

"We have decided!"

I could see that it was useless to argue and ridiculous to offer any protest. Ridiculous and dangerous. We were standing in the meeting room of the praetorium beside the window that opened onto the forum. The wind, puffing up and gathering in the drapes, was allowing the rather shadowy light to illuminate the faces of the decemvirs. Seen from a distance—without the details of the sweaty brow of one, the tight lips of another, the fingers obstinately buried in the toga of a third—it might have looked like a spontaneous, informal, almost friendly gathering at the baths or under the shade of a portico. They'd come to inform me that for the moment they were forgiving me. For the moment! Hostilities were only suspended because it wasn't proper at that time for dissension to interfere with the euphoric rites. And the rites were their principal conception of Romanness. But . . . until when?

On Tarcisis' humble scale, the decemvirs' scheme—aiming to declare a truce they knew and hoped would be temporary—represented a laughable palace conspiracy. I was being coerced. I objected, "I don't feel I have the authority to keep Iunia Cantaber in jail!"

"We've discussed the matter, and it's our understanding that you have! We put her in your charge! As for the practical side, Caturus has already spoken to the centurion. Isn't that so, Caturus?"

The decemvir named Caturus, who never opened his mouth at any meeting, agreed with multiple nods of his head.

"We consulted with the senator," Apitus added, "and he was of the same opinion."

Calpurnius, of course. But . . . Aulus? Had the members of the curia questioned and convinced Aulus without my knowledge? I'd passed him a while before in the gallery. Nothing had been visible in his demeanor.

"Aulus?" I muttered, imprudently.

"Ah, yes, Aulus! So much the better that you mention him. It would be good now if the duumvir relayed the decision of the curia to the guard."

And Apitus took a few steps, drew back the curtain that closed off the tablinum room, and called for Aulus, who appeared from the other side, from the gallery that gave entry to the curia, as though he'd been hiding behind the drapes, waiting to be summoned. Very formal, he thumped his cuirass with his good fist. The two lictors entered by the curtain of the tablinum, dressed ceremonially and with the fasces on their shoulders. Standing stiffly, Aulus didn't want to face me. He stared at Apitus and awaited orders.

"Perhaps you would care to transmit the decision of the curia to our centurion."

Apitus, quite at ease, was stroking his toga with a loose, casual hand. For a brief moment the hilt of the dagger fastened to his belt glinted. Spurinna's words to Caesar came to me: "Beware the ides of March!" I must have smiled. There was an exchange of looks all around me.

"You tell him!" I replied.

"The followers of Christ are to be arrested. All of them!" Apitus put an imperious and triumphant stress on the last words.

With military gravitas, Aulus asked permission to withdraw. Apitus gave it, extending his arm graciously. But Aulus drew back for an instant. He faced me, finally, awaiting my assent. I looked down outside at the forum. Not many people. Most of the city was still milling about alongside the encampment out there, acclaiming the men of the VII Legion Gemina. When I pushed aside the curtain and turned back inside, Aulus had left.

They'd already agreed upon certain issues of protocol. The decemvirs were taking their leave one by one. I thought I heard some bantering in the gallery. Apitus remained until the end and then, with a signal, sent the lictors away. Before leaving he observed, "Order is being restored. So much the better."

<hr/>

I returned home as soon as I got rid of the edicts to be posted announcing the curia's decisions. There was no water in the baths because of the orders I'd sent to the superintendent at the start of the siege. I ordered the connection to the aqueduct reopened and the hypocaust lighted. I had trouble eating. Mara endured my silence until I asked her suddenly, without warning: "What's going on, then, with Galla? And Aulus?"

"I'd rather not have to tell you."

I took Mara's hand and squeezed it slowly. I tried to smile. *There's nothing a man can't bear* was what that gesture was trying to remind her.

"Calpurnius has seduced Aulus. He's promised him promotion to first centurion and to intercede on his behalf for admission to the knightly order. He's leaving him twenty iugera of arable land in his will."

"Was it Galla who told you this?"

"No, friend. Galla's stopped dropping by. This is what the slaves are talking about."

"And I was always praising Aulus' loyalty."

"Aulus' loyalty is still intact. Calpurnius and the others are the ones who can count on it now."

I made a surly gesture of uncontrolled fury, and a goblet rolled along the table and fell to the floor with a loud clank of dented metal. A slave woman appeared. Mara picked up the goblet and put it on the table.

"About Aulus still," she said, "it would be good for you to be aware of something, Lucius. That poet who came to the house . . . the one who fell off the aqueduct . . ."

"Cornelius Lucullus."

"Yes. He was sending poems to Galla secretly. He was asking her to meet him."

"And Galla?"

"Galla is fickle and curious."

"Do you think Aulus found out?"

"In Tarcisis everybody finds out everything. Except you, Lucius Valerius."

Mara pulled me over and hugged me.

⚜

The basilica was shrouded in an aura of thick, heavy silence. The walls were dimly lit by torches whose bluish wicks were guttering down to their tail ends. I told the half-asleep jailer not to make any noise but to bring Iunia Cantaber to me. The man went over to the door, held the bars with one hand, and with the other slowly began to work the lock. I peeked inside the cell. An odor of rotting straw and a musty heat were wafting out. In the rear, in a niche on the wall, the exhausted wick of an oil lamp was sputtering. Iunia had given the cot I'd sent her to someone else. Wrapped in a cloak, she was sleeping next to Arsenna on the straw.

Their heads were quite close; they were almost breathing into each other's face.

"Waking me up like this? Is this part of the method for reconverting me to . . . Romanness?"

The jailer had withdrawn and was sitting in a corner on a greasy hide. My slave Luciporus was waiting at a distance, beside the door that opened onto the stairs.

"Don't quibble, Iunia. Listen: you're going to escape! And I'm going to help you."

"Don't even think about it!"

Her answer was immediate, forceful, and rude. I still hadn't learned—would I ever learn?—not to be surprised by Iunia's reactions, so I was left stupefied, speechless.

"Now that I have an opportunity to be a witness of the living God and redeem my past life, Lucius, would I throw it away by fleeing?"

"You could be condemned to death, Iunia. It's such pointless madness."

"And that's just what I want. The divine Master was also condemned to death unjustly. Why should I want to save this miserable body? This false existence isn't the one that counts, Lucius Valerius."

It was the salvation of the soul, then, the ethereal life; I'd already heard that speech. Inside, next to the door, someone had tried to draw a fish on the dirty wall with some kind of grease. The incomplete sketches were visible from time to time in the dull lamplight.

"I didn't have you arrested, Iunia."

"Maybe not. I've got nothing special against you, Lucius."

"What if I were to make you come with me?"

"I'd wake up the whole city just as long as I had any breath left."

"What have I ever done to you, Iunia? Why won't you ever listen to reason from me?"

"That's foolish, duumvir. It's just that you're on the side of error. That's all."

And after a few moments during which, without moving, she witnessed my trepidation and suffering: "Is that all, Lucius?"

With a snap of her fingers she summoned the jailer.

⚬━━◆━━⚬

The cock hadn't crowed yet, and the barber was already combing my hair and trimming my beard, which he sprinkled with the spray of a mysterious perfume. The flames in the tripods had disappeared and left strange and indecisive embers. The oil in the lamps would have to be replenished. All that was coming in from outside was the whispering of the litter bearers as they got ready by the door. Mara, with the help of a slave, was pressing my toga, using irons heated on a copper brazier resting on the floor. Every fold was studied, undone and redone, with methodical skill. A coarse-bristled brush gave luster to the small band on my tunic. Mara, holding the comb, curled my beard again, dissatisfied with the barber's work. She was demanding, impatient, autocratic. The toga was picked up once, extended, folded, put on, and pressed again. Mara checked to see if my right hand could move freely, set the height at which I should hold the cloth with my left arm; and when, fretful, I finally left, she still didn't seem satisfied.

The city gates were wide open, and the lights on the legion's palisade glowed in the distance. I was puzzled, when I reached the pomerium, by the absence of any delegations—especially that of Calpurnius.

"They've already gone on, duumvir." A gatekeeper wrapped in a felt cloak came out of the guardhouse and pointed toward the camp. I gave my people orders to proceed.

That short stretch seemed quite long to me. On the shoulders of the men carrying me I passed the graves, whose stones, greeting travelers and praising the dead, were being lighted now by the wan glow grudgingly irradiated by a still-sleepy Helios. "Pink-fingered Aurora" had once more fulfilled her annunciatory task. In that narrow span of land, in sight of everyone, my friend Maximus Cantaber had perished. Over to the side, in the gorse, Iunia had buried the lost Moor one day. Next to those distant thickets, Clelia had been absurdly sacrificed.

The city behind me was slowly waking up. Cocks were crowing. I could already make out the movements of the sentries by the encampment's stockade.

I had fewer than seventy paces to go when several groups began to assemble at the camp's gate, headed out; they were as relaxed and merry as if, relieved, they were exiting a recitation. They immediately formed a boisterous procession and started toward me. In front were three lictors with purple hems on their tunics. Calpurnius' chair was swaying behind them on the shoulders of his slaves. A ray from the rising sun softly reflected off the metal tip of the staff that one of those accompanying me was carrying, and Calpurnius' gaunt hand noisily closed the curtains of his litter. Voices were suspended and expressions became serious as my retinue and the others converged.

"Keep going, don't stop!" I ordered.

We passed each other. First came Calpurnius and his complicated entourage. Following, deferentially, was Apitus, on foot at the head of the decemvirs and other knights and decurions. Then Aulus—my Aulus—with some vigilantes from the city. Finally, in his immaculate white toga, Rufus Cardilius, along with the lively mob and the swarm of slaves that always attended him.

They now looked like a procession of spirits preparing for the eternal silence of Hades. They filed past me almost at arm's length and didn't even look my way, much less greet me. I kept the curtains open, conspicuously staring at this one and that while my men continued on. Behind me, as the retinues went off, I once more heard the outburst of shouts and laughter. With foreboding I got out at the gate to the officers' quarters and identified myself.

I was received at once. The tribune appeared jovially at the door of the praetorial tent and was gracious enough to take a few steps in my direction and clasp me by the hand to lead me inside.

"So late, duumvir?"

"The sun is barely up."

"I didn't even get to bed."

Nothing about him indicated a bad night. This very young man's beard was so sparse that it was scarcely visible in the dawn light. His name was Marcus Agneius Scaurus, and—I found out later—after this mission he planned, despite his youth, to get admitted to the senatorial order and to seek the Tribunate of the Plebeians. There were precedents, and it seems that his senatorial family had had so many consuls in its ranks since the founding of the city that nothing could be denied him. And he was clever: he'd managed, in a few smiling, bland, and casual words, to sneak in a couple of rebukes.

On the other side of the rough wooden table that took up most of the tent stood a first centurion and a standard-bearer, the latter at rigid attention. From the looks Scaurus cast surreptitiously at the centurion from time to time, I could see that the subaltern's experience would be called upon, when needed, to compensate for his superior's greenness.

The formal phrases of protocol continued. He insisted that I sit down, and he settled himself elegantly beside me on a carved ivory stool that was out of keeping with the table's military austerity. He played distractedly with a small baton of command topped by a gold eagle, twirling it between his fingers. He began every sentence of greeting and thanks with the formula, "As I've already had occasion to say to the distinguished senator and the delegation from Tarcisis."

I noticed that the band on his tunic, unlike mine, dangled slackly and had no gleam. This carelessness was one more mark of distinction, showing the strip's daily use and emphasizing its provisional status—it would soon be replaced by the senatorial laticlave.

He offered me wine and explained, almost deferentially, that his mission at the head of three cohorts of the VII Legion Gemina was part of the campaign of the procurator Gaius Valius Maximianus, who at that moment must have already crossed the strait on his way to relieve Volubilis and Septem Fratres. Another column was reinforcing the garrison at Emerita. Having come from the Danube by forced marches, the XII Legion Fulminata was arriving in Africa. It wouldn't be long before the Moorish hordes were pushed into the sea, where they'd find the arms of Maximianus facing them. In a while, the young tribune observed, laughing, they'd be saying in Rome that a Moor could be bought even cheaper than a Sardinian— an allusion to the famous saying about the superabundance of slaves captured in the Sardinian campaign.

Reaching the end of that topic, he congratulated me on the defense of the city, "worthy of a Cincinnatus," and he expressed relief that my life had been saved at a propitious moment. They'd told him about the extreme valor of a freedman, whom the delegation from Tarcisis had already honored, besides, by including him in their embassy and whose name escaped him for the moment. The centurion leaned over and reminded him of the name, whispering, "Rufus Glycinius Cardilius!"

I invited Scaurus to enter the city and was prepared to give orders for him to be received with festivities, as was customary. He lamented that such, sadly, wasn't possible, as he'd also explained to the most worthy senator and the distinguished delegation. He could never enter a city in solemnity without first having obtained express authorization from Gaius Maximianus. Also, he had to clear the territory of barbarians and continue his mission to the south. Perhaps—if I didn't object, of course—he could entertain the idea of an informal visit as an ordinary individual. And, suddenly, nonchalantly, tracing the rim of his wineglass with the tip of a forefinger: "They told me the attack of the Moors was quite strong. But . . . was there any need to reduce the perimeter of the wall, to tear down houses?"

"If I hadn't ordered the wall repaired, the Moors would have got in."

"Obviously. Oh, it's always easy afterward to criticize a person who had the courage to make difficult decisions at the right time."

He raised his glass to me and smiled indulgently. And I understood that Calpurnius and the others—contrary to what I'd thought—hadn't made their visit a little before mine. They'd kept the tribune company the whole night through. They'd defamed me, made complaints. Marcus Scaurus, commander of the military force on campaign, now constituted the highest authority in the region. The improvised meeting of the night before, arranged by the decemvirs, also had had the objective of keeping me away while they worked to influence the young man.

But the worst was yet to come. The tribune called the centurion with a flick of his ivory baton, whispered something in his ear, and smiled at me. The centurion left. Scaurus was looking at me now very cheerfully, his chin resting on his fist. I'd already noticed that this young man's words—whatever they might be—never corresponded to what he was really thinking. My countrymen also cultivated that art, if indeed in a less skillful and less genteel way.

"It seems there's going to be an interesting spectacle in your city shortly."

I remembered Arsenna. But I didn't say anything and sat there in mute interrogation.

"The Christians are going on trial, aren't they?"

"It doesn't seem to me that a trial would be a spectacle."

"Don't you think so? Won't the people attend it? Won't they be making bets? Won't there be claques and cheering? Won't there be comments in the forum? Won't it be the dominant topic of speculation? Couldn't it be the forerunner of a second act, that of torture and executions? Won't the plebs exult in it and be contented and pleased in that way?"

"I limit myself to administering justice in the name of the Senate and of the People."

"Of course, duumvir. I can only congratulate you. And immediately after that, you'll have the privilege of offering the people the death agony of a contemptible bandit. How lucky you are! Have you seduced Fortuna? Did you know that one of my grandparents was kidnapped by thieves in the time of Trajan?"

Before I could find words to reply amid the perturbation this had caused, Scaurus blithely changed the subject and went on without transition to praise his troops and the healthful military life. Then he yawned discreetly, hiding his mouth with the palm of his hand.

I don't know by what trick, but the first centurion appeared in the tent again, very solicitous, and I could see that it was time for me to leave.

XVIII

I COULD HAVE summoned the decemvirs one by one and demanded explanations ... if they deigned to appear, which was doubtful; and they would always back themselves up with the wishes of the senator: Calpurnius had decided to visit the encampment as soon as night came on. Who would dare go against an order from Calpurnius? If I, in retaliation, were to seek out the senator at home now, he probably wouldn't let me in. Or, condescending to receive me, he would say he'd decided on that the night before because, being who he was, he'd felt like it.

And Aulus? Aulus had a look of complete innocence about him. He'd hastened to accompany a delegation from the city—presided over by a senator—to greet the commander of the cohorts. They'd ordered him: "Come with us, bring an escort!" How could he have refused? In his current state, and after the unsettling news I'd heard about him, I would spare myself the pain of listening to that excuse. He told me nothing when, crisp and proper, he came to request the password for the night. Was he obliged to say anything? Maybe at the time he didn't know ...

I couldn't attest to what course the long nocturnal conversation in the praetorial tent had taken as concerned events in the city and the Empire, but it wasn't hard to guess. After the customary praises and flattery, I imagined, Calpurnius had voiced the first anxieties, Apitus had given details, Rufus, the hero, had provided color, with Calpurnius synthesizing and letting himself doze off from time to time. Aulus would have remained silent, and Scaurus, smiling, perfumed, and relaxed, would have reserved judgment until he could discuss the part pertinent to him with the centurion, his counselor, later on.

Could Calpurnius have suggested, feigning distress and a heavy heart, that I, despite being worthy of all praise, had let myself be misled by a jealous hatred of Pontius Modius? And that later I'd inexplicably fallen under the spell of the Christian Iunia Cantaber? And that I'd been derelict in my duties, softened by impulses that, reducing my principles to a shambles, went against my very will? Perhaps Calpurnius hadn't expressed himself in such a frank and outspoken way. It was more his manner to insinuate—a phrase here, a phrase there, heaping concern on top of concern—until, gradually, the callow and inexperienced Scaurus would grow alarmed.

I set about reviewing my own case coldly, as if sitting in judgment of myself. A procedural question: had I indeed been bewitched by Iunia? I went over all my encounters with her, acknowledging the strange and subtle pleasure I got from them, even though most of the time my words and attitudes had seemed ungentle and distasteful to me, even though I had been constantly testing the limits of my self-control as I tried to choke back my fury. It was true that Iunia attracted me, even against my will, like those magical crags that loom loftily over the sea and call ships to them, smashing their hulls against the rocks.

But considering Iunia's personality—so fragile and at the same time so firm, so ingenuous and so authoritative, so sure of herself and so contradictory—remembering her ways of looking at a person, the calm and tranquility of her manner on one side, the hauteur and challenging hardness on the other, it was impossible for me to accept that she could call upon any occult powers. In any case, why would she have wanted to ensorcell me—a simple magistrate, tied to the law, the Governor, and the Senate—and not

Calpurnius, Apitus, Rufus, or Aulus (even her own father or her sister Clelia, neither of whom she ever succeeded in convincing of a single word of her beliefs?). And Iunia hadn't brought on any certainties in me, but, rather, perplexities . . . not so much concerning the propositions of her religion, full of fantasies and intricate arcana like any other, but with regard to Iunia herself.

She spoke to me as an equal; she always treated Rufus with the superciliousness of the daughter of a knight; and I could even swear that the pilgrim Milquion, her putative supervisor, was, alongside Iunia, more the one being supervised.

She believed, with unwise firmness and excessive enthusiasm perhaps, in that god, that doctrine, and those prophets. But most of the city's men and women believe in even more absurd beings and miracles. Some worship the same animals as the Egyptians; the Jews wear special sandals on the seventh day to stop them from walking more steps than their strange law prescribes. Every religion lays down the most surprising prohibitions regarding food. Once I had to suppress the wish of the priests of Cybele to have themselves castrated—after I consulted the decurial judges, it became clear that mutilation was incompatible with the customs of Lusitania, if not of Rome. Every afternoon I watch the old slave women pass as they leave their masters' houses, kettles in hand, to oil and perfume the statues of Apollo.

And it isn't just the ignorant plebeians who cling to these cults, these superstitions, and these practices. Pontius told me once that every year on the beaches of Byblos, always at the same season, a living head arrives, drawn by the waves from Egypt, to pay homage to the Syrian goddess. He guaranteed that his physician had seen it. Pontius was a decemvir, well-read in Epictetus and Metrodorus, one who devoured Cicero and Licinius Calvus, and yet he let himself believe in that seagoing cranium . . . And wasn't it true that in Rome itself Senator Publius Mummius was the patron of the charlatan Alexander of Abonuteichos, a worshipper of Glycon, the serpent with a human face? Why not? I myself sometimes accept fantasies that seem unreasonable and even silly to others. The only person I know who doesn't allow herself any illusions is Mara. But Mara is so exceptional . . .

Everybody knows that the Christians are experts at drawing evil spirits out of people. I saw with my own eyes the instance I related before. In Judaea, Christ had the reputation of a great magician, one of the Egyptian school, which produced so many marvels and miracles. Maybe Milquion, also an exorciser of spirits, had learned some of those arts and was using them to hold Iunia in thrall. But this wasn't easy to believe when you saw them side by side.

I had no reason to think that Iunia could have bewitched me. Did she dominate my thoughts all the time? But it was natural for me to be concerned about her. She was the daughter of Maximus. She was a widow. She was vulnerable. She needed protection, understanding. And now she was even more exposed and surrounded by threats. My interest originated, finally, not in oriental enchantments but in my sense of responsibility, my duty as magistrate, citizen, friend.

Could that be it?

That's how my thoughts were drifting as, taking long strides, I paced about the meeting room of the praetorium. By thinking about Iunia I was quelling the temptation to go down to the jail to visit her once more. What for? My instincts might have wanted to lead me there, but my reason didn't see any sense in the visit. After all, I couldn't tell her anything I hadn't told her already . . . and what I'd heard would certainly not be pleasing. I reviewed and rejected all the pretexts, some of them flimsy, that came to mind. But they wouldn't stop infiltrating my mind in a most pressing, most insidious, most subtle way. Bewitched, I?

She shouldn't have been in that squalid, stinking jail in close contact with a bandit and worthless trash. From the looks of it, Iunia's religion had great esteem for those outside Romanness—founded, as it had been, by a barbarian, and on top of that, by one who'd been crucified. Out of that came the gentleness with which she treated Arsenna, contrasting greatly with the way she addressed her servants or a tradesman like Rufus Cardilius. But might not Arsenna be trying to milk some advantage out of the fact that he was imprisoned in the company of the daughter of a knight? That mildness of gesture; that honeyed look; that closeness, sleeping on straw almost breath to breath. I didn't stop to reflect before giving the order: "Put Arsenna in the stocks!"

When, moments later, they came to tell me that Iunia Cantaber wanted to talk to me, I almost relented. I took a few steps alongside the lictor. But the reason behind the request immediately occurred to me. Iunia, of course, wanted to keep me from holding Arsenna in chains. She was trying to intercede for the bandit. I turned back, dismissed the lictor.

It didn't take me long to reconsider, and I revoked the order. But I'd succeeded in resisting the urge to see Iunia, a forbearance that gave me some painful inner satisfaction.

⚬━✦━⚬

I tried to write to the Emperor that morning. For the first time in ten years I would make use of the privilege he'd granted me. Perhaps Marcus Aurelius didn't remember, and I would have to begin by reminding him. But how?

"From Lucius Valerius Quintius, duumvir, magistrate of the law in Fortunata Iulia Tarcisis, Lusitania, to Marcus Aurelius Antoninus, Emperor, in Rome" . . . several times I sketched out the heading of a letter on the wax, and just as many times rubbed it out. Iunia was imprisoned two floors below me. I could imagine her sitting quietly in the weak light from the window. Furious with me? Having forgotten me already? What could she be doing now? How might she have taken the news that I wouldn't see her? How had she reacted to the cancellation of Arsenna's torture? What could she be thinking about?

I went down the stairs, yes, but not to approach Iunia. To flee from her. I ran home in a frenzy, almost without an escort. There was no possibility of my concentrating in the praetorium. The noise of the forum would reach me in aggressive waves now. I thought I was hearing moans and chants from the floors below; even the whispering of the slaves in the archive room bothered and distracted me now.

⚬━✦━⚬

Mara couldn't help being bewildered by the haste with which I went to the tablinum and sat down at the table without changing my clothes. But she knew enough to remain silent and keep her

233

distance. I wanted to write an unforgettable letter. I would present the Emperor with all my perplexities; I would call upon his benevolence and tolerance; I would advocate the freeing of Iunia Cantaber; and I would justify myself, too, in the face of the intrigues known and those surmised. All that came to me were disconnected, inconsistent phrases, banal rhetorical expressions, sentences that were sometimes grandiloquently bombastic, sometimes miserably common. You don't write to an emperor the way you would to an ordinary citizen; you have to ponder your words well so that nothing in them will show any pride, ingratitude, or calculated humility. What's called for is an elevated, oriental-like style, ornate with images and figures, worthy of the palace.

I did what I could. I'm not a rhetorician, nor am I extraordinarily well-lettered. Perhaps my style of a provincial from Hispania would bring a smile to the faces of the Palatine functionaries. I think in any case that my worries, the description of events, the appeal to the magnanimity and clemency of the Princeps, and my plea for the safeguarding of social peace were expressed clearly in the missive, which was brief.

Before putting a seal on the tablet, I called Mara and asked her to listen to what I'd written. She made some observations regarding the style, I explained that one didn't treat the Emperor as "sir," as the result of an indication he'd made himself, which Mara must have been aware of since we'd talked about it so many times. Then I noticed that the reservations Mara was trying to voice weren't exactly those. She was biding her time before bringing up what she now stammered out with a rare hesitation: "So much and to one so high because of Iunia Cantaber?"

"Am I doing the wrong thing?" I asked.

Mara didn't answer. She pretended to hear sounds inside that called for her attention. She got up, smiled, gave me a quick kiss on the forehead, and I was left alone, fiddling with the stylus between my fingers.

The letter was never sent. I went so far as to summon two trusted slaves and order them, to their great perplexity, to get ready to leave for Rome at any moment. I intended to avoid the official mail, which would of necessity have to pass through Scaurus' hands; he would, certainly, be constrained by honor from breaking my seal and examining my correspondence, but he might hold it back out of natural mistrust. Was I committing an offense? What was at stake made it worthwhile from my point of view. And I could always admit it and delay events as I wished, with the pretext of Marcus Aurelius' silence. Perhaps in the meantime Scaurus would march south with his cohorts, and civil authority, free of the military hand, would return to its customary axis. But underneath it all I wasn't sure if it was preferable to postpone or to expedite events . . .

With surprise I saw a centurion enter my atrium, following the steps of the nomenclator. The man was unarmed, alone, and helmetless. Under his arm he was carrying some writing tablets, larger than usual, and in his hand a papyrus scroll. He saluted me in military fashion, handed me the scroll and one tablet; only afterward did he hand me the second one, with a stylus attached for me to inscribe my receipt. He saluted again with martial pomp and left. The nomenclator hadn't had time to say a word.

On the wax a message was written in Marcus Agneius Scaurus' own hand. After a few cordial remarks, he stated that he was sending a copy of an edict from the Emperor that had only just reached his hands. He had hastened to pass it along because it had seemed to him that those words were providential for resolving the doubts that I, as high judge, couldn't help having. In that way any natural reluctance that might impede the course of an exemplary trial was removed. He'd had only the applicable part copied, feeling that I didn't need the labyrinthine harangues that preceded it and that displayed (or, he said ironically, "obscured") other items irrelevant to the matter at hand now. He assured me that I could have complete confidence in the legion copyists, but if I required it he would send the complete transcript of the original, which was at my disposal in the praetorial tent.

The extract was categoric, detailed, and it left no room for doubt: all new religions were prohibited; it recommended that magistrates pay special attention to members of the sect called Christian, bent on spreading sedition in the Empire and confusing the loyalty of citizens, and dedicated to practices offensive to the peace, health, and well-being of the people. It had been verified that some had poisoned wells, and there were those who even attributed the outbreak of pestilence in Rome to them. The authorities should not take action or seek these cultists out except in the case of public turmoil. But if—as a consequence of disturbances of civic order or following a specific accusation by citizens—the Christians were brought to trial for their practices, they were to be incarcerated immediately in the public jail, judged with all the rigor of the law, and punished with the same stringency if found guilty, always in conformity with their social status. Only those who swore by a sacred object to renounce their superstition and to conform to the rites proper to Romanness would be freed.

Neither Scaurus' note nor the extract of the edict bore a date. The tribune had probably had news of the law even before he'd received me. It wouldn't have surprised me to learn he'd reported it to the notables of Tarcisis who'd gathered in his tent without me. Had he let a few hours pass before communicating it to me in order to judge whether my spontaneous reaction would be in accord with the will of the Princeps? Or could he have found out somehow that I was in the act of writing to the Emperor? Could I have done a poor job of erasing the tablets in the praetorium? What trust could I have, after all, in my archivists? In any case, why so much perfidy? I didn't deserve it. I wasn't that important; nor was the city whose governance had fallen to me.

Facing me, the bust of Marcus Aurelius Antoninus was almost smiling, eyes lifted. Stone-cold marble, thinking about posterity, heedless of me and my pleas. How could a man so lenient, so aware of the relativity of things and opinions, publish such inflexible and arbitrary rules? Why persecute the Christians more than the Mithraists, the followers of Cybele, those of Isis, those of Sostratus, the Jews? What could the Emperor know that I hadn't witnessed myself? What harm was there in the inclusion of that god in the multitude of divinities that swarmed in the Empire or above it? And what did it matter what the ignorant commoners ruminated on in their dungheaps?

Why would a sovereign I respected and venerated want to do harm to Iunia Cantaber?

I felt like cursing the images of the Emperor. Hurling them against the wall. Removing them from my home altar. And it was in that state of mute despair that Mara found me. I showed her the letters and dropped onto a stool. Mara read, took her time, sighed, ended by snuggling against me.

"Maybe it's time for me to resign."

"Showing your disagreement with the Emperor? The trap's all set. The judgment of the Christians would have your own added to it. The Julian Law of Treason is still in effect. But you can always recuse yourself from judging Iunia . . . because, in the end, it's only a question of Iunia, isn't it? Declaring yourself ineligible as a friend of the family. They'd all understand the scruples of a judge."

"And by whom would she be judged, then? By Apitus, by Cosimus, by one of those spineless decemvirs? Or by Scaurus himself, a man who, in all candor, compared a trial with a spectacle? Would that be better for her? More just?"

"Iunia doesn't interest me so much. The one who interests me is you, Lucius Valerius," Mara said with crisp syllables, a precise and sharp intonation, a half-smile. Then she took my face between her hands, looked into my eyes for a long time, and held me again. Mara pressed her hand against my chest and exclaimed suddenly: "Iunia!" To my amazement she repeated: "Iunia!" She squeezed my pulse between two fingers and leaned her head against my chest. "A heart that doesn't rest, a cold sweat, a rebel pulse that beats at the mention of a certain name. What is it that I can't guess? Do you remember the story of Seleucus' physician?"

I pushed Mara away gently and stood up. She was looking at me serenely, with rueful irony. She got up too and, already on her way inside, stopped, made an elegant gesture of indifference with both hands, lowered her head, and left.

All alternatives were blocked: if I refused to judge Iunia, someone would take my place, and I would be accused of a denial of justice, of being in collusion with the Christians; if I absolved Iunia, they would arrange some way to annul the decision, accusing me of disobeying the imperial edict, and they would invoke the Julian Law of Treason; if I condemned Iunia, they would see their hatred

237

for the Christians fed and—they were quite aware of this—my suffering would be matched by the animosity they felt for me.

I unsheathed the dagger that was lying on the tabletop and with which I sometimes cut sheets of papyrus. I ran my knuckles over the polished, icy steel; I tested the tip on my palm. All alone I would never have the courage. I didn't possess the determination of Pontius, theatrically stimulated by the presence of an audience. Maybe that slave, Luciporus, could help me . . . In the end would I betray the motto of Epictetus—"Stay! Endure!"—that I'd always tried, with such a signal lack of success, to adopt as the guiding principle of my life?

When Mara entered rapidly through the tablinum and snatched the dagger from my hands, I'd already decided to take whatever was going to come. She hid the blade behind her back and faced me, tight-lipped, with a determined look. Slowly she retreated to the wall.

I raised my hands in a peace-making gesture, went to the door of the tablinum, returned to the table. I tried to assuage Mara's fright by talking banalities.

❦

Aulus, in the praetorium, facing me, stiff, arms hanging down. I'd decided to proceed with the case against the Christians as quickly as possible, so that the anticipation would come to an end and I would see myself finally delivered from that nightmare, even if it meant getting into another one. I ordered the centurion to undertake right away a search of the houses of all Christians, free or freedmen, who were held in jail. They should confiscate books, symbols, idols—any objects that looked sacred or only strange.

Aulus saluted me stoically. Before he could take a half-turn, I confronted him. I couldn't resist. I still had friendly feelings for him. I was paternal: "What's going on with you, Aulus?"

"Nothing, duumvir. I'm doing my duty as always."

"Why have you abandoned me, Aulus?"

"I'm not Sabinus' dog, duumvir. I serve the republic."

"What have they offered you, Aulus, to guarantee your so-fearless zeal for . . . the republic?"

"Do you have any further orders, duumvir?"

Aulus was answering me inexpressively and coldly, his eyes fastened high up on the wall frieze. I stood, went around the table, took him by the shoulders, and repeated, "What's going on with you?"

"You must be confused, duumvir. Nothing's going on. I've never disobeyed your orders, have I?"

It was useless to reproach him, agonizing to persist in this line of questioning. It wasn't worth the trouble to confirm the reasons for his sad submission, obvious reasons I'd either guessed or learned by devious means. I'd treated him harshly at the time of his attack on Rufus. I'd been sarcastic about Arsenna's going about as he pleased on the highways. I'd rewarded him stingily with praise and a phalera after he'd freed the roads of a dangerous bandit. All things considered, what else could I have expected? I released him. "No one forced Sabinus' dog to drown. He leaped into the Tiber out of loyalty."

"He was a dog."

Aulus left, interpreting—and rightly so—my reconciled silence as desistence.

❦

In midafternoon the lictors brought a tent cloth held by the corners and deposited the spoils of their search on the floor of the curia. All jumbled together there were assorted baubles, most of which had nothing to do with the Christians. Some statuettes, already cracked from careless treatment, represented Mithras and the Bull. One of the "fishes" was nothing but the remains of a gargoyle. Pouring out as the cloth was shaken were pendants, brooches, and amulets representing fish, anchors, and even a cross. Every object displayed a leather label with the name of its owner. I left the pile of wax tablets for later and pulled the two cases of books flagged with Milquion's name toward me. I opened a scroll and read at random: "*And they heard the sound of the Lord God, strolling in the garden in the cool of the evening . . .*"

There it told, in vulgar Greek, a myth of the world's creation by a divinity who strolled in gardens in the evening breeze. The narrative seemed primitive to me, a bit incongruous and poorly thought out, nothing that could compare, for instance, to the legend of Deucalion and Pyrrha. I went along picking up scrolls and unrolling them, still randomly: there were endless lists, heroes who lived for hundreds of years, lamentations, curses, betrayals, wars, exterminations—everything put forth in a barbarous, repetitive, obscure style. It all seemed brutal, intolerant, and bloody to me. It probably wasn't any more so than our own myths and legends; but in ours, amid the violence and crimes there's always an instance of clemency and greatness of soul that makes things better and remains as an exemplar for humanity in future times. Some of Milquion's texts, by contrast, praised envy, contempt, and the thirst for killing as if they were virtues. That's what those barbarian gods are like: they accept human sacrifices, are gratified by blood and the smell of charred flesh. Of that type was the abominable god of Carthage, Bel, who never had enough of the ashes of adolescents and who, at an auspicious moment, was overthrown by us Romans.

I admit that my brief and therefore superficial reading of those books was insufficient to form an idea of the whole. Perhaps I was being unjust, and the edifying parts were contained on the many pages I hadn't read.

I searched for and couldn't find in the scrolls that prophet, Isaiah, whom Milquion and Iunia had cited to me. But in the second case, up against *Letter of Hermes the Shepherd,* a book stood out called *The Good News of Matthew,* which spoke to me finally of that Christ whom they said was the son of god. After a detailed Judaic genealogy, along with a string of teachings and miracles that were quite ingenuous and alien to our milieu, there were tales of a virgin birth. Finally, a conspiracy, a trial, a crucifixion, and a resurrection on the third day. Not on the second, not the seventh, not the fifteenth: on the third . . .

And what did all that matter to me, after all? I thumbed through those texts, and they left me completely unmoved. This person segregated foreigners and massacred priests, others ate from a forbidden tree and were expelled from a garden, still another one cast out demons, cured paralytics, and came out with maxims and incomprehensible parables, letting himself be crucified between thieves later on.

Our sibylline books are quite entangled and abstruse. The Books of the Dead of the Egyptians are even more so, according to those who understand. That's the nature of things. Belief isn't philosophy. But a religion that needs so many texts and is based on so many millions of words can't help but be eccentric.

Nevertheless, if those tales didn't affect me in any way and all I felt, reading them, was the gulf that separated me from other people, other mentalities, other notions of the city and of things sacred (and, with that, a certain disdain for the low language in which they were written), I was bothered and almost indignant over the fact that they'd been accepted by Iunia.

Maximus Cantaber hadn't been a man to neglect the education of his daughters. Iunia certainly must have been familiar with Homer, Catullus, Virgil. How could she have let herself get enmeshed in that verbosity, so foreign and so common, so lacking in style and beauty? What was going on with that woman?

And there I was, letting every pretext lead me to Iunia. What was going on with me, I should have asked instead . . .

On the tablets were written artless prayers, copies of psalms, and even lists of names. It wasn't up to me, according to the terms of the imperial edict, to track down those who weren't formally accused. I put the tablets aside, along with the rest of that symbolic junk. I ordered them to take everything to my house. I set the trial for two days hence, and I immediately dispatched slaves to put up notices and notify the accusatory parties and the military authority of the legion.

Then I called for an escort and, heavy-hearted, descended to the dungeons. I myself would advise the prisoners of the trial, also because I had something to show them.

⌒══✦══⌒

On my orders the jailer opened the doors to the storage room, which squeaked raspily from lack of use. This was where the instruments of torture were kept, and he went about laying them out on the floor. They were so varied in shape and size that if this one could be picked up with two fingers, that other resisted even the strength of shoulders. I commanded the attendants to open the cell and call out all the prisoners except Iunia Cantaber and Arsenna. They were soon surrounding me, silent and downcast. Some were

241

trembling; others were praying in a faint whisper. The voice of Iunia Cantaber, who could see nothing from where she was clinging to the bars, then rang out: "It's not fair to separate me from my brothers and sisters. I demand that you let me join my brothers and sisters! Lucius Quintius? Are you there, Lucius? Listen!"

Unconcerned, forcing myself, I acted as if I couldn't hear Iunia's protests. She insisted, shouting, "Brothers and sisters! My brothers and sisters! Remember who you are; remember Him who suffered for your redemption. Earthly powers cannot prevail over the omnipotence of God!"

Faced with silence, Iunia began to call them by their names, one by one, in a loving, almost maternal tone. In a low voice I ordered, "Nobody answer!"

And nobody answered.

"Your trial is set for the day after tomorrow, at the third hour. You may speak for yourselves or designate a lawyer."

No one said anything. Around me were weakened faces, forlorn expressions, crossed arms clutching their bodies. Iunia, in a clear tone, continued to exhort them from inside the cell.

"Explain to them," I calmly told the jailer, pointing to the iron chair. And their eyes were more attentive to the instrument than their ears to Iunia's plaints.

"This is the iron chair," the man muttered in a hoarse voice. "The one to be judged is tied here, and coals are lighted in this drawer under the seat. When the chair turns red it makes a fine spectacle: smoke comes off, and the smell of scorched flesh begins. On that rusty hook over there . . ."

It could be seen that the vile jailer was taking pleasure in describing those gloomy objects destined to cause pain and suffering. Sometimes he hesitated, unable to remember exactly what a certain pulley or serrated plate was for.

I was paying heed only to Iunia's shouts and cries, which, as she stood only steps away from us, shaking the iron bars, seemed to make the cell door jerk and rattle all the more. Her fellow Christians all showed terror in their expressions, in the uncertainty of their glances, in the tears running down their cheeks. Milquion had buried his face in his hands. The jailer had described in detail the methods and effects of the chair, the rack, the pulleys, the hooks, the saws, the tar, and the brimstone. He was preparing for a second round of explanations, to encompass what he'd left out the first time, when I interrupted: "All right! You've done your duty! That's enough!"

I slowly looked over the prisoners before me. They were smothered in prostrate silence. Iunia's appeals, as she continued shaking the bars, sounded like some distant noise, absolutely alien to the very material reality of the murderous iron implements they had before them.

Milquion, his cheeks flushed, wiped his watery eyes before asking, "Are you going to torture us, duumvir?"

"I want you all to see the torture awaiting you so that you won't blame me later on for your ignorance."

"I haven't done anything wrong."

"That's what's to be determined." And I asked, "Is everything clear to you all?"

There was a chorus of mumbled pleas. A woman gave a deep sigh, wavered, fainted, was held up. Iunia kept on with her grievances. And the more she shouted, the greater was the anxiety and discomfiture of those poor devils. Milquion, taking me by the hand: "Duumvir, have pity on these people!"

"And on you?"

"On me also."

The men of the escort and the jailer had opened the cell. They pushed Iunia back, and she fell silent as the prisoners were led back onto their straw. When I passed by the cell door, all of them began to intone in unison a chant that followed me as I climbed the stairs to the outside. Depression had given way to rage, to judge by the hardening of faces and the vigorous way they finished the versicles. I gave a quick look over my shoulder: Iunia, her hands grasping the bars, had been the first to sing. When she saw me turn my head, she interrupted the psalm to yell, "We're ready, did you hear, duumvir? We're ready!"

When I got upstairs, the heavy door thundered closed behind me with metallic echoes. The bustle of the basilica. Normal people.

XIX

I DIDN'T LEAVE the house the next day. My subalterns came from the praetorium with business right after daybreak. I ordered them to carry a statue of Jupiter from the temple to the basilica in the middle of the night and without making any noise. At dusk I sent the password to Aulus on a sealed tablet, before he could come to me. Words from Virgil: *"How changed he was . . ."* I didn't receive anyone all day. I learned that Proserpinus had sought me and that Calpurnius had sent a message, the contents of which I did without.

I didn't have to prepare the judgment; no one was expecting any oratorical flights from me. A preliminary hearing of the accused wouldn't add anything. They all knew what awaited them. Iunia had understood, certainly, that she was exempt from the tortures applicable to the Christians of lesser station.

Distractedly, I passed my eyes over Milquion's books once more. Christ—I read—had ascended to heaven, like Romulus; Augustus; Faustina, the wife of Antoninus; or . . . Drusilla, the mistress of Cato. Original, that idea of a dead god—if we forget the announcement of the death of Pan, which was proclaimed on Asian shores and carried to Rome on a cargo ship during the time of Tiberius.

But I didn't go on with the reading; Iunia and the others weren't being charged with reading. For almost the whole day I dedicated myself to doing nothing or to utterly trivial tasks such as transferring rare little goldfish from the tank in the peristyle to the one in the impluvium or pruning the rosebushes in the garden. Mara helped me in those pastimes with false, exaggerated merriment.

Cautiously, assisted by only one slave, I conducted a propitiatory sacrifice in the garden, consecrating a small white calf garlanded with flowers to the god who took the evening breeze, asking that he not abandon his faithful and, especially, that he might intercede for Iunia.

I don't believe in that god any more than I believe in our old Roman gods, and I give even less credence to the divinities of Lusitania. But what means do I have to communicate with Providence if not through this language of rituals, this calling upon intermediary beings that our ancestors taught us?

I took steps so that later on I wouldn't be accused, spuriously, of complicity. I addressed the offering to Justice in a very audible voice, but secretly I invoked Iunia's god and his crucified son. And I hoped that the supreme being who lays out the destinies of the world would hear my prayer and turn misfortune and bloodshed away from Tarcisis, receiving in exchange the blood of the innocent animal.

At nightfall I lingered a long time in the bath with Mara, who'd done everything to give me an agreeable day, never mentioning the distasteful chore that awaited me on the following one. Before we went to bed, a slave read us a passage Mara had chosen from the *Satyricon: ". . . the master of eloquence who does not do as the fisherman does and does not place on the tip of his hook the bait that he knows will be valued by the little fishes, will remain for long hours on his rock, despairing of ever catching anything."*

At dawn the lictors came for me at the house. On the street a small, excited crowd was waiting for me; they encircled my chair and accompanied me to the forum in a procession. I gave orders that the gawkers were not to be allowed inside. In the dim light of the basilica there was already some movement. In the center of the main nave stood the statue of Jupiter, which—it was said—was a replica, much smaller and with minor differences of detail, of the figure of Zeus of the Thunderbolt of Olympia. Close to its base was a small three-legged altar of wood.

At the rear of the nave was a wide platform where the stools for the decemvirs and the table and chairs for the judges, were arrayed. As assessors I had Apitus and Cosimus, who had just arrived and were huddled nearby, chatting about unimportant matters. The decemvirs were trickling in, forming conversational groups. Their indiscernible words echoed hollowly through the open space of the nave. I ended up learning that an armed force of G. Valius Maximinianus was coming down along the coast and that the main body of the Moorish hordes, pinched and pressed on three fronts, was beginning to mass on the banks of the Galpe, ready to retreat to Africa, where the XII Legion Fulminata was waiting for them. The barbarians' folly would end up on the steel of this miraculous legion—ironically, through the favors of Jupiter, favors that the Christians (it was reported) abusively claimed for their god.

Slaves noisily dragged in a table and placed it close to the platform, for the cartularies and scribes to use. Others set up a water clock, laid out tablets and writing materials, and purified the air with incense.

Scaurus then presented himself. He entered wearing a gathered toga and made it clear to those who went to greet him that he was there only as a private citizen and didn't wish to meddle in the affairs of the city. The centurions and soldiers who attended him were unarmed and could be recognized as military men only by their short tunics, belts with metal aprons, and iron-soled boots that clanked on the paving stones. He addressed me quite correctly and urbanely. After the exchange of greetings he declared, "Don't wait for me to give the signal, Lucius Quintius. You may begin whenever you wish."

Proserpinus, holding books under his arms, came to greet me. Behind him Rufus, quite humble, dressed in an unadorned tunic, was letting himself be led along as if he were the defendant and not the plaintiff.

Missing was Calpurnius, who made us wait. As soon as his inlaid chair entered, a fawning group surrounded it and led him to a place beside the dais. He gave me a nod as he passed. Ahead of Calpurnius' chair marched Airhan, imposing, glittering, and pompous, like a master of ceremonies.

Half of Tarcisis was jostling for position around the doors to the basilica. The cloth in which the material proofs were wrapped was laid down in a bundle near my table. I could hear the sound of objects grinding against each other and the crumbling of ceramics. The water from a jar gurgled loudly as it was poured into the clock.

Aulus arranged his vigilantes in a row, and the guards unbarred the doors. The notables took their places. I raised an arm, and the wide double-doors were opened to the people. It was already going on the fourth hour.

There they all came, swarming in, and in an instant the basilica was filled. There was fighting over places; altercations broke out. The crowd mounted the steps, and the upper galleries seethed with people dressed in all colors. Little attention was paid to the priorities of social position: mingled in agitated rows were men and women, decurions and plebeians, artisans and slaves, and even peasants who'd come from a distance, people who were usually uninterested in public affairs. A chaos of voices, laughter, and footsteps filled the open space.

"The trial should have been held in the forum," Apitus whispered into my ear. When he moved his face away, I could read a trace of censure on his lips.

In the front section, beyond the statue of Jupiter and the space marked off by Aulus' men, behind a rope strung there, I recognized with gratitude the friendly smile of Mara, who'd come, half-veiled, accompanied by a single slave woman.

I turned to Calpurnius and then to Scaurus; each nodded agreement. I ordered a lictor to bring in the prisoners. When he went off between the rows of guards, the mood of those present grew tenser; the nervous murmur permeated the vastness of the nave to such an extent that I was unable to hear the cartulary who was consulting me on details.

Mingling with the roar of the audience, a chant was beginning, faintly, to be heard. The guards used their spears to hold back those who pressed too frantically against the restraining rope. The Christians were walking behind the lictor through the cordon of guards. I immediately recognized Iunia's voice rising up over the others. My alarm made the stylus cut sharply into the wax.

She was marching in front, holding hands with a slave woman and singing at the top of her lungs. Not all the others were joining in. The crowd stirred, shouted, insulted. When the prisoners lined up in front of the tribunal, silence returned.

I asked the name and status of each, beginning with the slaves and purposely leaving Milquion and Iunia for last. They all stated their names, their affiliations, and the house to which they belonged or of which they were freedmen or clients. Milquion declared that he had been born in Trabesh, in Syria, and that he was not a Roman citizen. Iunia limited herself to saying, in a crystal-clear voice, "Iunia Cantaber, Christian!"

I pretended I hadn't noticed the provocation. I asked the prisoners if they wished to speak for themselves or if they had masters or patrons who would represent them. I passed my eyes over those present, caught sight of some figures slipping away, some faces turning aside: no one wanted to assume the patronage of the accused. Proserpinus got up from his place and very confidentially came over to whisper, "You should know, duumvir, that I wouldn't hesitate to represent them if I hadn't been entrusted with the accusation. If you want an adjournment . . ."

But Iunia Cantaber raised her voice: "The men and women you see here don't need anyone to speak for them. Even those of lowly status have a patron in heaven who is worth more than all the lawyers of Rome."

Loud guffaws and hooting echoed off the walls of the basilica. One of the lictors began to read the accusation, and silence, interrupted by an occasional outburst, took hold.

Who were the poor wretches I was to judge? There were fourteen of them, not counting Iunia and Milquion. Almost all were downcast, visibly distressed by the solemnity of the tribunal and the jeers of the crowd. The small clutch of slave women, wrapped in their veils, exchanged random looks and nervous smiles. Three other slaves in torn and filthy tunics stood there amazed, it could even be said flattered, at being the target of so much attention. Two couples who were looking at me with terrified eyes were holding hands. The old man I'd heard reading a letter in the Cantabers' gardens, who wore the matted beard of a philosopher (less clean than his clothing), was hunched over, wringing his hands. An artisan dressed in leather was compulsively scratching his chest with a fingernail. Tall, hollow-eyed Milquion seemed very attentive, his breathing shallow, accelerated. Iunia was staring at me, her face taut, arms at her sides, very stiff. And farther off, obscured by the movement of the crowd at times, the tender face of Mara, tranquil and supportive.

One slave woman who'd been smiling before suddenly began to weep, hiding her face with her rolled-up veil. Another one embraced her. Milquion lowered his head. The lictor finished reading the charge and gravely rolled up the scroll. Then he picked up his fasces and put it back on his shoulder. The voices in the hall grew louder; there were fits of coughing; a few scattered comments could be heard.

"You"—I pointed to the slave woman who was crying—"you heard the accusation. What have you to say to it?"

The woman opened her mouth wide, shook her head from side to side, and was unable to answer. Another spoke for her: "We're Iunia Cantaber's slaves. If we did anything wrong, we did it out of ignorance, because we haven't got the head to decide for ourselves."

"Are you Christians?"

"We're nothing, sir; we do what we're told to do. Where our masters go, that's where we go too."

The slaves quickly closed ranks around this girl, who knew how to give a quick answer. They all affirmed their weakness of spirit and laid the responsibility for their acts on their masters.

"We don't kill, we don't wound, we don't do any harm," added the slave who'd been thrown into the cistern with Milquion.

"Are you a Christian?"

"Me, sir? I only did what they ordered me to."

"Why were you singing a while back?"

"Because my mistress was singing."

"Why weren't you at the wall defending the city?"

The man looked at Iunia Cantaber and cast down his eyes. Others made a sign of agreement by dropping their chins onto their chests in the same way.

"Answer, all of you!"

"Sir, we weren't authorized."

"By whom?"

"By our mistress, Iunia Cantaber."

"Is that true, Iunia?"

"It is!"

"What about you"—I addressed the other group—"who are free men? Who stopped you from going to the wall?"

"I'm a foreigner, duumvir."

"I'm not talking to you, Milquion. I'm referring to those there."

The men pressed closer to the platform, bent over, wringing their hands: "I'm an old man, I'm no good for war," said one. Another said, "I'm a blacksmith, and in my shop I was repairing the tips of spears. I was fighting in my own way."

"Are you Christians?"

"I don't know anything about religion, my lord. I can barely read capital letters," the blacksmith volunteered fearfully.

And the old man, who couldn't excuse himself by illiteracy: "I watched Iunia Cantaber grow up. I could never deny her anything, no matter what. I owed so many favors to her father, whose life is over now. If Iunia asks . . ."

"Are you a Christian?"

"No, sir, if the truth be known, no . . . deep in my heart, no."

I got up, my steps making the dais creak. I pointed to the statue of Jupiter, beside which a praetorium slave stood with a jug of wine and a cup.

"I invite you to make a libation to Jupiter Optimus Maximus!"

All rushed to the statue in almost hysterical haste and tried to snatch the wine from the slave. The crowd grew excited and pressed forward to get a better look. Mara's eyes fell, sad, compassionate. Iunia, implacable, adjusted her veil. The accused were wrangling with the slave for the cup to pour the wine on the altar. Milquion was restless. He didn't know where to put his hands, kept alternating his gaze from me to the ones worshipping Jupiter. My assessors, the decemvirs, and Scaurus smiled disdainfully. Calpurnius was dozing.

Proserpinus then raised his arm and asked if I would be so good as to ask one more question of the prisoners interrogated thus far. He wanted to know if it was true that Maximus Cantaber's slaves had stopped their master from attending the sacrifices in the temple on a certain day. They all replied, in a clamor, that they didn't know or that it had been a matter of disagreement between father and daughter, both of such high station that it wasn't up to slaves to interfere.

"Are you satisfied, Proserpinus?"

"I reserve my questions for later!"

Confident, he made a dismissive motion, drawing his free hand out of his toga. Rufus, flush against him, was speaking into his ear incessantly. Now it was Milquion's turn.

"So, what about you, Milquion, aren't you a Christian either?"

"I'm interested in everything with respect to the only God."

"That's not what I asked you." I raised my voice and leaned toward the foreigner. "I asked whether you were or weren't a Christian."

"My interest in this religion is purely spiritual."

"I ask you once more if you're a Christian. Can't you understand Latin now?"

Milquion looked falteringly at Iunia. She didn't return his glance. Then he sighed and made his decision: "I've ceased being a Christian, duumvir."

"When you saw the iron chair?"

"I've been doing a lot of thinking, duumvir."

"*Episkopos*, bishop, is what I have in my notes. Weren't you the one who distributed the bread, who presided over the mysteries, who read the texts, who administered the lustral water, who drove out evil spirits?"

"Always with the conviction that I wasn't offending the laws of Rome or the will of the divine Princeps. In Maximus Cantaber's house they listened to me, gave me shelter, fed me. I did what they wanted me to; I read them the texts, explained the rites . . ."

I had to impose silence. A swell of surprise was rippling through the hall, cut here and there by caustic words of indignation. Insults poured down from the balcony. Proserpinus laughed, wagging his head. Milquion edgily went on justifying himself: "I was translating Matthew into Latin verse. You can consult my documents, duumvir. It was only intellectual curiosity."

He ran his fingers over his beard, inhaled deeply, held his open hands out to me, and lamented, "Have pity on me, duumvir, I'm an unfortunate man."

Proserpinus stood up slowly, with composure, and raised his voice: "You sacrilegious man! Do you deny that you spat when you passed the temple?"

"I did not spit!"

"You snorted, you swine, which is the same thing."

"I may have inadvertently coughed beside the base of the temple. But I never spat or snorted. I swear!"

I asked Proserpinus to hold off as he made ready to lash out at Milquion. "Do you deny your Christ?" I asked the bishop.

"Yes, duumvir, absolutely."

"Do you venerate the Emperor?"

"Yes, duumvir."

And before I could order him, Milquion ran over to the statue, seized the cup from the slave's hands, filled it with wine himself, and poured it over the altar, which was already sticky from so many libations.

"Did you see, duumvir; did you see, judges?" Milquion asked frightenedly, looking at one and then another of the notables on the dais, who appeared solemn and indifferent this time. The catcalls erupted again in the hall. Milquion went back to his place beside Iunia, who didn't seem to notice him.

No sooner did I look at Iunia Cantaber—having reached, finally, this moment I had delayed as long as possible—than she got ahead of me: "Before you ask, I repeat, I am a Christian, yes. I feel sorry for all who are not, and I feel compassion for those who have just recanted, and I swear that I will pray for them."

"Don't anticipate me, Iunia. You've seen what has happened. Do you want some time to think?"

"May God grant that I am worthy of Him and of His Son, who sacrificed Himself in order to save us. I don't need any time, duumvir. I've been ready ever since I accepted the Christ!"

"You heard the accusation! Do you accept the accusation?"

"I am indifferent to the accusation."

My two assessors cast their wrathful eyes on me. And once more, despite the circumstances and beyond my bitterness, I felt deeply irritated with Iunia Cantaber. Apitus took the floor and pointed a finger at Iunia. "If you wish to die, why do you come here? This is a tribunal, not a slaughterhouse. There's no lack of nooses in this city. There are poisons, precipices, deep waters! Why do you provoke us?"

A wave of applause ran through the basilica. But Iunia was there to defend a point of view, not to capitulate to the orthodox reasoning she knew to expect from our tribunal. She took a step toward the platform and raised her arm. Apitus lowered his. "You're the ones who are all condemned! You, not I! Can't you see the signs? The plague in Rome? The floods on the Tiber? The invasion of the barbarians? The end of time is approaching. The city of God is descending over the Earth. When the moment arrives, woe to him who doesn't recognize the word of the Lord."

For the first time, Cosimus the haruspex whispered a comment into my ear: "How can you let her talk like that? They're nothing but half a dozen frogs around a little puddle."

Once more I questioned the bishop, who was covering his face with his hands. "Do you agree with that, Milquion?"

Milquion hunched over and began to weep again. The tears running down his stringy beard gave him a gummy, pitiful look: "I don't know what to say anymore, duumvir."

Iunia walked in front of him and lifted both arms: "Let me speak! Lucius Valerius, let me speak!" And, turning her back on the tribunal, Iunia addressed the people. I could hardly make out the words: "Yes, it's a matter of salvation . . ." An uproar arose, louder and louder, and drowned out her speech. I saw among the spectators faces crimson with rage. From the balcony, fists were shaken at Iunia. Mara, buffeted by the surging crowd, was swaying from side to side, her head lowered. Rufus was smiling, triumphant. Proserpinus was making vague, ineffectual gestures to calm the crowd. On the platform the notables were looking at each other with expressions that oscillated between scoffing and nervousness. Calpurnius, awake now, was measuring Iunia with his dull little eyes.

With great effort and the intervention of the lictors, a semblance of order was restored. Iunia, perspiring from her tirade, was gasping for breath. No one had heard anything of what she'd said. Suddenly she turned to the tribunal and roared, hoarse now: "Yes, duumvir, I choose martyrdom! I want to die for my faith the way the Savior died for us, and I offer my sacrifice for those who are jeering at me!"

The taunts and mockery redoubled and only quieted down when, with a gesture, I gave the floor to the accusation. I removed the cork from the water clock, and it began to drip into a clay cup. Everyone fell silent to hear Proserpinus, who, standing now, was still exchanging some private words with Rufus as he rearranged his toga to its customary form. Then he took a step forward, raised his hand, assumed the gesture of the orator with his fingers, and began his speech in praise of the Emperor with a profusion of adjectives and figures of speech.

Alas, the generous Princeps, like the heroes and the gods, could not be immune to the betrayals that are the insidious weapon of his inferiors. And while he spread his benevolence across the territory of the Empire, from frozen Britannia to the dry deserts of Nubia, corrupt beings were plotting the republic's downfall. And how were they doing it? Sometimes by the direct action of corroding people's spirits; sometimes by offenses to the accepted procedures of piety; sometimes by affronts to the divinities who, up in the spheres, outraged, ponder their revenge.

Why had the Moors abandoned their desert mountains by the thousands to pass over the Pillars of Hercules and spread their fury across Lusitania? How is it that they had spared all cities, contenting themselves with laying waste to the countryside, until they came to concentrate their forces before the walls of Tarcisis, the only city in all of the south that they besieged?

Because the spirit of Tarcisis had been offended—Proserpinus asserted with a roar, making his toga fly—because the news of impiety in Tarcisis had risen to the ears of the aggrieved gods, and soon they were meeting in council, deliberating punishments, and demanding expiation.

The basilica was festive now. Rhythmic applause broke out to accentuate Proserpinus' flights of oratory. I, as was my custom, was running my finger over the rough glass of the water clock. It was a gesture well known to Proserpinus, who, interrupting his sublime delivery, promised in a humble parenthesis that he wouldn't be long.

And, surprisingly, he wasn't. Pointing to the prisoners, he disparaged the role of the slaves, ridiculed the artisans and the working people, and made the assemblage laugh. What had that one done, how did this one dare, who does the other one think she is? He seriously censured Milquion, his opportunism in having exploited the weakness of a widow and the benevolence of an old man. And when Iunia Cantaber's turn came, he dramatically fell silent for a few moments with his finger pointed witheringly at her and his brow hardened.

But, unexpectedly, he tempered the verbal thunder. He made his voice clearer, softened his syllables, went on to reflect aloud with bland and discursive phrases. He recalled Iunia's early widowhood, the death of her mother, and her natural fragility, exposed to all dangers after the first blows fate had dealt her heart . . . all of which opened the way for other blows to her understanding. That religion was criminal, certainly, had done damage to the republic, had enraged the gods with its sacrileges; but happily the VII Legion Gemina, represented there by the honored presence of Marcus Agneius Scaurus, had restored peace, healed the injuries, and removed the threats. The spirit of the city could well consider himself appeased. And Proserpinus, raising his eyebrows and addressing now the spirit of the city, asked him if he didn't consider himself compensated. After a few seconds had passed with no reply, the advocate lowered his eyes and folded his arms.

A puzzled murmur ran through the basilica. Citizens gaped at each other. Coughs began, conversations broke out. Mara clutched her veil against her breast, bit her lower lip, and with questioning eyes made me a wry face of support. Rufus, calling Proserpinus over, tugged at his toga with both hands; meanwhile Proserpinus, in view of the divinities' continuing silence, let his thin arms fall to his sides.

Nor did Proserpinus lean over to Rufus. He was coming to the end of his allegation. He marshaled his gestures and his words in one last breath. He praised me and the other judges, praised the decemvirs and all the notables present, and, taking in all the accused with a broad sweep of his left hand, he limited himself to asking that justice be done, knowing that each would be judged for his acts in accordance with the equity that was to be expected, given the excellence of the tribunal.

A buzz of dejection zigzagged through the great nave, higher, lower. Arms waved. There were flurries of conversation in the gallery. Proserpinus hadn't presented any witnesses. A group of potential testifiers protested that they wanted to be heard. There were those who demanded the questioning of witnesses, the reading of documents, the display of proofs. A tumult was beginning to break out; to my left there was shoving, gesticulating, shouting. Mara, luckily, was far away from the rowdies.

The water clock still held three fingers of water. Rufus, visibly vexed, was remonstrating with broad gestures as he faced an impassive Proserpinus, who, sitting with great majesty, wasn't paying him the slightest attention. Rufus grew weary. On an impulse, with a show of impatience and an angry voice, he leaped up and asked to be heard. I denied him the floor. I was jeered. He shouted and flailed—and this time it was Proserpinus who held him back . . . I couldn't hear Rufus' spiteful words. And it was amid derisive hooting that I announced that the tribunal was retiring to reach its decision.

What moderation had come over Proserpinus? Why had he spared the accused so much and cut short his intervention when every sign seemed to predict a detailed and thunderous screed? He owed no special favors to the Cantabers; he was involved with other clientele; his horror of the new religion seemed sincere; and his complicity with Rufus was undeniable. Why had he strayed so far from his nature and his usual techniques? Proserpinus had done only the minimum. It was habitual with him to harangue for hours on end, demanding clock after clock, and to end, interrupted and annoyed, by parading his hurt over the tribunal's incomprehension. It was, furthermore, a style that was very pleasing to spectators. He'd had the opportunity of a lifetime in his hands, the largest audience ever. He owed me nothing, nor did I owe him anything, and yet . . .

A curtain was drawn behind the platform. In that narrow space Cosimus, Apitus, and I met to deliberate the verdict. More than once, out of courtesy, we had Calpurnius and Scaurus called to take part, but they both refused with the message that they didn't feel worthy of such an honor.

"So?" I asked my assessors in a low voice.

The din in the hall almost prevented us from hearing each other. Cosimus drew back the curtain and shouted for stools, and there we three settled, knee to knee, like friends in an intimate consultation. My counselors had tablets with Marcus Aurelius' edict resting in their laps.

"In the end, this has been nothing but a flight of birds," Cosimus sighed. "When you think about it, what importance does it have? Slaves. Unimportant, gullible people. They don't know what they're doing."

Iunia's resounding voice reached us from the other side of the curtain as she tried to be heard over the turbulent crowd: "Over the city of Pepuza, in Anatolia, the skies opened up and the new Jerusalem was seen, radiant with light! From all corners of the Empire, pilgrims headed there in hopes that they could arrive in time. In Rome, on the graves of the martyrs, roses bloomed out of season. And you, you allow yourselves to disregard the great change in the times."

A huge peal of laughter followed this, reaching the highest and remotest nooks of the ceiling. The floor seemed to tremble. Doves that nested among the beams and tiles took flight. When voices were lowered, the flutter of wandering wings still crisscrossed the nave.

"The slaves, it's clear, had no choice," Cosimus continued, thoughtfully. "Are we going to condemn deluded slaves? It would be stupid!"

"A few lashes?" Apitus asked, not entirely persuaded.

Cosimus shrugged. "What for? Will the justice of Tarcisis be elevated by whipping a few poor wretches?"

Beyond the curtain, Rufus' voice was rising up, perfectly clear, amidst the laughter and noise: "Iunia Cantaber! Show respect for the tribunal!"

"Show your respect for what's holy, you contemptible freedman!"

Proserpinus intervened, but his voice could barely be heard: "Rufus, Iunia, let's allow the court to deliberate. We don't have the right to disturb the seclusion of the tribunal!"

The overwhelming hubbub of the furious crowd swallowed his words and, it seemed to me, almost made the curtain hiding us flutter.

"Also," Apitus went on, "they all showed repentance and consecrated the wine to Jupiter."

Cosimus: "Do you think they were sincere?"

Apitus: "What difference does that make? I saw them run to the statue and pour wine on the altar. Everybody witnessed it. That's what counts."

Cosimus stretched his arms out in front of himself, with a brusque, peremptory shake: "Set them free! Rome must show clemency. The ones to blame are the ones who dragged them into it, prevailing on their weak wills."

"There you are, foolishly convinced that you're witnessing the application of justice! Have you thought yet about the time you will have to face the Supreme Judge? How your limbs will tremble and how your laughter will be changed into a scowl?" It was Iunia again, taking advantage of a lull; her pronouncement sparked a new round of taunts.

"The tribunal is deliberating! Why are you disturbing justice?" Rufus' deep voice.

"Quiet! Quiet, everybody! Lictors! Lictors! Order in the court!" The serious, angry voice of Proserpinus.

"What about the foreigner?" I inquired.

"A poor devil. We can expel him from the city, at most," Cosimus said.

"What for? He humiliated himself to such a degree that his presence in the forum is the best way of dissuading others against the Christian superstition." Apitus shrugged.

"A clubbing?"

"It's not worth the trouble."

Outside, the whispering was rising now, in unison, filling the whole space; then it dissipated into separate shreds of phrases and isolated sounds.

Behind the curtain, we didn't take our eyes off each other. No one dared to be the first to broach the fate of Iunia Cantaber. Finally, I ventured: "Sufficient proof wasn't presented to incriminate Iunia Cantaber. Proserpinus, always so fiery, was moderate and didn't bring any facts before the tribunal."

Cosimus touched me on the knee with the wax tablet in a friendly way. "Ah . . . Lucius!"

"Poor Proserpinus is getting old," Apitus sympathized.

Beyond the curtain there was now a strange calm, as if all the shouters had grown fatigued at the same time. It was hot in that narrow enclosure. I was perspiring. Apitus broke the uncomfortable pause, declaring that in good conscience he considered Iunia Cantaber guilty, and that the prisoner's social position only aggravated the situation.

I tried to argue. Proserpinus himself, in his allegation, had put forth extenuating circumstances for Iunia . . .

Apitus and Cosimus were condescending toward me; they took my hands and told me how sorry they were for my suffering at this decisive moment. What mattered, however, was not their esteem for me, nor the esteem they sensed in me for someone on trial. It was the interests of the republic. Iunia Cantaber—they both lamented it—had done everything possible to have the maximum penalty applied to her. Her behavior excluded her from any chance of clemency.

"I know," Apitus whispered to me, "I know that among us you're outvoted. But in public, as duumvir and presiding judge, you will have to announce Iunia Cantaber's sentence of death."

"We don't have the jurisdiction to pronounce sentences of death."

"Of course not! Iunia will go on to Rome, and the sentence will be confirmed or overturned by the praetor. Iunia's blood will never be on our heads. Shall we go?"

When I announced the acquittal of the slaves, the hall filled with hostile bellowing. An intense and interminable ovation erupted when I announced Iunia's sentence. She looked at me with an expression of triumphal happiness. I had never seen such joy on her face.

XX

"A BRAVE WOMAN, Iunia."

Scaurus, with one hand on the edge of the wall, was speaking to me. I hadn't known he'd followed me up to that tower. I gave a start and must have shown some annoyance, because the tribune made the calming sign of someone who would go on his way out of respect for my solitude. I turned my back and with my eyes followed the cart that was carrying Iunia as it receded amid the dust raised by the escort of horsemen.

They'd been quick to implement the sentence. The day after the decision, still early, a dispatch was sent to Rome, another to the governor. Iunia left the next morning.

In the meantime, the major event in the city had been the suddenly announced adoption of Rufus Cardilius by Ennius Calpurnius. The ceremony took place in the forum, under my window, in my sight.

I preferred not to say farewell to Iunia. I learned that Arsenna had wept and that she'd blessed him. As soon as I heard the sound of carts on the pavement of the forum, I ran to the wall from the basilica's rear entrance. I spotted the procession going through the city gates. I went up to a tower so as to keep sight of the cart for as long as possible. The curtains on the canopy were drawn. I knew that in the first cart some slave women who wanted to accompany their mistress were traveling. Iunia was in the second cart, therefore. But I couldn't see her.

The procession passed close by the encampment, which bordered the highway. The soldiers were pulling up stakes, rolling up tents, and were unhurriedly forming up into ranks. I could faintly make out the bleat of a trumpet. The cohorts, too, were making ready to leave. At last I turned to Scaurus, who was waiting, leaning against the wall, his arms folded. He was wearing his military regalia.

"The time has come for good-byes for everyone, Lucius Valerius. I ask your forgiveness for having interrupted your . . . meditations. As you can see, I came alone, without formalities, and it's without formalities that I want to have a few words with you."

"Shall we go to the praetorium? To my home?"

"Here is fine. I won't lose sight of my troops. You have a villa some distance from Tarcisis, isn't that so?"

"It was destroyed by the Moors."

"Well, you'll have to rebuild it."

In an amiable tone, as if begging my pardon for everything he was saying, and stressing that he didn't want to use his prerogatives as a military authority in time of campaign, Scaurus was inviting me to quit the city.

He wanted to leave Tarcisis in peace, and from the information he had at hand, my remaining in the duumvirate would not be looked kindly upon by the many people who hadn't forgiven me for Pontius' suicide or for my tolerance toward the Christians. Had the judgment turned out otherwise, there would have been many citizens who foresaw for me the ignominy of a charge of treason.

He, Scaurus, sensed a certain ingratitude and even injustice in those rumors. It was for that reason that he was telling me and asking me—not ordering me—to resign the duumvirate and withdraw, at least temporarily, from the city. I had the notables and the people against me. Human fickleness . . . I've known it well . . . Scaurus sighed.

"I've got no liking for power. I was almost forced into the duumvirate."

"I know, I know . . . even if it's hard for me to understand. But explain to me: why didn't you organize games or even promise them? No one has forgiven you for that. And that Arsenna—why have you spared him?"

"There's been enough blood shed in my land."

"Ah, Marcus Aurelius, Marcus Aurelius. The private dislikes of the Princeps are communicated to cities buried in Lusitania."

"And yet . . ." I was going to mention the recent matter of the Princeps and his criminal edict, but Scaurus interrupted.

"Let's drop that, Lucius Valerius. Are you in accord with my proposal?"

"Exile?"

"Let's not exaggerate. Only a pause, at a distance, while things put themselves back together."

"Tomorrow I'll call the curia together and give an accounting . . ."

"Oh, no, don't worry about that; I've already taken care of everything. It would be better if you left discreetly."

"I'll put my mind to it."

"Of course. And you may avail yourself, if you wish, of an escort from the legion."

Scaurus saluted me with an elegant gesture, offered some final warm words, and went down the tower steps.

I had some carts rented; and all that day, sitting in the atrium among slaves who went about the arrangements, excited by the prospect of the trip, I waited for someone to come and say good-bye or have a word with me. I sent the password to Aulus by a slave. Once more, a line of poetry: "*Popular favor . . .*" Then I retired to the tablinum.

Mara was giving orders inside. From time to time she would appear in the doorway, give me an encouraging look, leave behind a quick caress, some affectionate words. Her face became gloomy, however, when she saw the scroll I'd spread on the table: a diagram of the highways of the Empire. With luck and ideal conditions, I could reach Rome in twenty days . . . probably before Iunia. In a low voice I kept repeating the names of the unfamiliar places that rose up as I unrolled the itinerary. Mara came in, pulled up a footstool, and sat there staring at me. She'd perceived my intentions immediately. She waited, not moving. I couldn't bear that painful expectation; I rolled up the scroll again and tossed it among the other books.

c━━◆━━○

When we left the city the next day, no one went along with us. At a glance I saw Milquion in a crew that was using brooms and buckets of water to wash the symbol of the fish off a wall. He averted his face and hid behind a corner. At the gate, Aulus pretended not to see us pass. He disappeared into the guardhouse.

Near the military encampment, where the rear guard was still finishing preparations for the column's departure, a voice called out behind us. It was Proserpinus, approaching at a run. He sprinted alongside the cart: "Lucius Valerius! Have a safe journey! May the gods be good to you and make you return soon!"

Sincere tears ran down his cheeks. He was panting with fatigue. I felt extremely moved, but I couldn't manage to say anything. Proserpinus' tall figure was being left behind, all alone, in the middle of the heath.

When we arrived, we found the villa in the state I've mentioned. Ashes and ruins. And for some time the work of reconstruction filled my spirit like a gift of Providence to deliver me from vexatious memories.

The days ran on. I took in with some detachment now the bits of news about Tarcisis and the world that were brought to me by travelers and merchants. The Empress Faustina had died, and I felt nothing. Gaius Maximinianus had finally swept the barbarians back to their mountains and deserts, and the safety of highways was reestablished in the south of Hispania. Young Scaurus had distinguished himself in the Moorish war, earned the laticlave, and sought the Tribunate of the Plebeians—I don't know with what success. Ennius Calpurnius had died and left the bulk of his holdings to his adoptive son, Rufus Cardilius, who hastened to add the name Calpurnius to his own. Along with Apitus, Rufus rose not to the aedileship but to the duumvirate. He'd given a considerable fortune to the city and was quick to order games, in which the main attraction had been the tearing to pieces of Arsenna by Cale-

264

donian mastiffs. Marcus Aurelius Antoninus finally went his way, and I didn't shed a tear. The momentous decisions of the republic passed on to Commodus, who made them while in gladiator schools. I never heard any further news of Iunia. Nor did I hear talk—just between us—about that religion of Christians, condemned like so many other fads to be swallowed up in the abyss of time. The will-of-the-wisp smoke of a straw fire.

I was troubled, it's true, by the little slave's drawing of a fish in the sand yesterday. But today I feel calm again. After all, the boy didn't know what that sign meant. He'd never heard, no doubt will never hear, any mention of the god who strolled through the garden in the cool of the evening.